THE STRAWBERRY BIRTHMARK

BY

A. TRAURING

This edition published in 2019 by AT Press, Atlanta, Georgia

ISBN 978-0-9915291-8-6

© 2019 AT Press, Atlanta, Georgia
v 5.5

Those who do not recognize this as a work of fiction should seek professional help. Names, characters, and incidents are products of the author's dubious imagination; all persons and events depicted are fictional. Any resemblance to actual persons living or dead is an unintended coincidence.

While some places depicted may exist in what some refer to as the real world, they are used fictitiously.

Mycology is a serious thing. Be careful out there!

Other books by the author in the Amy & Paul Saga:

A Different Kind of Twin

The Beaded Necklace

The Wedding Fatality

The Rothschild Jewels

Available at Amazon.com at
https://www.amazon.com/kindle-
dbs/entity/author/B00JCC9RCO?_encoding=UTF8&node=283155

Dedicated to Cindy, who has put up with my telling her of all the possible plot lines, all the 'clever' dialogue, and all my fantasies about Amy, and Paul, and Christine, for years and years and years.

Thanks to Sue Sandell for editorial support. Once again, she has made my work into a better book.

Thanks to the EPC Book Club for fellowship, good reading, and wonderful support.

Amy and Paul live at
http://atrauring.weebly.com

℘ TWENTY YEARS EARLIER (2010) ℞

He let himself into the dark bedroom and slowly felt his way toward the bed.

"Honey?" her voice came, groggy and startled, "What are you doing home?"

He whispered, "I snuck out. I missed you." He moved toward her voice. He heard her move in the bed, and a softer tone as she said, "Well, come here. I missed you, too."

She felt the bed move as he knelt on the mattress and then lowered himself. She laughed, then reached for him, and whispered, "Take those clothes off."

The couple giggled like schoolchildren as they readied themselves to make slow love.

Afterwards, the woman snuggled against him, tired and relaxed. "I love you, Ryan," she said.

"You're the best, Sammie." His smile was enormous. "I snuck out. I have to get back to my reserves base."

When the woman fell asleep, Jeffrey gathered up his clothes quietly and tip-toed out of the dark room. As he left the house for his car, he wondered if his twin brother would ever know what just happened.

✄ 1 ☾

"Our first job!" Amy jumped in the air and high-fived Paul with both hands over their head. Her smile was enormous.

"I guess we're a private detective now," Paul said aloud.

"Puh-lease," she replied, "that's private investigator." A pause. "And yes, we are!" She danced around the living room, excited that her plan to leave NOPD and set up a private practice was working. "You've got to call Christine. She has to be with us tomorrow when we meet the client." She pushed the buttons on her phone, then withdrew to let Paul lead to speak to his girlfriend.

"What are you doing for dinner tomorrow?" he asked.

"Paulette!" she squealed. "I was going to call you later. Dinner? What do you have in mind? Amy?"

"I'm here," Amy said, of course sounding the same as Paul - uh, Paulette. "I just set up my first meeting as a private investigator. Come with us to meet the client!"

"Uh—wouldn't I just be in the way? It's a business dinner, right?"

"No!" Amy cried. Then, "I mean, yes it's a business dinner, but I need some moral support. Besides, I want the man to think he's hiring a team, not just one woman." She was open-mouthed, hoping for Christine's assent.

"I don't know..."

Paul took the lead. "It's a free meal at Dockside–business expenses are deductible."

They heard her laugh. "This is fun. Any other reasons why I should come?"

Amy wasn't prepared to tell the truth, that she told the client that she would bring the company's principals with her. When she was silent, Paul said, "I don't want Amy getting all schoolgirl crush-y on the guy. Besides, I always like to sit next to you. How's that?"

Another laugh. "You had me at 'dinner', but I love how entertaining you can be. Dockside? When? What should I wear?"

"Six-thirty," Amy answered, excited that Christine had agreed to her scheme. "Wear black. Businesslike, okay?" Even before Christine responded, Paul added, "You can stay over with us. Or can we go to your place?"

"I love your silver tongue, Paulette. If you've got wine, I'll stay with you and Amy. What's the job? Tell me it's not dangerous!"

"I can't imagine any problems," Paul said. "The man's son ran away when he turned eighteen; now he wants to find him. Should be simple." Then, "It's Amy. Should take two days, but I'll hit him up for a week's fee in advance."

"Thanks for thinking of me, Amy. This should be fun. Look, I have to get back to studying, the boss is paying for my real estate license class and there's a quiz tomorrow on covenants. But I'll be there tomorrow. I love you, Paulette."

When they finished the phone call, Paul thought to her, *She doesn't know she's one third of Clear, Hodges and Owens, does she?*

Amy shook their head. *She'll be excited, right?*

Oh, I'm sure she'll be excited. Dunno if that'll be good or bad.

✍ 2 ✍

"Where is this place?" Paul asked aloud in the privacy of Amy's car. He was leading to drive, but Amy was navigating.

"When the Earhart Expressway ends, make a left. The client said it was near his house."

"That's a help," he snorted.

She cried, "The Shrine on Airline![1] I didn't remember it was near LaSalle Park." Amy had grown up in the Metairie suburb of New Orleans, and used to climb trees with her younger sister at that park. "Maybe we can climb a tree for dessert."

"We did that when I first met Christine," Paul said, nodding. "That was a fun day."

Paul turned left onto a big street with a typical New Orleans neutral ground, a grassy median between the two directions of traffic. "Dickory," he glanced at a street sign, "at the corner of Hickory Creek? Where is Dock?"

The restaurant is in that shopping center, Amy thought to him. He saw it–a corner suite in a strip of stores with a fake mansard roof, sandwiched between the Daiquiri Express Cafe and the stand-alone Fat Hen Grill. Paul parked the old yellow Benz and switched off the ignition. "This looks like a dive," he said.

---

[1] The minor league baseball stadium. When the New Orleans Zephyrs changed the team name to the Baby Cakes [oh yes, they really did!], they changed the ballpark name, too; Zephyr Stadium had become obsolete. By any name, the field was adjacent to and virtually part of LaSalle Park, on the major Airline Drive thoroughfare.

"Sure does, but the customer is always right." Still, they sat looking at the menu of special dishes and drinks written in soap on the sectioned glass walls.

When Amy saw Christine's Smart Car pull in, she took the lead to get out and lock her Benz. Paul said, "I don't know about this place. I'll bet this used to be a liquor store. Or a laundromat."

"We'll ask."

Paul jumped to the lead and ran to his girlfriend's car.

"Paulette!" she cried when she saw them. "Hi, Amy. Are you sure about this place? It kind of looks like a dead laundromat."

Paul wrapped their arms around her and kissed her. "You look great," he said, sounding like Amy. "Even greater than usual."

She stepped back and did a twirl, "How do you like my little black dress?" The sun glinted off her crooked front tooth as she smiled. "Is it business-y enough?"

"Thanks for coming," Amy said. "Uh, what happened with your hair?"

"Paulette?" she asked. He responded, "Yo."

Knowing it was her lover leading, Christine leaned against them. "It's always been the different shades of blonde. And I know yellow is Amy's favorite color. But yours is blue and I want you to be glad to see me. It's just a little streak. Is it okay?"

"You make it look great," he said. "And just for the record, you could be covered in an oil slick and I'd be glad to see you." She smiled. "I like it," he added. "Amy?"

"Have I ever told you how glad I am that you don't have piercings on your face?"

Christine wrinkled her nose. "Thanks, I think. I don't have a hat, so you're stuck with me like this."

"Maybe the lights are low," Amy said. "Look, would you mind taking notes?" She handed a spiral notebook to the woman; "We need to look professional. Let's see if my first client is here yet." Christine searched her purse for a pen as Amy let her into Dockside Seafood and Oyster Bar.

Despite the appearance from the parking lot, the interior of the restaurant was clean and well lit. A chubby young woman in jeans shorts and a red-and-white check bib apron greeted them, "Welcome to Dockside!"

Amy said, "We're supposed to meet a Mister Doublet. Is a gentleman waiting for us?"

A man two tables away turned when he heard his name. "Over here," he called as he waved and stood up.

Amy took two steps toward the client when Paul felt her inhale sharply. *You okay?* he thought to her. He heard her, silently, *Ba-ba-oh-ba-ba.*

You're too young to be having a stroke. What is it?

Amy stood in front of the client, staring. *Hunk alert!* she thought to Paul.

Christine stuck out her hand and introduced herself. "And this is Amy Clear. You are Ryan...?" She had forgotten the surname.

His voice was deep and melodious. "Doublet," he answered, shaking Christine's hand. "DOO-blay, like in French. Miss Clear?"

Amy roused herself. "A pleasure to meet you. Shall we sit down and discuss your needs?"

Ryan Doublet was about forty years old. He was five-ten, perhaps one hundred seventy pounds. Amy couldn't tear her eyes away from the handsome face: hazel eyes, thick eyebrows, a full head of black hair; a compelling face that showed the virile need for an afternoon shave across his top lip. The man pulled out her Windsor hoop-back chair, and then Christine's. "I appreciate you meeting me on such short notice," he said as he took his own seat. "My father died recently, and I need your help to satisfy part of his will."

The same woman who had greeted them came by to take their orders for drinks. Christine asked for a Dixie beer, while Amy ordered a limeade and Ryan asked for bottled water.

"My father's will leaves a large sum of money to my son. Trouble is, Lucas ran off two years ago and I have no idea where he is." He smiled sheepishly, as if embarrassed to admit the child had disappeared. "I need to find him so the estate can be discharged. My father doted on my boy. I think he will be pleased at what is waiting for him."

Christine opened a spiral notebook and clicked her ballpoint pen.

"How old was your son when he left?" Amy began.

"Just past eighteen," Ryan said, then turned to thank the waitress for bringing their drinks.

"Why did he leave?"

Ryan held the water bottle up to his forehead. "I ask myself that a dozen times a day." He unscrewed the cap and took a gulp, then poured the rest into a glass. "A rough adolescence, and I probably was overbearing. I never imagined he would run away."

"How rough? Drugs? Alcohol? School? Trouble with the law?"

He sighed, and Amy's heart went out to him–this incredibly attractive man, in a dress shirt and blue sport jacket, no necktie; an image of power, confessing vulnerability with a sigh. The man didn't answer, and Amy was silent, so Paul prompted, "Mister Doublet? Why did your boy leave home?"

"You want your children to be prepared for real life, to be able to earn a living and keep a roof over their head. I wanted him to go to college. He didn't." He looked up at Amy and shrugged.

It was an effort to keep from reaching for the man's hand. She forced herself onward. "Were there any other issues? Did he owe money? Pregnant girlfriend?"

"That's pretty offensive, but I guess you have to ask."

"Yes, Mister Doublet, I do. So?"

Ryan shook his head.

"Any guess where he'd have gone? Friends or relatives in another area?"

Another shake. "My father–his grandad–lived across the lake in Pearl River, but I'd have heard about it if he had gone there. My former in-laws are in Kentucky, but they say they haven't seen Lucas." He leaned forward, as if sharing a secret, "Our, uh, our families are not on great terms. But I don't believe they would lie to cover for the boy."

"So, any ideas where he'd go?"

"He's got a strong background in IT. Maybe he went to Miami or Dallas or Raleigh. But for all I know he's still in New Orleans."

"How long ago did he disappear?"

"Two years ago in June."

What! Paul bellowed. Before Amy could react he challenged the man, "You've waited twenty-three months to find him?"

He heard Amy think, *Don't be hard on him. The poor man is in pain.*

While they waited for Ryan's response, Paul thought back, *That's too long to wait. He only wants him back for the legacy.*

Another sigh. "Pride," Amy's client finally said, and Christine wrote it down. "Lucas was a jerk, but that's how kids are supposed to be. I was the adult, and I wasn't ready to admit I was a bigger jerk."

When Amy nodded, the waitress thought it was directed at her, and she stopped to take everyone's orders. Ryan asked for a crab platter with collards and baby limas. Amy wanted an oyster loaf with extra Remoulade sauce. When Christine ordered a chicken salad, Ryan tried to kid her, "You come to a seafood place to order chicken?"

She blushed, and leaned to whisper to Paul, "I get plenty of fish from my Paulette." Amy gasped in surprise, even as she heard Paul silently snicker. Christine sat upright again and said, "But I'm on some medication, have to limit fish."

Amy looked at Christine's notes. "You have no idea where he may be," she said to Ryan. "You think he'd be doing computer work. How advanced?"

"He had Microsoft Server certification when he left, but not CISCO. He shouldn't be in charge of a department, but he's better than some tape jockey."

Amy nodded, not really understanding the last expression. "Here's what I need. The most recent photographs you can give me– ah," taking them, "thank you. His full name, date of birth, Social

Security number. Does he have a passport? Did he have credit cards when he left? Has he accessed his savings or checking account?"

"All that?" Ryan said, surprised.

Paul smiled angelically and said, "Not really. If all you're doing is going through the motions to satisfy the lawyer and probate, no, we don't need any of that information." He heard Amy shouting at him silently. Even Christine was looking at him, slack-jawed; somehow, she always knew which of them was speaking. "But if you're really trying to find him, yeah, we need all that."

He sat back, looking at the paper placemat in front of him. "No, it's serious. The attorney at Goode at Law explained what we need, what Lucas needs." He rubbed his chin as if he were thinking about it. "Offhand I don't know his social security number, so we'll have to talk again. Will tomorrow be soon enough?"

Amy took the lead back. "Sorry if I was too blunt, Mr. Doublet. Yes, tomorrow is fine."

She looked at the photographs of her target. Most were snapshots, candid photographs around the house and in a park. One was clearly the formal high school senior picture, where the boy was in suit and tie. Amy nodded, "I can tell he's your son. He is beautiful." She looked up at him, while Christine tried to peek at the picture. "Why isn't he a model?" She saw Ryan's mouth and hazel eyes in the boy, with carefully unkempt curly hair. The arrangement of straight nose, wide mouth, dimpled chin and light complexion made her think of magazine ads she'd seen for Calvin Klein or Benetton. She heard Paul think, *I see what you mean. Too bad I like women.*

"You are most kind," Ryan told her, "but if you knew his mother, you'd know where his looks really came from. And he's not a model because he has a brain."

There was a silence, and then Amy plowed on, "Uh, let me explain the ground rules, okay?"

He frowned, creases above his nose, between those hazel eyes.

"I charge $250 a day plus expenses," she went on, "a week in advance. I will respond to your phone calls or emails within 24 hours.

You will respond to mine likewise." Christine was staring at her, the first time she had heard Amy's sales pitch. "Lucas Doublet is an unusual name, so I should get results within a week. If he was Bob Brown it would take a lot longer. Write me a check for $1,750 and I'm all yours."

"Pretty steep."

"And if somehow I don't locate him, you get your money back." She thought to Paul, *Crap. I was hoping I didn't have to tell him that part.*

The man swallowed, but he reached inside his sport jacket and pulled out his checkbook. "Who do I make it out to?" he asked as he began writing the amount.

"Clear, Hodges and Owens, LLC."

"What?" Christine exclaimed.

Amy held her index finger to her lips and thought to her, *Not now. We'll talk later.*

"Paulette?"

He hadn't heard what Amy thought to Christine, but he thought, *Let's wait to talk about that, okay?*

Doublet didn't notice Christine's outburst. He ripped the completed check out of the book and handed it to Amy. "How do I get in touch with you?"

She took three business cards out of her purse and handed them over. "Call or email me first. If I'm unavailable or you get impatient, call Christine Hodges here. And if you're desperate, call Paul Owens."

Doublet looked at the cards, and at the two women. "Where's Owens?" he asked.

It was Paul who said, "He's in the back seat of the car with a migraine. You'll meet him later."

After their meals were delivered, it was Ryan's turn to question Amy. When she mentioned spending spent three years as a detective with NOPD, Ryan said, "That's how I got your name. I called the Parish police. A Sergeant Francks recommended you."

"I must thank Walter for the referral."

When they were done, Amy grabbed the dark blue folder with the check. She heard Paul think, *Eighty three dollars? No way!* She slapped her Optimum card on it and flagged down the waitress.

"I'll call you tomorrow for the information I need," Amy said, holding out her hand. The man shook it vigorously. "Tomorrow. All in good time. Please, Miss Clear, find my son. I'm proud of him, and I need to tell him that."

Amy and Christine stood by the Smart Car in the strip mall parking lot. "Paulette, will you tell Amy I'm angry at her?"

"I think she can hear you," he replied.

"I'm not talking to her. I'm so angry." She stamped her foot.

Paul wrapped their arms around her. "You're a brave woman to say so. I guess we need to talk. Our place or yours?"

She buried her face in their chest, inhaling the mingled scents of shampoo, deodorant, soap, and sweat. "I don't know if I'll be able to stay," she said, muffled. "You have that wine?"

"Wine. Check."

"Okay. I'll follow you." She stood on her toes to reach up and kiss her Paulette on the cheek. Then she disappeared into her car.

"What is going on?" Amy said aloud as they drove home. "What is she angry about?"

"I don't know, but I don't like it. I don't like my Christine to be mad."

"She won't talk to me?"

"You heard her."

"This is the silliest damn thing."

He thought to her, *You're sounding like Tracey. Christine thinks you did something. Maybe you didn't, but she thinks so.*

Out loud, Amy said, "Oh! Never tell me I sound like my mother! God, of all the insults!" Hearing his silent laughter did not improve her outlook. "This was an important meeting for me. I wanted Christine to share it. And she's mad? Oh!"

Paul looked in the rear-view mirror and saw Christine's yellow Smart Car two lengths behind them. "Can you do something for me?"

he asked, trying to sound innocent.

"What do you need?" she said, concerned.

"I need you to take Christine seriously when she explains what's going on."

"Only because she's your girlfriend."

"Maybe because she's your best friend?"

It was half an hour before Paul parked at the curb by their house in the Carrollton section. He was encouraged to see in the mirror that Christine was pulling in behind.

He kept leading to put his arm around Christine and hold her as he unlocked the door. He heard Amy thinking, *She'd better have a good reason. She could have ruined this job for me.*

Inside, door locked, Christine looked down as she said, quietly, "I'm really angry."

"What is it, sweetie?" he asked.

"Do you know what it's like to discover you're one third of a company you didn't know existed? When maybe–"

"Oh, come on!" Amy interrupted. "It's not like–"

Christine looked up and said, "Paulette, ask Amy to hear me out. Please?" Her face was red with anger, even as she kept her voice level.

Silently he said to Amy, *Remember what I asked you to do?*

Amy dropped her arms. "Okay. I'm sorry, Christine. Tell me."

"Thank you," she said, taking a step back, because she could tell the person leading in the body in front of her was Amy, not her lover Paulette. "You want to be a private eye, that's great. I'm proud of you; you've always done exciting things. I worry about how dangerous it is. I'd hate for anything bad to happen to Paulette or you. But it's your heart's desire, and I'm rooting for you. Do you believe me?"

"Of course!" Amy knew Christine was one of her biggest fans.

"Good. But being a private eye isn't <u>my</u> heart's desire."

"But it would be so much fun!" Amy blurted. Christine frowned, and Paul thought to Amy, *You said you'd listen to her.*

"I'm sorry. Go ahead. What is your heart's desire?"

"Paulette. She's turned my life around. I want to be with her all the time. But there's this rest of my life, when I'm not around her." She turned her head toward the futon and said, "Can we sit down?"

"Sure," Paul said. "Oh, and the wine we promised!"

She grabbed their hand and pulled them to the futon. "Never mind the wine. I need to talk to Amy."

A sigh, "I'm here."

"I've been a receptionist at Lincoln Realty for five years. They're finally helping me pay for the classes I need to get a license. I'm going to be a real estate agent. Finally, I'm going to make some real money."

"And that's your heart's desire?"

She shook her head. "No, Paulette is my heart's desire. But getting my license, selling houses–it's my challenge, it's my goal. It's me deciding to do something and making it happen."

Paul took her hand. "That's exciting. Oh, Christine, this is great! What can I do?"

"Tell Amy I'm not going to be her receptionist." Her lower lip was stuck out.

Amy led. "But we'd have such a good time! Think about how we can help people, maybe fight crime, and–"

"Paulette, tell her to listen to what I'm saying."

"–and, and—oh." The three people in two bodies sat silently for a moment, until Amy muttered, "Crap. What am I going to do with all that letterhead?"

"Tell Amy she can turn it over and use it for scratch paper. Tell her she had no right to assume I wanted this. Tell her–"

"Tell me what?"

"Amy, what you did was wrong. It disrespected me. It made me angry, and instead of Jilling up and saying 'I'm sorry,' you're doubling down on it." She stood and grabbed her handbag. "I'm too mad to stay tonight. Paulette, we'll talk tomorrow. And tell Amy–tell her I love her but right now I don't like her." She didn't wait for a response, not even her lover's hug; she was out the door, and they heard the peculiar sound of the motor starting on her Smart Car.

"That didn't go well," Amy said aloud. Then, "Can't you control your girlfriend better? You know she'd have a good time if she joined us."

Paul started to get up off the futon, but he felt Amy tense all their muscles, her technique to keep him from moving their body. "What are you doing?" she asked.

"I was going to walk us to the mirror. I want to see our face when you're saying these things."

He felt her shrug, then get up and walk to a narrow but tall mirror on the arch that made a sorry effort at dividing the big living room in two. "Okay. What do you see?"

Paul saw her–their–pretty face: small nose, thick dark eyebrows, and grey eyes. He smiled so he could see the turned front tooth that he still thought was her cutest feature. "I see the Amy I live in. But she's been talking like some pod-person."

Amy saw the same image he did, but she knew Paul was lurking behind the eyes. "What? Because I'm disappointed that she won't play with us?"

"That's fair," he answered, staring at the eyes in the mirror. "Giving her a hard time because you're disappointed isn't."

"You're just taking her side!"

He moved their left hand, 'his' hand by their custom, to hold their right arm, but she flapped her arm to slough it off. "I thought it was 'Amy first.' You say that all the time, 'Amy first.' Now it seems like it's Christine first." Their jaw was set tight, with a vein pulsing on the side of their neck.

He tried to calm her anger. "That's what it looks like to you, I get that. But what I see is Amy losing sight of a boundary with another person. She–"

They coughed, the sound of both trying to speak at once. She thought to him, *Boundary? What do you and I know about boundaries? We share the same head!*

And he laughed.

"What?" Amy said out loud, but she was beginning to laugh, too.

He wrapped their arms around themself for a moment. "Touché. Tou-fucking-ché."

Amy went to the bedroom to begin her nightly ritual. "That doesn't solve anything," she said, picking up a clean towel. "But now it's okay with me that we sleep together."

"Me too. Uh, let's not talk about it any more tonight or I'll volunteer to sleep on the sofa."

℘ 3 ℞

Not having a real job anymore, Amy slept in. It was eleven before she was dressed and ready to start her day.

She called the NOPD station on Rampart Street, where she spent three years as a detective. "Sergeant Francks," she told the front desk.

"Hey, what?" came the voice on the phone.

"Walter, Walter. It's Sugar. Amy!" There was a big smile on her face.

"No kidding? It's good to hear your voice, honey, I tell you what. You know I was thinking about you the other day–"

"I know," she interrupted. "I'm calling to thank you for the referral."

"He sounded helpless, and I figured you could use the business. What's his story, anyway?"

Amy explained the client was looking for a runaway son because of a legacy. "It was the first dinner I can write off for business."

"This is from my lips to your ear, Sugar," he said, lowering his voice. "You check out your clients every bit as much as you do their job. There are some creeps and weirdoes out there."

"Advice received and welcomed. You're a doll, Walter. Still got the pony tail?"

"If I ever cut it, throw me in a wacky ward 'cos I've lost my mind."

"A lot of men shouldn't have one," she confided, "but on you it's cute. It's sexy."

"Oooh, don't start me up, Sugar," he laughed.

When the call was over, Paul asked, "Now what? Do a background check on Ryan Doublet? Let's cash his check."

"Not a bad idea. Huh. I'm glad Walter said that. It wouldn't have occurred to me to make sure the client was legit."

When she was ready to drive to the bank, Paul said, "I want to call Christine at lunch. What can I tell her?"

"I'm still angry," she said as she waited for the diesel engine to smooth out. "I don't want to hire some stranger to watch a phone that never rings."

"How about your sister?"

"Christine would be perfect."

He paused before putting the old Benz in gear. "What do you know about Fleetwood Mac?"

"Who?"

"Christine Perfect."[2]

"That's what I said. I trust her and I know she'd do a good job. Plus she could help in the field."

Paul let out the clutch and headed for the Iberville Bank. "Except for one little factoid. She doesn't want to."

"Can't you change her mind?"

"No. And now I'm getting angry. Really, Amy, she said 'no.' That's an end to it." He felt her stick out their lower lip.

Amy turned on the radio and they finished the drive without further conversation.

The teller spent a moment at her computer before, satisfied, she counted out $1,750 in hundreds and tens. "I guess the client checks out," Amy said as they went back to the car.

"I don't know," Paul laughed; "he might still be an axe murderer."

---

[2] Christine Perfect McVie was one of the lead singers during the most commercially successful period for the English band Fleetwood Mac. Earlier she had released a solo album under her maiden name. Back in 1978 Paul and his wife Mary Pat wore out a copy of Fleetwood Mac's Rumours...just like everyone else in the western world seems to have done.

At 12:05, Paul used Amy's phone to call Christine during her lunch hour. Before he could say hello, he heard the woman say, "I don't want to talk to Amy. Just you."

"That'll work. I told her to put her fingers in her ears while we talk."

After a pause, Christine said, "But if she does that, how can you hear me?"

"Inside fingers, inside ears. I don't know how to explain it, it's just something we can do." He tucked the phone under their chin and leaned against the inside of the car door. "How did that real estate quiz go?"

He could hear the smile in her voice. "A ninety-one. Did you know that a deed covenant is binding even if the seller doesn't bother to tell you about it?" They talked about her class, and her excitement at getting closer to her goal of becoming a licensed realtor.

"I'm so proud of you," he said. "You took control of your life. It's exciting to watch. I'm sure you're over the moon."

"Yeah." A pause. "I wish Amy was as reasonable about it as you are." Another pause. "I miss her. She's my best friend, after you." And then, "And I miss you, too."

Paul hoped Amy didn't interrupt; he didn't have the ability she did to tighten their muscles to prevent her from taking control of what, in fact, was her body. He was grateful she remained silent. "When will you have time for us to get together? I'll work on Amy to make it happen."

"Class tonight. Did you know it's not really real estate? It's 'immovable property.' Uh—" she made an odd noise, as if she were blowing out to make her lower lip vibrate while she was thinking "— Tomorrow night. Friday night. Want to come over?"

"I sure do," he laughed. "I'll call you tonight and let you know if I can get Amy to promise to behave."

"I hope so. I love you, Paulette!"

"Me, too. Talk to you tonight."

When he ended the call, Amy said, "You didn't badmouth me to your girlfriend. That's hopeful."

"Hey, I don't remember anyone calling you names just because you disagreed with them," Paul said. "Well, your sister, but that's what siblings are for."

"Scarred for life," she held the back of her right hand against her forehead. Then, grinning, she counted the seventeen-hundred-fifty dollars again. And again.

Amy waited until she thought Ryan Doublet would be home from work to call his cell phone. "Mister Doublet, do you have the information I need on your son?"

"Yes, yes. Well, most of it." He rattled off the son's date of birth, middle name, cell phone number from two years earlier, and a physical description to complement the photos he had given her the night before. "I have no idea what his Louisiana driver's license number was," he added, "and I don't have his social security number. Do you really need them?"

She squeezed their eyes closed and rubbed their forehead. "Ryan, his social security number is on your income tax forms from when you claimed him as a dependent."

"Oh, yeah," an embarrassed laugh.

It was Paul who added, "And unless he was a privacy freak, it's likely his license number, too."

"Ah. All in good time. I think my tax records are in the vault. It'll be tomorrow before I can look at them. Is that okay?"

"The meter is running, Ryan. The sooner you get me the numbers, the sooner I can find him." Amy was uncomfortable being firm with him because she still had the image of his handsome face in her head. "If you like we can meet tomorrow to–"

"Christ! I'll call you tomorrow morning, okay?" There was silence on the line, and then he said, softly, "I'm sorry, Miss Clear. This has been a tense time for me, you know?"

"So I see," she said. "Look, you can call me Amy."

"Amy. Okay, Amy. I'll call you tomorrow when I get to the bank."

When the call was over, Amy said, "Let's get started." She took a fresh legal pad and wrote "Lucas Claude Doublet" at the top of the first page. "We categorize the skip," she said, mostly to herself. "It's an intentional disappearance, but he's not running away from the law, we don't think he owes anyone money, he just was escaping that sexy, sexy father of his." She wrote some notes on the pad. "Do you think he was trying to cover his tracks when he ran away?"

"Hmmm," Paul considered it. "I didn't. Of course, I was fourteen and didn't even make it to White Sulphur Springs."

"You ran away from home? You really were a bad boy." She sat back, pen in hand, to talk with her dyad.

He laughed out loud. "I don't remember why I was so pissed at my dad. Anyway, the last thing I considered was hiding my steps. Hell, I called mom from the Lewisburg bus station." A moment later he added, "I wasn't very good at being a bad boy back then."

Amy nodded and bent back over her legal pad. "There are some searches I can do with just the name." She shook the right-hand mouse to wake up Windows Umpteen. "Let's see what we can find for Lucas Claude Doublet."

She heard Paul think, *What kind of name is 'Claude'?* She snickered and said out loud, "An old-fashioned one. Maybe that was grandpa's name."

She started with a public paid website. Its teaser front page found five people in America with the son's complete name. "Now I see if one of the free places can dig it up."

"Already there," Paul said; while Amy had done her search, he had used the lower monitor and the left hand mouse. "ZabaSearch says San Francisco and Atlanta."

She grabbed his mouse and printed out the few details the website gave on the two possibilities. She said, "I'll try a dark database on IT workers. Let's see if I get a hit there."

The occupational index site found four people named Doublet in information technology. Two were in New Orleans: their client, Ryan, and someone named Jeffrey Doublet. "He's got a relative?" Paul asked.

Amy drummed the fingers of her right hand on the desk. "Walter said to do a check on our clients. Let's see–" She brought up a Google search page and entered 'Doublet New Orleans'.

There were more than one thousand results, although she quickly realized almost all of them were for Doubletree Hotels. One of the remaining ones was a year-old news article from the *Times-Picayune:*

38-Year-Old A Suicide In Kenner:

Jefferson Parish Police called the death of a Kenner man yesterday a suicide. Jeffrey Doublet, an area computer specialist, was found hanging in the living room of his home on East Glendenon Road. The 38-year-old's body was identified by his twin brother, Ryan Doublet of Orleans Parish. Police say a note at the scene revealed the man was depressed over personal matters.

"I've heard there's some psychic bond between twins," Paul observed, "maybe like you and me. This must have been awful for Ryan." Then, "Why does the IT vocational website still have the brother listed? He's been dead a year."

"The poor man." She realized she wanted to comfort her client in a most unprofessional way. Shaking her head, she clicked on a link to an older article from the paper:

Deranged Mother Stabs Infant to Death

Orleans Parish police arrested Mrs. Samantha Doublet of Plum Street yesterday afternoon after receiving calls from neighbors saying a half-dressed woman with a bloody knife was knocking on doors and asking if her daughter was there. Police found Mrs.

Doublet sitting on the curb at Birch and Hollygrove, holding the weapon. Examination of the woman's home led to the discovery of the body of her four-month-old daughter, Brooklyn Doublet, who had been stabbed repeatedly. Her husband, Ryan Doublet, and their son, Lucas, were not at home and were not harmed.

Although in police custody, Mrs. Doublet has been transferred to East Louisiana State Hospital in Jackson[3] for psychiatric evaluation.

"Holy crap! That poor, poor man! I've got to help him."

Paul thought for a moment. "He's had some tough luck. But this isn't the same thing as checking him out, you know."

"What is it, then? If it were me, I'd be a pool of jelly on a nuthouse floor."

You're tougher than that, he thought to her. *So's Ryan. I'm sure he's got some quirks from it, but he appears to be a survivor. Good.*

Amy said, "You're resisting. Is it because I think he's good looking?"

"Nah," he laughed, "it's because he's a total stranger and I don't trust anyone I don't know." Then, "At least his check cleared."

The phone startled them at 9:15 in the morning. Amy grabbed for it, dropped it, and somehow accepted the call while she was fumbling under a chair to retrieve it. When she finally said "Hello"–after a string of 'crap crap shinola's–she heard Ryan Doublet laughing. "Did I interrupt anything?"

"Good morning, Mister D–uh, Ryan. Took awhile to find my phone, that's all."

"I'm still at the bank, and I have my son's Social Security number

---

[3]Long-time New Orleans residents still use the name of the previous location, Mandeville, as shorthand for the state psychiatric hospital. However, that facility closed in 2012 and the nearest state mental institution now is in Jackson.

for you. Just as you said, it was in my tax records."

Doublet dictated the nine digits. Amy repeated them back, and he confirmed them.

She rubbed their cheek with their right hand. "I started work with just Lucas' name. Now I can get serious." A quick thought to Paul, *Wish me luck*; then to the client, "Look, let's meet up on Sunday, I should have something to report by then."

"Why did I pay you for a week's work if you'll find Lucas in four days?"

"Because I asked you to," she answered. "I'm not saying I'll have his current address by then, but I should have some news. A progress report." She thought to Paul, *Am I going to have to tell the guy I have a crush on him and I want to see him?*

Paul thought back, *Did you think that to me, or did you say it out loud?*

"Oh, crap!"

"What?" Doublet asked.

"Nothing, nothing. I, uh–I just remembered I have to get to the, uh, the dry cleaner."

"Can you bring Owens with you tomorrow? I want to meet the guy who runs things."

Oh, let me, Paul thought to her, then said, "Owens? He's just another investigator. I'm the boss. Christine is the office manager, sort of. But yeah, I'll get him to come. Dinner at Dockside? Eight o'clock?"

"Make it seven. I have a security conference early on Monday."

"Okay. Ta-ta for now," Paul finished and ended the call.

Amy said, "Don't make fun of the customer. He's the only one I have."

"So far. Yeah, I'll be good. Let's call Christine, tell her we're coming over tomorrow?"

He felt her roll their eyes. "Yes, of course. All things Christine must be stamped and counter-stamped and approved by the board."

He was dialing their phone. "Now who's making fun?" he said.

Later Amy opened the subscription Social Security Number trace site and carefully keyed in Lucas Doublet's number. It took a few minutes for results to scroll down the screen. Not as detailed as she had hoped, but a twenty-year-old didn't have all that much history to explore. "That's him before he ran away," Paul said, pointing at a few entries marked Louisiana. Amy nodded their head; "He worked at a Popeye's franchise; must have been high school."

Records for auto registration came from North Carolina and Georgia. No property ownership, no arrest records, no tax liens. Weird names of what she took to be employers, also in North Carolina and Georgia. Checking account still at Iberville Bank in Metairie, but no indication when it was last accessed.

And that was all. If she hadn't been using her leftover NOPD ID to access the database, she'd have felt cheated at how little information she got.

"Two states," Amy mused. "At least that narrows things down."

"Yeah. He's a computer geek, North Carolina would mean the Research Triangle. And Atlanta is the only thing in Georgia, right?"

Amy went through eight proprietary databases with her leftover police login. Paul asked, "How much will these cost when we have to start paying for them?" which made her snort with a laugh. By 10:00 PM she had narrowed Lucas Doublet's whereabouts to Raleigh, North Carolina, and Tucker, Georgia.

"But where does he live now?"

"I'll worry about that in the morning," she said, closing her web browser. When she stood up, she bent their neck and stretched, "Ow, my shoulders are stiff." One of them yawned. *I hear you,* she thought. *Let me brush my teeth and I'm headed for the sack.*

Amy was laughing, "I can't believe you're the one saying that!"

"I get the joke," Paul said. It was true–usually Amy was the one asking him to behave, pleading with him not to interfere with her talking to a man, begging him not to draw attention that might lead to their biggest joint fear, a rubber room in Mandeville. "But the last couple of times we were with Christine you pissed her off and she went away. I miss her!"

Paul was driving her old yellow Benz, on the way to his lover's double in West End. "If you're going to set her off again, can you at least wait until morning?"

He could feel her pouting their lower lip. "I just don't understand why she won't do this," she said. "The three of us would have a blast if she worked for Clear, Hodges and Owens. Why can't she see that?"

He sighed. "Why can't you see she doesn't want to? She doesn't have to justify herself. Although she's explained why. We're lousy business people, and she's excited about setting herself a challenge, meeting it, and making money. Good for her!" He turned down Christine's street. "We'll be okay."

"You're just taking her side, damn it," but there was a smile in her words. "I promise I won't get in your way tonight. Let me drink, okay?"

He pulled up her driveway. "It's a deal."

The blonde woman was sitting on her tiny porch, a real estate textbook open on her lap. Paul turned off the engine–it rumbled a bit, as diesels do–and drank in his view of her. Her hair was a multitude of lengths in a rainbow of hues, hanging at the sides of her face as she looked down; the recent blue streak was over one ear. She was wearing a bright yellow T-shirt and faded blue shorts, and was jiggling her legs as she studied. The reading glasses were a recent addition, now that she was thirty-eight. She was bouncing a pink hi-liter off her lower lip as she read. Paul couldn't help but smile. He was in love.

When he tooted the horn, the woman looked up and smiled. "Paulette! You're here!"

"You bet I am," he said, and ran to her. It was their first hug in a week and it filled him with relief and comfort. "I'm glad you got here," she said to their chest, "the mosquitoes were about to send me inside."

"Are you hungry yet? Chinese? Our place on South Broad Street?"

She squeezed them, then backed off to say, "Let me get my purse."

During the meal Paul asked about her coursework. "What was yesterday's class?"

"Ethics," Christine said, between forkfuls of crawfish lo mein. "You have to tell a potential buyer if a house was ever flooded. Even if it's all been fixed up." Her tongue wrestled with a wayward noodle. "Umm, umm–" a quick swallow, "–A house is the single most expensive thing most people ever buy, and lots of people only do it one time. I like the idea of hooking people up with the right place."

Paul listened carefully. He was used to Christine being passive, credulous, and child-like. It was exciting to hear her enthusiasm and her unexpected confidence. "I'll bet you didn't know that New Orleans property values are the highest they've been since 2023. No major hurricane since then," waving her fork like an orchestra leader, "and while prices were low, people made repairs and built extra rooms. Now they'll be able to make back their investments."

Paul reached across the table to hold her free hand. "I swear, you've never been as pretty as you are right now. You're so self-assured; it looks great on you."

"Oh, Paulette." She dropped her fork and put her hand over theirs. "I love being able to share this with you. You've been such a fan, even when I was having trouble with my medication and I was always scared you'd never call me or come back." She wore that wide, childlike smile that always made him optimistic about life in the universe. Leaning over, she kissed Paul on their lips, then sat back just a few inches. "Do you like the new me?"

Still smiling, he nodded.

I don't! he heard Amy think, and his smile collapsed into a frown. "What's wrong?"

"Argument with my co-pilot," he said, as he thought, *Maybe I don't like the new Amy.*

Christine grasped both sides of their face. "Amy, talk to me. What is it?" At the same time, Paul was shouting silently at her.

"Stop!" Amy barked. She shook her head free of Christine's hands. "If you both talk to me I can't understand either of you."

Paul thought to Christine, *You go ahead.* The woman was comfortable hearing her lover's male voice in her head. She nodded, and said, "Amy? Are you okay?"

Amy dropped her head to the table, carefully missing the half-filled bowl of won-ton soup. "I'm sorry. I'm–I'm sorry." She felt Christine pet her hair, and heard the woman say, "What can I do?"

When there was no answer, Christine said, "Paulette? Amy's okay, isn't she?"

"I think she's conflicted. Talk to us, okay?" He tried to rub their body with their left hand, 'his' hand, but all he could reach was their left leg. "Please?"

When Amy sat up, her face sagged. "I'm a horrible person," she began; she was disappointed when no one protested, but went on anyway, "You know I love you, Christine. We've talked about how we're sisters. And–" Anger and resentment still roiled her insides, but Amy made the decision to lie to her friend, to Paul's lover. "–And I just got carried away about starting a business. I've been bad." Nervous, she reached for her fork for something to do. "Can you forgive me?"

A huge smile bloomed over Christine's face. "Yes," nodding, "yes, of course I can. I do. I know you'll have as much fun as a private detective as I'm going to with real estate."

Amy couldn't meet the woman's gaze. She looked down at her Assorted Vegetable Delight. It didn't look delightful anymore.

Earth to Amy, she heard Paul think. *How about I'll eat and you drink. What is wrong with you?*

She smiled at the woman across the table and thought to him, *I lied, okay? I'm pissed as hell but I don't want to louse up your love life. Or my friend life.* When she let Paul take the lead, he dipped their fork deep into the rice and vegetables on their plate. *I'm only angry with her; it's not like I hate her.* Paul was enjoying the food and didn't reply. *I am such a loser. Where's the booze?*

He flagged down the waiter for a Tsingtao beer, and dutifully let Amy lead when she asked for a sip.

"Why is Amy getting drunk?" Christine asked. She always could tell which one of them was leading.

"Because I feel bad. I haven't forgiven myself yet for being such a bitch."

"Suit yourself," Christine said with a smile. Then, "Paulette, I'm thinking I'll work on the west bank. Property values are lower than in the city, there should be less competition. Still plenty of opportunity, though. What do you think?"

Enthusiastically he said, "I never thought about it, but what you say sounds reasonable. Everybody's got to live somewhere."

Amy had three beers at dinner. By the time they returned to Christine's double she was asleep.

Paul and his lover giggled while they brushed their teeth, poking and hugging and building anticipation of Christine's floor mattress. Abruptly, she asked, "Can I talk to you, Amy?"

"She passed out. She's the one who drank all that beer."

"She's not happy, is she?"

He took a deep breath. "No, she's not. She'll be okay, though."

"Is it me?" She stood in front of them, messy toothbrush in hand.

"Absolutely not," he said. "Amy's having trouble adjusting to you becoming so independent. So wonderfully self-assured." He smiled and hugged her.

"It's because I don't want to work for her, isn't it?"

"That's not quite right," he said, moving their left hand to her butt. "It's fine that you have other plans. She's just having trouble accepting that the world doesn't revolve around her."

"So it is my fault?" Her chin quivered. "Oh, no. Amy's my best friend!"

He wrapped their arms around her and held her close. "She's still your best friend. And you're hers. Really, Christine, you haven't done anything wrong."

"You're sure?" she said into their chest.

He kissed the crown of her head, the multi-colored, multi-length hair that was *le coif Christine*. "I am positive."

After a moment she stepped back and smiled up at him. "Come on, Paulette," she took their hand and tugged them toward her

℘ 4 ℞

Amy spent more time at one of the subscription skiptrace sites that had proved useful when she was a detective with the New Orleans police. It was providing dates attached to credit report entries. Where earlier she had narrowed Lucas Doublet's travels to Georgia and North Carolina, now she was sure he was living in a place called Tucker, Georgia. He was paying his rent on time, and keeping up with his utility bills. "He's still using his real name," she said to Paul. "I think that means he's honest. He wasn't trying to hide, just be left alone."

I agree, he thought back. *Do you tell Ryan tonight at dinner?*

She stretched her neck and scratched the front of it with her left hand. "Kind of. I'm not ready to give him the street address. Hey," she sat back with a new thought, "I'll offer to charge him to collect the boy. When's the last time you were in Georgia?"

"Mary Pat and I celebrated our thirteenth anniversary there," remembering the woman he had married when he still had his own body. "We ate at a seafood restaurant that was on an indoor boat. It was weird, but kind of neat. As I remember, the natives were friendly, they didn't bite. Well, hardly."

"You come to New Orleans, you eat a muffuletta or crawfish and a beignet. If we go to Atlanta, I want fried chicken and a peach. Oh, and peanuts."

"All we have to do is convince Ryan to pay us to fetch Lucas."

She pushed their chair back from the computer. Her state Private

Investigation Agency license was hanging on the wall in a three-dollar frame. "Do you think it's too soon to make a pass at him?"

She heard Paul snicker. "Maybe wait until you're ready to tell him the boy's address." Amy got up to drag dirty clothes to the utility room and the washing machine. Paul went on, "I think the etiquette is that once you sleep with him, you can't ask him for more money."

"Really?" stuffing jeans and towels into the old tub washer. "Then I'll wait until we settle the–wait! Who says so?"

"*Cosmo*, I think. No, Helen Gurley Brown."

"Who?"

"Or Carrie Bradshaw. I don't know, maybe it was Miss Manners. It's just something I read somewhere."[4]

"You're making it up, aren't you?" she smiled as she started the machine. "I can tell when you're just funning me."

"You see through me like I was made of Saran Wrap," he laughed. "Seriously though, would you be comfortable asking Ryan for another check after you do the deed?"

"Expenses, sure," she shook her head at Paul's euphemism. "Salary or rates, umm–I don't know. Yes, that might be awkward. Crap. I guess I just flirt for now."

She went to the kitchen, but before she turned on the water at the sink she thought, *I can't do the dishes, I just turned on the washing machine. Crap and a half.*

"Are you going to introduce me to Ryan when you sleep with him?"

"He says he wants to meet that Owens guy."

"That definitely waits until the paying job is finished."

Amy was thinking about getting into the car to drive to dinner when Ryan Doublet called her. "I'm running late," he said. "I went up to see my wife, and there's a wreck on the Causeway that's got traffic fucked back to Slidel."

---

[4] If *Cosmo* is still publishing in 2030, Amy never noticed it. She has never heard of Helen Gurley Brown, *Sex In The City*, or Carrie Bradshaw. She is used to Paul referring to 20th century celebrities and mostly ignores them.

"You got an ETA?"

"Shit. Give me thirty minutes–no, forty-five minutes. I should be at Dockside before eight, anyway."

She heard Paul say, "Be careful;" then he thought to her, *Dead clients don't pay their bills.*

"I'll be there soon," Doublet said and rang off.

As she put her phone away, Amy said, "That's an invitation to ask him about the wife. What was her name? Uh, Samantha. Do you think she's still locked up?"

"Ask. We'll find out."

Smiling, she said, "Guessing is where the fun is. Don't you want to play?"

"She killed a four-month-old baby. The less I know about her, the better."

"Oh, you old grump. You geezer."

"You got that right, kid."

"Maybe you can help with this, geezer," she began as she settled in on her futon. "Suppose Ryan does have me collect his son. How do you think that will work?"

"Knock on his door and say John Beresford Tipton[5] sent you and you have a million dollars for him. Child."

"What? Am I supposed to know who John Barefoot Tipsy is?"

"Hmm. He won't, either. I guess, Tell him his grandfather left him a wad of money in his will. Let me ask you–if you say that, will his first question be 'when did pepaw die?' or 'how much did he leave me?'"

"Tsk, tsk. You're so cynical!"

Paul laughed out loud. "Maybe it comes with age. But cynical or not, I'm the happiest man in the world. I'm not dead."

"Too bad they cremated your body when it died. Wouldn't it be

---

[5] The unseen benefactor of a TV golden-age program, *The Millionaire.* Actually it was his assistant, Michael Anthony, who would knock on an unsuspecting recipient's door and hand them a cashier's check for one million dollars. I mean, one meellyon dollars.

great to visit your tombstone? We could dance on your grave."

"I wish we could. And that's why I'm happy. I'm an 75-year-old man with the body of a 30-year-old. And a pretty 30-year-old woman at that. Life is good!"

After a moment Amy giggled. "I'm sure Ryan will think that's just peachy when I introduce you."

Allowing for Ryan's delay, they drove out to Harahan for dinner at Dockside. They arrived at ten before eight, and he was waiting at a corner table, a nearly empty highball glass in front of him. He stood up when he saw Amy come in the door.

"I hope I haven't kept you waiting," she said as she sat. "Is everything all right with your wife?"

"No such thing." He drained his glass and motioned to the waitress for a refill. "Will you join me?"

"Glad to. A Dixie?"

"Since you ask, nothing is all right with my wife. Everything has been all wrong for the last eleven years." He shook his head.

She thought to Paul, *I guess she's still at Jackson,* and heard him think back, *Let him tell us.* A nod, then, "What's the issue?"

"It was quite a big deal–" to the waitress bringing drinks, "Thank you," then, "Sammie is at East Louisiana State. She had a breakdown and–" he stopped, took a sip from his refilled bourbon "–there was a trial. She'll probably spend the rest of her life up there."

The old news article she had found on the internet told her what Ryan didn't, that the woman had stabbed to death their infant daughter.

"How is she?" Amy fought the urge to take the man's hand.

"The same," he sighed. "A lot of the time she seems normal, and then she'll get confused and think she remembers things that never happened." Looking up at her, he said, "I love my wife. I've loved her since the day I met her in college. This–this is hard."

Amy's fingers fluttered over the back of Ryan's hand, then closed on it. "I'm so sorry."

They sat silently for a moment, hands touching. Finally Paul–

sounding exactly like Amy–said "Does she know about Lucas going away?"

He pulled his hand back. "Yeah. She blames me. That really hurts because it is my fault. Today I told her about hiring you. She's excited that she'll get to see our boy again."

While they looked over the menu and placed their orders, Paul and Amy argued silently about pumping Ryan for his take on his wife's rampage and his brother's suicide. She wanted to pry, while Paul thought it best to drop a hint or two and let the man respond or not. *Maybe,* he thought, *start out asking him if we can go to Atlanta to get Lucas. Then see where it goes.*

She took a long sip of the Dixie–in a glass, no less–and thought, *You don't mind that I'm going to make a pass at him?*

Hell, no! You deserve a good time. Even I can tell the guy is a looker. Just make sure you don't end up finding his son for free.

Ryan didn't know why Amy flashed a smile when she asked, "Have you thought about what we'll do when we locate your son?"

"You said you wanted to give me an update." He glanced at his wristwatch, "Christ, I've got a meeting at oh-dark-thirty tomorrow."

"My traces indicate Lucas spent some time in Durham, North Carolina, and now he's in a suburb of Atlanta. It might be another day or two before I get a street address for him and for his job. What then?"

She heard Paul think, *That dumb look on his face means he hasn't thought about it.*

"Uh, I guess, uh–well, I can–" and he stopped.

"He ran away from you, so I don't think calling him up will work. How about if I go get him?" When he made no reply, Amy went on, "I can find him at home or at work, tell him there's a legacy waiting for him, and bring him back with a bow on his forehead. It's the same $250 a day plus expenses." She tried to hide it, but she was holding her breath, waiting for his answer.

"I'd lose more money if I took off from work to do it myself," he muttered. "Yeah, fly the goober back to me." He smiled. "I think you'll like him."

Amy said, "I hope so, if I'm going to sit next to him on the plane ride back." Silently Paul was cheering, *Yes! Money! Yes!*

With all their business settled, Ryan wolfed down his shrimp loaf. He threw a twenty dollar bill on the table when he made his excuses to leave, "You got the last check."

"Go ahead, Ryan;" thinking about the rest of the grouper on her plate, she said, "I need the ladies' room before I'm ready to go. I'll call you when I nail down Lucas' address. We can talk about the flight to Atlanta then."

The busy man stopped still for a moment and said, "You're doing a great job. Thank you for finding my son."

When he was gone Amy sat back down. *Food tastes better when someone else pays for it,* Paul thought. He swallowed, and put the fork in their right hand for Amy to take a bite.

As she chewed she thought, *No way I was going to leave this behind. Why didn't I know about this place earlier?*

They traded the fork back and forth, because whichever of them was leading got more taste and more satisfaction. When they were done, Paul thought, *Let's get on the internet and figure out where we'll have fried chicken and peach pie in Atlanta.*

Amy got a callback from Experian on Tuesday morning. Their legal department had checked out her police credentials and were willing to give her access to Lucas' credit record. It was the final piece of the puzzle. There was a street address in Tucker, marked "Apartment C-5;" his Social Security tax was being paid by an S Corporation called Anthropomorphos.com. She was so close to Lucas Doublet that she could smell his aftershave.

"Maps!" Paul called when she got off the phone. "Let's find him, and the place where he works, and call Ryan and–"

She knew she couldn't speak while Paul was talking, so she thought to him, *I'm glad you're excited about this.* He stopped, and she felt him smile. Amy went on, *If only your gal pal was on board.*

Now, now, he thought back. *Be glad that I am. Mapquest? We'll use GPS when we get there, but for now we can get the lay of the land online.*

"Like the time I went to Nashville with Kowalski to bring back that museum murderer. Their PD used big digital maps to work up a strategy."

She let Paul find the address on his monitor. A few clicks on his left-handed mouse and he brought up an aerial view of a close-in suburb of Atlanta. "The Baron DeKalb Apartments. Lots of trees around it."

Using her right hand mouse, she turned the screen image to a road map, and widened the range. "That circle road must be the difference between the city and the burbs," she said. "Like the Westbank is here."

"When do we go? Me for fried chicken."

Working together, Amy and Paul found and printed maps to show where Lucas lived and where he worked. With no knowledge of the city's insane rush hours, Paul thought he plotted the man's likely commuting pattern. When he began a Google search for chicken restaurants, Amy laughed and said, "We're not going on vacation, you know. It's a work trip."

"Does that mean we don't get to eat while we're there?"

"Find us a cheap hotel, okay?" Mentally she rehearsed what she'd say when she called Ryan to tell him she was ready to go get Lucas, while Paul found an EconoLodge and a Motel 6 near where Lucas lived, both around $75 a night. "Nice. I'll call room service an expense, maybe I can get a hundred a night."

Later Amy was sitting on an aluminum folding chair in the tiny courtyard of her back yard. Most of the patio was covered with red bricks, but there were two banana palm trees and a stand of Christmas ferns that had decided Louisiana was a great place to grow. Paul asked, "What happens when you get another client?"

"If someone calls today, I'd have to put them off. If they can wait until next week, maybe I'll be able to make a living." She was facing her back fence, made of old grey boards; beyond was a neighbor's huge live oak, and the top of their two-story house. Prodded by Paul, she was part way through an ancient book about an interstellar hitchhiker, and was beginning to warm up to the people with funny names.

"Christine opted out," he said, "and that Owens guy isn't really carrying his weight. It's just you. How will you juggle clients?"

She closed the book in their lap. "On the police force, there were plenty of cops and detectives to pick up little things when I was working something intensive or out of town. I guess I figured I'd do the same thing solo."

"But it's just you. That won't work."

"I guess not," she said, and opened the paperback. "I'll worry about it when I get a second client. How do you say this guy's name - Za-Zaphod?"

"Let's visit Christine before we go to Atlanta. I need a honeybunch fix."

"Sure," really paying more attention to the book. "Maybe we'll end up alternating days between her and Ryan."

She felt Paul shake their head. "I'm sure there's a rule against getting involved with a client."

"Probably. You going to report me to the P-I ethics committee?"

"Only if you stop sleeping with me." Amy smiled and wondered if she could get a third arm like the crazy man in the book. It would be so handy!

"We're ready to go."

"You found my boy?" Even over the phone, the tone of Ryan's voice pulled at Amy's heartstrings. She was still sitting in her back courtyard with her book, her second glass of cheap white wine, and a citronella candle.

"Yes, Ryan. I haven't talked to him yet, but I have his address, I know where he works, and I got his cell phone number. Now the—"

"Oh God, this is wonderful," he interrupted. "How can I ever thank you?"

"Thank me when I bring him to your door. I think the best way to go forward is for me to go to Atlanta, explain things in person, hogtie him, and drag him back. What do you say?" Silently she thought to Paul, *I am required to consult with the client, no matter how wrong they might be.* She heard him snort.

"Yeah. Definitely. I thought about it after you suggested it at dinner. If I get him I'd have to miss a bunch of work and pass up some side business I really can't afford to do without. You said your same rates?"

The Amy Demon on her shoulder said, "It's out of town, jack up your price." Paul thought to her, *You already told him it would be the same fee.*

But I need the money! she thought back.

"Miss Clear? Amy?"

"Yes, I'm here, Ryan. Yes, the same $250 a day, plus expenses—that's air fare and a half-way decent motel, a rental car, meals, and whatever bribe I have to give Lucas."

"Bribe? Do you think he might not want to come back?" He sounded worried.

Paul was impatient and jumped to the lead. "Well, duh! He ran away from home. Whatever his issue was, he may not be done with it." He heard Amy think, *Down boy. Don't scare away the paying customer.*

I guess. There are some mistakes that you can't undo. You pay for them forever.

"I didn't mean to make you feel bad," Amy said, leading again, "but we'd be foolish to ignore the possibility."

It was a few seconds before the man finally said, "I guess my dad's legacy will have to be enough of a carrot." A sigh, "All in good time. Damn."

"Ryan, we ought to do this right away. I can meet you so we can go over the flight schedule, and you can buy the plane tickets. With all the government stuff it's tricky when you pay for a ticket for another person, I need to be with you. Uh, when you do that." She held her breath. *Is he going to invite me over?* she thought to Paul.

Another pause. "Christ. I'm going to an I-triple-E meeting right now, it's in the CBD. I won't get home until ten o'clock."

Amy jumped. "Airlines sell tickets twenty-four hours a day. If I come over tonight, I can be in Atlanta tomorrow."

Hey! What about my honeybunch fix?

Change in plans, I hope. You may have to settle for a phone call.

Paul thought their heart had stopped beating, as Amy waited on the man's answer.

"Yeah. Yeah, okay, let's do it." Amy was flush with excitement. When Ryan dictated his address in the West Carrollton section, she thought to Paul, *That's not even a mile from here!* To her client she said, "Great. I'll see you around ten. Call me if you're going to be very late, okay?"

The neighbors wondered why they heard Amy screaming, "Yes! Yes! Yes!" She knocked the chair back when she jumped up and danced a jig around one of the banana palms. Then she rushed inside and hauled down a suitcase from the top shelf in the spare bedroom closet.

"How much will you charge him for this?" Paul asked aloud.

"Never mind the money. Tonight I get him." She found a black canvas overnight bag in the back of the closet and took it out. "I'm thinking three days of clothes for Atlanta, in case Lucas needs some time to see the light." She dragged the bag and the suitcase into her bedroom and threw them open on the bed. Underwear, jeans, black dress slacks, three nice shirts, two not-so-nice tee shirts, a maxi-skirt, her various holsters, and a hard case for her gun for the plane ride. "Is my pistol permit valid in Georgia?" she said to Paul, even as she tossed a box of 9mm ammunition in the valise.

Then her attention shifted to the overnight bag. She stood in front of the open top drawer in her chifferobe, wondering if she owned the kind of lingerie the man would, uh, appreciate. She heard Paul think, *How about the flannel nightgown? Some men are into that.*

The words "It's June, why would --" were out of their mouth

before her brain caught up. "Thanks for the advice," she smiled, "you're a big help." She held up a gauzy black babydoll. "I don't know what I'd do without you." Amy rolled up the scanty piece of clothing and tossed it in the bag. "Really."

When she added Paul's current reading matter, *Sir Harry Hotspur of Humblethwaite*, she said, "Haven't you read enough books from two centuries ago?"

He laughed, "There were good things in the world even before you were born in 1999. I don't give you a hard time about those cop mystery potboilers you like, so --"

She couldn't speak while he was talking, so she interrupted by thinking to him, *You do so! You give me crap every time I read myself to sleep with one.*

"Oh. Yeah, I guess I do. Never mind. Pretty day, isn't it?"

Smiling, she sat next to the open overnight bag. "Paul. I'm going to get Ryan."

You're an angel for putting up with me and Christine, he thought back, *and our deal is I have to put up with your men. You deserve a good time. I hope he's a keeper. Will you introduce me?*

"Not tonight, I won't." She was trailing the fingers of her right hand up and down her left arm, touching Paul. "Maybe later. I love how honest we can be with Christine, it would be nice to do that with a man."

"I'll try to stay out of the way," he said. "Uh, if there's booze..."

"Yes. You get the booze."

"I'm on board."

After packing, Amy attempted to take a nap; "I hope I don't get much sleep tonight," she told Paul. But the anticipation kept her awake. Finally she got up, changed into workout clothes, and went for a run. Forty minutes later she was back home, sweaty, tired, and just as wide-awake as before. "I want this to work!" she shouted in frustration.

"I vote for a shower," Paul said, "then maybe a warm glass of milk. If we don't get a nap, I'm going to sleep through all the fireworks."

She snickered. "That's all right for you, but I want to be awake for them."

So she showered, then lay down to read. She turned the television on and off half a dozen times. Half-heartedly she opened a crossword book but gave up after she didn't guess four clues. Somehow the sun moved west in the sky and it grew dark. Despite herself, she did doze off.

She had set the alarm, so at nine-thirty she was blasted awake. Instantly she was smiling. She was excited. She was going to mark her client as her own.

Amy put on the shortest skirt she had, a brown one that wasn't all that short, but at least the hem was above their knees. She reached for a pullover blouse, but stopped. *What's wrong?* Paul thought to her.

"Undoing buttons is sexy," she said, and took a shirt with ruffled front instead. After two minutes in front of the makeup mirror she was ready to leave. First she wheeled the suitcase to the street and put it in the trunk of her old yellow Benz. Then, purse and overnight bag in her right hand, she let Paul lock the front door behind them.

"I want to call Christine," he said as she fastened their seatbelt.

"Sure. I'll drive, you talk." She pressed the glow plug button and mentally counted to eight before turning the key and cranking the diesel engine.

When they were underway, Paul called Christine. Her outgoing message reminded him she had a class that night. "Leave me a message," her voice said, "especially Paulette. Bye!"

"Heads up, Honey," Paul said, sounding just like Amy. "We're probably flying to Atlanta tomorrow to find the kid and haul him back. We're on our way to the client's house now, and Amy expects to be knocking boots—well, it's Christine I'm telling!—uh, Amy expects to be getting closer to the guy very soon now. I'll call you tomorrow from Georgia. I love you."

When he ended the call, Amy said, "You are the crudest, rudest, garbage-mouthiest person I have ever known." She was smiling.

"Yep, that's me. And you are the prettiest, most skinniest Private Investigator I have ever known. I think we make a good team."

"I'm glad you're in such a good mood, " she told him. "Let's see, a right on Dante—" she made the turn,"—and he's just past Oak Street." When she parked she sat back, both hands on the steering wheel. "I will get you as drunk as I can," she said aloud. "In return, you will not mess this up, okay?"

He said, "It's a deal. That's how much I love you."

The house on Plum Street had two stories, with a small porch on the ground level and a railed-in terrace above it. A wrought iron fence protected the tiny front yard. She thought the home was painted grey but couldn't be sure in the darkness. As she locked her car door, Ryan Doublet turned into his narrow driveway. "Is that you, Amy?" he called from the open car window. Amy hefted her overnight bag and walked across the street towards him. "Our timing is perfect," she answered.

She inhaled sharply when she saw him get out of his white Passat; he put his fists on his hips and leaned back, stretching. Ryan wore a khaki colored suit, creases still sharp on the trousers. His shirt was light blue, with the striped tie, undone, hanging down the front. She heard Paul think, *Make him shave,* and laughed.

"I appreciate you being willing to work so late," he said, straightening up and holding out one arm, inviting her to walk with him to the front door. "Are you hungry? Christ, the meeting went on and on and I haven't eaten since lunch."

"No, I'm good," she said; somewhere she had read that a woman who eats hearty on a first date comes across as a pig. But wait -- they'd already shared dinner twice, and this wasn't really a date. Was it? "I'll watch you."

She followed him through the door, down the hallway, and into the open-floor-plan kitchen, listening to him complain that computer vulnerabilities cured in 2004 were suddenly showing up again in new applications because the youngest programmers were reinventing the mistakes of twenty-six years earlier. "Punks think they invented digital," he muttered. "It keeps me employed, but it's so frustrating."

He's so self-assured, she thought to Paul. *I thought only cops and my dad acted like that.* Her mouth was hanging open.

Ryan opened the refrigerator and took out a lunch plate covered in wax paper. He lifted a corner and sniffed. "Good," he said, "it's still edible. Do you like mushrooms?" He took a skillet off a hook above the stove.

"Are you kidding? That looks like half a cauliflower."

Oil in the skillet, a medium flame on the range. "I'm a mycologist. This is a puffball I found on the north shore last week. *Calvatia gigantea.* Sautee 'em with some garlic, spread some cheese, and they make good eating. You should try some."

Amy heard Paul silently shouting *No!* "Umm, no thanks. Like I say, I already had dinner."

As the olive oil began to spit he dropped the mushroom in the frying pan. The fungus was bright white and looked firm. "Are you chicken?" he smiled. "Did I hire a coward to run down my missing son?" He slid the skillet back and forth and held a spatula in the other hand.

The evil Amy demon on her shoulder told her to say "Gimme that thing," but Paul again shouted silently, *No! Please, no!* Trying not to sound as defensive as she felt, she said, "I've wrestled alligators. I've talked murderers into throwing down their weapons. I've killed bad guys, and I have the scars to prove it. Bravery, Mister Doublet, means taking chances when something important is at stake. Showing off for nothing is fools' courage."

"Well, I guess you told me," he said, still smiling. He was flipping the thick slice of mushroom in the pan. "Me, I like knowing how to live off the land. I've got a garden in back, and when I go hiking I'm always looking for plants I can eat."

After an uncomfortable pause Amy said "So we're cool," even though it was a question. She thought to Paul, *I'm shaking. I can't believe I did that.*

"Yes, Amy, we're cool. And you can call me Ryan."

At the dining table Amy watched him enthusiastically attack the grilled puffball. "It's filling, too," he said between bites. She nodded, then let Paul have another gulp of beer from the glass Ryan had provided. "What is this?" Paul asked aloud; he could tell it wasn't Dixie or the hated Abita.

"Home brew," he answered; with a mouth full of puffball it sounded like "Hm bwew."

"You make your own beer?" Paul went on. "Now I am impressed. What's the alcohol content?"

He hoisted his own glass and said, "Eleven-point-one percent," then took a very long draught. "I use special yeast. Like it?"

"Boy howdy, yeah!" Paul replied and drank some more.

Now you hush, she thought to him. *Tell me when you want more beer, but let me do the talking.*

Yeah. Hey, home brew. I like the guy!

"Where is Lucas?" Ryan finally asked. "What have you found?"

"He's in Georgia," she told him, "a suburb named Tucker. He works for a software company, Anthropomorphos.com—do you know them?" He shook his head, so she went on, "I checked them out. They develop video games."

"Really!" A smile spread across his face, and Amy thought she saw how proud he was of his son. "I can imagine—" and he stopped. "Well, you want to collect him?"

Paul interrupted to say, "Can I have more of your homebrew? It's really good." When Ryan rose to get the growler, Amy said, "It would be a mistake for you to contact him. A lot depends on how grown-up he's gotten; if he's still in adolescent rage mode, even a legacy won't bring him back." She retreated long enough for Paul to drink half the new glass in one go. "I won't drug him or kidnap him. Either he can be convinced or not."

"I understand." As he sat back down, he pulled the undone necktie from his collar and tossed it on a nearby chair. "If he won't come back for you, then I'll go up there and drug him or kidnap him."

Smiling despite herself, she said, "That's not legal, even for a parent. But I'll be off the case by then." Paul drank more beer, then said, "This is so good! Please, sir, may I have another?"

"You be careful, Amy," Ryan said. "That stuff'll knock you on your ass."

Paul thought to her, *I'm counting on it.*

This time Ryan left the growler on the table after refilling her glass. Amy asked, "What exactly is the legacy?"

"My father wrote his will a very long time ago. I think Lucas was two. He was the only grandchild then, and so my father made a provision for him." He sighed. "Dad was not always aware of reality his last few years, but his investments did well anyway. Lucas stands to inherit about two hundred thousand dollars."

"Wow," Paul slurred, and he took another drink. "I like how full this tastes." Amy banished him again, then probed Ryan, "Any stipulations?"

"If he had lived longer, my father would have become the crazy guy down the block with a house full of cats. He always was a cat person. The will says that if the stock and cash don't go to his grandson, they will go to the Cat Fanciers' Association." He made a face. "I mean, I like cats fine, but two hundred thousand dollars' worth?"

"So Lucas is the only person in the family who can inherit." Her face was creased as she was thinking, trying to ignore Paul silently singing about having a drink drink drink for Lily the Pink Pink Pink.[6] "I hope my parents don't do anything like that. Besides, my sister already has three kids; they'll get whatever money is left."

Paul drank more. Amy said, "You're good with this plan, then. I figure three days to convince Lucas and bring him home. That's $750 plus expenses --"

"Ah! I paid you for a week in advance, and this is just six days. Can I get a rebate?"

---

[6] The song sounds as old as Ireland herself, but Paul knows what actually was the original recording by The Scaffold, thank u very much.

"Sounds fair," Amy said, feeling her face turning red from embarrassment; Ryan probably thought it was from the beer. "Five hundred plus expenses. I can leave tomorrow, so let's get me a plane ticket."

He wrote out the check and handed it to her. When he looked at his watch he said, "It's after eleven. It wouldn't be fair to book you on a red-eye. Damn, are there any cheap flights left?"

"You're watching your pennies?" Paul slurred.

"That beer's getting to you," Ryan grinned. Amy heard Paul silently shout *Amen!* Still, he went on, "I'm doing much better, but yeah, I watch pennies. After Lucas ran off I got depressed and stopped working. It's only the last year I've been back in the saddle. I'm still paying off some long debt."

"Good for you!" Amy said. "I'm sure it's tough, but I'm impressed that you've turned things around." To Paul she thought, *He's tough. He's a winner.*

"Let's get you a ticket. Come on—" he stood up, motioned for her to follow, and went up the stairs. "—my office is in a guest room. Booking online is the way to do it."

She followed, noticing family photos on the wall beside the steps. The walls were a neutral ecru, as was the carpet. When he flicked on the overhead light in the office, she saw framed posters of ancient movies. Groggy, Paul pointed to one of a motorcycle film and thought to her, *I saw that in a theatre. There were naked girls in it.*

"I think BravoAir has the best rates," Ryan said as he sat in front of the monitor.

"Does Bigger Rubberband fly to Atlanta?" Amy asked. Silently she was trying to make Paul stop singing.

Musing as he typed, Ryan said, "MSY to ATL, open round trip. How about eleven o'clock? In the morning?"

"Yes, I can do that."

There were more clicks. "A hundred forty seven dollars. Sweet!" She watched him retrieve his wallet and take out a credit card, then type numbers into the computer. Then he said, "Give me your driver's license. I have to show them who the ticket is for."

Amy took her license out of her wallet and handed it over; then she moved behind him to see what he was typing. Deliberately she leaned over his shoulder, pressing her right breast into his back. "When does it land in Atlanta?" she asked, trying to sound innocent. She heard Paul gurgle silently, then think to her, *More beer!*

Ryan wriggled in his seat, pushing harder against her. "Twelve-fifty-three," he answered. "Direct flight. I'm printing your boarding pass." The work done, he looked up and around at her. "You want some more beer?"

He was so close. Yes, he needed a shave, but shadow or not, his square face was so handsome, his mouth was inviting, and his hazel eyes were so, so hazel. "That too," she said, and she leaned closer until he finally got the hint or worked up the courage and kissed her.

What she paid attention to was the kiss. The feel of Ryan's lips, their pressure on hers. The embrace. She was aware of Paul periodically silently shouting *More beer!* but she didn't bother to answer him. As much as she loved Paul, she missed these physical sensations, and the anticipation of what was to come.

When Ryan broke the kiss to stand up next to her, Amy put her index finger on his nose and said, "If you go shave, I'll be naked on your bed when you get back."

There was a huge smile on his handsome face, a twinkle in his hazel eyes. He began to unbutton her shirt. "I love to unwrap my presents. Don't you?" and he kissed her again.

ॐ 5 ॐ

"Wrztf?" Ryan flailed with his left hand until he hit the alarm button, sending the clock off his night stand and halfway across the room. He hoisted himself up on his elbows.

Amy wasn't asleep. She had spent the last hour staring at Ryan's sleeping profile, wishing he'd wake up to make love to her again, and wishing Paul would wake up from his drunken stupor so she could talk to him about her conquest. "Good morning, handsome," she said. "Sleep well?"

"I slept? I don't think so." He kissed her on the forehead, and she rubbed his chest with her hand. "That -- that was tremendous."

"Sure was," she replied. "When I get back with Lucas, maybe we should try it again. On a weekend."

He closed his eyes. "Get up. Get up. Got to go to work." It took a few seconds before he leaned forward and sat up, throwing off the sheet.

She inhaled sharply at the sight. That handsome man, thin, well muscled, who had spent most of the night bringing her pleasure and release. She reached out but missed as he stood up, back and bare buttocks toward her. "I don't know how I'm going to stay awake at work," he said, looking over his shoulder at her and smiling.

Amy lay back and stretched lazily. She watched Ryan stride to the bathroom, then heard the sound of the shower behind the closed door. Silently she shouted, *Wake up, Paul!*

"Huh? What?" aloud.

"Thank you for behaving last night. I had a wonderful time."

"Good. I don't remember a lot of it. Damn, my head is killing me."

She snickered. "That's funny, my head feels fine, and it's the same head you're in. Think it was that beer?"

"Ow. What did he put in it, anti-freeze? Sure was good though."

"I've got an eleven o'clock flight, and the suitcase is in the car. What do you want to do until then?"

"Sleep? Can I have some aspirin?" After a moment he added, "Ow. Why does our face feel funny?"

"Five o'clock shadow. Takes some kind of man to have that kind of stubble." She put her palm to her cheek. "It's okay, I packed makeup."

"Who are you talking to?" she heard Ryan call from the bathroom. He opened the door and stood there, toweling off.

"I talk to myself," she said. "A lot. And I answer me, too. Is that okay?"

"You can walk on the ceiling and I'm good with it." He flicked the towel in her direction, even though he was on the other side of the room. The fleeting view of his naked genitals made her grin. At the same time she heard Paul think, *I used to have one of those.*

"There's not much in the kitchen, so don't even bother looking. Let yourself out the back door and it'll latch behind you." He fumbled in a bureau and pulled out underwear. "I've got a security team meeting at nine-fifteen, so I have to hurry." He turned to face her and saw her big smile that showed off her crooked front tooth.

"Damn, you're cute." As she began to blush he added, "Call me tonight to let me know you made it okay." He was getting dressed as he spoke. "Anything I can do here to help you get Lucas back, you let me know." He was fastening a tie that had some geometric design.

"That beer was great," Paul said. "Can I order a couple gallons?"

Ryan walked to Amy's side of the bed, then leaned down to kiss her on the mouth. She put her arms around his neck and tried to pull him down to her. They both laughed. "Get up," he said, "let me take a look at you before I go."

Paul thought to her, *At least he's got his clothes on.* Amy pulled back the sheet and stood up in front of the man. His expression of pleasure made her feel proud to show off her thin frame. She closed her eyes and willed him to do what he did next, put his arms around her and hold her nakedness against his office dress clothes. Paul blurted out, "Your belt buckle is cold!" even as Amy snuggled against his shirt, inhaling the odor of his deodorant and soap and shampoo.

"Yes."

He leaned away to take another look at her, and murmured, "All in good time." Then he hugged her tight again; he nuzzled her hair and said, "Bring my son back." He kissed the crown of her head and was gone.

Amy fell back on the bed, smiling. "Ow!" Paul said out loud. She hugged themself. "That was wonderful." She thrashed their legs and shouted, "Wonderful!"

"Doctor Owens diagnoses you with an acute case of lust. Can we get those aspirin now?"

John Moisant was an aviation pioneer who was killed in 1910 when his plane crashed at a makeshift runway on a farm just west of New Orleans. The modern airport on that site is named Louis Armstrong International, but its government monogram remains MSY -- Moisant Stock Yard. From humble beginnings it has grown into the tenth largest airport for a city of its size.

The BravoAir attendant watched Amy fill out the form to check a bag with an unloaded firearm, and directed her and her suitcase to the TSA kiosk. A bored agent with blue laetrile gloves pawed through the underwear and unfolded her shirts, then held up her box of ammo. "You use round nose?" he asked, dismissively. "Get yourself some hollow points."

"Thanks for the suggestion," she said, hiding her irritation at the delay, "I'll do that."

He opened the hard case, checked that her Ruger was unloaded, then closed the padlock on the case. "Zip it up and you can go," he said, already turning to another victim—uh, customer.

With that behind her, she waited on the security checkpoint line for another eight minutes. Her earrings set off the metal detector, and the agent called her back. Angry, she removed the cheap jewelry; she tossed it in a trash can and walked through the scanner without more incident.

Amy wished she had a skateboard to get from the back of the security checkpoint to the far end of Concourse B. She felt as if she'd been walking all day when Paul shook their head and said out loud, "All right. I'm awake. How are you doing? And where the fuck are we?"

Her annoyance switched to him. *The airport,* she thought to him sharply. *"I'm tired and cranky. And you've been asleep all morning while I've been dealing with all these little dictators.*

Let me lead, he thought back. *You can tell me about Ryan and sleep on the plane.*

She retreated, and her mood improved. *Thanks. Tired and cranky, you know?*

So you said. Hey, where are we going? He nodded at an elderly couple walking in the opposite direction. Paul loved it when Amy let him lead; there was a huge smile on their face, despite the beard burn.

"Gate B-17," she said. "BravoAir flight 2153."

Paul walked faster, and started to whistle a tune. Amy called silently, *Slow down! I'm sore from last night. Don't you feel it?*

This is weird, even for us, he thought back. *This morning I had a headache and you didn't. Now you're sore and I'm not.* He began walking slower.

I'm used to us having private thoughts and memories, Amy mused, *and whichever one of us is leading gets the buzz from beer or food. But personal body sensations? Paul Owens, what are you doing to my one and only body?*

"I don't know," he said softly. "I slept through most everything last night."

In the gate waiting area Amy drifted to sleep. Paul dragged his paperback out of her purse, then sat and read until the flight was called. She did not wake up until they were circling Atlanta.

"Much better," she said out loud, startling Paul as he read, and leading the businessman in the center seat to say, "What is? Better than what?"

"Awake is better–" and she heard Paul think, *Stranger next to us.* "Oh, uh," she turned, embarrassed, to the man in the dark grey suit. He had a question mark on his face. "I was tired and I took a nap. I feel better now."

"Excuse me," the stranger said, "but I've been watching you read and not fifteen minutes ago we talked about The Braves' season." She could feel Paul slap his inside face. "Really?" she said. "I hope you were a gentleman and did not take advantage of me." She smiled and looked down at Paul's book. *You could have told me,* she thought to him.

Nah, she heard, *this is too much fun.* Meanwhile, the businessman actually undid his safety belt and moved into the aisle seat. *Did he, you know, make a pass or anything?*

Of course, Paul thought. *Believe me, Ryan is a better kisser.* Amy squinted and slammed his book shut, losing his place. She stared out the window at the green countryside south of Atlanta. It wasn't until she heard Paul laugh that she realized he was kidding. *Yank my chain, why don't you?* she thought, but she wasn't angry anymore.

The two baggage claim areas were enormous, each the size of three football fields. The steward had announced luggage would be at the North Terminal in carousel four, and within twenty-five minutes the conveyor belt began to disgorge suitcases onto the moving metal sections. A man grabbing for his own valise pushed her away, prompting Paul to think to her, *Too bad our pistol is in the bag. Asshole!* She had to wait until the carousel made a complete circuit before she could claim her case.

Then it was downstairs to the car rental kiosk, and from there a long drive in a strange city to the Motel 6 Paul had identified. "I thought roads in NOLA were bad," Amy said, swiveling her head, looking for a gap to meld into the traffic on the interstate. "These people are insane." She finally fit the tiny rental car into the flow of cars. Three minutes later she glanced at the dashboard and cried, "I'm doing seventy and everybody's passing me!"

"Want me to drive?" Paul offered. His offer calmed her down, making her realize she didn't have to be the one who navigated these strange speed-demon urban-jungle roadways. She took two deep breaths. "No, I'm okay. But thanks. You can get us to that place where he works, okay?" She felt Paul's excitement. She thought, *You really do like to drive.*

"Nah. I love it. HEART IT!"

It was after two when Amy parked outside the lobby of the motel. The middle-aged black man behind the counter greeted her, and almost immediately he found her reservation. *At least this is going fast,* she thought to Paul. The clerk gave her a key card and instructions on taking the outside stairway to the second floor, and then going most of the way down the hall.

Amy let Paul lead to bounce her suitcase up the stairs. *I have got to wash my face,* she thought to him, *and change clothes.*

And load our gun, Paul thought back. *Christ, it's as humid here as it was back home.*

She let Paul use the key card to open the room door.

Everything was beige. The carpet, the bedspreads, the textured wallpaper, the curtains, the lampshades, even the abstract prints hanging over each of the queen-size beds. Paul threw the valise on the near bed and unzipped it, then retreated. Amy kicked off her shoes, and was walking to the bathroom as she pulled off her shirt. The water was hot, the bar of soap tiny, and the washrag was beige. Slowly she rinsed and washed her face, then rinsed it again. When she dried off she said out loud, "Much better. I almost feel human again."

"Good. No time like the present to meet Lucas. Anthropomorphos-dot-com, here we come."

"Yes." She loaded two seventeen round magazines, then inserted one in her pistol; she racked the slide to put one round in the chamber, and decocked the hammer.

"Are we wearing a skirt?" Paul asked.

"I'm thinking - I'm thinking these slacks and the hip pack. And it's going on the right side." Amy felt the left-handed Paul stick out their tongue. "What?" she said, "I'm letting you drive."

She pulled a gray bow blouse over her head, then stood in front of a mirror and tied the bow to show off just a hint of cleavage. "Okay, I look decent," she declared. "Let's get there before they close for the day."

Paul had entered the address in Amy's GPS the day before. While he drove, Amy practiced what she'd say to Lucas. "'Hey, rich boy!' No, too flippant. I know, 'The bad news is that your grandfather is dead.' No, no, no. Maybe, 'Your dad wants to know if he should set the dinner table for you.'

"Oh, for crying out loud!" Paul laughed. "Pretend I don't know what's going on. Tell me."

"Okay. There's this man who just got left a ton of money in his grandfather's will. I'm going to convince him to go back to his father, after running away two years ago, so he can collect. How's that?"

"Pretty good," Paul said. "He only has to stay long enough for the legal rigmarole, right? It's not like he has to quit his job and live with dad." He made a left onto a wide street called the Glenridge Connector. It was surrounded by hotels and modern office buildings.

"I hadn't thought of that," Amy said aloud. "Yes, you're right. If he thinks his sexy father is some kind of monster, he doesn't have to stay with him." She laughed. "Besides, my life would be easier if sonny boy wasn't underfoot."

"It's over there," he pointed across the intersection. A quick left on something-Ferry Road, then into a parking lot at number 780. The office building was five stories, dark glass and brown stonework. Paul took a space labeled "Visitor" and turned off the engine.

"You ready?" he asked.

Amy looked in the rear-view mirror and patted an adventurous lock of hair into place. "Show time," she said, using one of Paul's favorite expressions.

When the elevator opened on the third floor she found that Anthropomorphos.com occupied the entire floor. The lobby was decorated in an industrial loft style, with exposed pipes and ductwork at the ceiling. The walls were textured concrete, covered in places by huge posters advertising some of the games Anthropomorphos.com had developed. Two concrete floor-to-ceiling pillars appeared to be keeping the fourth floor in place, like Atlas carrying the world on his shoulders. The floor was hardwood with a brilliant polyurethane finish.

Amy went to the minimalist blonde wood desk where a bored receptionist sat. "Hi. I'm looking for Lucas Doublet."

The receptionist was high contrast—a translucent complexion surrounded by black hair, a black sweatshirt, and kohl eyeshadow. "Who can I say is here?" the woman asked as she reached for the intercom phone.

"That's just it," Amy said, smiling. "He doesn't know me. I'm a private investigator and I have some important news for him. Uh, he's not in trouble or anything. Can I just surprise him?"

She put phone down. "Gee, I can't just let you in. We've got security—"

While she spoke, Amy took out her PI badge holder and held it in front of the woman, just as she did so many times with her police ID. "Talk about security," Amy said. "I'm not here to cause a problem."

"Gee, detective. Uh, okay." She stepped on the remote door lock and pointed, "That door. Lucas is about halfway back on the left."

She heard Paul think, *What a sweet talker you are. That smile - that's the one that always works on James, right?*

Dad tested and Dad approved, she replied silently.

The work room was almost as big as the baggage claim area at the airport. An outside wall with windows was brick, but the other three were concrete, textured by having been poured into a frame of wood boards. In addition to ducts and pipes overhead there were rows and rows of daylight LED tube bulbs. Cubicles were everywhere, an out-of-place cloth and plastic labyrinth that clashed with the industrial design of everything else.

Amy walked to the left wall and started toward where the receptionist told her she'd find Lucas. Three steps down she recognized the boy from the pictures Ryan had shared, suffering a tirade from an older man who seemed to be a boss. The older man's anger or displeasure was evident, even before she could make out his words. But she stopped and thought to Paul, *My God! I knew he was good looking from the pictures, but this is insane. He's—he's gorgeous.*

You had daddy, it would be too kinky to ball the son also.

You can talk all the trash you want, she thought back, *but I'm busy looking at God Almighty.*

"Who are you?" the supervisor barked.

"I am Detective Clear," Amy answered. "I'm here to talk to Lucas Doublet."

"Detective? Are you a cop?"

Asked the direct question, Amy had to answer, "I'm a private investigator."

"Then get out of here." He turned toward the back of the big work room and shouted, "Garibaldi! I need you here!" The man turned back to Amy and said, "If you don't leave, my security chief will make you leave."

Paul took the lead to talk past the man at Lucas. "Here's my card," he said, sounding just like Amy. "I'll be at your apartment later. Six o'clock?" Lucas nodded, examining her business card.

"What's up, Mister Travis?" The security man was tall, bald, broad, and wearing some ad-hoc uniform. He stared at Amy through squinted eyes.

"I'm out of here," Amy said. "*À plus tard*, y'all." She stepped backwards until she was satisfied the muscle with the bullet head wasn't following her. Then she turned and left.

It wasn't until she got out of the elevator at the ground floor that

Paul thought to her, *We never heard his voice. He didn't say anything."*

Maybe he's mute, she thought back, *like Igor[7].* She heard Paul add, *Or Wiley Coyote. Or Gromit the dog. Or Harpo Marx—well, without the bicycle horn.*

"You're making them up, right?" she whispered as they walked to the rental car.

She felt him shake their head. "May as well be," he answered.

After Amy got comfortable in the rental car, she said, "I think we wait on his doorstep." Both of them liked the privacy of a car, where they could speak aloud without attracting stares or making bystanders uncomfortable. She leaned forward to start the engine. "Do apartments have back doors?"

"Let's find out. I'll drive."

What had seemed to Paul to be a short drive when he looked at the online map in New Orleans took nearly an hour in the dense rush hour traffic, even with the GPS pointing the way. Once he reached the huge Baron DeKalb Apartments sign he drove slowly through the parking lot, trying to find Lucas' building. There were four long structures, each the same three-story white stucco topped with maroon Mansard roof. Four trees were kept safe in six-by-six foot concrete islands in the parking lot; the only other green (aside from the occasional Toyota) was from low, decorative bushes growing along the face of each building.

"5942 ahoy," Paul said when he spotted the right one. He found a parking space without a painted stencil number and turned off the engine. "It's not six yet," he said. "What do we do?"

Amy led and got out of the car, locking it behind her. *Sit by his door and play rock paper scissors,* she thought to him. *You beat me last time.*

---

[7] Paul had dragooned Amy into watching *House of Wax* more than once. For whatever reason, she felt sorry for the character played by a young Charles Bronson.

The building lobby was a large room, painted the same landlord beige as the motel room, with nondescript curtains flanking the four windows facing the parking lot. There were several chairs with pale green upholstered seats, and a sagging green sofa. On the left wall two chrome elevators waited for their buttons to be pushed; for the impatient, there was a stairwell on one side. Amy called for the elevator.

When she entered the shiny cube, she pressed the button for the top floor, the third. Paul said, "Unit 315. He must be in apartment 15," and she nodded.

The hallway was dim, with whatever low power incandescent bulbs were still legal. The wallpaper was a dull yellow pinstripe, vaguely matching more beige carpet. *You get to knock,* Paul thought, *you're the boss.*

She expected silence, but her knock brought the sound of nearing footsteps. Lucas Doublet opened the door, arms wide, and said "Kali, it's—" before it registered on him that Amy was at his door. "Hi, Lucas," she smiled, and started to walk into his apartment. "I'm sorry we didn't get to talk at work."

The man lowered his arms but did not move from the doorway, so Amy walked into him. She felt a warm glow at having touched the beautiful boy.

"What do you want?" he shouted. "I nearly got fired because of you. I was already in trouble before you showed up."

She smiled. "I think I can fix that. May I come in?"

"NO! I don't even know if I want to talk to you."

"Here's the deal. Your grandfather died and left you a big pot of money. You have to come back to New Orleans to sign some papers."

Still blocking the doorway, Lucas' eyes popped open. Amy heard Paul think, *Which question will he ask first?* Instead, the man surprised them both by saying, "Who are you, now?"

She gave him another one of her cards. "Amy Clear. I'm a private investigator. Your father asked—"

"Oh, fuck, no!" and he stepped back to try to close the door. Amy held out their hands and said, "Two hundred thousand dollars."

He blinked.

"And it's not like you have to move home. You just have to take care of some legal stuff."

They looked at each other silently for several seconds. Paul said, "Look, my feet hurt. Can I come in?"

This time Lucas stepped back and let Amy pass.

The apartment echoed the lobby's decor, with beige carpet and pale yellow walls. He led her to the living room, where the furnishings led Paul to laugh out loud—brick and board shelves, with half a pyramid of empty beer cans on the top.

"What's funny?" Lucas asked, getting defensive.

Paul responded, "Reminds me of my first couple of apartments. How long have you been working on the Great Beer Pyramid?"

He looked up at the display. "I don't know. Eight, nine months? I don't drink that much."

"The only reason I finished mine," Paul said, nodding, "was it was only four across on the base."

Lucas looked around and led Amy to a second-hand sofa in what appeared to be surprisingly good shape. As she sat, the man said, "When did Grandpa die?"

"Sometime in the last few months." She slipped off her shoes and began massaging her right foot. "I didn't feel like I could intrude on your dad and ask him when. Or how."

"Gramps was a great guy. He loved cats, last time I saw him there were six or seven around the house." He looked out a window for a moment, then turned back and said, "So, what happens next?"

"You come back to New Orleans with me. Your father and the lawyers explain everything, you sign some paperwork, and you'll be wealthy. You can stay there or come back here."

"Really?" He drummed his fingers on the arm of the sofa. "How's dad?"

"He's okay. He says he's proud of you and he wants to tell you so."

"Did he say why I left?"

Amy said, "He told me why he thinks you left. Why don't you tell me the real reason?"

He turned on the sofa to face her. "I went to Edward the Confessor High School and I hated it. I got good grades and all, but it was so boring. So regimented. It was like prison with prayers. When I finally graduated, all I wanted to do was play on the computer. And sit in a tree in the back yard."

"He, uh, he didn't mention the tree."

"Yeah. So when dad got heavy about wanting me to go to college—Louisiana Tech, of all places—I said no. He said yes. I said goodbye." He chewed on the side of his thumb. "I was so mad. I'm still mad."

"I'm no therapist," Amy said. "Our parents love us, even when they're wrong. I can tell you your dad regrets everything now. He says he was a bigger jerk than you were."

"He called me a jerk?" defensiveness rising.

Paul took the lead. "Relax. All of us are jerks some of the time. At least he recognizes he was worse than you. He said he was the adult, he's the one who should have known better."

"No kidding?" A smile slowly crept onto his face. "Maybe the old man's wising up. All in good time, I guess."

She heard Paul think, *That's what Ryan says, 'all in good time'. Guess he's a chip off the old block.*

"Tell me about your dad." She tucked her bare feet under their butt.

"Well, he's a—wait, how long have you known him?"

"Nine days? He hired me to find you."

Lucas shook his head. Amy thought to Paul, *He really is so good looking!*

"My father is a slug," he finally began. "He lives on the couch and watches old movies on cable. I could never get him to come out to shoot hoops with me." She heard the resentment in his tone. "He's not mean or anything, just—I don't know, lazy? But he works hard.

He really knows computers and he taught me enough to get a job like what I'm doing at Anthropomorphos.com."

"I don't know why I thought he was into gardening. Hiking."

"Dad?" he laughed. "Not unless he's had a personality transplant since I left. I'm telling you, the TV is his best friend. His office has all these old movie posters."

Ah, she thought to her dyad, *we saw those posters while Ryan was buying my plane ticket.*

Paul untucked their legs and rubbed their left foot. "If you can tell me, what happened with your mom?"

They watched Lucas' posture sag. It was a while before he said, "She killed my little sister and she's been locked up ever since." He was biting his lower lip. "I love my mother. But how do you trust someone who kills a baby?" Then, "She's never coming home. It fucked over my dad. He still loves her, I understand that, I still love her, too. But they'll never let her out of Jackson."

"So, the last time you saw her?"

"A couple of weeks before I left. I told her I was going to move to North Carolina for a job and she said that was a good thing. She wished me well. And she said she wouldn't tell dad." He turned on the sofa to face her, eyes squinting. "Why do you want to know all this?"

"I like your dad," Paul said. Amy shouted silently at him. She began to sputter out loud to Lucas, but the man said, "Oh."

"I was out of line," Amy said, "it's none of my business and your dad is just a client and I guess I'm just nosey. I used to be a police detective so I'm used to asking questions but—" She heard Paul think, *You're babbling. Stop.* She took a deep breath. "I'll stop now."

They sat in silence for a minute.

"What am I supposed to do now?"

"Come back to New Orleans with me," Amy answered. "Meet the lawyer. Sign some papers. See if you and your dad can't be friends, I guess. You'd be free to come back here, you know."

"I need to think about it. I want to talk to my girlfriend about it."

Amy nodded. "Right now, the plan is I can stay in town until

Monday. Can we talk tomorrow? You can let me know what you're thinking."

"I guess. But Kali's going to be here soon, so you have to leave. She's the jealous kind."

She let herself laugh out loud. "With your looks, she should be." She heard Paul think, *He's blushing. Isn't that cute?*

"Let me think about what you've said. Uh, how much money again?"

Amy smiled. "Two hundred thousand dollars. Before taxes. My number's on my card," she handed him another one. "Talk to you tomorrow." Lucas followed her to his apartment door, and waved as she began walking down the hallway.

I want to talk to the girlfriend, Amy thought to Paul. He answered, aloud, "You still think like a police detective."

"Wish I still got paid like one." She sat on the beige carpet across from the elevator bay to watch.

It wasn't long before the elevator went "ding!" and a woman stepped out of the car. Amy heard Paul silently shout *Hellooooo Nurse![8]*

She had to be the girlfriend. The woman was tall and skinny in a loose knee-length shift. Its eggshell hue set off her dark, wavy hair and her exotic Asian complexion. Paul and Amy both thought she was a match for Lucas in the looks department. The woman stopped as Amy struggled to her feet. "Hi, I'm Amy, I'm a detective," she said. "You're coming to visit Lucas Doublet?"

Smiling but uncertain, she said, "Is there anything wrong? Lucas, he's okay?" She had no accent.

"He's fine, I just talked to him. There's nothing wrong. He can come into some family money." She offered her business card. "Ask him about it. And please remind him to call me. I'm the go-between."

The dark woman looked at the card and nodded. "Thank you,"

---

[8] "We're Animaniacs! We have pay or play contracts. We're zany to the max, There's baloney in our slacks..." Paul's favorite was Yakko, who reminded him of Ringo Starr.

she said.

Paul then jumped to the lead. "And if I may say, you are lovely. Absolutely lovely."

She smiled broadly. "Thank you. I was on the cover of *Atlanta Magazine* in April." Then she headed down the hall to Lucas' Apartment 315-C.

Alone in the elevator, Amy joked, "I'm going to tell Christine what you said to the girlfriend."

He snorted. "I am a Christinavore and an Amyoholic. But just because I'm on a diet doesn't mean I can't look at the menu."

"At least you don't say crude things."

No point, he thought back as the elevator opened at the ground floor. *All that is understood anyway. What is she—Indian? Pakistani? She really is—tch!* as if he had kissed their fingers.

You got that right, Amy thought back. *But she's skinnier than me. I hate her.*

Understood. And it's not like she's going to sleep with us, so I hate her, too.

Walking back to the rental car, safely away from people, Amy said aloud, "You and I, we have so much in common. Whatcha doing tonight, big boy?"

"Fried chicken and peach cobbler. With luck this is our only night in this town. I wonder what's the local beer?"

Paul led to drive back to their Motel 6. A different desk clerk was on duty. Amy asked for a restaurant recommendation for fried chicken.

"There's a Popeye's across the Perimeter."

Laughing, "I'm here from New Orleans. I want real fried chicken."

The man thought a moment. "There's Mary Mac's."

Paul led to ask, "As in the Monitor and the Merrimack?"

"I don't know what that is." Carefully, slowly, the man repeated and expanded the name: "Mary Mac's Tea Room. It's downtown."

Amy thought to Paul, *What are you two talking about?*

"A tea room? I don't know."

"Their collards are so good you can drink the pot likker."

What language are you two talking?

Southern, he thought back. *Alcohol content of pot likker is zero point zero.* Then, to the clerk, "Anything else? For fried chicken."

Laughing, the man said, "If you don't mind being half the age of anyone else there, the Colonnade. There might not be a long wait this early."

"I like being the youngest woman in sight," Amy answered, and she asked for directions.

She showered and put on clean clothes, a pale yellow shirt and dress jeans. "We didn't ask if there's a dress code," Paul said.

"There is never a dress code for a pretty girl," she answered, applying makeup before the bathroom mirror. "In NOLA, a flash of boobs would get me anywhere."

Did I miss something? he thought back, not wanting to move their face while she wielded the eyeliner pen. *Have you ever done that?*

"God, no, I'm a lady. But how many times have we seen it work?"

"Ah. Mardi Gras throwers. Check."

"And that fake concert you dragged me to at Tipitina's."

Paul replied, "Tribute concert. Yeah, that was a bit strange. It's not like those girls were trying to kiss the real George Harrison."

She dropped the closed pen in her purse. "Are you still talking southern?" she said out loud.

"No, now it's fab scouse. I'm tri-lingual."

"No wonder Christine is so crazy about you."

"Did—did you just make a dirty joke? Who are you and what have you done with the real Amy Clear?"

"A girl has to have her secrets," she smiled as she locked the motel room door behind them.

It took Paul three-quarters of an hour to find the restaurant, even with the help of the GPS. The place was on a schizophrenic street that put nudie bars cheek by jowl with old southern establishments of taste and refinement. *This is just like the French Quarter,* Amy thought as they got out of the rental car. *Antoine's right next to Sleazy McBimbo's Skin Emporium.*

Paul thought back, *First time I went to New Orleans, you—my God, James and Tracey weren't gleams in your grandparents' eyes. I'm walking up Bourbon Street and some bored barker in a shiny suit is repeating 'Here's where they do it, folks. Stripped raw.' He wasn't talking about oysters.*

Did you go to those kinds of places when you were a man? Out loud she told the manager at the *maître d'* table it was just one for dinner.

Well, sure. I think it's a law, every guy has to go once or twice.

The manager offered, "As soon as I get that table bussed, miss."

She smiled at him, but kept thinking to Paul, *So, you went once or twice? That's all?*

Paul could tell she was just teasing, that his answer didn't matter except as friends like to know one another. *A guy rite of passage. Every time one of my friends got engaged, or divorced, or fired, or found a new job, a bunch of us would have to take them to some slime pit to throw dollar bills at mostly naked women.* Silently he laughed. *It would have been unsupportive not to participate. Rude, even.*

"I understand," Amy whispered. "It was the man's code, the unwritten law, you had to do it. Your friends needed your help with all those bare boobs."

Something like that. The worst part was knowing that if you so much as touched one of the girls a bouncer who looked like the entire defensive line of the Saints would rearrange your face. Naked women, great. Spending money, not so much.

"This way, miss." Amy followed a waiter in a red jacket, threading their way through the noisy crowd of diners. She heard Paul point out the walkers propped up at so many tables. *You really are the child in this place,* he thought.

Eventually Amy was seated at a small table surrounded by a

mixture of Red Hat Ladies and Gulf War veterans. There were two younger people nearby, bored children in single digits who had no choice about keeping Grandma and Grandpa company. Amy thought, *Not a good place to pick up a man. The chicken better be good.*

It was. The entrée was half a chicken, fried with batter and breading that was to Popeye's as a Cadillac is to a tricycle. Amy thought, *My mouth wants more but my stomach says no.* The side dishes were just as good—collards for Paul, although he did not drink the pot likker, and cucumber salad for Amy. As usual they juggled the fork, for the taste was strongest for whichever one was leading at the moment, but no one seemed to notice. And they both approved of the local Sweetwater 420 beer.

The only disappointment was the lack of peach cobbler. "We only serve that on Fridays, miss," the waiter apologized.

"Just as well," she said, "I don't have room for dessert. May I get a doggie bag for the chicken?"

Waddling through the dining room to leave, Amy noticed there had been a big change in the clientele. *The walkers are gone,* she thought to Paul.

So are the old ladies, he thought back. It occurred to both of them that somewhere around eight o'clock the senior citizens had gone to sleep and Atlanta's gay men had come out for dinner. *Can't blame 'em,* Paul thought. *The food is great and it's not grossly expensive.*

When I get back to the motel, remind me to add this to the expense report. Then, out loud, she said, "Thanks for dinner, Ryan."

Back in the parked car, Paul led to put the key in the ignition, then sat back. "Are you as stuffed as I am?" he asked aloud.

"Absolutely. I can't believe anyone could have eaten that entire meal. Impossible."

"We need a Coke. Bubbles pack things down and make you burp."

One of them did just that.

"Oh, Lord," Amy said, "take me home so I can sleep in the bathtub."

"Yeah, let's take advantage of the Motel 6 courtesy forklift."

After a minute of labored, over-stuffed breathing, Paul said, "If Lucas isn't ready to go back to New Orleans when we talk to him tomorrow, let's take him and that girlfriend we both hate to dinner here."

A wicked smile spread across their face. Amy said, "It might be a violation of the Geneva Accords. Yes, let's. That'll fatten her right up."

Paul started the rental car to head back to their motel room. He made one stop, at a Quik Trip, to buy them a sixteen-ounce diet ginger ale. The empty plastic bottle was rattling around on the back seat long before the blue-and-red Motel 6 sign welcomed them back to their home away from home.

Paul dialed Christine's number. Her "Paulette!" perked him up. "Have you found the boy yet?" she asked. "When are you coming home?"

"We found him. I hope tomorrow we can convince him to fly back with us."

"All that money. You'd think he'd jump at it."

"That's what we're hoping. Hey, how was your class yesterday?"

"Contracts 101. It's hard. Maybe I don't want to do this."

"I'm sure it is hard," Paul said, "but I'm sure you can learn it. That's what classes are for. If you already knew this stuff you wouldn't need the class."

"I guess," glad for Paul's support but still dubious about her own ability and ambition.

"I'll call you as soon as I know when we're coming back. Amy says it'll be Monday at the latest."

"I miss you," she said. "You're better than the medication. Sometimes my head gets fuzzy when you're not with me."

"See if brushing your hair helps the fuzzy," he laughed. "I miss you too. We met our target's girlfriend today. She's super pretty, and all I can think about is you."

He heard Christine laugh, then the sound of her phone hitting the floor, and of the woman scrambling to retrieve it. Still laughing, she finally said, "You are my favorite little liar in the whole world. Tell Amy 'Hi,' and come home soon, okay? I love you, Paulette."

"Oh, Christine. I love you, too. Bye."

As Paul ended the call, he heard Amy think, *She didn't want to talk to me? I'm hurt.*

"She did tell me to say 'Hi' to you."

She wrinkled their nose. "I'll bet she's still mad that I want her to work for me."

Paul placed the phone in their right hand, 'Amy's' hand. "Don't borrow trouble," he said. "Ryan asked you to check in. Hurry up so we can go to sleep."

It took Amy less than a minute to tell Ryan about her two meetings with Lucas and her plans for the next day. He said, "Okay" a couple of times. Then there was an awkward silence. Finally Amy said, "So how was your day?"

After fifteen minutes Paul silently whispered he was going to sleep, and did so.

By the time Amy found the ringing phone somewhere in the pile of yesterday's clothes on the floor, the call had gone to voice mail. She groaned. "Wake me up, why don't you," she shouted at the empty room, "and then run away." She sat on the edge of the hotel bed, wearing a wrinkled yellow shirt from the day before.

"What time is it?" Paul asked out loud. She heard him making the noises one makes when stretching, which fleetingly struck her as odd, since no one was stretching their—her—body.

"A quarter after nine. Who the crap is calling me at a quarter after nine?" She pressed buttons on the phone until it showed her she had a new message.

"Miss Clear," they heard Lucas Doublet's voice, "I am very angry at you. You had no right to drag Kali into this, and now she's hounding me with a million questions. I don't know that I want anything to do with you. I must hear you apologize, and then maybe I'll consider going to see my father. Maybe."

Amy groaned and let herself fall back onto the bed, her feet still on the floor. "Crap. One step forward and a mile back."

Paul said, "You can practice apologies on me."

A mischievous smile. "How's this? 'Lucas, I get paid even if you stay here and wave goodbye to all that money.'"

"Pretty good, but I'm still waiting for the word 'sorry'."

"Ah, my mistake. 'Lucas, I am so sorry that you are a pig headed adolescent.'"

"I'm not feeling it," Paul said, laughing.

Amy called Lucas. "Good morning, it's Amy Clear. I got—yes, yes Lucas, I got—" She rolled her eyes and waved the phone at arm's length while the man spewed his anger and outrage. "I'm sorry—Lucas, please, listen to me—I said—okay. Yes, I—okay." When he finally finished venting she said, "I am sorry that I intruded on your privacy. It was wrong of me and I do apologize." Then she waited for a response

There was a long silence. Lucas's anger was blunted by her accepting his feeling and for taking enough responsibility for it to ask for forgiveness. "Well... all right," he said, a little at a loss.

"Let me make it up to you," Amy went on. "I'll take you to dinner, we can talk more. And if your girlfriend is available, she can come, too. What do you say?"

"Let me run it by Kali. Can I call you back in a while?"

The plan to make a plan being established, Amy ended the call and fell back on the bed. This time she was smiling. In no time she was laughing so hard she had pulled their legs up and rolled to one side, in a fetal position; she was pounding the mattress with one hand with each snort and cackle. She thought to Paul, *Damn, I'm good! I wound him down and I didn't even have to bat my eyelashes at him.*

"Well done, Ace," he said out loud.

When she had regained her composure, Paul asked about how her conversation with Ryan went after he fell asleep.

"Good. We talked more than an hour."

"That long? About what?"

He could feel crimson moving up their face. "Oh, you know," Amy stammered, "this and that."

"Oh. So I missed the phone sex?" he laughed.

"Uh, yes, you did."

After a long silence, Paul said, "I think I'm sorry I asked. No. No, I know I'm sorry I asked."

Tension resolved, she said, "I'm so glad you put up with me."

"I always wanted to be a pretty girl, and then I go and miss the good parts."

"Sometime I'll tell you all about it. All the magic and mystery of being a woman."

"Fuck that," he said, "I mean the sex."

She stuck her tongue out and blew, "Ptthhhhh!"

Lucas called back within an hour. "Kali says we'd love to have dinner with you. She's always wanted to know a detective." Paul noticed he sounded enthusiastic. He thought to Amy, *Don't know what he thinks about us, but he likes that Kali girl.*

"I'm so glad," Amy replied. "I'm looking forward to really meeting her. And I want to hear what you think you might do with all that money."

"Yeah," he laughed, "me, too. Kali may have some plans."

She relayed directions to the restaurant, and they agreed to meet there at seven o'clock.

When she hung up, Paul thought, "We picked this motel because Lucas lives nearby. We could have picked up him and the girl."

"I'm not sure how this meal will go," she answered, shaking her head. "We're all better off with separate escape vehicles."

"Someday, when I grow up, I'll be as careful as you."

Sitting in the surprisingly comfortable motel chair, Amy mused, "Not bad. Twenty-two hundred dollars for what, eleven days' work? Now all I need is a second client."

Paul thought, *Lucas is tight about this girlfriend. He said 'we', and he sounds resigned to letting her spend his money.*

"I let you spend my money," Amy said aloud.

"So, you think Lucas and what's-her-name are like you and me?"

Rubbing their left arm with their right arm, Amy said softly, "Of course not. No one else is like you and me." Now letting their fingers trace their forearm, "And you don't spend much of my money."

"What am I going to spend it on? You're good about letting me get things for Christine. I'd buy you presents, but I haven't figured out how to surprise you."

"I tried to buy a birthday card for you one year, but when I was looking at the ones in the store you asked who it was for. Yes, we can't surprise each other with things."

Paul wrapped their arms around themself and squeezed. "You've got Ryan," he said, "and I've got Christine, and we've got each other. Life is good."

"Yes." She let herself feel Paul's hug, the closest they were able to come to physical contact. Then, "Mister Love of My Life, what shall we do with this fine day." She was surprised to hear her own voice as Paul led to sing a verse of an ancient song she had never heard before about "One fine day You'll look at me And then you'll know It's meant to be..."[9]

Paul was leading when they got to the restaurant parking lot at a quarter to seven. It was more crowded than the day before; he had to park near the back of the lot, where another driveway led to some dingy motel that he assumed charged by the hour.

"I'm leaning toward the pot roast," Amy said as they walked to the entrance. "It's that or the liver."

Paul thought back, *Liver's okay, but pot roast--that lights my fire. How come we never try to cook pot roast at home?*

She replied silently, *I know how to make three things. Four, counting the spaghetti sauce you taught me. Pot roast is a little beyond my, uh, my culinary vocabulary.*

---

[9] The Chiffons, with composer Carole King on piano. Amy has never heard of them or her.

Paul was mentally explaining the low cost of a used crock pot, the ubiquity of internet recipes, and the availability of friends like Christine and Florence for test-driving new dishes, but Amy smiled at the host and said, "I'm back! How bad's the wait?"

"About thirty minutes," he said without looking up. He was the same middle-aged man in a dress shirt, open at the collar; his hair was salt-and-pepper, wavy and trim, and his gold-rimmed glasses were perched on the end of his nose. When he came up for air he said, "Wait—weren't you here last night?"

"Can't stay away," she smiled. "A young couple will be joining me at seven."

He looked down at his table chart. "I think I can seat you in a few minutes. How will I know your guests?"

"Oh, easy. They are stunning. The woman is tall and skinny and gorgeous, and the man is—well, he's tall and skinny and gorgeous, too. They'll be hard to miss."

It was only a few minutes before a host came to escort Amy to a table in a different part of the restaurant. Paul snorted silently as he pointed out walkers and canes to her. "Your server will be with you shortly," the host told her and disappeared back toward the front desk.

I want to know what he'll do with the money, Amy thought. *That'll give me an idea of whether he's coming back with me or not.*

She heard Paul think back, *Also, just what kind of character he has. Is he going to quit his job and blow it all on drugs and tattoos?*

When a waiter in a red jacket arrived, Amy explained she was waiting on friends. "Could you bring four glasses of water?" she asked.

Their watch said 6:01—still on Central Daylight Time—when she saw the host with Lucas and Kali in tow. Lucas was wearing a blue pinstripe dress shirt open at the collar, and khaki trousers. The woman was in beige knit slacks and a beige pullover blouse with a deep blue bow low on her chest; she appeared to have no cleavage to show off, only light brown skin that gleamed behind her outfit. Amy heard Paul think, *Don't leave me alone with her.*

Amy stood when they reached the table. Lucas apologized for being late, then said, "I know you've met, but let me introduce you." His girlfriend leaned forward and hugged a surprised Amy. "Amy Clear, this is Kali Goswami. Kali, meet the detective my father hired, Amy Clear."

It was Paul who said, "Glad to meet you. I'll say it again, you are lovely."

When they were seated, Amy said, "I don't mean to be tacky, but are you related to Sanjay Goswami?"

"That is my father's name," she answered. Her teeth were blindingly white.

"Is he a mathematician?" When Kali nodded, Amy went on, "I had to read his *Treatise On Differential Equations* in graduate school. It took me two months to digest it, but to this day I understand standard deviation. It was a big help when I worked in market research."

"He will be happy when I tell him," she smiled. "Perhaps you can meet him? He teaches at Georgia Tech."

"I hope I'm going back to New Orleans very soon. But on my next trip, it would be a treat."

Lucas and Kali opened their menus and discussed the entrees. Overhearing their conversation, Paul thought, *They're looking for two meals she likes, one of which he can stand. Doesn't matter what he wants.*

"Just like us," she said out loud.

In stereo she heard, "I'm sorry, what?" from Lucas in her ears, and from Paul in her head.

"Ah, thinking out loud. Sorry. I can vouch for the chicken, but tonight I'm all over the pot roast."

Kali said, "I am going to have the salmon salad. We're deciding what Lucas will have."

Can I talk to her? Paul thought to Amy. She nodded, so he took the lead and said, "How long have you been modeling?"

"What? Oh, two years. It's just extra money while I'm in school."

"When we were, when I was on the Parish police, I met some models. Isn't it tough? Competitive?"

"Competitive? Yes. That is why I am having salad."

"Where are you in school?" Paul noticed Lucas was beaming, obviously proud of the woman.

"Agnes Scott," she answered. "My major is chemistry."

Amy interrupted. "What's an Agnes Scott? Remember, I'm not from around here."

The woman laughed. "It is a women's college. Think of Smith or Bryn Mawr with a southern accent. My father agreed with me that math was not my strongest talent. I decided on chemical engineering, and he thinks that is a good idea."

"It is a pleasure to meet such a strong woman," Amy said; to Lucas, she added, "You are a lucky man."

"Strong? Feh!" Kali said. "I am in school, I earn money as a fashion object. But you! You are a detective. You were on the police force." The smile was gone. "You are strong. You are brave. You make a difference."

Amy was stunned by the complement, since she didn't think she had made much of a difference with NOPD. In her silence, Paul led to say, "Thank you. We all do what we can. You'll probably make a great engineer."

The waiter returned with their drinks. "Uh, where does the limeade go?"

"Here," Amy raised an index finger. "Limeade and that Sweetwater."

Lucas said, "I don't think I could handle both of them."

It was Paul who smiled and said, in a fake film noir accent, "Sweetheart, I'm a two-fisted drinker."

Amy turned to the waiter to order, giving Lucas and Kali a chance to decide on his meal. "Pot roast, with cabbage, and, uh, can I get tomatoes and okra?"

When the waiter finished writing her order and looked up, Lucas asked for the salad for Kali, and pork chops for himself.

Amy took a sip of her limeade, holding the glass in her right hand. "Lucas, have you thought about what you'll do with your grandfather's inheritance?"

"A nicer car," he said. "At least I don't have student loans to worry about—that's one of the things I argued about with dad."

She nodded. "Ever considered starting your own business?"

"Not really. But now --"

Kali interrupted. "Did you ever kill anyone?"

"Say what?"

"You were on the police. Did you ever, you know, shoot anyone?"

First she thought to Paul, *Does that strike you as inappropriate?* then she said to Kali, "I'd be happy to regale you with tales of danger and derring-do, but not now. I'm working right now." She turned back to Lucas, "You were saying?"

The man seemed uncertain—not about what to say, but whether or not to speak when his lover had wanted the floor. He looked at Kali, and she smiled back, so he continued. "I like making video games. They have a big share of the electronic entertainment market. It might be fun to do that as a manager."

"Ah. You can be that man who was busting your chops yesterday," Paul said aloud. "You know, you could buy the company and fire him. Or better yet, not fire him, but let him know he's not the boss anymore."

"Travis is so old school," Lucas said. "He knows business, but he'd be just as happy at a used car lot."

"Did you have to take classes to become a detective?"

Amy frowned, "I didn't." Then she pointedly turned back to Lucas. "Do you like your job? What exactly do you do?"

"Anthropomorphos.com makes video games." His eyes swiveled to Kali to see if she was okay with him talking. "I'm on the planning team, and I code a lot, and I help test-drive the results." A smile broke across his face, "That's my favorite part. I'll learn how to do the video rendering if I stay long enough."

The red-jacketed waiter brought their meals. Amy said, "What are these? Sliced tomatoes and fried okra?" She looked up at the waiter. "This is what you call tomatoes and okra?"

"I don't understand, miss. Is there a problem?" He put the salmon salad in front of Kali.

"No. Not a problem. Just a surprise. I guess I expected them to be chopped and mixed." She heard Paul think, *This pot roast smells great. Hurry; take the first bite so I can get some.*

For a few minutes the conversation was full of "That looks good," and "You've got to try this," and "This is better than that place we went to last week." Then Kali said, "Excuse me. I do not mean to be in the way. But why do you change hands with your fork?"

"Uh-oh," Paul said. Then Amy led. "Part of me is left-handed. The left-handed part of me needs to eat with the left hand to taste the food. The other part of me has to do it with the right hand." She smiled. "That way both parts of me get to enjoy this excellent pot roast. Would you like a bite?"

"Oh. You are making fun of me."

"Actually, Kali, I'm telling you the God's honest truth. And really, this pot roast is superb." Paul reached for his beer with their left hand and Kali blinked rapidly and repeatedly. He thought to Amy, *I think we've spooked her.*

"You're ambidextrous," Lucas noted. "So was Michaelangelo. That's cool."

"Tell me about your granddad," Amy said. "Why did he leave this money to you?"

"Gramps had twins, my father and Uncle Jeffrey. My uncle hasn't married, and I'm the only grandchild left. I think he figured his sons are grown up and don't need financial help." He cut more off his pork chop.

Don't tell him, Paul thought. *Let his dad be the one who gives him the news that Uncle Jeffrey is dead.* Amy nodded their head.

"You like your uncle?" Amy asked.

"He's a great guy! He's even better at computers than my father, and he always was up for playing catch or camping out." He frowned at a memory and said, "My father is glued to the sofa."

"And your grandfather—"

"How long have you been a detective?"

Paul stared at Kali, mouth open in annoyance and surprise. Amy quickly took the lead; she stood up and said, "Please excuse me, I need the powder room. Kali?" and she reached out to grab the woman by the wrist.

Once she understood what was happening, Kali followed willingly. When they were in the dim, fancy restroom, Amy turned to face the woman. "I'm flattered that you are so interested in what I do. I'll answer all your questions sometime, but not tonight. I'm working tonight. There are some things I need to find out from Lucas."

"I am sorry," Kali said, even though she was smiling. "What you do, it is fascinating to me. I was born in Kashmir, but the family moved to America when I was little. I have led a sheltered life. A privileged life. But you, you have faced danger."

Amy heard Paul think, *Fans are great, but this is just a little creepy.*

The woman went on. "I admire you, what you do. I would love to be you. I mean, for a day, or a week."

The notion tickled Amy. "If we could trade places for a day or a week, I'd do it. You are stunning, your boyfriend is gorgeous, you're smart enough to major in chemistry for crying out loud. And you're skinnier than I am, damn it." Paul added, "If we did that, though, you'd know all my secrets, and I'd know all yours."

A grin. "I drink bhang," she whispered, "and I smoke ganja."

I used to, Paul thought to the woman, *but Amy won't.*

Kali turned her head, looking for the source of the male voice that had popped into her head. They were alone in the women's restroom. She looked back at Amy, who recognized the confusion in her face. "I'm guessing that was the left-handed part of me," she said. *Damn right,* she heard Paul think. She went on, "You don't need to be me. I'm sure you have your hands full being Kali. And I have to insist that you stop interrupting me and Lucas this evening. I'm working. Don't make me ask the waiter to bring you a dozen bad oysters, okay?"

She looked as if she might start crying. Paul touched her on the arm and said, "Call me in New Orleans. I'll be glad to talk to you. Honest."

"I will behave," she said. "Give me your card? I will take you up on your offer."

Amy handed one over. "That first number is mine," she offered. "It's flattering, that anyone cares as much as you do about my work. Please, please call me."

They walked back to find Lucas holding a bone in his hand, working at getting the last bit of pork chop. "Oh, what can I do with you?" Kali laughed. She play swatted him on the shoulder as she sat next to him. "Women are the only force that can civilize men."

"Amen," said Paul, grabbing the fork in their left hand and stabbing a piece of pot roast.

With Kali forcing herself to observe rather than intrude, Amy and Lucas were able to talk about his plans. He would miss his grandfather, for instance, even though the old man's mind was largely gone the last time they were together. He wanted to see his mother, to tell her how he had succeeded in supporting himself in a different city. Cautiously, he thought maybe he and his father might reconcile. He looked forward to camping with Uncle Jeffrey (Paul reminded Amy not to disclose the man's death). A decent car. Meet up with some people he knew at Edward the Confessor. "When do you want me to fly back to New Orleans?" he finally asked.

Amy was excited that her plan had worked; she had guided Lucas into convincing himself to return home. "Can you get a leave of absence from your job? We can fly down tomorrow."

That provoked an interruption from Kali. "I am not so ready for you to leave!" She put her hand on Lucas's and stared into his blue eyes. "When will you come back? Do not make me say it, Lucas, but please do not leave me."

"We'll talk about it tonight," he said softly, patting her hand. Then he looked at Amy, sheepish. "I'll call you tomorrow, okay?"

"That's fine, Lucas." She picked up the bill—she heard Paul silently shout, *Ninety four dollars!?!* –and stood up. It was after nine o'clock, and the restaurant was emptying out. "Where are you parked?"

As they walked out together, Amy said, "I'm glad we got to talk, Kali. Call me when I get home to New Orleans. And please give my regards to your father." At the same time, Paul thought to her, *Nice to meet you. You really are just lovely.* The woman dropped her purse, and Lucas bent to retrieve it. "Are you a bhoot?" she whispered.

I don't know what that is, he thought to her, *so I guess we are. The left-handed part of us, anyway.* "It's okay, I'm really harmless."

When Lucas handed the purse back to her, Kali whispered something to him. "Thanks for dinner," he said to Amy, "we'll talk tomorrow," and they left. Amy lingered in the vestibule to give them a chance to get away.

Did you mess with her? she thought to Paul.

I didn't mean to. But, yeah. Yeah, I messed with her.

When she hadn't heard from Lucas by noon, Amy called his cell phone. Once again, her greeting was met with anger. "Kali says you were rude to her. You told her to shut up, that's just uncalled for. And then she said you were playing some mind tricks with her. I'm pissed, I tell you what!"

"If I could play mind tricks, Lucas, I'd keep you from getting mad at me." Sitting in the motel's comfortable chair, she leaned forward, elbows on her knees.

"You told her to shut up! What kind of person are you?"

"I'm the kind of person who takes it seriously when I'm working. I was working last night, trying to get to know you and see if you were going to visit your dad. Kali kept interrupting, so I explained that I'd be happy to talk to her another time, but not then. Lucas, I gave her my card and phone number."

"So, all I am to you is a job?"

Amy thought, *Paul, please talk to this man before I tell him to hurry up and die.* He took the lead and said, "The important thing here is your family, and your chance to be given two hundred thousand dollars. Your dad pays me even if you decide to cut off your nose to spite your face."

They could hear Lucas breathing, but he did not respond. Paul went on, "I'm sorry if I upset Kali. She is delightful, she's real smart, I love the way she talks."

"A-ha! So you did play some mind trick on her. She was frightened and upset. Why did you have to attack her?"

"Whoa!" Paul called. "No attack. I thought to her, it's something I can do when I'm near a person. It doesn't work on the phone."

Amy screamed silently at Paul. *What are you doing? Telling him what we can do? Are you insane?*

Maybe I am, Paul thought back to her. *What were you going to tell him?*

She fumed. *If we end up in Mandeville[10] I will say 'I told you so'.*

"Sorry, Lucas. What did Kali say?"

"She said she heard a man talking to her when you two were in the ladies' room, and again when we were leaving. Only there wasn't anyone around."

"That makes sense to you?"

"Damn it! Kali is my girlfriend. If she says that's what happened, I believe her."

Amy was startled to feel Paul smiling. "Good," he responded, "because that is what happened. Remember what Amy said about moving her fork from one hand to the other? Well, I'm the left-handed part of her. I'm a man. And when I think to a person, they hear my

---

[10] Into the 1970s Mandeville, on the north shore of Lake Pontchartrain, was the location of the Louisiana psychiatric hospital. The facility has been moved to Jackson, but to any long-time New Orleanian (or child of long-time New Orleanians) 'Mandeville' is the regional expression that means a state institution with padded walls and rubber flatware, staffed by men in white coats who take tax deductions for oversize butterfly nets as work expenses.

man's voice."

"You've been reading too much Lovecraft," he snorted. "That's a crock of shit and you know it."

"Let's say you're right, and what I've said is bull. You got a better explanation for what Kali told you?"

When he had no response, Paul thought, *He's all yours,* and retreated.

"Lucas? You there?"

"This makes no—I'm having trouble—What can–"

"Hmmm?"

In a conspiratorial voice he said, "Kali can be a little strange."

"She seems fine to me," Amy grinned. "Smart, pretty, what more could you want?"

"So, you really can do that? That thinking thing?"

"Lucas, I've said all I can say about it. You and Kali are safe. She's not crazy and neither am I, right-handed or left-handed." She paused. "How about you? Are you crazy enough to wave goodbye to everything you grandfather wanted you to have?"

"How much did he leave me?" He didn't sound angry anymore.

"You just like to hear me say it," Amy laughed. "Two hundred thousand dollars. When do you want to go back to NOLA to talk to the lawyers?"

There was a long silence.

"Lucas?"

"Kali is afraid I won't come back."

"You can if you want. You don't have to."

"You're no help."

Amy said, "You mean I'm not telling you what to do. You've got lots of possibilities. Look, I'm no therapist, and I can't say I'm all that successful at the boy-girl thing."

"Yeah, I—I'll be all right. I like her, I really do. She's a little strange, sometimes that scares me—uh, makes me worry. I just hate to make her unhappy, you know?"

Paul felt the need to weigh in with his perspective of seventy-five years. "She's outstandingly beautiful, just breathtaking. And she's smart. And you're only twenty. Tough call, I have to admit." Amy added, "But it's your call to make. Look, can I book our flight? I'd rather be home with my friends than hang out up here waiting for you to make up your mind."

She heard some vague sounds while the man thought. Then Lucas said, "Sunday afternoon. Pick me up around noon."

"I will hold you to that, Lucas. See you Sunday. Call me if you want to talk in the meantime."

After she ended the call, Amy said, "Where is a tacky tourist souvenir shop? I want to get stuff for mom and dad. And my sister and her kids."

"And for Christine," Paul added. "When Mary Pat and I were here for our anniversary there was a tourist trap called Underground. Every bit as tacky as lower Bourbon Street. I wonder if it still exists?"

Amy packed her suitcase Sunday morning, shoehorning in the Hot 'Lanta T-shirts and coffee mugs she'd bought as gifts for her family and friends. She heard Paul ask, "Aren't you packing our metal friend?"

"I'm going to wait until I turn in the rental car. Roskette doesn't do us any good in a suitcase." She patted the concealed holster on her right hip.

It was just before noon when Paul parked the car near Lucas's building. The day already was hot, in the mid-eighties, but the humidity was unusually low, and the colors of some of the vehicles in the lot popped in their eyes. He retreated to let Amy lead. When she reached his apartment, she knocked and shouted, "Airport taxi!"

Lucas was in a bathrobe when he opened the door. She saw he was tall, handsome, and unhappy. "Hey, we've got a two o'clock flight. You better get dressed."

From the living room came the sound of a sobbing woman.

"I'm not going," Lucas mumbled.

They walked into the living room. Amy stared at his back in

disbelief while Paul thought to her, *I will drag this pampered baby to the airport whether he likes it or not.*

"What? Not going? What happened?"

He held out his arm to point at Kali, who was sitting, red-eyed, on the sofa. Her mascara had run down her face, leaving streaks like a Hallowe'en mask. She was clutching a wad of tissues.

Silently, Paul thought to her, *You! How can you be so selfish?*

Her sorrow seemed to sidestep the vague anxiety Paul's voice had provoked at the restaurant. "I love him!" she declared. "I am afraid he will not come back." She held the tissue up to her nose.

Amy did not hear Paul's private words to the woman. She said, "That's it, Lucas. You can stay here and be poor. I told you I get paid either way."

He said, "Can we wait until tomorrow? Give me and Kali a chance to sort this out?"

Amy shook her head. "I've already waited. I've wasted a weekend away from my friends to babysit a grown man." She poked her index finger into his chest. "I mean, you're supposed to be a grown man."

Lucas hung his head, ashamed but helpless at being called childish. Kali's dark eyes burned with determination and anger. Amy threw one arm in the air, shook her head again, and actually turned in a circle. "Call your father if you change your mind, but I am out of here."

Before she could move to leave, though, Paul took the lead and said, "Wait a minute. Wait a God-damned minute. Fuck that. Lucas, you're coming with me. Put some clothes on. You don't need a suitcase because I'm sure you've got clothes in New Orleans. Move! Now!" Paul pushed Lucas, catching him by surprise and almost toppling him. "I said 'move'!" He pushed again, in the direction of the bedroom.

What are you doing? Amy thought to him. *I don't need to put up with him.*

He's pissed me off," he thought back. *We'll get a better reference if we bring him back.* Out loud he taunted, "That's right, get dressed!

Don't make me come in there and do it for you!" In fact, Paul was enjoying going off on the man.

"No!" Kali cried, finally standing up and coming toward Amy. "Leave him here with me! Do not take him away." She slapped them on the shoulder.

Do not touch me, Paul thought to her, and she took a step back. He continued, out loud, "If you think Lucas isn't coming back, you don't have a very good relationship. Get it behind you while you're young and beautiful. And—"

"No! No!" she shouted, "Do not take him away!"

Lucas had stopped to listen to Kali, so Paul said, "Are you in the bedroom yet? No? So why have you stopped?" He reached up—Lucas was seven inches taller than Amy—and grabbed and twisted the man's left ear. Lucas bent in pain, and Paul pushed him toward the bedroom.

"No! No! Do not!" Kali continued to yell. Paul thought to her, *If he comes back he'll be a rich man. And if he doesn't come back, you're better off without him. Now please SHUT THE FUCK UP!*

When Paul had finally pushed Lucas into the bedroom he slammed the door behind them. "Clothes," he barked. "Chop-chop."

"I'm not wearing anything under this," he said, tugging at his robe.

"Won't do you any good," Paul answered, "I'm into girls. GET DRESSED!" They heard Kali banging on the closed door, shouting and keening.

Slowly, Lucas took a clean pair of boxers out of a drawer and stepped into them, pulling them up in place under the robe. "How can you treat Kali so bad?" he asked as he sat on the bed to put on socks.

"I'll ask you the same question," Paul said. He heard Amy laughing silently.

Moving slowly, like a robot with a weak battery, he donned a silk shirt, and then grey trousers. When he stuck his feet in his loafers, Paul said, "Yay! Gold star, Lucas, you've done good. Ready to say goodbye to Kali?"

Expressionless, Lucas walked to the door and opened it. Kali fell against him; she wrapped her arms around him and began kissing him wildly, all over his face. "Say goodbye for now, Kali," Paul said out loud. "Come on, Lucas, they're not going to hold that plane for us." He went behind Lucas and pushed their hands against his back, shoving him—and Kali—toward the apartment door. "Oh, you lovebirds are so cute," he said. "Just think of how happy you'll be when you're back together." To Kali he thought, *Please get out of the way. You're just making things harder.*

When Paul finally got Lucas to the open door, he turned to face Kali. "I'm the left-handed part of Amy," he said aloud, sounding just like her. "You are stunning, and I know you're smart. You've got a lifetime of joy and heartbreak in front of you. Please grow up; don't get hung up on this."

A moment later Amy added, "I meant what I said about your dad's treatise."

When Kali began to cry again, Paul thought to her, *Stop that!* He turned away and pushed Lucas down the hallway toward the elevator lobby.

Lucas was docile if slow as they walked across the parking lot to the rental car. Amy thought to Paul, *Well done! I was all for leaving the baby behind, but you took charge. Maybe I'll get a bonus.*

You forfeited a bonus when you slept with Ryan, he thought back. *I was so angry at this kid. And Kali is beautiful, but she's as big a baby as sonny-boy here.*

I liked that ear twist thing. The Mother Superior used that trick on me a few times at St. Giles Academy. Did you think more to Kali?

Out loud he answered, "Uh, yeah. I actually did tell her to shut up. There's something about the sound of an irrational crying woman to make me go ballistic."

I'll keep that in mind, you sexist pig, Amy thought back.

"Oink."

Lucas stopped and turned to them. "How can you say that about her? She's the love—"

"Save it, Lucas," Paul interrupted. "You were having the same problem I was, but you handled it differently. Badly, I must say."

"I just—" He stopped speaking, and let Amy guide him into the passenger side of the rental car. "There you go," she said. "All comfy? Let's see if we can get to the airport in time for our plane."

Paul led to start the car and maneuver out of the apartment complex. "Make a left," Lucas suddenly said. "That'll take you to the highway. Then go east and south."

"I appreciate that," Amy responded. "Are you okay now?"

"I—I think so." He looked directly at her. "You are one strange lady, but you get the job done."

"Yes, indeedy, I do. Thanks."

After a few blocks of silence, Amy asked, "What happened back there?"

"Back where?" He turned to look out the window, then grasped what she meant. "Oh. Kali didn't want me to go. She's convinced I'll never come back."

"Is it just geography? She can transfer to Tulane or something."

"I don't know."

She glanced at him. "Don't know what?"

"I don't know a damn thing. I don't know why Gramps would leave me money. I don't know why I'm going home. I don't know why Kali got so demanding. I don't know why you bothered to drag me away." He smiled. "Thanks. I think."

"Good luck figuring all that stuff out. I'm not sure yet why I bothered."

He pointed, "Change lanes. You want to go east here." Paul flicked the turn signal.

"Did you do that mind game thing with Kali again?"

Amy thought, *Paul? You're on.*

'Yeah," he said. "Your girlfriend is beautiful, but she was too intense for me today."

"How do you do that?"

I don't know, Paul thought directly to Lucas. His jaw dropped.

"How do you <u>do</u> that?" he repeated, more urgently.

"I told you, I don't know," this time aloud, sounding like Amy. "Don't worry about it. It's not catching or anything."

"This has been a crazy weekend," he muttered, and looked out the passenger window.

When Paul pulled in at the car rental station, he let Amy lead to unload her pistol and pack it in the suitcase she was checking. "You have a gun?" Lucas asked, looking over her shoulder.

"I was a police detective for three years," she said, wrestling with the case's zipper. "I got used to it."

"I'm glad I didn't know you had it."

Amy didn't answer; she pulled out the valise handle and wheeled it into the rental kiosk. After she settled the bill, a courtesy van took them to the BravoAir section of the North Terminal.

Waiting at the gate for their flight, Lucas seemed content to study his shoe-tops while Amy, having silently and successfully whined to Paul about *Sir Harry Hotspur of Humblethwaite*, opened her paperback whose cover bore the legend, in large, friendly letters, "DON'T PANIC."

It wasn't until they were strapped into their seats for the two-hour flight that they returned to meaningful conversation. He offered, "Thank you."

"You're welcome," Amy said reflexively. "Uh, for what?"

"You got me away from Kali. If you hadn't pushed me, I'd never have left."

She loosened her seat belt so she could turn in her seat, tucking one foot under her butt. "Sounds like you have a, uh, complicated relationship with her. Do you like her?"

"Oh, yes, I sure do." He smiled, and paused until it faded. "I like how things were before you showed up."

Amy heard Paul think, *Uh-oh. Does he have the hots for you?*

She raised an eyebrow to prod him on.

"Kali's busy in school, she's got her modeling, and she stays over maybe two or three times a week. I've got work, I'm totally into the gym every other day, I've got some friends—it's been comfortable. No pressure, just a lot of fun."

Amy sighed. "So, what happened when I showed up?"

"When she realized I'd go home, she panicked. The only reason she was calm at dinner was she smoked a couple of blunts on the way over. God, she was a wreck."

Paul said, "I'd be wrecked too if I smoked two joints."

"Not what I meant," he shook his head. "As soon as we got back in the car she started crying and talking crazy shit."

Amy waited for him to go on. It was a useful tool she had learned as a police detective. Silence makes anyone nervous and they will talk more than otherwise. Finally Lucas went on, "I knew she liked me. Hell, I like her! But she freaked me out, she was so intense. I couldn't deal with her feelings. I started to, I don't know, shut down."

She thought to Paul, *He played like a grown-up but he's just a kid.*

I don't know that I was any more mature at his age, he thought back. *That doesn't change the fact that I was a despicable creep back then. But him? Freak out because a beautiful woman loves you?* Amy felt Paul shudder.

We don't know about Kali. She may be a queen bitch from hell.

Maybe. Or this poor guy's life may have peaked at age twenty.

"I'm sorry, what?" Amy said. "I was thinking about something."

"I said I guess I'm not ready to settle down, and Kali is."

"So, will you go back to Atlanta?"

After a long pause he said, "I don't know."

"Fair enough," Paul said.

Amy asked, "Do you see other women?"

"What? No! No way. I'm faithful to Kali."

"What about in New Orleans? Old flame there?"

He shrugged. "I had some girlfriends in high school, but I don't know if they're still around or not."

They were quiet for a while, and then a steward pushing a cart down the aisle offered them drinks. Amy settled for a ginger ale, and Lucas asked for water.

Amy asked him to talk about his father. Since she had slept with the man, since she hoped she was in the midst of sleeping with the man, she wanted to know more about him—even from as biased a source as the returning prodigal son.

"Father is okay," he began, "when he's not being a bully. And he doesn't do that very often. Just about college." As he talked, he seemed to put the emotional scene with Kali behind him; he became more talkative and more comfortable. "Mostly he was lazy unless he was at work. You know what mother told me? In college she dated father and Uncle Jeffrey."

"No kidding!" Amy cried, truly surprised. "Why did she pick Ryan? Uh, your dad?"

"I didn't press her. It's not the sort of thing you ask your mother, you know? But she said she had no regrets. Later I asked father and he said it was part of the sibling rivalry they'd always had."

"Let me get this straight," Amy said, tilting her head in thought. "Your Uncle Jeffrey had a thing for your mom?"

A shrug. "I'll ask him about it. We're pretty good friends. I used to wish he was my father instead of, you know, my father. We went camping, he'd play basketball with me. I could talk to him. Huh—" a sudden new thought "—maybe he's got advice about what to do about Kali."

Even though she heard Paul think *Don't do it!* Amy said, "There's something you need to know. Your Uncle Jeffrey died about a year ago."

Lucas's face fell. "No. No, I don't believe you. Father would have told me."

"No one knew where you were," she countered. "You did a very good job of running away."

"Shit, shit, shit," he muttered. Then, "What happened?"

"All I know is what I read in the *Times-Picayune*. Suicide. He hanged himself."

Lucas turned away to look out the little window at the tops of clouds and patches of dull green 28,000 feet below. Amy put her hand on his forearm and said softly, "I'm sorry." She saw him nod, but he continued his sudden interest in nephology.[11]

One hundred miles later he turned back to her. "I remember visiting Uncle Jeffrey in the hospital when he had his appendix out. There were tubes coming out of him, he looked pitiful and scary at the same time. For awhile I hid behind father, but finally I went to him—hell, I think I was eleven or twelve—and I told him if he needed another appendix he could have mine." He smiled at the memory. "He mussed my hair and said, 'You're a big boy, Lucas. A good boy.' I loved my Uncle Jeffrey."

"No reason to stop," Amy said.

The BravoAir jet landed on time at Armstrong International. When they left the secure area so Amy could get her checked bag, Ryan Doublet was waiting for them. "Son!" he called, and came toward them. Lucas grinned reflexively and ran to meet him. They embraced, a long hug with arm pats on backs and even a few tears. "Dad, I'm sorry—" "Sshhh, it doesn't matter, you're here." Amy sat on her suitcase, enjoying the sight of genuine emotion. She heard Paul think, *When I came back from trying to run away, the greeting was not so, so, uh, happy. I couldn't sit down for three days.*

She whispered back, "Look at that. I think maybe Ryan is worth the risk."

But we're staying with Christine tonight, right?

Of course, she thought back. *They deserve time alone together. And I've got laundry to do. Think Christine will come over to our place?*

Amy pulled out her phone, then let Paul dial his lover. "We're back, honey!" he said. "Amy's got stuff to do at the house. Do you want to come over tonight?"

"Anything for Paulette," she giggled. "You've been gone four days; I'm sure Amy's got nothing to eat. I'll stop at Rouse and bring some rotisserie chicken. And I've got a new booze."

---

[11] Study of clouds. Now you're ready for trivia night at the bar.

"Is that new as in you haven't opened it yet?"

"Silly. No, it's something I never heard of until the contracts teacher talked about it. You'll see. How's six o'clock?"

I'm glad Ryan is busy, Amy thought when he ended the call. *Otherwise he'd think I just made a date.*

You have to tell him about me. It'll be great; we'll be able to relax around both our lovers.

The two men stood very close, talking softly, oblivious to the people and sounds of the busy baggage claim area. Amy wheeled her suitcase to them and interrupted, "Mission accomplished, Ryan. I'll--"

"Oh, you have to come to the house," Ryan said. "The two of you, I'm thrilled at what you've done." He smiled at Lucas and patted him on the side of the neck.

"No. You two deserve some bonding time, and I want to make sure my house didn't up and move to St. Bernard Parish. Let me come by tomorrow? I'll have an expense voucher for you."

Ryan Doublet was glowing with happiness. His son in front of him, finally home; the woman who made it possible and who had warmed his bed, the agent who made it so. "Yes, tomorrow. I'll cook dinner. Bring wine. And that overnight bag."

She blushed at the invitation but made a forceful nod. Ryan kissed her on the cheek, then turned back to his son. Amy's hand went to the wet spot on her face as she watched the two men walk away. Paul said aloud, "That seems to have gone very well."

The moment Amy opened her door, Christine threw bags of groceries to the floor to empty her arms so she could embrace her Paulette. "I missed you," she said, and she kissed him again and again. "Next time Amy leaves town for four days, can I come with you?"

"It's great to see you," he returned the hug and kisses. "We had to deal with a crazy woman up there. You're even more of a relief than usual."

When Christine had satisfied her Paulette deficit, she picked up the grocery bags. "So, it was a success, Amy?"

"Yes, it was," Amy answered. She thought to Paul, *She's thrilled to see you but she remembered me. I love your girlfriend.* Amy went on to relate some of the events in Atlanta. As she talked, they migrated to the kitchen. Christine took charge of dinner. She got out two dinner plates, flatware, and highball glasses. She cut up the rotisserie chicken and spooned out the cole slaw she had brought.

"The kid we brought back was overwhelmed by his girlfriend not wanting him to leave," Paul summarized. "And when I say girlfriend, I mean a tall, skinny, exotic fashion model girlfriend. Amy was ready to leave him behind, but I dragged him around by his ear and made him get dressed and come with us. What a baby!"

"Was she really a model?" She took a liquor bottle out of another bag.

"It's Amy. Actually, yes. She was on the cover of the hometown magazine. But she's smart, her father wrote a math book I studied in graduate school. She was great. A tad emotional, but great."

"What on earth is that?" Paul asked.

"The teacher in my real estate class turned me on to this. It's absinthe."

They coughed, the sound they made when they both tried to speak at once. Paul backed off so Amy could say, "I've heard of it, but I thought it was illegal. Doesn't it make you see pictures?"

"That's what he told us," Christine said with an enormous smile, "but it's legal. I got this at Vom Fass on Magazine." She twisted off the cap and poured some of the clear green liquid into the highball glasses. "This is so different! Do you have any sugar?"

Paul said, "I've had single malt scotch, I've had moonshine, I've had Olde English 850. Hell, I've even had Yoo-Hoo[12]. But I never had absinthe. This is fun." As he spoke, Amy turned to a cabinet and took out some packets of sugar. "Here's what I have," she said, and handed them to Christine.

---

[12] If you don't know Yoo-Hoo, ask somebody old. Preferably from the north, and ideally a New York Yankees fan. Yogi Berra had something to do with this.

"We're supposed to do this with sugar cubes, but I guess this will work." She ripped the top off the white packet and poured some of it into each glass. Then she slowly added a few ounces of cold water. The drinks turned milky, with a green tint.

"Give it a second and it'll be ready." Christine was happy that she was bringing something new to share with her lover and Amy. She moved her arm in time, as if she were counting to ten, then picked up one of the glasses. "Tell me what you think."

Amy sniffed at the glass. "I know that smell. What is it?" Then she shrugged and took a small sip.

"Licorice!" she shouted, slamming her glass down on the tiled kitchen island. "God, I haven't had licorice in years. I --" Abruptly she thought to Paul, *I guess it would be rude if I told her I hate licorice.*

"Yes," he replied aloud, then led to take his own sip. The taste of food or drink was always much stronger for whichever one of them was leading. Their mouth puckered, and then he said, "Like ouzo, but twenty times stronger." When he drained the glass, Christine clapped, and finished her own.

Does licorice really go with chicken? And cole slaw? Amy thought.

Tonight it does, he thought back. Then out loud, "Greeks drink a lot of ouzo and eat a lot of chicken, so this will be a great dinner. Thanks for handling it." The woman hugged him, then picked up the plates to carry into the living room. Paul followed with the drinking supplies.

It's not so bad when you're leading, Amy thought. *Do you really like it?*

No, he thought back. *But I really like Christine, and she's excited about sharing something from her world.* By the time they were at the sofa he went on, *I'll add more water to the next one.*

To his lover Paul said, "So people bring booze to the real estate class? Well, this is New Orleans."

"You mean this wouldn't happen somewhere else? I think the teacher just found out about absinthe. He was very excited." She cut into her chicken breast. "And I think he was trying to get one of the girls loaded."

Amy volunteered her hopes about turning her night with Ryan Doublet into a relationship. "He invited me to come over and stay, right in front of his son."

"Encouraging," Christine said. "Is this one married?"

"Uuh... Well, yes. His wife has been in a criminal psychiatric ward for ten years and is never getting out."

"Paulette, what book was that? It wasn't Jane Austen." They both were fans, although Christine preferred the movies and made-for-TV dramatizations to the novels.

"Jane Eyre," he answered. "Charlotte Brontë. Exactly, but she's in Jackson instead of the attic. No one's going to set the house on fire."

Christine nodded, head down over her plate, more cole slaw on her fork. "Not ideal," she said, "but he sounds available. And you know he won't spend Christmas with her."

"I'm hoping my taste in men is improving. Otherwise, I peaked with my dad and Paul."

Christine spent the night, her spat with Amy about the detective company now over. But as she and Paul rested after making love, she suddenly said, "I have to go home."

"What? Why? Is something wrong?" A burst of fear flew through him.

"My mom is sick," she was hugging their body. "I take the last class on Thursday, and the next morning I'm flying to St. Louis. My brother says she's not doing well."

Paul was torn between concern that his lover's parent was ill and relief that she wasn't leaving their bed right then and there. In the meantime Amy said, "Oh, no. You've said how close you are. This is terrible."

"Thanks, Amy—" she always knew which one of them was speaking "—Nathan says she may have had a stroke last night. I want to look after her when she gets out of the hospital."

Paul led to pet her hair and rub her arm and back. "Honey, I'm so sorry."

She squirmed closer, now that Paul was leading in Amy's body. "I'm going to miss you. Amy, too. I don't have any friends in St. Louis anymore."

"I guess you'll have to help her get better fast so you can hurry back to us." They caressed one another. "After your class, can we come over?"

She squeezed them. "You better," she said. A few tears were leaking down her cheek.

The phone line Amy had installed for Clear, Hodges & Owens was silent on Wednesday. For awhile she sat on her sofa, unread book in her lap, staring at the telephone. When that didn't make it ring, she poured herself a glass of limeade and sat in the courtyard behind her house. "Any idea on drumming up business?" she asked aloud.

Paul answered, "Call Walter. He got you the Doublet job; maybe he's got ideas."

"We're brilliant," she said. "Look out, world." She reached for her cell phone.

"Rampart Street, Sergeant Francks," she heard.

"A gracious good afternoon, Sergeant. How's every little thing?"

"Sugar! Great to hear your voice. How'd that job go?"

"Success. Tracked down the missing adult son and brought him back. Been paid, and I hand in the expense report later today."

"So he checked out, huh?"

"First thing I did was cash his check," she laughed. "Then I checked him out. Ten or eleven years ago his wife snapped and killed their baby girl."

"Doublet!" Walter exclaimed, "I should have recognized the name. I worked that case, Sugar. It was so sad. The husband was a wreck, but the wife was real calm, she wasn't any trouble. I remember she said that 'Now everything belonged. Order was restored.' Never figured out what that meant."

"What do you remember about the husband?" Her heart was

beating faster.

"Whoa, nothing, really. He was practically comatose. He didn't have a clue."

"Yes. Look, Walter, you got me my one and only job so far. Any advice for drumming up some business?"

"Sure, Sugar. If you want domestic investigations and lost dogs, put ads up in laundromats."

"Euuww. I don't know that I want that business."

"If I knew the first thing about promoting my own business I wouldn't be taking care of the gun safe for NOPD. Sorry."

Paul took the lead, sounding just like Amy, to ask "Did you ever want to be in business?"

"When I got out of the army I ran a numbers and drug racket in Detroit. The Commander rescued me."

"Is—is that a joke?"

"Walter speaks with straight tongue, Sugar. Commander Ramirez saved me from myself. No, I'm not interested in running any business anymore."

"Okay," Amy said, uncertain. "I'm sorry if I dredged up bad memories."

"Nah, it's just life. Look, Sugar, you know I'll tell people to call you if they need a PI. You were great on the force. I'm not surprised this Doublet job went well."

When she hung up, Paul thought, "Maybe you should call the Commander. He likes to say he's an Amy fan."

She shook their head. "I'm afraid to call him. He was so disappointed when I resigned."

"Yeah, he sure was. You know, you can brag about this job. I bet he'd be glad to help."

"Maybe tomorrow. I have to work up my courage first."

Amy tossed a bug-out bag in the back of her old yellow Benz and led to drive the mile or so to Ryan Doublet's home. "Will you introduce me?" Paul asked. "With Christine leaving town, I'll be a wreck if you're the only person I can talk to."

"Why, Paul Owens. You sound like that would be punishment."
She was smiling.

"Okay, that came out wrong."

"It's alright, I know what you mean. We'll see how it goes."

She parked across the street from Ryan's house. His car was in
the narrow driveway, and lights shone from most of the windows.
"Looks homey," she said wistfully.

"You belong," Paul said. "I hope I do, too."

When she knocked, Lucas answered the door. "Dad's in the
kitchen," he said, ushering her in. "We're having spaghetti."

"How are things going?" she asked in a low voice,
conspiratorially. "I hope it's better than when you left."

"Oh, yeah. Dad's been cool. And I'm a little more mature now."

Amy ignored Paul's silent snicker as they walked into the kitchen.

"Amy!" Ryan called. He was wearing a bright red bib apron, and
was holding a long wooden spoon that dripped red sauce onto the
hardwood floor. He leaned toward her and kissed her on the cheek.
"I'm glad you made it. Open that wine, will you? And then you two,
scoot! No one gets to see my kitchen magic."

Lucas gave glasses to Amy, then took the bottle of Shiraz and a
corkscrew and led her into the living room. As he uncorked the wine
he said, "How long have you and my father been dating?"

"It's still new," she said, holding out her wine as she felt a blush
come up on her face. "Is that a problem?"

"Not at all." He poured her wine, then his own glass. "Mom and
dad are still married, but it's not a practical arrangement. He tried to
date a few times before I left, but—I don't know, I think he wasn't
sure he wanted to. We never talked about it." He took a sip. "He likes
you, you know. He talked about you today."

She heard Paul think, *All Ryan knows is that you found Lucas and
you're good in bed. What else could he talk about?*

"What's he say?" she asked; silently she answered Paul, *Damn it,
I am good in bed.*

"He says he likes you. You surprise him all the time."

"I do?" She took a long sip of wine; then she let Paul lead to take a longer one.

"And I told him about your mind games with Kali."

"You said things are good with Ryan—I mean, with your dad. Any word from Kali?"

The man swirled the wine in his glass. "She emailed me to say she was thinking about dropping out of school and modeling full-time. That way she could travel and come down here." He took a sip. "Do you have any idea how much she makes for a fashion shoot?"

"Actually, I do. When I was on the force I worked a murder that involved a big league fashion model. If Kali saves her money she can go back to school after the modeling dries up."

"You think this is a good idea?" he challenged her.

"Model now, make and save a ton of money, go to school later? Yes. The part about her coming down here to see you is your problem."

He turned from her, but she saw the vein in the side of his neck pulsing. "I see why Dad says you always surprise him."

Paul led to say, "I'm not judging you, Lucas, but I won't help you hide from your issues. You can't make the right decision for yourself if you don't let yourself understand what's at stake." He heard Amy think, *Well done. Now back off. I want to find out more about Ryan.*

"I don't know," Lucas said. "I just don't know."

Amy put a hand on his forearm. "That's okay. Sometimes it takes a while before you can figure out what you think about something. What you feel about it."

"I feel like a bonehead that I don't have an answer yet."

"Give yourself a little slack. Things—"

"Dinner is served!" Ryan shouted from the kitchen. "Lucas, did you set the table?"

"Yeah, Dad," he yelled back as he headed for the dining room. Amy juggled the bottle of wine and both glasses and followed him. *You were never this young,* Paul thought to Amy. *When you were eleven you were older than this kid.*

"Thanks. I think."

The dining room was an eighteen-foot square. Gauzy white curtains covered the windows that made up one entire wall. There was a heavy, dark china cabinet on the opposite side of the room, and a matching sideboard on another wall. The table was large enough to seat ten people comfortably. It looked nicer than her parents' dining room, very clean and very grown-up. The only jarring note was the red-and-white checked tablecloth on the third of the table where the plates were clustered, at the end of the room near the doorway from the kitchen. Candles were burning in two wicker-wrapped Chianti bottles. Paul thought, *A little bit of Mama Rienzi's Pizzaria in the middle of a really nice dining room.*[13]

Ryan had put out plates overflowing with pasta, and a serving dish with two loaves of homemade garlic bread. "You sit over there," he told his son, pointing to a steaming plate in front of the window; "Amy, over here," pulling out the chair on the opposite side of the table. He disappeared into the kitchen again, then returned with two tureens, one with sauce and the other with more noodles. Finally he sat at the head of the table.

"My two favorite people in the world," he announced. "I'm glad you both are with me tonight." He lifted his wine glass for a toast, met by Lucas's and Amy's half-empty glasses.

Paul took the first bite and told everyone, "Excellent!" To Amy he thought, *This is as good as what I make.*

"How long have you been a *chef de cuisine*?" Amy asked.

"Oh, I've always—" She noticed Lucas' jaw dropping, while Ryan began again "—uh, I, uh, I started cooking after Lucas left. I made a lot of changes then."

"Dad, this is very good. I love spaghetti; I'm glad you learned how to cook this sauce."

He smiled proudly. "I remembered that you like it. I even dressed

---

[13] Mama Rienzi taught the author the spectacular spaghetti sauce recipe at the Café Shalom Rienzi in Greenwich Village a couple of lifetimes ago.

up my usual recipe for you." The son greedily took another forkful of noodles and sauce. "Mushrooms for you," Ryan added.

"Tell me what the deal is with the lawyer," Amy said. "Sorry to talk shop," she said to Lucas, then returned to Ryan. "I won't feel like the job is done until your father's will is satisfied."

"I called the probate lawyer today. We have an appointment for a week from Monday. Lucas will sign some papers, and then, eventually, the legacy will be released. It would have killed me for all that money to go to a bunch of house cats." He looked at his son. "You're going to be a rich young man. Maybe not going to college wasn't such a bad idea."

Lucas dropped his fork, splashing sauce onto the checkerboard tablecloth. "Dad! So you're not angry anymore?"

"I've been telling you that since you came home," he said. "Every parent wants his children to do well. Usually going to college is a help. As it turns out, you're doing fine on your own terms." He held up his wine glass again. "No, son, I am not angry anymore."

Dinner conversation covered the shopping spree Ryan had taken Lucas on that day, because he outgrew all the high school clothes he had left behind two years earlier. Ryan clucked about the expense involved in replacing some rotted soffets on the house. Lucas said he gave up looking for high school friends after calls turned up two who were away in college and an old girlfriend who now was married.

Ryan had taken the day off work to go shopping with Lucas, but even so he got several calls from his employer. "One of the multi-core units stopped multi-coring," he fumed. "I told them to reboot the machine and not to call unless something was on fire."

"Multi-core?" Amy asked. "What is that?"

"Many CPUs on one chip," Lucas said. "If the computer is set up right, different applications are handled by different CPUs so they don't compete for brainpower." Ryan nodded and added, "They've been around for maybe twenty-five years. They've got 256-core chips now, but the early dual-core units were breakthroughs."

"Dual core," Amy mused. "That's it. That's us."

"Us?" Ryan's fork was in mid-air, dripping sauce onto his plate.

"The left-handed me and the right-handed me. Two minds in one brain."

There was a long silence, long enough for Amy to think to Paul, *Maybe this isn't such a good idea.* Finally, Lucas said, "I told you about that, Dad. She played mind games with Kali. And she can make her voice sound like a man's."

There was an amused expression on Ryan's face. "Lucas said you helped him escape his girlfriend. How did you do that?"

"That was easy. I dragged him around until he got dressed and left her behind." She made a motion with their hand, "Grab 'em by the ear and twist; they'll go wherever you push 'em. I figured I'd get a better job reference if I brought him back."

"Not that. The boy said his girlfriend told him you talked to her without saying anything."

"In the ladies' room," Lucas prompted. "And then at the apartment."

Yes, she thought to Ryan, *I can do that.*

The amusement on his face turned into a grin. "Well, how about that."

Out loud she said, "Do you want to meet that Owens guy?"

Everyone ignored Lucas saying, "Who's Owens?" Paul thought, *Pleased to meet you, Ryan, I'm Paul Owens. Amy has an invoice for expenses and I'd appreciate it if you'd settle up.*

Ryan laughed. "That is amazing." His smile looked as if the man was about to burst. "Just great. You really are one surprise after another."

"Wait until you see me tap-dance." To Paul she thought, *I survived. I think this is going to be okay.*

I don't—we can tap-dance?

"How did you learn to do this?" Ryan asked, even as he went back to his dinner.

"I'll explain it all some time. I'd rather hear how you two are getting along."

"On Saturday we'll go see Sammie. Lucas's mother. I've told her I was looking for him, and she's excited." He turned to his son, "Your mother misses you."

When the meal was done, Amy picked up empty plates and put them on the kitchen counter. There were three bowls on the other side of the sink, near the stove; she saw one had chopped onions, one had broken mushrooms, and the third, sliced green and red bell peppers. "Out!" Ryan shouted. He was carrying the tureens of spaghetti and sauce. "No one sees my kitchen magic. Out!" She rinsed her hands at the sink and retreated to the living room with Lucas.

"Cooking is a new thing for my dad," he said. "I think he's embarrassed or something about anyone watching him. He yelled at me when I came in to get a glass of juice."

Amy relaxed on the dull red sectional. "He didn't cook before you went off?" She liked the way the ultrasuede felt as she patted the cushion next to her.

"Nope, I was the luckiest kid in the world. I had pizza three nights a week."

"And ice cream the other four?" They both laughed.

Ryan joined them, sitting on the sectional near Amy. "What have I missed?"

"Lucas was telling me about how you've changed since he left. What happened?"

"Oh." There was a long pause. "I felt lousy. I thought I had driven Lucas away, that it was my fault, and that maybe I'd better change my ways. I drank. I stopped working. And then my brother died."

"Dad, you said—"

"Yes. Jeffrey committed suicide." He shook his head. "He killed himself. Mother long dead, father senile, wife in a prison hospital, my son gone, and then my twin. I—I hit rock bottom." Amy put her hand on his arm, and he placed his other hand over it. "But I bounced," he went on. "It occurred to me that I hadn't worked in months, and that it hadn't harmed anyone but me. I owed a ton of money on a second mortgage I took out to be able to pay for the first one."

Lucas left his chair and sat on the beige carpet in front of his father, his chin on the man's knee. "But it wasn't all because of me. Was it, Dad?"

A smile, "No, Lucas. It was Jeffrey who pushed me over the edge." He turned to face Amy and said, "So I shook myself and went out and got a job." There was a long pause. He still held her hand. "I learned to cook. I started to exercise. I planted a garden. I didn't want to turn my brain off in front of the TV anymore."

"I wish I'd been able to help," Lucas said, guiltily.

"Thank you, son. You're home now; that's what matters."

Abruptly Ryan stood up and said, "I want a beer. Amy? Lucas?" Paul answered, "One of your homemades? You bet!" while Lucas shook his head. "I'm not feeling so good," he said. "I think it must have been the peppers. Dinner was very good, thought."

When Ryan came back with refreshments, Lucas said "Think to me again. Now that I understand it, I want to hear it some more."

Amy heard Paul think, *He has to pay in advance before I'll do a trick for him.* Amy shook her head and said "No. I don't do magic tricks and parlor games. In fact—" she pointed her right index finger at him "—never ask me that again." Less sternly she said, "Both of you, please, don't tell anyone that I can do this. We used to be afraid of spending the rest of our lives in a padded cell. I don't much worry about that anymore—yes, Paul, I know you do—but our life will be easier if no one else hears about this. Besides, people will say you're the crazy one for thinking you can hear me. Okay?"

"I don't believe you," Lucas countered. "It's not possible. Kali was upset and misunderstood what was happening."

You're right, Amy thought directly to the man. *It's not possible.* He did not know that he was watching Paul laugh behind Amy's closed mouth.

He nodded, then slowly stood up. "Please excuse me, I'm not feeling well. I think I'll go to bed."

"Come here, boy," Ryan said. Dutifully the man stood before him. Ryan put his palm on his forehead. "You're not running a fever. I hope you feel better fast." Amy waved and said, "Me, too. See you tomorrow."

When he was gone, Ryan put an arm around Amy and pulled her to him for a kiss. She put her hands on the sides of his face and returned it.

"I missed you," he whispered to her ear.

Good, she thought to him.

Beer! she heard Paul think. She broke the kiss, laughing, and said, "Paul likes your beer." It looked to Ryan as if Amy picked up the glass and took a long, un-ladylike guzzle. "You done?" she asked, looking up at the ceiling, then added, "Good, I'm busy." She looked at Ryan and said, "Where were we?"

"Wait, wait, wait. You're not kidding?" He was staring at her.

Let me, Paul thought to her, and then directly to Ryan he thought, *We've already done this. I'm Owens. I'm real. Who do you think just chugged your eleven per-cent homebrew? And when Amy doesn't get tipsy it's because I hope to be floor-hugging drunk before the night is over.*

Amy was watching Ryan's handsome face. She recognized the confusion on it. "What did he say? I can't hear him when he thinks to someone else."

"I do computers. I don't know a lot about psychology and biology, but I'm pretty sure what you're doing is impossible."

"Oh, yes, totally. Do me a favor, though; pretend it's real," she said, and she leaned in to hug him, to feel his solid body and smell the combination of scents that came from him.

"I can do that." He stood and picked her up, and carried her to his bedroom, kissing her most of the way. As they entered his room, they heard noises from behind the bathroom door across the hall. "Poor kid," Ryan muttered. And then he threw her on the bed.

Amy had a wonderful, passionate, satisfying night. She was positive that Ryan did, too, considering his stamina and thoughtfulness. And Paul behaved himself.

A few times Amy thought directly to Ryan: things like, *I like that*, and *Ohmygodohmygodohmygod.*

When they paused to rest, each clutching the other tightly over the twisted sheets, Ryan asked, "So what is Owens doing while we're, uh, getting to know each other?" She swore candlelight was glinting off his smiling teeth.

"Hiding," she answered. "He closes his inside eyes and tries to forget it's a man making our body feel good." She wiggled against him. "He imagines it's his girlfriend." She was tracing lines in his chest hair with her index finger.

"His girlfriend? Your—your—what do you call Owens?"

"Dyad. We are a dyad." She kissed his chest and inhaled his scent.

"Okay. So, your dyad has a girlfriend?"

"Yes, indeed. I assume Paul does the same things when I'm with you that I do when he's with her. Although Christine is a sweetheart; she's a good friend."

He stared at the dark ceiling, trying to make sense of it. "Oh," understanding dawning, "you're bisexual. Wow, that's cool. That's downright exciting."

"No threesome, Christine hates men. And I'm not bi. Paul and I both are very hetero."

He kissed the side of her head and rubbed his hands up and down her back. "Sure. If that's what you tell yourself, I won't argue."

She pushed him away only to climb on top of him, leaning forward to press her body against his. "Let me explain how this began," and she told him about the simple accident at her father's hospital when she was eleven, how Paul's mind escaped his comatose and dying body in a splash of fluid and took up residence in her, how her father investigated and discovered Paul's memories were accurate, how even Paul's sister came to believe in his resurrection in Amy, how she came to Metairie to visit Paul and her family several times. "It's impossible. It makes no sense. But it's what happened."

A long silence while the man smiled openly at her. "You really are an amazing creature."

"Yes, I am," she said, and reached her hand between their bodies. "And you're no slouch either."

When she awoke, she was alone in Ryan's bed. His clock said six forty-five. Amy lifted herself up on her elbows. "Paul?" she whispered.

Good morning, dyad, he thought back. *Did you have a good time?*

"Oh, God!" she said aloud. Then, whispering, "Was it awful for you?"

Nah. I remembered that trick Christine showed me. Whoa!

She was hugging themself. "I like him," she said.

"And we've been introduced. I have high hopes. It'll be great if we can be as open with Ryan as we are with Christine."

"Who are you talking to?" Ryan asked as he came back in the room, towel wrapped around his waist.

"Comparing notes with Paul. He's glad he's met you. And he really likes your beer." She let the sheet fall and she reached for Ryan's towel.

"Uh-uh," he said playfully, stepping back, out of her reach. "If we start up again I'll never get to work. That's no way to pay for home repairs."

"Meanie," she frowned, arms crossed. "Were you checking on Lucas?"

"Yeah. He's fine. Did you two bring some bug back from Atlanta?"

"No. Just him." She swung her legs off the bed, sheet demurely covering part of her body.

"Come over tonight," Ryan said. "Let me treat you to a steak."

"Steak good, tonight bad. Paul's girlfriend is flying home to St. Louis tomorrow because her mom had a stroke. We want to give her some moral support. How about Friday?"

"Want to talk about it in the shower?" He dropped his towel.

Amy jumped up to hug the man. "You're a sweet talker, you know that?" While he started the shower, she took her dopp kit from her overnight bag.

"Is Friday okay?"

"Yeah. Are you sure Paul won't let you come over tonight?"

Ryan heard Paul's masculine voice in his head. *We have a deal. We put up with each other's love life. And as long as I'm with Christine, the best we'll do is alternate nights.*

"Oh crap, what did he say?"

He was holding a dripping face cloth. "You'll alternate nights? What is that?"

She continued soaping their body. "Imagine you're a Siamese twin. One body, but two heads. Everything has to be a compromise. Unless both heads agree, nothing happens."

"But that's stupid. I'm not a Siamese—hell, you're not a Siamese twin. You're just an imaginative woman with issues."

"Suit yourself," Amy forced herself to say, even though her heart was sinking. "But if you want to spend time with me, that's how it works. Alternate days." She was holding her breath, afraid that Ryan might end their budding relationship. She felt Paul move their left hand, 'his' hand, to pat their right arm in support.

"A very sexy imaginative woman," he said. "I'll try. The most I can do is say that I'll try."

Relieved, she said, "I can live with that." Paul thought directly to him, *That's all any of us can do, is try. Thanks, Ryan. And I hope we get to be friends, too.*

When she saw Ryan shaking his head, Amy thought to Paul, *What did you say to him?*

He's a trooper. I think I'm going to like him.

ß 6 ঔ

Even though Amy let Paul lead to drive to the police station on Rampart Street, she felt bittersweet pangs of *déjà vu*. "We used to drive this six times a week," she said out loud, enjoying the privacy of the car. "We had fun, didn't we?"

"Sure. We got shot. We got hit on the head. We fell off a cliff. We got thrown in a bayou and left for dead. Good times, good times."

"Well, yes, that too. But I had fun. I learned a lot, tracked down some bad people, made friends—Yes, I had a good time."

"So tell me again why you quit?" At the traffic light Paul turned onto Magazine.

"Too regimented. I kept getting dinged for paperwork. And two internal affairs investigations a year. I wasn't making friends in high places. They'd have fired me eventually."

Paul laughed. "You weren't making friends, but we're on our way to see Commander Ramirez. If you <u>had</u> made friends, would we be going to meet President Christie?"

"Maybe Christie would be going to meet President Clear."

The officer behind the entryway desk was new to Amy, and made Amy fill out the various permission slips. Then she slipped a plastic "VISITOR" badge under the bulletproof glass and said, "Someone will come get you shortly." As she took a seat in the waiting area Amy thought, *This is too strange. They used to let me barrel right through this place.*

It wasn't long before a two-stripe yeoman came to the waiting room. "Brossard!" she called, "Great to see you, Officer."

"It's a pleasure to see you again, Detective. Come on, the Commander is ready for you." She followed him down the familiar corridors, getting him to gossip about her former colleagues. Detective Veronica had been hired away by Baton Rouge, but Doctor Jermaine was still the Parish's Chief Medical Examiner.

The yeoman knocked at the Commander's inner office door. Immediately the door swung open, with Ramirez standing in his white uniform shirtsleeves. "Okay, Brossard, she's here. Lock the front door." He smiled at her and said, "A treat to see you again, Detective." It had been four months since she handed her resignation letter to the man. Four months since he tried to talk her out of leaving the police force. Four months since she had cried in his office, feeling guilty about leaving in the face of his professional faith in her. Silently she thought to Paul, *Don't let me cry again.*

"Commander, thank you for seeing me. You are looking well, believe you me." She touched his arm and kissed him on the cheek. Commander Ramirez had been her friend, her supporter, ever since she was eleven and he was just a Sergeant.

He stepped back to let her in, and motioned her to his conference table. She saw a pistol with its breech open, a badge, and paperwork on a clipboard. *No!* she thought, *He thinks I want to re-up.*

"Sergeant Francks tells me you're doing well as a PI." He held out her chair. "What's the story?"

She described her success with the Doublet case. "But I need your advice. I stumbled onto this job, thanks to Walter, but how can I attract new business?"

His kind smile shone through a careworn face. He had gained some more weight since the last promotion. "Depends. What kind of cases would you like?"

"Not lost dogs. And maybe not divorce. Important stuff—you know, murders, big robberies, that sort of thing."

"You could do worse than come back to NOPD. I know, I know," both hands up when she began to protest, "I just want you to know that door is open as long as I'm here. Look, if you want to parallel the police on murders, make presentations to some of the big criminal law firms. Tell them you're available, tell them about some of the big cases you worked, and drop my name."

Amy let Paul take notes in her notepad, scribbling furiously with their left hand.

"And if you want insurance fraud investigations, go to the local office of the big insurance companies. I don't mean two hundred different State Farm agencies, I mean the big local claims office. Same thing–introduce yourself and brag about those fraud cases where you found the policyholder playing volleyball. And mention my name."

She let Paul write, then said, "Is it really that easy?"

"No," the Commander laughed. "Then you have to call to remind them you exist. People tell me it's the 'hurry up and wait' part that gets them."

"Thank you, Commander Ramirez, I—"

"Please. I'm Johnny to you."

She blushed. "And I'm your Junior Commander.[14] Johnny, I can't tell you what a big deal this is to me. I appreciate your advice."

"Advice?" he smiled, eyebrows raised. "Do you have liability insurance? Have you incorporated? Are you paying your self-employment tax? Quarterly filings? A lot of the things that have to be done are boring as can be."

"Do you know my accountant? He tells me the same thing."

"I don't want to embarrass you, Amy," Ramirez said. "but I would love to have you back here. You're a creative thinker—maybe because I never could get you to go to the Police Academy. You've shown your courage, you've risked your own life to save other officers. And I know you are absolutely honest. My department needs three dozen

---

[14] When Paul first appeared in Amy, her father, Doctor Clear, brought her to the police station so Paul could look through a mug-shot book to identify the thugs that kicked him into the coma that eventually led to his death just hours after his personality switched to her in a splash of medical fluid. The then-Sergeant Ramirez helped them, and he gave 11-year-old Amy a "Junior Commander" sticker to put on the school blazer she was wearing.

people just like you."

For a second Paul imagined thirty-six Amys and laughed aloud. "Sorry," he said. "I was seeing a bunch of Amys running around." When he stopped, Amy continued. "Comm—uh, Johnny, I need brain bleach to get rid of that image. Thirty-six me's, wow!" A serious look replaced her smile, "I made a deal with myself. I've got two years to start making a decent living as a PI. If I'm still struggling in 2032, I'll be back here begging you to let me direct traffic at Carrollton and Claiborne."

He nodded and said, "If no one blows up the intersection, I'll still need help there."

They exchanged some pleasantries—the Commander asked to be remembered to Amy's father, while she asked after his grown children, Pete and Consuela. She thanked him again, and Officer Brossard walked her back to the entryway.

Standing in the July sun, Amy thought, *Phone book. Top criminal lawyer firms. Insurance claims offices. I want ice cream. You?*

"Ice cream," Paul said out loud. "Definitely ice cream."

Paul and Amy found a glum Christine when they got to her double that evening. "I finished the class, yay," she said listlessly. "I'm worried about Mom, boo." She held her Paulette in a tight hug.

He petted her hair and inhaled her scent, a mixture of soap and perspiration and shampoo. "Mom is worth being worried about," he whispered back.

"I knew you'd understand." She squeezed.

"Tell me what you know. What's the latest from Nathan?"

Christine started sharing the news she had gotten from her brother in St. Louis. Suddenly she interrupted herself, saying, "Oh, you must be hungry. Hi, Amy, how are you?" She led them to the bare kitchen table, then went back to telling her story without another thought of food.

"How are you holding up?" Amy asked.

"I haven't cried in an hour or so. I guess I'm doing okay. Thanks." She continued with details: an apparent stroke at home, Nathan and his wife finding her and rushing her to a hospital, the vigil outside the ICU, guarded news from three doctors, and finally, transferred to a private room. "She still can't talk, but Nathan says she knows who he is and that he's there. I've got to help her."

"Yes," Paul said, hand on hers on the tabletop. "Yes, you do."

After a moment he said, "We brought you something." Paul poked around in Amy's purse, and finally came up with a small doll. It was plastic, about four inches tall; a cartoony freckled pink face with comically big eyes, blue coveralls, and hair as long as the doll was tall. The hair—really thick plastic strands—was as multi-colored as Christine's own. "No matter what happens," he explained, "when you hold this you're holding me, and Amy." He lifted it up and kissed it, like a Bishop laying on hands. "It's Amy," she said, and she kissed it, too. Ceremoniously, Paul held the doll out to his lover. "I'm going to miss you like crazy. And I'm going to be worried about your mom."

Christine held it. It was an ugly little doll, sold as a joke troll, but given meaning by Paul and Amy's actions. The woman looked up at them, a couple of tears working their way down her face. "I'll have this with me every second," she said, working hard to control her voice. "I'll sleep with it. I'll—I'll—" and began sobbing.

Paul held her. He cooed, "It's okay. Let it out. It's okay to cry; I'm here." Amy thought similar things directly to the woman.

"What if she dies?" she exclaimed between sobs. "She's my mommy and I love her so much!"

Amy thought to Paul, *Dad says some stroke victims would have been better off dying.* Out loud, to both of them, Paul counseled, "Don't borrow trouble." Then, to Christine, "Tomorrow you'll be with her. You and your brother will take good care of her, I know."

Later that evening Christine asked, "Paulette, how did you end up inside of Amy? Can I get my mom inside me?"

"I love my mother," Amy said aloud, "but the last thing I'd want is having Tracey inside my head." When Christine let out a new wail, she said, "What?"

Not a good time to share that, Paul thought to her, then went back to comforting his lover. It hurt him to see Christine in such pain. But he knew from his own history, the death of each of his parents, and more recently, his sister, that all a person can do is let the grief wash over and through them. *There is no shortcut,* he thought to Amy. *No matter how you look at it, it takes a few gallons of tears before you begin to get a grip on the reality of a parent aging, or declining, or dying. But the only alternative is a parent burying a child, and that's just wrong. It's the most wrong thing in the universe.*

When they went to bed, Christine said, "Just hold me, Paulette. Make me feel safe." She was wearing an ancient white cotton nightgown, an article she'd not worn to bed with Paul in many years. Amy thought, *Oh, good. Uh, I'd rather we hug than get so physical.* She could hear the laugh in his thought when he replied, *Just think of Ryan making our body feel those things. Last night I was thinking of Christine, not him. I had a pretty good time.*

"So did I," she whispered.

"Did what, Amy?" The woman always knew which one of them was speaking. She was curled up on her side, her head resting on their shoulder. They could feel her jiggling her feet.

"Paul said something about Ryan. I had a good time with him. I understand if you don't want to hear about it."

"Please, tell me! Make me think about something else. About Paulette and you being happy. Will he keep you two out of trouble while I'm gone?"

She told Christine about her evening with Ryan. "I told him about Paul. He thinks I'm crazy, of course. And I told him that I couldn't come over tonight because Paul was visiting you." Christine smiled against the side of their face. He picked up the story, "She didn't hesitate for a second. I was so proud of her. She told him she could alternate nights with him, but that our time together was non negotiable."

Amy added, "I was scared. I was afraid he'd tell me to get lost. As it is, he just said he'd try."

"I wish I was as brave as you. Uh, do I have to spend time with him?"

A cough, then the sound of one of them laughing. "I told him there wouldn't be a threesome," said Amy. "After I know him better, I'll let you know if I think you two would like each other."

Christine kissed their cheek. "Thanks, Amy. I love how you take care of me and Paulette."

Paul leaned their head against hers. "I had a little private chat with Ryan. I think it's going to work."

"You mean you and Amy can be yourselves with him, too? Like with me?"

"That's the plan, *ma belle amie*."

"Amy, don't you love it when Paulette speaks French?"

"*Oui*," she laughed.

Paul spoke in a low, serious tone. "I'm going to miss you so much. I understand, family always comes first. But—"

Christine put her index finger against their lips to stop him. "I'm trying not to think about how awful it'll be without you. I was such a mess before you, I'm afraid I'll be a mess again when I'm away. I love you, Paulette. I can't live without you." She threw her arm around them; it felt like she was crying again.

Get the GooGone, Amy thought to him. *That's a little co-dependent for my taste.* He was rubbing Christine's back, rocking to comfort her. *If it weren't for you,* Paul replied silently, *I'd feel exactly like she does. You're my rock. I'm hers. And I love her, you know that.* To his lover he whispered, "Shhh, it's okay. You can cry. I'm not afraid of your tears."

Christine was distant in the morning, preoccupied with concern about her mother and anxiety over flying. Paul respected her brooding but tried to keep physical contact to reassure her she wasn't alone— holding hands, a hand on her arm, thighs touching in the car as he led to get her to the airport. Amy tried to be motherly, asking if the woman had packed her medications, did she have the right clothes for St. Louis' July weather, where was her boarding pass. It was a car full of sadness that parked at Armstrong International.

Paul and Christine hugged a long time just outside the security line entrance; they were ignored by other travelers more concerned with their own flights than with the apparent sight of two women kissing. "Call me when you land," Paul said, and he felt her nod. "I want to—I need to talk to you every day," she whispered. This time it was Paul who nodded.

Amy said she was hungry, but Paul insisted on standing outside the secure area, watching Christine's multi-colored hair slowly move to the metal detectors, and finally beyond. "Okay," he said, "I'm ready. Uh, can we eat someplace else?"

"What? You don't like overpriced airport concession food? That's why I love you."

On the drive back home, Amy and Paul talked about Christine's mother having a stroke. "Dad says some people recover. But some people get all brain dead. It's tough."

"Yeah. My fear is that Christine won't come back. If her mother is disabled, she might stay to take care of her." He thought a moment. "And that's the right thing to do, but damn, I'll go bonkers."

"This is like Lucas and Kali," Amy reflected. "He was relieved to be leaving because she was too intense for him. But you're an adult. You support Christine going even though you'd rather she were here. And she's just as clingy as Kali, but you're okay with it."

"And?"

"No, nothing. It's like that English lit class at UNO, just compare and contrast."

"I'm taking it as a compliment. Love isn't just emotion, it's behavior. And I love Christine. I want what's best for her. And I believe her that helping her mom is what's best for her." He sighed. "I hate being a saint."

Amy snickered. "When I was at Saint Giles, the boys at Archbishop Rummel used to say that chastity was its own reward."

"Another reason I hate being a saint."

"Can I say it's convenient that I'll get to spend a bunch of time with Ryan?"

Paul said, "Not only can you say it, I won't hate you forever for it. Getting to know him might take away some of the sting of Christine being gone. Can't you get him to shave?"

"I wish. He won't do it. Something about liking to open his presents."

They were at their computer desk, each browsing their separate monitors. Paul took advantage of their ability to read different things if they were placed in a certain way; he was going through an essay about the Brontë sisters on the higher monitor, while Amy was going through Craigslist on the lower one, trying to determine where she could post a notice about Clear, Hodges & Owens Investigations. When the cell phone rang, it was Paul who jumped to lead and grabbed it out of their right hand. As he had hoped, Christine's number was blinking in the display.

"Christine, it's Paul. Are you home yet?"

Despite the background noise, he could hear her say, "Paulette! I just got off the plane. Nathan and his wife are going to meet me."

"How was the flight?"

"We didn't crash, so I guess it was a good one. I—I miss you."

"Yeah," he said softly. "I miss you, too. When will you get to see your mom?"

"I hope that's where Nathan takes me now. I've got to see her. I'm so worried—" he heard a catch in her voice that made his heart ache "—I—I'm so worried about her."

"I know. I know. And she loves you for it. It will be so good for her to see you!"

"You think so? I hope I can do something for her. I miss—Oh, Nathan! Nathan! Over here!"

"Your brother found you, good. Christine, listen to me. I love you. You are an angel of mercy to go to your mother. And Amy wants to say something."

The voice was the same, but even over the phone Christine somehow always knew which one of them was speaking or leading. "I've got my fingers and toes crossed for you, Honey," Amy said. "You're my best friend. Save your mom and come back to us soon."

"Oh, Amy, thank you. I don't deserve you, either of you. I love you and—just a second, Nathan, just a—oh, Sheila, you look great. Let me finish—" back to her phone, "I love you Paulette. I love you Amy. I'll talk to you tomorrow." They heard her start to say something to her relatives when the call ended.

Paul looked at the silent phone. "I really miss her. Already."

"Yes. I hope her showing up is the magic cure for Mrs. Hodges.

Then she can come back soon."

"Yeah."

When Amy got to Ryan's house, the front door wasn't open—it was sitting on sawhorses in the yard. Ryan was crouched, back to the street, massaging the side of the door with a piece of sandpaper. She heard Paul say out loud, "That looks like fun."

"Ryan!" she called as she stepped through the wrought iron gate, "Is this your part-time job?"

He looked up, startled, then smiled. "Amy, what do you know about getting a door unstuck?"

Paul said, "I've fixed a few in my time. Where does it stick?" Ryan, of course, saw Amy and reached to hug her; Paul was concentrating on the door. "What do you know about carpentry?" Ryan asked.

"Oh, I'm Paul." Ryan stopped his reacharound abruptly. Looking up, Paul said, "Amy, we have to remember to announce ourselves with him."

Ryan had no way of knowing Amy was the one who said, "Oops. Sorry."

Amy took the lead and laughed at the puzzled look on Ryan's face. "Hi, I'm the right-handed me. I'm your date tonight," and she kissed him on the cheek.

Paul said, "Hi, I'm the left-handed her, and I'm helping you fix your door." He stuck out their right hand, and Ryan mechanically shook it.

"Hey! This isn't funny," Ryan said. He wasn't exactly pouting, but he stood with hands on hips.

"I don't mean to make fun," Amy said. "You'll get used to me. Uh, to us. You've met Paul. Maybe he'll convince you he's real with the door, because I sure don't know anything about sandpaper. I draw the line at emery boards." She saw the anger or defensiveness slip off Ryan's face, replaced by confusion. "It's Amy. Can a girl get a kiss?"

"You're sure?"

"That's the spirit! Yes, I sure am Amy and I sure do want you to kiss me." She smiled, showing off the slightly turned front tooth that Paul and Christine found irresistible. Tentatively, Ryan leaned forward, stopped, then leaned some more. Amy threw her arms around his neck and kissed him. *It's okay,* she thought to him, *it really is me.* She heard—and felt—him laugh, and his kiss became more confident, more enthusiastic, more erotic.

When they came up for air, her voice said, "It's Paul. Show me where the door was getting caught." Ryan took a step back, leading Amy to think to him, *He likes to help, but I'm not going anywhere.*

They turned to look at the door laying on the supports. "Uh, how—how do I know, you know, which one of you is, uh, talking, or, uh, or—"

"If it's physical contact, it's Amy. You're too butch for my taste. I like women," said Paul. He knelt to examine the leading edge of the door. "Look, here—" he pointed "—the paint is worn down and scuffed. We'll plane that down." Ryan nodded, looking over their shoulder. Paul sidled around to look at the bottom of the door, and pronounced it fine. He stood to get a view of the top of the door, and whistled. "See that?" pointing, "That looks like the worse problem. Let's see the doorway." Without waiting for a response, Paul in Amy walked to the opening where the front door belonged. "The jamb shows the friction here," near the top of the doorway, "and on top. Ryan, have you had some water damage up above?"

"Uh, I've got some bad soffits. Would that be it?"

"Could be, could very well be. Depends where they are." He turned to face the man. "Okay, sandpaper's not enough for this job. Where's your plane?"

Amy enjoyed the changing expressions of surprise, confusion, and amazement on her lover's handsome face. She wanted to pat him and tell him to have fun playing with Paul and she'd take him to bed later. It startled Paul when she laughed.

"Amy?" Ryan asked; it sounded like a plea, "Are you there?"

"Yes. It's Amy. I'm always here."

"How do you know all this stuff about fixing a door?"

"I told you, I don't. It's Paul."

"I'm Paul," he said as he took the lead. "I know it's confusing, we both sound exactly the same. We got spoiled because my girlfriend— God knows how she does it, but she always knows which one of us is talking or leading. Anyway, I owned a house when I had my own body. I've done this kind of thing before. Only, I'm no good at plumbing, so don't ask." After a moment of looking at the immobile Ryan, he added, "Uh, the plane?"

"Your own body?"

"Yeah. I thought we explained that. Kicked into a coma, body died, mind inside Amy. Uh, the plane?"

"I'll, uh, I'll get it," he said, and headed toward the house.

"It's Amy. Bring back some beer, okay?"

Paul thought to her, *This is going to be fun. It's a simple project, but I'm guessing Ryan hasn't spent a lot of time with lumber.*

I think it's going well, she thought back. *It'll be great, we'll be ourselves with both our lovers.*

Paul ran his finger over the part of the door that awaited planing. *It's about time you found a winner.*

Ryan came out of the house holding a general purpose metal plane. It was ten inches long, made of black metal, with wooden handles on the front and rear. Paul could see the blade was not fastened for use. "That's the right tool for the job," he called to Ryan.

"You seem to know what to do," he said, handing it over to Paul.

"You have to set the blade." Paul placed it on the door. He fitted the blade and pushed a tiny bit to expose about one sixteenth of an inch of cutting surface. Then he twisted the thumbscrew to fasten it in place.

Ready to work, Paul said "Hold your hip against that side of the door while I'm using the plane here, okay?" Ryan nodded and braced himself.

When Paul bent to the troubling part of the door he thought to Amy, *It's not difficult. And if the blade is sharp, you don't even have to push hard.* But the blade was dull, so he had to put their back into the work. Thin shavings spiraled out of the plane's mouth, gradually showing the various colors the door had been painted over the years— red, yellow, a different yellow, and red again. After every three or four strokes Paul would feel the door with his bare hand. Finally he said, "I think we've got this part fixed. The other one will be a bitch, though."

Paul pointed out to Amy and Ryan how the wood grain was vertical where the top of the door showed signs of sticking. "That's why I asked about water damage. Moisture could get in the grain and swell up. Planing against the grain is tricky," he warned. As he readied themself, he told Ryan, "It's even more important that you hold the door. We don't want to split the grain." When the man nodded, Paul scraped the dull plane across the swollen sticking point. Instead of spirals of wood, what came out of the mouth of the tool were small, short hunks of broken grain, almost like big pieces of sawdust. He grunted as he worked the wood with ten, twelve, fourteen strokes. He heard Amy think, *Whoa, I'm getting tired,* before he felt the raw wood and decided the problem was gone. "I think a candle or some soap, and we're good to put the door back."

"Candle? Soap? What's that for?"

"Seal the wood so you don't get more swelling from moisture. And make it slippery so it opens and closes easier. Think of it as WD-40 for wood."

"All right. Bar soap okay?"

"Candle's better, but soap will do," Paul answered, and Ryan turned to return to the house. Amy added, "Don't forget the beer this time!"

Amy wrapped their arms around themself. "You know so much different stuff. I'm in awe."

Smiling, he said aloud, "You already know a lot. When you're my age you'll know way more than I do."

"How old are you, geezer?"

"I'm a youthful seventy-six. Kid."

"Seventy-six what?" Ryan said. He had a cardboard beer caddy in one hand and the kitchen bar of Ivory soap in the other.

"It's Amy. Beer!" He handed the soap to her, then gave her a beer. "Can I get you to open that for me?" she asked. "I know it's confusing, two of us but only two hands."

He put the caddy on the ground, and used something on his keychain to take the cap off his home brew. "You want first sip?" she said to the air; then, "Okay, I'll go first." She took a healthy but feminine swig. "Paul says he'll wait until you get the door back up. This stuff is great, you ought to bottle it. Sell it, I mean." She took another sip.

Ryan shook his head and began laughing. "What am I going to do with you? With you two?" He hoped it was Amy he was about to hug, and her "Mmmm, nice," convinced him it was.

"Let's finish the door. Uh, it's Paul." He wielded the bar of soap in their left hand, rubbing it up and down the leading edge and the top of the door. He dropped the Ivory and said, "Ryan, help me get this back to the door frame." The two of them, looking like Ryan and Amy, stood it up and slowly walked it up the three steps to the entryway.

"You pulled the hinge pins," Paul called. "Way to go!"

Ryan said, "I thought about unscrewing the hinges, but this looked easier."

"It's a little tricky getting it back, but you're right, it's a lot easier than dealing with all those screws. C'mon, help me get this up. Just a little more, a litttttle more..." Paul stuck their foot under the door to hold it level, leading Amy to let out a yelp. "It's Amy. Sorry. Don't you ruin these shoes, Paul."

"It's Paul. With our foot like this I can't reach," he told Ryan. "Can you set the bottom hinge pin?" Ryan took the metal cylinder and slipped it in the upper knuckle on the bottom hinge. He poked at it. "I can't get it into the second hole --" Paul moved their foot, changing the door's angle, and the pin slipped into place.

"You're a natural," Paul said. "Now the top one." Ryan reached up to start the pin, and Paul again jiggled the door's position until the pin fell home.

As Paul wiggled their foot free, "It's Amy. I want to put that last thing in. Is that okay?"

Ryan heard Paul's male voice in his head, *It was her body that did the work, so let her control the pin. That alright with you?*

"Uh, yeah. Yeah, sure. Amy, go ahead."

Smiling, she held the pin over the properly aligned knuckles on the middle hinge, then ceremoniously dropped it in place. "I hereby declare this bridge open!"[15] she intoned.

"Give them all a tap with the hammer and we're done," Paul said. "What did you do with that beer?"

Ryan opened and closed the door a half-dozen times. Satisfied with the results, he said, "Amy—uh, Paul, thanks for your help."

Amy and Paul seated themself on the top step of the entryway, taking turns sipping from the beer. Meanwhile, Ryan picked up the sawhorses and put them on a hand truck, then took them away somewhere. He came back to collect the plane, hammer, and screwdrivers from the lawn. "Are these wood chips going to hurt the grass?" he asked Paul; he wasn't sure which of them laughed and said, "I doubt it."

Lucas appeared at the doorway, clothes rumpled from a nap. "Dad, you fixed this. It works now."

"No, son. It was the left-handed part of Amy that did it." On cue, Paul stood to make a curtsey and to give a Queen of England wave of the hand.

"Are you doing okay? It's Amy."

"Yeah," the boy answered. "My stomach's been unsettled since I got back here, but I'll be okay."

"But you're up for the movie, right?" Ryan said.

"Yeah. Maybe popcorn will calm down my insides."

They spent the evening at the Prytania, the last large, single-

---

[15] Paul once dragooned Amy into watching the film *A Hard Day's Night*. This silly comment stuck with her, although she doesn't remember who John Lennon is. Uh, was.

screen movie theatre in the entire state. Ryan and Lucas both had seen *The Room* four or five times and looked forward to the camp humor and cult audience atmosphere, but Amy and Paul had never heard of it. Ryan sat with Lucas on his right and Amy on his left. A few minutes into the film Paul thought to Amy, *This is like a car wreck - you don't want to see it, but you can't not look.* When she giggled, Ryan whispered, "Yeah, that affair gets even weirder."

Amy relaxed, laying her head on Ryan's shoulder and munching popcorn. But after awhile she drifted to sleep, so Paul took the lead to keep their eyes open. "What the hell," he thought, and continued to lean against Ryan. He ignored his occasional pats and rubs, knowing they really were for Amy. But when two characters began an oral sex scene, Ryan reached around their body to fondle their breast. Paul smiled and thought directly to the man—with his man's voice, of course— *What kind of a girl do you think I am?* He felt Ryan's head turn. "Amy's asleep," Paul whispered. "Save the romance for her, she'll like it. Can they really show that in a movie?"

Later Ryan heard Amy's voice in his head, *What did I miss?*

"Uh, the left-handed you told me not to feel him up."

Yes, that would be Paul. Homophobic creep but a real sweetheart. But I'm awake now, so, what were you trying to do? She leaned back, against his shoulder, to present her mouth for the kiss he indeed delivered. It lasted until Lucas and half the audience, reacting to something on the screen, exclaimed, "Oh, gross!"

"It was fun, Dad," Lucas said when they returned to the house. "I never get tired of that silly movie. And you know, none of my friends in Atlanta have ever heard of it."

"Their loss," Ryan replied. "What did you think, Amy?"

"What I saw of it didn't make a lot of sense. Lame dialogue. I mean, incredibly, phenomenally, painfully, lamefully lame."

"That's the idea."

"So now I'm ready for trivia night at the Seven Seas."

A moment later her voice continued, but it was Paul, saying, "Ooh, ooh. How 'bout me, Boss?" He was waving their left hand overhead. Lucas laughed, and Ryan, smiling, said, "Yes, Paul?"

"I liked it. Amy's right, it didn't make a lot of sense. And, yeah, the dialogue sucked. And he starts to push someone off the roof and then they go back to whatever they were talking about. And the sex scene, that was hilarious. I don't think it was supposed to be, though. Anyway, I thought it was great fun. Amy, how come we didn't know about this movie sooner?"

Still smiling, Ryan said, "So you haven't made up your mind yet?"

A cough, then, "It's Amy. Yes. I didn't care for it and Paul did."

"That's what I mean," he said. "You still haven't decided."

"It's Paul. I thought we explained this. We are different people. Amy didn't like the film and I thought it was funny. We are decided." To Amy he thought, *Damn, he doesn't get it.*

She thought back a plan. Then, out loud, Amy asked Lucas what he liked about the film, while at the same time Paul thought directly to Ryan, *We really are different people, we just live in one body. You don't have to believe it, but everything will make more sense if you do.*

Lucas explained he liked how predictably bad the dialogue was, while Ryan said, "But that's not possible."

"Dad?"

"It's Paul. He was talking to me. Absolutely impossible, you're right. But here we are."

"Dad?"

"Yeeeeeeah."

Amy laughed at his stunned expression. "Lighten up, Ryan," she said, "we really are a lot of fun. Hey," turning to Lucas, "are you feeling better?"

The man stopped to consider. "Yeah. Yeah, I feel fine. Popcorn must be a cure-all."

"Don't forget the Raisinettes," his father added. Then, "Everyone up for visiting Sammie tomorrow?"

"Yes!" Lucas shouted, "I miss Mom. I hope she recognizes me, it's been two years."

"Think I'll pass. Uh, it's Amy."

"Why? She was excited when I told her I hired you to find Lucas. I'm sure she'd like to thank you for bringing him home."

She shook her head. "We all have done things we wish we hadn't. The worst part about being a homewrecker is meeting the wife."

"Why, Amy, I never would have thought—"

"Oh, sure, like you've been a saint all your life! Look, this is a lesson I learned the hard way. Crap-and-a-half, his wife broke her arm in a car wreck and then Paul went and told her we hoped she was feeling better." Amy winced at the memory of her almost-but-not-quite affair with her police partner Officer Kowalski.[16] "I don't want to feel all that–that guilt. And the shame. So, no, I don't want to meet your wife tomorrow."

She heard Paul think, *Still a homewrecker, but now you avoid the wife?* Out loud she blurted, "Oh, shut up!"

"My, aren't the walls perpendicular," Ryan observed. "I think I understand. We'll get back to town pretty late—there's a fish place in Jackson I like. Besides, tomorrow is for Paul's girlfriend, so how about Sunday?"

She nodded. "Sunday. Sunday's good." Silently she poked Paul, and he said, "My girlfriend left town this morning to see her mom in the hospital. There might be some, uh, flexibility in our schedule for awhile."

"Son, don't you have an early day tomorrow?" Lucas said "Yes, dad," and began straightening out the newspaper he'd been looking at. Amy laughed and thought to Paul, *My God, they have a code! It's like that guy I went out with at UNO, he asked his roommates if they had an early class and it meant they were supposed to get lost.*

A strange thing between a father and son, I would think.

It's a great thing, she thought back. *He wants me. And I sure*

---

[16] Way back in *The Rothschild Jewels*. Like most of us, Amy learned from a bad experience.

want him.

In the morning, Amy was melting butter in a frying pan to make scrambled eggs when Ryan stormed in. "Get out of my kitchen!" he shouted. He grabbed her by the shoulders and turned her toward the door, pushing all the way. She could tell this was not a joke.

"Don't let the butter burn," she shouted as he ran back into the kitchen. After he turned off the stovetop, he came back to Amy before she had a chance to sit down. "I'm sorry," he said, "are you okay?"

"Yes. Kind of surprised, though. What's up with your kitchen?"

"It's haunted," he said. "I don't let Lucas hang out in there, either. If you need something from the refrigerator, get it and leave." She realized he was wearing a towel around his waist. He needed a shave, and his morning breath was awful. She leaned in and hugged him. "Okay. Teach me the rules and I'll behave."

"It's Paul. Haunted?"

"Something like that." Even though he was talking to Paul, he patted their back and arms.

"I don't want to make trouble," Amy said. "You want me to stay out, I'll stay out. But someday you'll stay over at my place and I'll show you that scrambled eggs *à la* Amy are to die for."

"I look forward to it," and he kissed the crown of her head. "Now go back to bed or something, I'm making breakfast for you and Lucas. Pancakes all right?" He was smiling. His brief anger had blown over, but there was a jaw muscle pulsing like a heartbeat.

"Pancakes," Paul said, "great." To Amy he said, *What is he hiding in there?*

I'm not a cop anymore, she thought back. *Just because he has some secret doesn't mean he's the reincarnation of Ted Bundy. Why, do you think he has jars of eyeballs in his pantry?*

Oh, jeez, now I'm dying to look. And you know how I hate to be told what to do.

Yes. Me, too.

Their parting was upbeat. Ryan and Lucas were excited about getting to visit Sammie, while Amy already was looking forward to visiting on Sunday. In the meantime she was glad to avoid meeting her lover's wife. Plus there was some housekeeping to be done. And she had to water the plants at Christine's double.

The routine developed. Christine called in mid-morning, and Paul phoned her after dinner. The good news was that her mother clearly recognized her and was glad to have her there. The bad news was that the woman still could not speak. The worse news was that the doctors said so much time had passed before the woman was brought to the hospital, that treatment possibilities were limited. "I'm okay when I'm sitting with her, but as soon as I go for a coke or something I start crying again," Christine admitted. "Paulette, I'm so scared. What if she never gets better? What if—"

"Oh, sweetie," Paul interrupted, "don't borrow trouble. I'm scared, too, and it's so easy to imagine disaster. You can't let yourself do that." He heard Amy think, *I'd freak out if something happened to my parents.*

"Nathan is so practical. I'm glad he's here. I told you he's a lawyer, right? He's making lists. At night he and Sheila go to mom's house to look for papers—" abruptly she sobbed.

"Yeah," Paul said, trying to be soothing. "Insurance. Powers of Attorney. Wills." He sighed. "It's got to be done. You're lucky he's there to take care of that part."

"I knew you'd understand," she whispered.

"The first night, I stayed at mom's," she went on. "It was nice to be in my old room, but the house was so empty, I just cried all night. I'm staying with Nathan and Sheila now."

Amy looked at the clean top page of the legal pad, but that wasn't enough to make words appear. She wanted to take Commander Ramirez' advice and create a presentation for local criminal law firms. Her goal was to get hired as a Private Investigator and independently confirm or prove false criminal charges against a client. It would be like the work she enjoyed doing for the Orleans Parish Police Department, but without all the rules, regulations, and paperwork. Or the dress code.

Her mind kept wandering to Ryan Doublet. Handsome Ryan. Nice Ryan. Lover Ryan. Weirdly secretive of his kitchen Ryan.

"You want to write this?" she asked aloud.

"Who, me?" Paul answered. "No, I want to go to St. Louis and hold Christine's hand."

She threw the pen down to the desk; it bounced and rolled off behind the computer screens.

It was just before noon on Sunday that Amy parked across the street from Ryan's house. The plan was for brunch at a local restaurant, then a hike on the north side of Lake Pontchartrain. As she locked her car door, Amy said, "Let's see if they remember me."

When she knocked, Ryan opened the door. "Well, don't you look great," he said, and wrapped his arms around her.

"Good to see you too, big boy," she answered, and lifted her face for a kiss. They embraced until they heard Lucas enter the room and bump into a table as he tried to turn around and leave.

"I was hoping you remembered me," Amy said. "How was your visit with your wife?"

"She said she wants to thank you for bringing Lucas back. It was nice to see Sammie so happy." He raised his right arm and motioned for Lucas to join them. "What did you think of your mother?" He had an arm around each of them.

"She looks well," he said, looking uncomfortable. "I didn't realize how much I missed seeing her." Amy heard Paul think, *Why is he wearing that expression? Do we have lettuce in our teeth?*

"She was thrilled to see you," Ryan confirmed. To Amy he added, "Sammie's affect is a bit flat, it was a big deal to see her so emotional. I hope you'll meet her next time we go?"

"Uh—by next time, probably." She couldn't hear Paul think to Lucas, *Is everything okay?* but she saw the man shake his head. *Damn,* she heard Paul think, *I wish he could think back to us. He looks like he's going to explode.* Meanwhile, Ryan continued to describe their visit to the mental prison in Jackson.

"It's Paul," he interrupted. "I could have sworn the tour director said there would be lunch."

"Ah, all in good time. No reason to stand here. Lucas, get yourself ready. I'll drive." When his son left the room, Ryan kissed Amy again. "How's Paul's girlfriend?" he finally asked.

Paul led to stare at the man. *I'm impressed,* he thought to Amy. "She's scared," he answered aloud. "A stroke is serious bad evil. I keep telling her not to borrow trouble, but it's hard for her." After a pause he went on, "Thanks for asking."

A nod for acknowledgement. "I'll get my mushroom basket. Then as soon as that boy of mine is ready, we'll go. I love the shrimp and grits at this place."

Lucas had been waiting in the hallway for Ryan to leave the room. Immediately he ran to Amy. "He's not my dad!" he hissed, trying to keep his voice down despite his anxiety.

"What?"

"Mom kept calling him Jeffrey. She thinks he's my Uncle Jeffrey, not my dad."

A cough, as Amy and Paul tried to speak at the same time; their jaw dropped.

That was the moment when Ryan returned with a large picnic basket. "Good, you're ready. Let's go!"

⚡ 9 ⚡

What once had been a sprawling frame house on Leake Avenue, across from the levee, was the Dante's Kitchen restaurant. Its weekend brunches attracted a large following, and not just from the nearby Tulane campus. It was an old residential neighborhood near the Carrollton Bend, making a strong comeback with upscale bistros, hair salons, and art galleries near the university. Ryan parked in a crowded lot belonging to the Dante Village strip mall across the street. When they all got out of the car, he remarked, "As crowded as the lot is, we may have a wait for brunch."

Lucas walked with Amy between him and Ryan, and he lightly held her by the upper arm. She heard Paul think, *This lad is freaked out. We have to talk to him by himself.* Meanwhile she held Ryan's hand as they crossed the street and then stood by the *maître d'* stand. Ryan barked instructions, outside table for three. A waiter grabbed menus and rolled silverware and asked them to follow him out to the patio.

"I'll catch up to you," Amy said, pointing to the ladies' room. "Lucas? You want to wash up?" The man looked as if she'd just thrown him a lifeline, and he came to her. They watched the server and Ryan go outside into the sunlight. Amy reached up and grabbed the tall Lucas by the shoulder, and dragged him into an alcove outside the restroom doors. "Well?" she hissed, "Is that Jeffrey or Ryan?"

"Mom kept calling him Jeffrey." Then, "But she also called him 'your father.'" He looked up. "I don't know. But it's creepy."

"Tell me if I have this right. Your mother is in a prison for the criminally insane. And she's not sure who Ryan is?"

He mumbled, "That's what father said. That she'd been like that for the last year or so."

To Paul she thought, *Any ideas?* He led to tell the boy, "I'm thinking your mom's not all there and nothing's wrong. But let me know if you notice anything that makes you think he's your uncle." He thought to Amy, *It's hard to tell someone their mom is coo-coo, but maybe it's less offensive than telling them that they're the one missing some parts. He seems cool with it.*

While she washed her hands in the lavatory she said, "Crap. He's got the detective part of me working. Ryan and Jeffrey were identical twins. I wonder if there was an insurance policy."

Come on! Paul thought back. *Just enjoy lunch and have a fun day with your boyfriend. Our biggest problem is finding our next case.*

Lucas was waiting when she left the ladies' room. "You feeling calmer?" she asked. They walked outside to join Ryan at a round wooden table covered by a thick canvas umbrella. At one time it had been bright red and blue, but now one could barely make out the word 'Cinzano.'

A half-full pitcher of Sangria was already on the table, with full, tall glasses waiting for Amy and Lucas; the glass in front of Ryan had only a few fingers' worth left at the bottom. He waved them over. Holding a menu, he said, "The shrimp and grits are the best in town. They're better than The Court of Two Sisters." Paul raised their eyebrows at the accolade as they sat. Amy looked at her menu and said, mostly to Paul, "Uh-oh. I want one of everything. Their house omelet sounds yummy." She heard him grunt, then think, "Yeah, but so does the salmon and egg."

"What are you doing?" Lucas asked.

"It's Paul. We're playing rock paper scissors to decide what to get." They went through several rounds, with Amy controlling their right hand and Paul their left.

Ryan laughed. "That's not possible." He looked down at his own hands, and attempted to do what he saw Amy doing. "Not possible at all."

"We told you, we're two people in one body." Another round and one of them moaned, "Ooooh, you win. We get the house omelet."

Lucas was staring, his mouth open. Amy thought to him, *What? You never saw a dyad before?* Her smile showed off the crooked front tooth that Paul liked so much. Lucas grinned back.

"We used to come here every few weeks," Lucas reminisced. "I liked their fancy version of a BLT." His mind made up, he closed his menu. "Did we come here with mom? I don't remember."

"Sure did," Ryan said. "Steamed mussels, every time."

The patio was not a typical New Orleans courtyard. Instead, it was converted from a residence side yard, with stockade fencing along Dante and Leake for privacy. Several magnolia trees provided a canopy above the canvas umbrellas. The waitress squeezed between theirs and a neighboring table to take their orders.

"Tell me about your wife," Amy asked. "Sammie? What's that for?"

"Samantha. I hope you meet her. She's not the woman she once was, but I will love her forever." He talked about meeting at Louisiana Tech, of the competition for her affection with his brother Jeffrey, and of the ten years of happiness together before, in his words, "It all fell apart."

"I read the newspaper article," Amy offered. "And one of my colleagues on the Parish Police said he worked the, uh, the incident."

Lucas said, "It was awful. I came home from school and there were police everywhere and they didn't want me to come in the house. I did anyway. I saw—I saw—I saw everything."

She heard Paul think, *He was what, nine years old? What a horrible thing to see.*

"We don't talk about it much," Ryan said softly, "but it's always there. Hey, Lucas?"

"Yeah, dad?"

"You're a good boy. I'm proud of you."

After brunch Ryan drove across town and across the Lake Pontchartrain Causeway to Fontainebleau State Park. He parked by the visitor center, where signs pointed to the various trailheads.

"It's Paul. I'm over 62, does that mean I don't have to pay?" Amy answered, "Shush! If they find out about you they'll want me to pay double." Meanwhile Ryan folded a ten dollar bill and slipped it into the honor slot for all of them.

"When's the last time you were here, boy?" Ryan asked.

"Ooh—three years ago? Uncle Jeffrey let me come on one of his hikes."

"Then it's about time you and I did this. Amy?"

"Never been," shaking her head. "A guy in college took me camping on the north shore but on the other side of the Causeway." She giggled at something Paul thought to her, then added, "I was not paying a lot of attention to the wonders of nature. Damn, it was cold!"

"First stop is the ruins." As Ryan led them past the visitor's center to the fenced attraction, he explained how the park had been a sugar plantation two hundred years earlier. "The chimney is impressive. This was where they ground up the cane and formed the sugar into cones."

"Do they let you climb on the ruins anymore?" Lucas asked. "I did that every time I came out here."

Ryan laughed. "They never let you. You did it anyway. So does everyone else."

Paul was excited by the ruins, and insisted on reading every interpretive sign. Even though he had made his living, when he had his own body, with computers, something about mechanical solutions appealed to him. "It's Paul. I have no idea how Dixie Crystal gets a pound of sugar on a shelf at Rouse, but now I understand how it used to happen." Very little remained of de Mandeville's husbandry—just the impressive chimney, parts of some walls, and two enormous bowls that were part of the evaporation process of extracting raw sugar from cane in 1829. For old time's sake, Lucas scrambled up a low wall, screened from the park office by the chimney.

"Nature trail is next," Ryan announced. "We'll go through the parking lot so I can get my basket, then we'll hunt the wily and elusive chanterelle."

Amy and Lucas lingered behind while Ryan went back to the car. "Uncle Jeffrey used to go hiking, not my dad."

"It's Paul. Was your uncle into mushrooms?"

"Not that I remember. But he had a garden behind his house. He liked growing things."

Paul considered that. "Do you really think Ryan might really be Jeffrey?"

He shrugged and turned away. Amy thought to him, *Does your dad have a birthmark? A tattoo? Does Jeffrey?*

"That's so weird!" but he was smiling. "Dad has a strawberry stain on his left thigh. And I told you about Uncle Jeffrey having his appendix out."

"It's Amy," she said aloud. "This is crazy, people don't do this in real life. God, I hope you are wrong."

"Wrong about what?" Ryan said as he joined them, patting his wicker basket. "Come on, the nature trail is this way."

The trail led through mangrove and cypress, under a spotty canopy. They saw otters splashing in a small bayou, where two great blue herons ignored them. Amy tried to encourage Ryan to include Lucas in the general conversation, instead of letting him concentrate on her; she thought to Paul, *If this man is worth hanging out with, he's good with his kid. I know what you mean about what a drag it is to be a saint.*

When they were confronted by a huge patch of mud and ooze, Ryan said, "Okay, detour. This way." He led, with Amy and Paul behind, and Lucas trailing. Suddenly he stopped, and Amy walked into his back. "Snake!" he hissed; he held out his arms to keep Amy and Lucas from walking into the danger.

Laying across their approach was a long, fat cottonmouth. It's big, scaly, grey and tan head was on one side of their intended path, slowly swinging left to right, with a forked tongue periodically shooting out and back. Five and a half feet away, on the other side of where they wanted to walk, the yellow tail twitched. "What is it, dad?"

At the sound of Lucas' voice the snake began to coil. It faced the group, gaping its big white mouth in a warning display.

Silently, Amy pushed Ryan to one side with her left hand while she unzipped her hip pack with the right. By the time he turned to see what she was doing, Amy was holding her pistol in a combat stance. The reptile sprang as the gun barked, and flame shot out of the barrel. The snake flew back, bounced off a tree, and landed somewhere in the woods to their right. They heard thrashing sounds for a few moments, amid the sound of hundreds of birds cawing and taking flight.

"What did you just do?" Ryan asked, incredulous.

She decocked the pistol and returned it to her holster. "What does it look like?" When she zipped her hip pack closed she looked up at him, smiling.

"My God. Have you ever killed anyone?"

"Why is that always the first question people ask? Ryan. I was a police detective for three years. I'm a Private Investigator. I carry a gun. Is this really a surprise?"

"Dad, I saw her gun at the airport when we flew home."

The man hadn't moved since he spotted the now obliterated snake. "I guess, yeah, I'm surprised. You're good—it can't be easy to shoot a snake that's in mid-air."

"It's Paul. I taught her. She's a better shot than I am."

"Can I see your gun?"

"No! Not now. Maybe later." She took the lead to resume walking the detour, and headed toward the dry main trail. "Have you found your mushrooms here before?"

"Sure. That puffball you wouldn't eat? I got it here."

From the back Lucas asked, "Puffball? How long have you been eating wild mushrooms?"

"Oh, I've always—uh, I don't know, maybe a year or so?" He

stopped walking to let Lucas catch up with him on the trail, and put his arm around him. "I changed a lot after you left."

As they hiked, Amy was surprised again and again by the variety of birds. Herons and pelicans are common enough in Louisiana, but the tiny red and green iridescent hummingbirds, the many types of ducks and coots and mallards, blue kingfishers, egrets, cormorants, noisy woodpeckers, yellow breasted meadowlarks, flycatchers, bright blue buntings and jays, gulls, red cardinals, hawks—she had never seen such a mixture of so many, so many different, and so many different colored birds in one place. "Is that an eagle?" she asked, amazed; she stood with one hand shading her eyes, looking at an enormous and majestic bird gliding above them.

Ryan rested a hand on her shoulder. "This is a prime bird-watching place. I've seen people with camera rigs." He snickered, "Not that I'd know the difference between any of them."

As they came upon a small clearing surrounded by traditional oaks and maples, Ryan shouted, "There!" and left the path. A few feet away he knelt by some lumpy yellow toadstools.

Amy and Lucas came alongside and crouched to see. "Yellow, like egg yolks," Ryan said. "The cap is dented in the center, and the edges roll over." With an index finger he pushed it sideways and said, "These grooves? They're called false gills. They go down the stem so far and then they're gone." The mushroom sprang back when he removed his finger. "Apricots," and he put his finger under her nose. Their eyes widened as Paul thought to her, *Yeah, apricots.*

"What will you do with them, Dad?"

"Cook them, my boy. They're great with scrambled eggs, but I use them in almost anything. They were in the spaghetti I made when you came back."

He wrinkled his nose. "I hope that's not what made me sick."

Amy chimed in, "Nuh-uh. I was fine."

Gleefully, Ryan twisted the chanterelles and dropped them into his wicker basket. "Look, more over there." A few feet away were several of the yellow toadstools. "And some over there, Dad."

"It's Paul. What about these?" Standing, he pointed to a brown mushroom with their left foot.

Ryan shook his head. "I don't recognize it, so I'm not going to touch it."

For the next quarter hour the four people in three bodies collected dozens and dozens of chanterelles. Paul and Amy were careful to avoid toadstools that weren't yellow or didn't have the peculiar odd shape of their quest. Quickly Ryan's basket was two-thirds full of yellow fungi.

"What's this, Ryan?" Amy asked. "Looks like a baby puffball." She was standing over a small egg-shaped mushroom with a slight green cast.

With just a glance Ryan said, "Might be. But it might be an Aminita. Early on they look exactly the same. Leave it be."

As they resumed their hike up the nature path, Amy asked, "So, don't trust a puffball until it's big?"

"Pretty much." He sighed. "Don't go picking mushrooms because of me. A lot of them will make you sick as a dog, and some of them will kill you dead. Hang out with an expert for awhile." He reached out to Lucas to hug him, saying, "Be careful."

"How did you learn which ones are safe?" he asked. He was smiling at his father's attention and touch.

"I used to—" he stopped, and started again. "Field guides. I've got books. And there's a state mycology group, I went out with them once." He sniffed. "Huh. They were just looking for psilocybin, the hippie monkeys."

Amy heard Paul think, *What did he start to say? 'I used to?' He used to what? I think he's censoring himself.* Amy let out a low "Hmmmm."

"But some of them are safe, right?"

"Yep. Just remember, if you make a mistake you can die."

"Teach me," Lucas said.

His father smiled and cupped a hand behind the boy's neck. "Sure. When we get home I'll show you the field guides. Then we can come back out here in a few weeks to look for mushrooms. And autumn is the best season, you know."

Despite the concern she shared with Paul that Ryan seemed to be editing himself, Amy had a good time with her new lover. Beyond his good looks, he was intelligent, with at least some knowledge about all sorts of things. He was open with his son. He humored her about Paul. And he was attentive to her. Back at his house, he even was understanding when Paul said it was time for him to call Christine in St. Louis. *He's such a winner!* she thought to Paul. He thought back, *I don't know that he believes I'm real, but at least he puts up with me. You done good.*

"Paulette, I'm so glad you called," he heard Christine's voice. "Aside from my brother and his wife, I've got no one to talk to here."

"Can you talk to your mom? How is she doing?"

"Oh, I talk to her non-stop, it makes her smile. But it's hard to have a conversation with someone who can't speak. Oh, I'm a bad girl for thinking that, I know."

"The only bad thing is that your mother is sick. You talk to her because you want to and because you see it matters to her. That's good. And if it's not completely satisfying—well, that's just something you put up with for now. Has her doctor said anything new?"

They could hear she was on the line, but she said nothing. "Christine, are you okay?"

"Yeah. I guess, Amy." How could she tell which one of them was talking, seven hundred miles away over a cell phone connection? "He says the more time goes by with no change, the less likely they'll ever be a change."

"Oh no, honey."

"Yeah," and he could hear her sniffling. "I'm not ready for this."

Paul sat them down on a leather chair in Ryan's den. "Nathan? Sheila? What are they saying?"

"Nathan says" sniff "he's going to check out" sniff "some nursing homes. I don't want my mom in a nursing home!" He could hear how hard she was working to keep from crying again.

"No, of course not."

They were quiet. Then Christine said, "Hug me, Paulette. I need you." He felt their stomach sink; that sense of helplessness, of being unable to provide his lover with the comfort she wanted, she needed, she was asking for.

"If you were here I'd be thinking to you," he said. "I'd be holding you and, and, and being here for you. I wish—"

"I know," she said weakly. "I'm looking at that doll you and Amy gave me, and it's a help, but it's not the same."

"I love you, Christine. You know that. Right? Right?"

"Yeah. I know."

Amy said, "Do you need anything from your apartment? Can we send you something?"

"Thanks, Amy. Just—just talk to me every day, okay? Paulette and you are all that's keeping me sane." They heard a beep, and Christine said, "Oh, it's Nathan. I've got to go. I love you Paulette! I love you, Amy. I'll call you tomorrow."

Paul ended the call and stayed seated. "Can we go to St. Louis now?" he asked out loud.

"I wish. She's breaking my heart. This is so grim."

A minute later there was a knock at the open doorway. It was Lucas. "I want to say good night. I'm going to call Kali, then hit the hay. Tomorrow I see the lawyer."

"Please give her my best," Paul said, sounding just like Amy. "And good luck."

They sat alone for a few minutes until Amy finally slapped their thighs and stood up. "Time to find out who we've been sleeping with."

꧁ 10 ꧂

She could hear Ryan washing up behind the closed bathroom door. Amy lay on his king-size bed, naked, but with the sheet pulled up to her chin. "What are the possibilities?" she whispered. "He's Ryan. Or he's Jeffrey. Yow."

Paul thought to her, "If he's Ryan, great—no change, you've got a great boyfriend, have a good time."

"And?"

He sighed and whispered, "If he turns out to be Jeffrey, you've still got a great boyfriend. You still can have a good time."

Amy pumped her legs under the covers. "If he's Jeffrey, my bedmate might be a killer."

"Wouldn't be the first time. But—" he turned it over in his mind "—maybe he just took advantage of a peculiar situation. Maybe he found his brother dead and for whatever reason decided exchanging identities would be a good thing."

"What? What's a good thing?" Ryan turned the bathroom light out as he walked into th e bedroom, a towel around his midsection. He was smiling. Then, "Are you cold?"

"What?" She looked down and realized she was shaking under the drawn sheet. "Oh. I guess so." She snaked her right arm out from under the covers and patted his side of the mattress. "Come to bed, big boy. You can warm me up."

"Let me get the lights."

"No," and she leaned over to snatch the towel away. "I want to see every bit of the glorious you." She heard Paul think, *No birthmark.*

Laughing, he fell on the bed and moved against her. Despite herself, Amy smiled and opened her arms for the man, whatever his name was.

During a lull she had a chance to look carefully at the man. Well-muscled, with just the tiniest bit of belly fat; a small five-pointed star tattoo on the back of his left shoulder; and a long, thin, purple scar on the left side of his abdomen. A shiver of excitement ran through her, a sense of danger that nevertheless did not frighten her.

"What happened?" she asked, pointing at the scar.

"Appendix. Turned out I didn't need it." He poked at the side of her right thigh, just above the knee. "What about you?"

"Souvenir from a murder suspect." She leapt on top of him, rubbing his chest. "And you know what? He wasn't even the killer."

He laughed and kissed her. "What did the real killer do to you?"

"He tried to do a lot, but Paul and I shot him dead."

He stopped caressing her. Slack-jawed, he was looking up at her.

"Uh—he was trying to kill me," she offered.

Ryan struggled to sit up, pushing Amy to the side. "It's a little weird," he said, "knowing that you killed someone."

"I guess this isn't a good time to tell you I killed more than one person as a police detective."

"Really?" He stared at her. "How do you sleep?"

She teased, "On a good night with you I don't." But she saw he was stuck in a serious frame of mind. "I'm not a murderer," she began. "What I did was with the force of law. And they were trying to kill me." His expression didn't change. "And every time it happened, I went on leave and did some soul searching. I don't know about you, but killing a person is not something I ever did lightly. Or for a personal motive."

He reached out and embraced her. "Please," he said, "forgive my curiosity. My morbid curiosity."

Amy felt reassured in his hug. "So what's it like for you? Did you ever kill anyone?" She heard Paul think, *An honest answer would be nice.*

She felt him shake his head, but he said nothing. Breaking his embrace, she said brightly, "I've got an idea. Let's be happy." She looked around. "There's all this skin, and I don't see anyone but you and me—"

He got the hint.

Later, before exhaustion engulfed a happy and tired Amy, Paul thought to her, *It doesn't bother you that Ryan is really Jeffrey?*

We don't know that. But... No, I guess not... He's still a fun guy... She yawned. *And he likes me...*

Tomorrow, let's call Walter to find out more about Jeffrey's suicide.

Umm... Sure...

Amy? Sleep had claimed her; there was no response. Paul turned their head and was looking at the man's unconscious face. *At least he's smiling*, he thought to himself. *As long as he's good to Amy and can tolerate me, it's okay.* But part of him felt it wasn't okay at all. If only to protect his dyad, the owner of the body he inhabited, Paul felt he had to know for sure who this man was. It was awhile before he joined Amy in sleep.

They were hurried in the morning; the appointment at the lawyer's office in the Central Business District was at nine o'clock. Amy hugged Lucas and wished him luck, then kissed Ryan. "I've got stuff to do today. Can I come out tomorrow?"

"Right. Paul's girlfriend. I'll call and let you know how things go with the lawyer. Tomorrow we can all go to dinner."

Amy rubbed his smooth, shaved face, and kissed him again. Then, "It's Paul. Don't let the lawyer cheat you."

They sat in Amy's old yellow Benz and watched Ryan and Lucas drive off for their appointment. "Call Walter," Paul said aloud.

"No. I don't care if he's Jeffrey."

Her reply was so unexpected that he stammered, "Wh—wh—what?"

"I like him. He likes me. I don't feel like I'm in danger. I don't care what his birth certificate says."

"There's a part of me that likes to know things. Like people's names. It makes me feel more in control. Please, can we check out the guy for my sake?"

Amy started the car–she had gotten used to the glow plug ritual the diesel engine required. "Is this your new way of trying to make me stop sleeping with a man?"

Cold! he thought back. *No, I just close my inside eyes and think of Christine, I'm good. I wish he'd shave at night, though.*

A smile. "Agreed. But now I have that fresh-faced, red-cheek look."

"Sergeant Francks?"

"Umm, I'm thinking Doc Jermaine."

She waited until she was home before she called her old NOPD station house and asked for Doctor Tallant. "I need some information," she told him.

"My goodness, Miss Clear. This is an unexpected pleasure. What can I do for you?"

Amy gave him the date of Jeffrey's suicide from the newspaper article she had found online. "Was there an autopsy?"

"Let me look," he said as he opened the search box on the police database on his computer. He repeated the date from 2028 as he keyed it in. "What's the name again?"

"Doublet. Spelled like double t."

She heard his snicker. "I know how New Orleans names work, Miss. Let me -- Ah, yes. Looks like the autopsy was done by a fraud and a charlatan named Jermaine Tallant."

"Oh, I hear he's pretty good," she teased. "Photos?"

"My God, Miss Clear, have you taken up some new and disturbing hobby?"

"No, sir. Just the same old and disturbing hobby, looking for criminals." The medical examiner had no way of knowing it was Paul who spoke. "Can I stop by and get some copies? Maybe look at the report?"

"Hmm. If you were to sit at my office computer, I could probably spend a few minutes looking out the window. We have rules about using police resources, but if nobody notices—well, then it didn't happen, did it?"

Amy smiled. "What can I bring you?" she asked. "A beignet? Muffuletta? Cheap stogie?" Jermaine had been her favorite colleague at NOPD: intelligent, desiccated sense of humor, eager to teach receptive ears, and full of courtly respect.

"I'm running low on eye of newt," he said. "See if Rouse has gotten any in lately."

Amy made a detour up Decatur Street to Central Grocery, where she picked up a muffuletta; then she ran across the street to Cafe du Monde for an order of beignets. It was twenty-five minutes before she reached her old headquarters, the police station on Rampart Street. Miraculously, she and Paul only ate one of the beignets on the drive.

The officer at the front desk made her sign in as a visitor, then slipped the plastic "guest" badge to her and let her in unaccompanied. As she walked down a flight of stairs to the medical examiner's floor, she heard Paul think, *Do you miss this place?*

Yes, she thought back. *Not the job, but I miss some of the people. I love Jermaine; he's like an auxiliary pepaw.*

I still can't believe you called him that, referring to Amy's paternal grandfather.

We all did, even dad, she thought. *I think it was on his birth certificate. Memaw is really named Hattie, but only you and her beau Mister Freddie call her that.*

The stairwell opened on a gloomy hallway across from the door to the temporary morgue and Medical Examiner's office. The glass inset was frosted, to prevent outsiders from getting unexpected views of vivisected bodies. In large red letters was written "JERMAINE". Amy knocked, then pushed the door open. She began to call, "It's the lunch fairy with—" but stopped when she saw the doctor in badly stained scrubs, standing over the opened carcass of what may have been a bulldog at one time, or perhaps a werewolf. "Uh, Jermaine?"

"Hello, Miss Clear," he said, not looking up from his handiwork.

"Are you still auditioning for *The Island of Doctor Moreau*?"

He harrumphed, "They said I was overqualified. No, one of our officers made an arrest, and the suspected drug dealer fed some things to this unfortunate pet, who was dead twenty minutes later. The pet, that is—alas, the perpetrator probably has been released by now."

"What was it?" she asked, finally standing beside him and looking down at the inside of a dog's stomach.

"Several little plastic bags," he said, poking at them with tweezers, "and one that either ripped or dissolved in the poor beast's guts." He used the tweezers to pick up some things Amy couldn't identify and place them in a Petri dish. Still staring intently through his magnifier loupes, the doctor used a tiny spoon to add some liquid to the small glass saucer. "We'll see what the test tells us in a minute," he announced, turning off the scorching light over his autopsy table.

Jermaine removed his magnifiers and finally looked at Amy. "Oh, Miss Clear, it is always a pleasure to see you. And you look like private investigating agrees with you."

"When you retire they should just burn this place down. It won't be worth a hoot without you." Smiling, she leaned over and up to kiss the man on the cheek; she loved the way it always embarrassed and pleased him.

"I understand you have work to do," he said. "Let me set you up at the computer while I sew Bowser back together." He led her to his work station. "Commander Ramirez told the IT department to keep your login, so you don't have to pretend to be me."

As she sat she realized she was holding the bag of treats from Café Du Monde. "You probably want to wash up before you open this," she said, handing it to him, "but I brought your favorites."

"Eye of newt?" he asked, breathless.

"Rouse said they're having a problem with their supplier," shaking her head. "They told me I should see that Marie Laveau woman on St. Ann Street."

"I'll try there after work," he said. Carefully he placed the bag on top of a filing cabinet, then set to closing the incision in the canine.

Amy quickly found the autopsy record for Jeffrey Doublet. The toxicology report showed a 0.14 alcohol level and a significant amount of chloral hydrate, a common enough, although prescription controlled, sleeping chemical. There was no physical indication of trauma, but the face–documented in the four accompanying photos— had become swollen and pale. Cause of death was asphyxia and venous congestion. The Medical Examiner—Doc Jermaine— estimated the body had been hanging for nine or ten hours. The evaluation was suicide for two reasons: the presence of a handwritten suicide note, and investigation of the disruption caused by the means of death, a twisted bed sheet, over the ceiling beam from which it was suspended. Notes indicated that a ruling of suicide was corroborated by the next of kin, who described the deceased's mental state and confirmed the handwriting of the note.

The next of kin was Ryan Doublet.

"Let's see the pictures," Paul whispered aloud, eliciting a snort from Jermaine.

One was a full frontal nude that clearly showed the wide ligature mark from the bedsheet used for the suicide. The strawberry birthmark Lucas described was visible on Jeffrey's right thigh. And there was no appendix scar on the abdomen.

"Holy shit," Paul said. "I've got chicken skin. What—" Amy silently interrupted him. *I don't believe it. I mean, okay, I've fallen in lust with Jeffrey Doublet, sure. But I do not believe he killed his brother.*

And the reason for that disbelief?

She considered Paul's question and answered honestly. *It hasn't had a chance to sink in yet. Plus, I don't want it to be true.*

"What have you discovered, Miss?" Jermaine had finished with the dog, removed his scrubs, and washed up. He was standing beside Amy, powdered sugar drifting down from his half-eaten beignet.

"We should call a press conference. I have just discovered that reality bites."

"Old news to an old doctor," he offered, grimly. "What is it that reality has done to offend you?"

Amy kicked the rolling chair away from the computer to let Jermaine see the screen. "Do you remember anything about this case?"

He knelt on one knee to look at the computer, licking sugar off his fingers. "Barely. The brother who was next of kin was an identical twin. You don't see them very often."

"Any reason to doubt suicide?"

"Actually—" he pointed at something on the screen "—the presence of chloral hydrate was curious. Considering the deceased's weight, the serum level I found could have caused unconsciousness, but not necessarily." He stood up, brushing imaginary dust from his trouser knee. "But the way the noose was set up, that bedsheet, that said 'suicide.'"

When she didn't respond, Jermaine stood by her chair and put a hand on her shoulder. "Why do you ask?"

I can't tell him I'm sleeping with the next of kin, she thought to Paul. *It would be like telling your grandmother that you're selling drugs at the middle school.* So Paul, sounding exactly like Amy, said, "I met the next of kin recently. He hired me for a PI job. He's a great guy, but his son said something that upset me."

Paul! Don't! she silently screamed at him.

Still seated, Paul walked the chair back to the computer console and clicked back to the full frontal post-mortem photograph. "The son of the next of kin—of Ryan Doublet—says his father has a winestain birthmark on his leg." He pointed at the screen. Jermaine peered at it, and said, "So the identifying mark on Ryan Doublet shows up on the autopsy photo of Jeffrey Doublet."

Jermaine stroked his chin and paced a few steps away and back. "Since they are identical twins, it is possible both men had a similar birthmark."

Paul heard Amy plead with him, but he said, "I've seen the next of kin, uh, in, uh, in a bathing suit. No birthmark. And an appendix scar."

"Oh. Oh dear. So you think that—" Amy's silent shouts drowned out the doctor. *I like this man. Don't make them arrest him! I'm not done with him yet.*

"I'm sorry, Jermaine, what?"

"Please, Miss Clear, you always had trouble paying attention. You are accusing the person calling himself Ryan Doublet of actually being Jeffrey Doublet? And of killing the real Ryan Doublet?"

Amy took back the lead. "I'm not accusing anyone of anything. But disturbing as it is, it seems that Jeffrey has been masquerading as Ryan Doublet." She stared at the computer monitor, trying to will it to change. "I don't know about murder." Looking up at Jermaine she said, "This doesn't have to be homicide. He may have just stumbled on his dead brother–"

The doctor held up his hand to stop her. "We have a dead Ryan. He was found hanging in Jeffrey's home, which made it easy for me to conclude the victim was Jeffrey and that it was suicide. But Ryan dead in Jeffrey's home, especially when Jeffrey goes on to claim he is really Ryan—it might still be suicide, but suddenly I have reasonable doubts."

Paul could feel Amy's fear. "You can't arrest him!" she blurted out.

"Not my job, Miss. Or yours anymore. Do I detect a personal involvement here? Hmm?"

Amy stared at her shoes.

"Well, no need for us to go into that." He pushed her chair sideways and knelt again at the computer. A few clicks to see different pages in the report; then, "Because the body was identified by the next of kin, and because no foul play was suspected by that quack of a medical examiner, there was no request for dental records."

She thought to her dyad, *It's all your fault. You just had to know who we were sleeping with. You couldn't just let me enjoy a decent relationship.*

He whispered, "I'm sorry, Amy. Really."

"What's that, miss?"

"Uh, talking to myself. May I say something?"

"Be my guest."

"CRAP!" she bellowed.

After a moment the doctor said, "Feel better now?"

Amy rested her head in her arms. "Finally. I finally have a decent boyfriend. He's good-looking, he's nice to me, he's got a real job, he's emotionally available—and he's hiding a death, if not something worse. Doctor Tallant, just take me out to the parking lot and shoot me, please?"

"If you insist, Miss Clear. Come along." His hand was on her shoulder again. When she looked up he was holding the Muffaletta out for her. It was missing three or four bites.

A smile spread across her face. "I'm not hungry, but thanks. You are a prince."

"I won't pretend to offer you personal advice," he said, dragging a metal chair over and sitting facing her. "But professionally—well, you know how NOPD works, and you're a licensed private investigator. I have no doubt you will pick at this sore spot until you convince yourself of the man's innocence. Or his guilt. And I have no doubt you will do the right thing at that time. In the meantime, though, I'd appreciate it if you would humor an old man who thinks of you like a daughter: be careful."

She nodded. It was Paul who said, "We haven't felt any danger."

"'We?' Yes, well, Ted Bundy encountered some thirty women who didn't feel any danger. Please, Miss Clear, take care of yourself."

Another nod. *I'm no threat to him,* she thought to Paul. He replied silently, *You will be if you confront him.*

"Thank you, Doctor Tallant. I appreciate your counsel. And making room for me."

"Please, everyone calls me Jermaine."

"And everyone calls me Amy."

"Ah. Yes, well. Is there anything else I can do for you, Miss Clear?"

Smiling, she said, "Yes. Don't you ever change." They both stood up, and Amy hugged the man. Awkwardly, he patted her back. As they took their leave, Paul said, "Good luck with the eye of newt."

Seated in the old yellow Benz in the PD parking area, Paul said aloud, "Now what?"

"I'm going to ask Ryan—uh, Jeffrey—his opinion of Jeffrey." She started to laugh, "That should be weird enough."

Paul thought to her, *That's a great idea. We need to find out if Jeffrey—if the real Jeffrey–had a motive to kill the real Ryan.*

Paul mashed the glow plug button and waited to crank the engine. Amy said, "I have to remember to call him Ryan, even though I'm convinced he's not."

"Yup. I think we're safe as long as Je—uh, as long as Ryan doesn't suspect we know his secret."

Paul backed out of the parking space and headed south on Rampart, towards home. "What's for lunch?" he asked.

"I don't know. Whatever's in the refrigerator, I guess."

"Should I stop at Rouse?" the supermarket chain to which they were partial.

"Why? They're all out of eye of newt."

"Ah, but sauté some toe of frog and fillet of a fenny snake—now, that's good eating."

Amy sat at the computer, trying to create a presentation for criminal law firms. Paul, working the other mouse with their left hand, was looking at an online version of *Macbeth*. "I thought it was from the Scottish play," he said, then quoted "'Double, double, toil and trouble, Fire burn and cauldron bubble.'"

What are you going on about? Amy thought to him.

"Eye of newt. It's from Shakespeare."

She snorted, "I thought it was from that occult store on Dumaine Street." Then, "What am I going to tell a law firm? Why should they hire me?"

"Didn't we take a marketing class at UNO? We need a slug line, some catchy—" Amy's phone rang, interrupting them. "I'll bet it's Christine," Amy said. "Go ahead, answer it."

"Paulette!" he heard his lover say his name—well, the name she used for him—as if he were her knight in shining armor. "Tell me everything's okay. Please?"

"We're talking to each other. We love each other. Everything will be okay, I promise. What's up with Mom?"

"Not much change," she sighed. "She still can't talk. But her face lights up when Nathan comes in the room, or when I do. It's sweet. But it's like she's turning into the daughter and I'm becoming the mother. I don't like that."

"Be brave, honey. You're doing good for her just by being there, I know it."

"I guess." It pained Paul to hear her so discouraged, but he understood her sadness.

"It's Amy. We're thinking about you and your mom. I want my best friend to be happy again."

"Thanks, Amy. I know you do. Paulette and you are what keep me going." They heard her blow her nose, then she asked, "How's your boyfriend?"

"Funny you should ask," she replied. "I'll let Paul tell you." He went on, sounding exactly the same, but Christine somehow always knew which one of them was speaking. "We went to visit one of Amy's old police colleagues this morning. Turns out her beau, Ryan, is really his dead twin brother Jeffrey."

"Wait. How can he be Ryan, and Jeffrey, and dead?"

Paul was tickled by her phrasing and let out a laugh. "The world thinks Jeffrey killed himself a year ago. We saw the autopsy photos today, and it turns out Ryan is the dead brother. Jeffrey is alive and pretending to be Ryan."

"Oh, no. You be careful, Paulette. Amy. Don't let him do anything bad to you."

"I don't think we're in any danger. He doesn't know we know. And you know us, we have to find out what's really going on."

Amy added, "Besides, I still like him. He's nice. He accepts Paul—either that or he's amazingly smooth about thinking I'm crazy. And I notice something in particular because you've pointed it out with some of my previous flames: he's emotionally available."

"That's good," Christine said. In the past she had wagged her finger at Amy for getting involved with a couple of married men and one ne'er-do-well folksinger. "You're happy when you're with him?"

"Yes. Yes, I am. And Paul is well-behaved."

"You won't forget me while I'm gone, will you?" Paul recognized his lover's fear, her lack of self-confidence, her occasional low self-esteem. "Never," he said. "Listen to me, Christine. I love you. Amy loves you." "It's Amy, it's true, I do. I love you." "I know you have to take care of Mom; family always comes first. But I'm counting the days until I see you again. I need my daily dose of Christine."

They heard the woman's sigh of relief. For a moment she sounded giddy, "Yeah. Me, too, Paulette. And you, Amy. Call me tonight, okay?"

When the call was over, Paul said, "Can we go to St. Louis now?"

"I wish. No, I have to dredge up more work. A slug line, you said?"

Amy had a legal pad with her when she drove to what she and Paul had decided they must continue to think of as Ryan's house on Tuesday afternoon. It contained half-a-dozen false starts on her presentation, and the one line she and Paul both liked: "Separating the saints from the dirt-bags." She thought she'd spend some time with Lucas before her lover returned from work.

She let herself in with the key Ryan had given her right after she brought Lucas back from Atlanta. *What's that smell?* she heard Paul think; she said aloud, "Eau de puke," and called Lucas' name. She followed the grunts she heard, and found the man in one of the bathrooms, door open, sitting in front of the toilet. "Are you all right?" Paul thought to her, *The boy is very far from all right.*

"Feel crappy," he mumbled.

She put a hand on his forehead. "I don't think you have a fever. What feels crappy?"

Slowly he said, "Head hurts. Back hurts. Thirsty. It's - it's --" and let loose with what little remained in his stomach. "Don't watch," he said, and retched again.

"Let me know if I can do anything," she said. "I know you don't want an audience for this performance. I'll be down the hall. Okay?"

"Yeah. Thanks."

Poor kid, Paul thought as they walked a few feet to the living room. *I wonder what he ate? Leave New Orleans for two years and your body forgets how to deal with cayenne pepper and okra.*

"I wish I could help him," she said aloud. "I remember mom holding my hair out of the way when I got sick once." She shivered at the memory. "Let's take another whack at this presentation," and she spread her false starts on the sofa.

You'll get Jef—uh, Ryan to help when he gets home, Paul thought. *Let's ask him about Jeffrey. Maybe he'll slip and give himself away.*

"Good plan," she said. "How's 'A Parish police detective doesn't just find the criminals. She also exonerates the innocent.'?"

"And finds prodigal sons," Paul added. Amy started to write, then paused and said, "Stop that!" She crossed out what she had put down. "You're supposed to be helping."

Every fifteen minutes or so she got up and checked on Lucas. She considered it improvement that he had returned to his room, laying on top of the bed in all his clothes. On one trip she saw he was shivering. "You want to get under the covers?" she asked him.

Weakly he answered, "No. In a. Minute. I'll be. Hot again."

"Can I get you anything?" She heard Paul think, *Don't catch whatever he's got!*

"Yeah. Water. So thirsty."

She nodded and made her way to the kitchen. "Get something bigger than a drinking glass," Paul said. He pointed at some high cabinets and said, "Maybe up there?" Amy took the stepstool from its place beside the refrigerator and dragged it to the likely section. As she climbed up the two rungs she looked down, and she saw three coffee mugs on the counter by the sink, each with something she couldn't identify from that far away. Once she was on the top of the stepladder she opened the cabinet and found Rubbermaid juice containers. She pulled one down and jumped to the floor. While it was filling with tap water she looked closely at those mugs. One had recently chopped onions; one had butter or margarine; and the other had some crumpled red and brown material she didn't recognize. She stuck her nose near it and waved air from above the mug toward herself. "Radishes?" Paul said. Amy poked her finger in the stuff. "Wrong consistency," she replied, "but that's what it smells like."

When the juice container was full she put the lid on it, then rinsed her finger. "Oh, a glass," she said, took one, and went back to Lucas's room.

She poured water into his glass and held it out to him. He struggled to hoist himself up on his elbows, then let Amy feed the water to him a little at a time. When the glass was empty, he dropped himself back down. "Thank you," he whispered. "So thirsty."

"There's more water in the jug. Yell if you need anything. I'll check back in a little while, okay?" The boy nodded. She patted him on the chest, like her mother used to do when Amy was sick in bed.

The next time she looked in on him, he seemed to be asleep. She called his name, softly, a few times, but got no response. Paul said, "I'll think to him," but she thought back, *No! You'll just give him bad dreams.* Then, aloud, "What he's been through, I'd be asleep, too."

Amy felt she and Paul had made some progress on the presentation for criminal law firms when she heard the side door to the house. Her car was parked in front, and Ryan called, "Oh, Amy! I'm home!"

She dropped her clipboard and pad to run to the door to greet him. "How was your day, Honey?" she said; she leaned against him, and bent her right leg to raise her foot in the air.

"I love computers," he answered. "They do exactly what you tell them. I spent four hours going through code to find some commas that should have been slashes." He kissed her forehead. "How about you? Been here long?"

"Couple of hours," she said. "I thought I'd visit with Lucas, but he's sick as a dog."

"Still?" He shook his head and began walking toward his son's room.

"It's weird," Amy said, following behind. "I don't think he's running a fever, but he's got chills and hot flashes and—"

Ryan growled, "He used to do this to try to get out of school. I wonder what he's avoiding now. Lucas? Lucas?"

The man was laying on his side on top of the bedcovers, panting.

Amy saw the water jug she had brought him was empty. "Boy, how are you doing? Lucas?" There was no response. "How long has he been like this?" he asked Amy.

"I've been here about an hour, hour-and-a-half," she answered. She had her hands in the front pockets of her jeans, her fingers playing idly with a small flashlight she always carried. "He seems real sick."

Ryan sat on the bed and leaned over his son, gently shaking him at the shoulder. "Lucas, talk to me." The boy's eyelid fluttered. "Dad. I'm glad. You're home. I don't. Feel well. Thirsty. Hurt."

"Is it worse than this morning?"

"Yeah." A feeble laugh, followed by a cough. "Yeah."

When he said, "We'll get you some water," Amy waved in front of the man and pointed at herself. She took the juice jug and went to the kitchen to refill it. She opened and closed a few drawers until she found the gadget drawer that every kitchen has, and found flexistraws. She took two.

Ryan was still sitting on the bed, his hand on Lucas' forehead, when she returned. "You're right," he said to her, "No fever."

Amy poured water in the glass and put a straw in it, then let Ryan attempt to feed it to the boy. Lucas seemed too tired to sit up. Ryan gave the glass back to Amy, then put an arm under his son's shoulders and lifted his head and chest. Amy pushed the straw to the Lucas' mouth. It took a few moments before he seemed to figure out what it was; greedily he drank almost the entire glass. Ryan let him down, while Amy refilled the glass and left it on the night stand.

"I think he needs a doctor," Amy said.

Ryan stood up. "Maybe. I'll see how he is in the morning."

Paul thought to her, *He wants to wait? Is that what any father you know would do?*

Not everybody's father is an M.D. like mine, she thought back, *But, yes.* She followed him into the kitchen, hearing him say, "...some things together for dinner. Maybe half-an-hour?"

"Can I help?"

"Nope. Now get out of my secret kitchen. You said you'd be working on a presentation?"

She nodded. "I'm sure I can use your help. too."

"After dinner. Now, scoot!"

When Ryan brought the quick meal out to the dining room—hamburgers, broccoli, and mashed potatoes—he called Amy to join him. "We'll save something for Lucas," he said, "but I don't think he's hungry."

"He was asleep when I checked on him a little while ago," as she served herself broccoli.

"It's Paul. How did the trip to the lawyer go?"

He nodded, then swallowed before answering, "It was smooth. Lucas had all the right paperwork with him. It'll probably be next year before he gets his inheritance, it depends on how the lawyer wants to deal with some tax issues. But he says that the conditions of probate have been satisfied."

"Okay. Did he say anything about talking to his girlfriend?"

"Paul? Why do you care about that?"

"Because I met her. Kali is stone gorgeous. I mean, hubba-hubba, drop-dead divine."

When he raised an eyebrow, Amy added, "Kali does part-time fashion modeling. She was on the cover of Atlanta's version of *New Orleans Magazine*. She is a very attractive woman."

"Really?" He took a forkful of potatoes. "He told me a little about her, but not that he was going to call her."

Smiling, Amy said, "Your grandchildren would be spectacular." Ryan snorted.

Here goes, Amy thought to Paul. Then out loud, "Tell me about your brother."

"What about him? He was a whiney, depressed, lazy man who took the coward's way out."

"Lucas said you and Jeffrey had a rivalry. That it even included your wife."

He put down his fork. "Why are you asking this?"

Amy placed both hands on the table, palms down. She took a deep breath and answered, "Because I like you, Ryan. I want to know more about you, and your family."

"Oh. I'm sorry," he reached over and put one hand over her left hand. "I'm not—I'm not—This being with a woman who likes me is a new thing."

"Don't let me intrude," she said, a serious look on her face. "If you're not ready to talk about him, it'll wait."

"No, it's okay." He went back to his burger. "We did have a sibling rivalry" –it sounded like 'sippng rivry.' "Things always were easy for him, and I always had to work at things like school." Another bite. "And it was like he never understood why I was—uh, jealous of him. People just liked him, and I had trouble getting people to notice me." He stopped, elbows on the table, burger in both hands. "Jeffrey loved me, he always was helpful, he shared things. He liked the world." Another bite. "Now, I loved him, too, but I envied him so much."

"My kid sister is three years younger than me," Amy said. "I can't imagine what it would be like if Kaylee was exactly my age, and looked just like me."

He shrugged. "It seemed normal enough to me because that's what our life was."

They paid attention to their meals for a few moments.

"The difference turned out to be sports. I like sports. My brother didn't. So I was on the football varsity and I got a letter in baseball. You know, he'd come to the games and cheer me on. He was happy for me when I blocked tackles or ran passes or hit a home run. And sometimes I felt like crap because he was so happy for me and I, I, I envied him so much. Does that make sense?"

No, Amy thought to Paul; it was Paul who answered aloud, "Maybe it will when I hear more."

"We both were interested in computers. So dad sent both of us to Louisiana Tech. We didn't room together—I was so excited at the chance to sort of live on my own that I threatened to punch his lights out." He laughed at the memory. "It was okay. We got along better. Well, he always got along fine with me, but I got along better with him. Until—" He took the last bite of hamburger, and chewed it carefully. Paul thought, *Is he stalling?*

Why would he do that? Amy thought back.

Finally he continued. "Our junior year we met this cute freshman. Samantha Fetters. I showed you her picture. She was a skinny redhead with a great smile and such a—well, I fell for her. And so did my brother." Ryan poked his broccoli with a spoon, but didn't take any to eat. "And she liked both of us. She went out with both of us."

Paul blinked. "That must have been difficult," he said, sounding exactly like Amy.

"You could say that. Sometimes the three of us would do things together, but that got to be awkward. He didn't like to see me kiss her." A snort. "Can't say I enjoyed seeing her kiss him."

She put down her fork and slid her chair closer to Ryan while he explained, "By our senior year, I was in love with Sammie. He said he was, too. We went to her and told her to choose, and she said she wouldn't. She said she liked both of us. She liked both of us courting her."

"It's Paul. Was that any kind of red flag to you?"

"What? No, of course not. What's wrong with you? Paul?"

"It's me," Amy said, stretching to put a hand on his. "Paul was married. His life was sure different from mine. Go on."

He stopped. "You really are different people?"

She nodded silently, while Paul thought one word to him, *Yup.*

Ryan stared at her—at them—for a long moment. He shook his head with a smile, then continued his story. "So I asked her to marry me. She said 'yes'." And my brother went berserk."

"What did Jeffrey do?" She was rubbing the back of his hand.

"He got extremely drunk. He trashed his dorm room. He came to my room and tried to fight me, but I guess we were an even match— nothing really happened. And he made Sammie miserable by hanging out by her dorm and begging and crying." He shook his head. "Like I said, berserk. When we got married after graduation, he wouldn't come to the wedding. I wanted him to be my best man, but he refused."

"I guess it really hurt him," Amy said softly.

"Yes. Yes, indeed, it hurt him. But it also hurt me. It was years before we got back onto decent terms. But we did. He was a big help to me after Sammie—well, you know. And again after Lucas ran away."

"Oh, Ryan," Amy said. "I had no idea."

"It's okay. We were on good terms before he died. I'd have hated myself if we weren't."

"Why did he—you know."

"He left a note," Ryan said, standing to gather up the dinner dishes. "His job wasn't going well. He had a lot of money problems. He was depressed." A pause. "Mom had died by then, and Daddy Doublet already was losing his marbles. I think he was lonely."

Looking at her shoes, Amy softly said, "I'm sorry, Ryan. I'm so sorry."

He put the dirty dishes back on the table and came around behind her chair. He wrapped both arms around her and hugged her from the back, and kissed the back of her head. "It's been a long time since anyone cared enough to ask." Another kiss. "Thank you." Amy lifted her arms over his, returning the hug as best she could from that position. She was excited. She felt he was grateful that she had intruded on his privacy. To Paul she thought, *Don't say it. I don't care that he's really Jeffrey, I like him and he wants me.*

After a long moment he kissed her again, then went back to clearing the dinner table. Amy followed him in to the kitchen. Paul thought, *Wait a minute*—he looked at the counter by the sink and saw only two of the mugs remaining. As best he remembered, the missing one held the crumpled black and red stuff that smelled like radishes. *Okay,* he thought, and abruptly she was leading again.

"I'm going to check on Lucas," she said. "He's been going through water like, uh, like water, I guess." A little embarrassed, she left the kitchen and walked down the hall.

She found the man sitting up on his bed, his arms wrapped around himself as if he was cold. "How are you feeling?" she asked as she sat on the edge of the bed.

A fleeting smile crossed his face. "I'm so tired," he said, slowly. "And my back and my sides. They hurt."

"Are you cold?" She put her hand on his forehead, but felt no sign of fever.

"Yeah. Right now. It'll change. In a minute."

"Do you have any idea what's going on?" she asked. "Did you eat anything spoiled or weird?"

He shook his head, then winced in pain. "Head hurts too."

"Let me get you some more water. Or would you rather have juice? A Coke?"

"Yeah. A Coke. Some ginger ale?"

She rested her hand on his arm for a moment, then pushed herself off the bed. "You wait here," she smiled.

Ryan was still fitting dishes into the dishwasher when she came back to the kitchen with the empty glass and jug. She ran cold water in the sink to refill the ewer. "Is there any ginger ale? Lucas says he'd like some." At Paul's silent direction she looked in the two remaining coffee mugs: one had fewer recently chopped onions, and the other still had butter or oleo. It was the radish-smelling whatever that was gone.

Ryan directed her to the refrigerator. She poured the soft drink into Lucas' glass, then picked up the water jug and went back to the sickroom.

His smile was feeble but real. *You poor boy,* she thought to him, and his smile flickered stronger for a moment. She put the jug on his nightstand, then sat on the bed again. "Here, I'll help you." She held the glass of soda and turned the flexistraw toward him. His sips were small, but they were many. He put his hands over Amy's on the drinking glass, and stared into her eyes the whole time. When he'd had enough he croaked, "Thank you."

"I'll check on you later, okay?" As she left his room, she turned like her mother had always done for a last look before she flicked off the overhead light and softly closed the door.

You would make a good mother after all, Paul thought to her. He felt her laugh and heard her silent reply, *Yes, if I could have twenty-year-old babies.*

Back in the kitchen she reported Lucas' condition to Ryan. "I think he's doing just a little better."

"Good. Hey, your presentation?"

Smiling, she said, "I've got a better idea."

They held hands as they walked to his bedroom. Paul thought to her, *How can you do this? You're going to sleep with a liar who maybe killed his own brother?*

"Yes," she replied aloud; then silently, *I don't know that he killed the real Ryan. And I don't care that he's the real Jeffrey.*

Ryan suddenly picked Amy up and carried her across the threshold of his bedroom, and dropped her on the bed. They embraced and kissed for a while. Then he said, "You take the bathroom first."

So Amy washed her face and brushed her teeth, listening to Paul plead with her to leave, to run away, to escape from the lying Doublet. She stamped her foot and barked, "Paul!" Then, silently, she told him, *I feel safe, I've got Rosckette. He's not going to hurt me. Since I know he's lying, it's like this is, I don't know, sleeping with a stranger, which is something you know I'd never do. But it's so exciting. God, this is turning me on. I am so going to rock this man within an inch of his life. And you—* out loud again, "you are not going to mess it up. Hush! I told you to hush!"

She stepped back into the bedroom, dressed only in her underwear. "Are you and Paul having a disagreement?" Ryan asked, smiling.

"It happens sometimes. He misses Christine."

"I don't know how to help him," he said, hugging her for a moment, then taking his turn in the lavatory. Through the closed bathroom door he heard the shout from Paul—sounding exactly like

Amy: "Shave!"

After Ryan had left for work, Amy dressed and went to Lucas' room. "Hey, Champ," she called, "how are you doing?"

"Amy," he whispered, a ghost of a smile on his face. "So thirsty." He was laying on top of the covers, still wearing his Monday clothes.

She took the jug and glass to the kitchen to rinse and refill them, then returned. He grabbed the glass greedily and drank it quickly, then coughed. He winced, "Head still hurts."

She thought for a moment and asked, "When's the last time you had to pee?"

"I don't remember."

"This morning? Yesterday?"

"Yesterday," he answered. "It was. Daytime."

"Do you still hurt?"

He nodded, "Head. Back. Sides. And tired."

The doctor's daughter said, "We're going to visit my dad. He's a doctor in Metairie. Can you get up?"

Lucas swung his legs off the side of the bed, but then lay back, feet on the floor. "Give me. A. Minute."

"We'll get you to my car. Come on." She stood by the bed, pulling up on his shoulders, but he was too heavy for her. "Come on, Lucas. I need your help. I'll pull, you sit up, okay?"

She heard Paul think, *Wait. Ryan said to wait.*

"You're the one who points out he may have killed his brother. Do you think he cares about his nephew?"

Lucas murmured, "What? Who. Killed. Brother?"

"Crap. Sorry, Lucas, I didn't mean to say that out loud. Look, you are right. He's your uncle Jeffrey. Ryan is dead. I don't know what's going on, but I'm worried about you being so sick. So, let's get going."

"What?" He felt Amy pulling on his shoulders, and he managed to sit up on the edge of the bed. "My. Father?"

"Your family is a little different from mine," she said, trying to pull him up by the armpits. "Walk with me, now."

Lucas tried to shift his weight but slipped and fell back on the bed. "Please, Lucas. I can't do this by myself. Come on. That's it," as he tried again, "you can—" He slipped again, bouncing off the side of the bed and landing mostly on the floor, taking Amy with him.

She cried to Paul, *What are we going to do? I've got to get him to Dad.*

Let me catch my breath, he thought back to her. Then he began thinking to Lucas. *Big guy! It's Paul*–even though he knew the man was hearing his male voice. *Amy and I need your help. We're going to take you to a doctor, Amy's father. James will fix you up. But you're bigger than we are. We can't drag you. Can you hear me?*

They heard him mutter, "Yeah. Yeah. I. Hear you."

Good, good. Now, first we're going to get off the floor. I need you to stand up. Amy needs you to stand up. You want to help Amy, don't you?

They heard another "Yeah."

He moved their legs back, putting the soles of their shoes on the ground. *Okay, Lucas. Help Amy and me stand up, okay?* He pushed up with his legs; he could feel Lucas struggling to force himself up. *That's great,* he thought to the man, *That's a big help. Up we go.* Paul pushed as much as Amy's five-foot six and one-hundred-nine pound frame could. When he felt Lucas begin to slip, he pushed back, and the man landed on the bed, legs dangling over the side. He and Amy landed on the floor, covering the man's feet.

"Groan," Paul said out loud. "Is there a fork lift in our car trunk?"

"Brilliant!" she shouted, and started to sit up. "A hand truck. Ryan used one when you fixed his door, he took the sawhorses away on it." Then, "Lucas, you okay?" They heard him grunt. "I'm going exploring; I'll be back. Don't you go anywhere."

"Does he have a shed in the back yard?" Paul asked aloud.

"Let's see." Finally on her feet, she set off to find the storage shed or workshop that might be home to a float.

She went through the kitchen and through the attached pantry to the back door. The day was hot and muggy, the haze barely tinged with blue here and there. The well-kept lawn was a dull green, but a medium-sized RubberMaid BigMax enclosure stood out in gleaming white. Amy noticed the padlock as she approached, and saw it was not clasped. She lifted it and swung open the door.

"Damn, I don't see it," she pouted. But Paul thought to her, *Over there. He left the sawhorses on it,* and he walked them to it. He led to offload the sawhorses, leaning them against a disused chest of drawers.

Amy said, "So I get Lucas to stand up on this thing. What keeps him from falling off?"

It's a convertible, she heard Paul think. *Let me*— and he lay the handtruck on the ground, its toe plate sticking up. He bent over and said aloud, "These cotter pins—" he pulled the two pins that held the handle in place "—come out. Now we pull out the handle—" he separated it from the wheeled portion of the float and stood up straight "—and slip it in these holes, and fasten it with the pins. Now it's a platform." Done, he leaned one arm on the handle and smiled.

Amy understood. "A blanket on the bottom and the back. He can sit. And—those are bungee cords? Great, just in case I have to strap him in. C'mon!"

She led to wheel what had been converted into a platform cart through the yard. She had to work at getting it up the two steps to the back door, but then it was an easy push to Lucas' room.

He hadn't moved while she was gone. "You hanging in there, big guy?" Paul called, sounding exactly like Amy. Lucas grunted. Amy pulled the blanket off the bed, then folded it and placed it on the platform. She was careful to make sure the fabric wouldn't hang down and interfere with the wheels. "How about you and me and Paul take a little trip?" she said as she worked, "it's a nice day for a drive out to Metairie. You'll like my dad; he's—he's—I guess he's pretty cool." Satisfied with her preparations, she turned back to face Lucas. "I need your help," she said as she grasped him by the armpits. "We're going to swing your butt off the bed and onto this neat little go-cart. Would you like that?" She thought she saw a fleeting smile behind his grunt.

She took a deep breath and tried to lift the man who was almost twice her weight. She did not hear Paul think to him, *Amy needs your help. Just for a second, lift yourself up. Come on. Yeah, like that.* They felt him struggle to come to his feet.

Amy was saying, "Now we're going to turn—no, turn this way, we're—" while Paul continued to think to Lucas, *Amy's so proud of you. Let's twist a little, you can do this for Amy, I know you can—* They lowered him to the platform float. "Are. We done?" he gasped. He was leaning against the upright handle.

Amy kissed him on the crown of his head. "You did great, Lucas." She lifted his legs and put them on the platform. "Comfy?" She saw a brief smile cross his face. "Okay, here we go." Amy stood behind the convertible handtruck and wheeled it through the bedroom door, down the hall, and across the carpeted living room. She opened the front door to determine their travel route. "Stairs!" she said. "How do I do this?"

Paul thought, *We go in front. We'll lift the foot of the cart up so Lucas' weight is on the back wheels. Then we pull slowly. He's going to feel a jolt on each step, though.*

She moved ahead of the cart and lifted up the foot, as Paul instructed. "We're going to play, Lucas," she said. "We're going to go 'boom, boom, boom,' okay? It'll be fun. Ready?" There was no response. Slowly she inched the cart forward, singing "Dum-de-dum-de-dum-de-dum" to an improvised tune; when the back wheels abruptly dropped to the lower step she shouted, "Boom!" The brief smile returned to Lucas' face, and he whispered, "Boom." Paul thought to Amy, *He's enjoying this? How do you do this?*

"Boom! Boom!" and they were on the cement landing in front of the house, level with the lawn. Amy struggled to push the cart across the squishy grass, finally getting it through the wrought iron gate and onto the sidewalk.

"Now to get him in the car," Amy said as she unlocked and opened the rear passenger door to her old yellow Benz. She leaned down to Lucas to say, "One more boom, okay?" He flashed that brief smile and softly said, "Boom."

Amy positioned the cart with the handle against the open door. First she chocked a cart wheel with a stone. Then she undid the cotter pins and pulled the handle free. Lucas fell back against her leg. "Boom," he whispered.

"Boom it is," she said. She climbed into the back seat, then grabbed Lucas by the armpits and began tugging. Silently, Paul thought, *Amy needs our help again. Can you get into the car? Just kind of push up where she's pulling? Come on, big guy. You can do it. You can help Amy.*

Lucas tried to push. He succeeded in forcing the blanket under him through openings in the platform, which helped the improvised wheel chock keep the cart in place. Finally his feet took hold. Amy was muttering "Come on, Lucas" while straining against his weight when finally he pushed himself up high enough for her to drag him onto the seat. *He weighs a ton,* she thought to Paul. She heard him laugh and think, *One of the very few things I don't like about living in a woman's body. I used to be strong. Really, I was.*

When she caught her breath, Amy let herself out the drivers' side door and went around the car to the comparatively easy job of bending Lucas' legs to fit inside the car. It was a relief to be able to close the door.

She pressed the glow plug button. "We're on our way," she called to Lucas lying in the back seat. She heard him whisper "Boom."

"Next time," Paul said aloud, "let's just call 911."

Amy stopped with her finger poised over the 'start' button, then tilted her head to look at the ceiling fabric, although that was only because her eyes had to be aimed at something. After a few seconds of complete silence she began to laugh. "Why didn't you think of that half an hour ago? Why didn't I think of that?" She started the engine and pulled onto the street. She looked into the back seat and called to Lucas, "Why didn't you tell me to call 911?"

When he said "Boom," Amy laughed again.

"We'll have to go back later," Paul said. "We left all the doors open, and the cart's on the sidewalk. Ryan's going to be mad."

"I hope he's more concerned with how sick Lucas is. But leaving the doors open, I guess that's bad."

It was a twenty-minute drive to the Jefferson Parish Medical Center where her father, Doctor James Clear, had his office. He had been an emergency room surgeon there for twenty years before he and a partner opened a joint practice. Amy tried to pull into the first emergency lane, but a late model BMW with an MD tag was blocking it, engine idling while the driver was doing something of vital importance like using the ATM machine just inside. "Dad would kill that guy," she shouted as she backed up and then drove around the jerk's car.

She threw open her door and yelled, "Emergency!" Two men and a woman in blue scrubs came through the automatic door, pushing a gurney. "Get him to James Clear," she ordered them, "Suite 218 North." By the time one of the orderlies challenged her, she was holding out her drivers' license. As Doctor Clear's daughter, Amy was widely known at the medical center. That—and one look at how sick Lucas was—was enough; the staffers agreed to wheel the man upstairs.

Amy moved her car to visitor parking, then raced to the elevator bay. She wanted to explain to Ashley, her father's triage nurse, what was going on. When she entered her father's office, the attendants were standing by Lucas' gurney, all talking at once to Ashley.

Amy added to the confusion by calling the woman's name. When the nurese recognized her employer's daughter, Amy told her, "My boyfriend's son. He's been sick as can be since Monday. Lethargic, pain in his head and sides, no longer urinating. Thirsty." Lucas, very plainly, said "Boom."

"No fever," Amy finished. "I'm scared for him."

She wrote something on the attendants' clipboard and began pushing the gurney past the waiting room and down the hall to an open examination room. "I'll get your father," the nurse said, and left.

Amy took Lucas' hand and looked down at the man. His eyes

were open, and there was a smile on his face. "How are you hanging in there, big fella?"

"Where. Am I," he asked.

"My father's office. He's a doctor. He's going to fix you up."

He nodded, and closed his eyes. When he heard Paul think to him, *You were great. You did a great job helping Amy,* he smiled for a moment.

"Are you all right, Amy?" It was her father's medical partner.

"Uncle Charlie!" she cried and hugged the man. Charles Eberhardt had been her father's best friend since medical school. He had been the pediatrician for Amy and her sister Kaylee. After the death of his wife he had aged noticeably, and now was semi-retired. "It's great to see you back at work!" The doctor was about six feet tall and one hundred sixty-five pounds, with a furrowed face full of experience, age, and sorrow. He kissed Amy on the side of her head.

"Hey, Uncle Charlie, it's Paul."

The man's eyes lit up; he had been part of the team that finally determined the reality of Paul's existence inside a then eleven-year-old Amy. "Good to hear from you, Son," he said, and held out his hand. Paul took and shook it.

"Uncle Charlie, my boyfriend's son is sick. I need you and Daddy to fix him."

Quickly, Doctor Eberhardt began an examination. Thermometer, 98.2 degrees; blood pressure, 100 over 65; eyes clear. Shallow breathing, no sound of congestion. He was preparing to draw blood when Amy's father joined them.

"Charlie, this man's yellow. We'll check his liver function."

"I was about to draw blood, Jimmy."

"Great. We'll put a rush on the lab for it." Finally, he looked up and saw his daughter. "Sweetie! Are you alright?"

"I'm fine, Dad. It's—"

"No gunshot?"

"No, dad. I'm fine. It's—"

"Maybe you need dinner and some laundry?"

"I told Lucas that you were cool, Dad. Don't blow it." She hugged the man, and explained what she had seen happen to Lucas since Monday, and described his symptoms.

Doctor Eberhardt chimed in, "No fever, Jimmy, but troubling low blood pressure." He removed the second full vial and inserted an empty one to finish taking Lucas' blood.

James Clear bent over Lucas. Amy said, "Lucas, this is my dad. I told you about him."

"Boom," the man whispered.

James applied the stethoscope to a few places. He probed the man's abdomen, getting a startling "Ouch!" from Lucas. When James pulled up the man's shirt, they saw a light red rash across his chest and down the side that was visible. He turned to his daughter and said, "I want to admit him. The blood tests will tell us a lot more, but I can see problems with kidneys and liver. How long has he been like this?"

"Off to the lab," Charlie said. "It's a delight to see you, Amy. And you, Paul." He left with the vials he had drawn.

"He started getting sick a couple of days ago, on Monday. He's been this blitzed out since yesterday."

The physician shook his head. "I wish he'd come in sooner. Can you work with admissions?"

"Sure, Dad. Thanks for looking after him." She leaned close to whisper to him, "And I'm excited to see Uncle Charlie back at work!"

"Yes, Pumpkin. Me, too." He improvised an admissions order on a clipboard and handed it to Amy. "Let's get him in a room. And, Honey?" Amy looked up, smiling. "Call your mother. She says you never call. She misses you, you know."

"Aw, Dad." Then, "It's Paul. Are you inviting us for dinner?"

He laughed. "Talk to Tracey. She's the entertainment director. Now scoot, both of you."

Amy waited in the lobby until a clerk called her name. She brought her father's admission order to the woman behind the desk.

"Are you family?" the nurse asked.

"Uh, no."

"Okay. Is the patient twenty-one?"

"Uh, no. He's twenty."

"I really need a relative to admit him."

Paul took the lead, sounding like Amy. "Doctor Clear wants him admitted. There's kidney and liver damage. If you don't admit him, he'll die."

When Amy saw the woman squint at her, she smiled. "Please. The man is important to me. I'll get his father here tonight or tomorrow."

Most of the questions an admissions clerk asks are about insurance. Amy admitted she did not know what Lucas' insurance company was, only that it was from his job in Georgia. "He works for Anthropomorphos.com. He's a computer programmer." The woman spent the next several minutes on her phone and at least was able to leave a message at Lucas' job.

"If insurance doesn't cover this, who will be the responsible party?"

"If you don't let him die, Lucas will be."

Finally, the clerk slid a wad of papers to Amy and said, "Sign at the Xes." She wrote her name four times, and handed it all back. "Where is he?" Amy asked. "Can I see him?"

"It'll be a little while before we hear what room he's in." Trying to be helpful, she added, "There's a coffee maker over there."

They ignored the coffee. Amy sat in a corner of the waiting room, by a window that looked out onto a pavilion.

Paul reached for her phone and dialed Christine's number.

"There you are, Paulette," he heard. "I was worried when you didn't answer when I called this morning."

"Whoa, what time is it?" He held the phone out to read the digital clock: it was twelve thirty-five. "Sorry, honey. Amy and I have been busy. How's Mom?"

A sigh. "She's still not talking, but the doctor says she is regaining her strength. She's getting better. Physically, anyway."

"She still knows you, right? And your brother?"

"Oh, yeah. Yesterday Nathan brought her a big helium balloon of Mickey Mouse and she actually laughed. She was still hugging it when I got here this morning."

"I'm thinking of you," he said, "and your mom." He paused. "I miss you."

"That's the right thing to say," she said. "I miss you, too. And Amy. Hey, isn't Amy's beau keeping her busy?"

"Uh, you could say that. I'm going to let her explain."

"Oh, good, girl talk. Amy?"

"Hey, Christine. I'm glad your mom is hanging in there. It's all because you went to take care of her, you know."

They heard the woman laugh. "I see Paulette's been teaching you how to give compliments. Tell me about your client boyfriend. Do you still like him?"

She thought to Paul, *Why wouldn't I?* but didn't wait to hear Paul rattle off the many reasons. "Yes, I do. But things are very strange."

"Of course they are. You lead a magic life, Amy. You and Paulette."

"I told you we discovered Ryan really is his twin. I still like him, but he doesn't know I've figured this out. And his son—actually, his nephew—got sick. I'm at my father's hospital for him."

"Is he sick like my mom?"

Paul took the lead to answer, "Sweetie, we don't know. Amy's father says kidneys and liver. We're going to wait to see him in his room, then we have to go back to Jeffrey's. Wait. Amy's boyfriend really is Jeffrey, but we have to keep thinking of him as Ryan or else we'll call him the wrong name. Something tells me that would cause trouble."

There was a pause. Finally Christine said, "And I thought when Amy quit the police force you'd be safe. Paulette, be careful! You too, Amy!"

They coughed, the sound they made when they both tried to speak at once. Finally Amy said, "We will. Thanks for caring."

"They just wheeled in mom's lunch, so I'm going to help her eat. Hmmm, orange sections." Away from the phone she said, "You'd better eat up, mom, or else I will!" Then, back to her phone, "Thanks for calling. I have to go. I love you, Paulette. You too, Amy."

"I miss you so much, Lover," Paul said. "We'll talk tonight or tomorrow, okay?"

"We better! Gotta go!"

Paul put the phone away in Amy's hip pocket. They sat in silence for a minute, until Paul said, "Can we go to St. Louis now?"

I wish, Amy thought. After a minute she said, wistfully, "I remember when life was calm. Normal. Me and my dyad and his lesbian girlfriend. We were so all-American, we could have been on the front of a box of Wheaties."

Paul snickered. Out loud he said, "Yep. And then some man with his creepy penis and his eleven percent homebrew beer and his dead twin brother entered the picture."

"Amy was happy for a little while," she nodded. "But then something happened. Something always happens."

"Boom," Paul said. She laughed and wrapped her arms around themself. It was how they could hug each other.

It was after two o'clock when James Clear called his daughter. "Is Lucas going to be all right?" she asked.

"I don't know. The lab test shows some liver dysfunction, and his kidneys are only working about five percent. I've got him hooked up on dialysis, that should make him feel better. But until I figure out what's attacking his organs, I can't give a diagnosis. Or a prognosis. I'll tell you this, honey, it's a good thing you brought him in. I think he'd be dead if you'd waited another day."

"Oh, Dad," she moaned. "What room is he in? I want to see him."

"Not today. I don't think he'd know you were there. Besides, he shouldn't have company during dialysis. Tomorrow might be better."

"Okay. I'll go talk to his father. Uh, do you have a minute? This is getting as weird as anything I ever did for NOPD."

"Are you okay?" he asked, intently.

"Oh, yes, I'm fine. But—"

"You're okay, and that's what matters to me, Pumpkin. I've got more people in exam rooms than Uncle Charlie can clear, so I've got to get back to the office. We'll talk tomorrow, okay?"

"Sure. Okay, Dad. Thanks for taking care of Lucas. And I'll call Mom later."

When she finished the call it was a dejected Amy who stood up and said, "I guess I go back to Ryan's."

I can feel how disappointed you are, Paul thought back. *It's because James didn't make time to hear about Ryan, isn't it? I don't think he's ever done that before. He must really be busy.* She walked out of the hospital lobby and headed for the parking deck.

That really hurt, she thought back. *I'm used to my daddy hanging on my every word.*

"Take it from me, getting older sucks."

"Thanks for the warning, geezer."

"Don't mention it. Kid." She got in the car and waited for the glow plug to warm up the engine, then started the noisy diesel and headed back to New Orleans.

Ryan—really Jeffrey, but Amy and Paul were still referring to him as Ryan—was standing by the hand cart, cell phone in hand. His car was parked on the street with the driver's door open. When he saw Amy arrive in her old yellow Benz he waved her to join him.

Damn, she thought to Paul as she got out of the car, *I was hoping we could close the doors and put away the cart before he got home.* As she neared Ryan she could hear him talking to a police dispatcher, telling them someone had broken into his house.

She pointed to the phone and shook her head.

"What? Uh, please wait a moment." Then, to Amy, "What?"

"No break-in," she said, "I took Lucas to the hospital. I didn't go back and close the door before we left."

He seemed paralyzed for a moment before he went back to the phone. "False alarm," he told the dispatcher. "I'm sorry to have bothered you, but there's no break-in. I'm good." He listened to the officer, then said, "I'm sorry" again and ended the call.

"I'm sorry, Ryan," she said.

"You took Lucas to a hospital? Why on earth?"

The question stunned her. "It's Paul. Amy's father said if she had waited another day, Lucas would be dead. That's why on earth. What's the matter with you?" The voice continued, "It's Amy. Didn't you notice how sick he was?"

"I don't have time for your 'two different people' rigmarole." He started walking toward the open gate. "Let me make sure nothing happened while the door was standing open."

Paul thought, *Don't you feel that warm glow of a father's pure love for his son?* Amy trotted after Ryan as he stormed his way up the three steps and into the house. "Damn it, Ryan, he was dying!" she shouted after him.

The man thundered through the house without saying a word. He stopped at Lucas' room and saw the disorder of the sheets and pillows. The kitchen was his next stop. He opened the refrigerator door and quickly closed it. Then his own bedroom, and finally his office. When he finished the tour he turned on Amy, who was just two steps behind him. "You had no right to do that," he hissed.

Amy's jaw fell open, until "It's Paul. You really want him to die?"

"No, of course not," he replied. "But he's my son, not yours. It's my call to make, not yours."

"So I'm bad for saving his life, and you're good for being willing to let him die? Uh, it's Amy."

Ryan stepped past her and walked to the kitchen; Amy followed. "Is that the equation?" she added.

In the kitchen, he turned toward her and said in a cold voice, "You just ruined everything." He was clenching his jaw, and the vein on the side of his neck was pulsing.

"Ruined what, Ryan? What?"

He reached for a drawer and pulled out a carving knife. "I have everything worked out and you have to go all Mother Theresa and ruin it all." He took a step toward her.

Amy stopped Paul from drawing her gun. *I like this guy—uh, when he's not threatening me. I'm not about to shoot him.*

Well, he's about to stab us. We have to do something.

She stepped back. From the corner of their eye Paul noticed the broom that's in every kitchen, standing between the refrigerator and a wall. Amy was surprised to feel and see her left arm reach out and grab it. Paul thought to her, *I learned how to use a quarterstaff in Boy Scouts.*

She let him lead and assume the basic defensive stance he'd been taught in West Virginia sixty-seven years earlier, the low guard: Paul's dominant left side facing Ryan; their right hand holding the top end of the broom stick and left hand holding the middle. The brush part was pointed at Ryan. *A little short,* Paul thought, *but it'll do.*

Ryan attempted to push the broom out of his way with his left arm while wielding the knife with his right, and Paul countered with what he remembered was called the middle guard, sweeping the broomstick against Ryan's knife hand. He followed quickly with a thrust to Ryan's stomach, but the flexibility of the brush kept it from being a telling blow.

Still holding the knife, Ryan grabbed the usual business end of the broom between both hands. Paul laughed and twirled the broomstick counterclockwise, which unscrewed the two parts; Ryan was holding the brush, while Paul now had better control over a shorter but more maneuverable stick.

Amy saw it all through her own eyes, but with Paul leading, she felt as if she was seeing it on TV. Her lover, with a knife, parrying to attack her, while her unseen internal dyad controlled her body, defending themself. In all their adventures together, she never had experienced this dissociation before.

Ryan threw the brush to the side and set himself in a crouch to present a smaller target. He feinted a few times until he finally drew Paul to block his attack, then he kicked out at Amy's left leg. They did not fall, but Paul stepped back and Ryan renewed the pursuit. Ryan held his knife with both hands and raised it overhead, to strike downward, but Paul remembered the level guard position (although not that it was called that), holding the broomstick horizontal, hands near the ends, to block Ryan's arm. He sidestepped Ryan's kick, and again thrust the tip of his stick against the man's chest. Without the brush to diffuse the blow, Ryan staggered backwards. Paul followed to finish the attack, but Ryan fell to the side, on purpose, away from the stick; at the same time, he slashed out and cut Amy's right calf through her jeans.

The pain brought Amy back to a more personal experience in Paul's fight with Ryan. Despite herself she shouted, "Ouch!" Silently she thought to Paul, *Don't let him do that again.*

"Oh, yes, ma'am" he said with a laugh. He considered an overhead blow on Ryan while the man was still on the floor, but he was afraid he wouldn't be able to block another ankle level attack. He poked at Ryan's face. When Ryan deflected the pole with his left hand, Paul spun around like a ballerina and whacked Ryan on the right side of his head.

He looked dazed, on one knee, still trying to stand up. Paul thrust against his stomach, then delivered the overhead down strike to end the fight.

Paul stood over the motionless man, breathing heavily from the exertion and the adrenaline.

"You didn't—you didn't kill him, did you?"

"Let's see." Paul used the broomstick to poke the man, the way a boy might test an animal he found on the side of the road.

Ryan grasped the broomstick with both hands and began to wrestle to take it from Paul and Amy. He pushed it and Paul fell backwards against the refrigerator door, then slid to the floor. Having taken control of the broomstick but without any experience, Ryan held it like a baseball bat. Paul locked eyes with the man as he slowly stood up, back still to the refrigerator. He smiled; it was something he and Amy both knew unnerved opponents. "Did I see you playing left out for the Zephyrs?" he asked, of course sounding like Amy as he referred to the local minor league baseball team. When Ryan rushed with an overhead strike, Paul took one step to the side to avoid it. He kicked Ryan's right leg and the man went down. Paul jumped and landed all one hundred and nine pounds of Amy on his lower back. Ryan was still.

"Did you—did you kill him this time?" Amy asked.

"Don't know, don't care," he answered out loud. "I'm thinking now is a good time to get out of here."

"I should close the back door."

Paul began to laugh. "Leave it open," he thought to her, "that way the police can get in when we call them."

"Okay, let's go," and she limped through the living room and out the front door. She saw the driver's door to Ryan's car was still standing open. Out loud she asked, "Why would I call the cops?"

"We're bleeding, for Christ's sake!"

"Oh, yes, I guess so. Why doesn't it hurt any more?" She had climbed in her Benz and pressed the glow plug button.

Shock? Paul thought back. *Excitement? Stupidity? I don't know, but why don't we pay another visit to your dad?*

Amy leaned over the steering wheel to look down at her right leg. There was a flap in her jeans where Ryan's knife sliced against her, and the fabric below it was red and gooey. "I paid thirty-four dollars for these pants, and my homicidal boyfriend has to go and customize them."

But he really, really likes you, Paul thought to her. *Can we go see James before this leg starts to hurt?*

For the second time that day Amy pulled into the first Emergency Room lane at the Jefferson Parish Medical Center. She threw open the car door. Her mouth was moving as she emerged, but no sound came out. Instead, she fell to the concrete.

When she opened her eyes, she saw her father looking down at her, a worried look on his face. "D—Dad?" she croaked.

"You got here just in time, Pumpkin," he said, breaking into a smile. "You were down three units of O-negative. What happened?"

"Oh. My leg." She tried to bend her knee to bring her right leg closer, but a flash of pain made her stop.

"You'll keep it, but you're the proud owner of seven of my best stitches. I'm afraid you might have a limp for a souvenir. What happened?"

"My boyfriend thought it was wrong of me to save Lucas' life. We had a fight and he had a knife."

James put his hands on his daughter's shoulders. "Looks like he used it, too. Tell me, what did he look like after it was over?"

"It's Paul. He was squished." He laughed. "I beat him up with a broom stick."

"Squished? Should I send out a meat wagon for him?"

"He's not worth it, Dad. How is Lucas?"

James dragged a stool to his daughter's gurney and sat. "He's stable. I hope he's out of danger. But he may need a kidney transplant. Something did a number on them."

Amy remembered how hurt she had been when she had tried to tell her father about Ryan being Jeffrey but he had been too busy to listen. "I want to tell you about Lucas' father. Do you have time?"

His smile filled her with relief, and a sense of security. "Yes, Pumpkin. I'll always have time for you. So, tell me."

"It's stranger than any of the cases I worked on NOPD," she began. "Doctor Tallant, the Medical Examiner?" James nodded; he and his hospital had occasional dealings with the Orleans Parish police. "We went over the autopsy report for my boyfriend's twin brother. Dad, my boyfriend is the dead twin!"

He put his hand on her head, petting her hair as she lay on the gurney. "You are one brave woman," he said. "You know how proud of you I am. But I worry. You've been shot, what, four times, you've been stabbed twice, you've been thrown in a bayou and left for dead— Amy, how many of your nine lives have you used up?"

She smiled at her father's concern. "It's Paul. I'm on my tenth."

James let his head drop, but there was a smile on his face. "What am I going to do with you two?"

"Commander Ramirez said I should talk to big criminal law firms about investigating claims. I think I need to talk to the lawyer who's handling the will."

"A will?" her father said. "Who died?"

"Lucas' pepaw. The boyfriend I thought was Ryan hired me to find Lucas so Grandpa's will could be satisfied." She was becoming agitated as she lay on the gurney.

"Easy, Amy, there's nothing that can't wait until tomorrow. It might take a little while for you to get used to that three pints of someone else's blood."

Amy stopped struggling. "I know you're right. But Ryan really being Jeffrey, and working so hard to get Lucas back, and then Lucas getting so sick—Dad, they're all related. I don't know if Jeffrey killed his brother, but he said me taking Lucas to you ruined his plans!" The right leg hurt, so it was only the left one she was wiggling.

"Paul? How do you see this?" James was one of the handful of people who had learned that Paul Owens was real and co-existed inside Amy, with his own memories and personality, and with his own judgments.

"Jermaine made a good argument that Jeffrey may have killed Ryan." The voice, of course, was Amy's, but the words were not. "What I noticed was, when Lucas first got so sick, Jeffrey didn't seem concerned. He even said he thought the boy was malingering."

He heard Amy think, *What does that word mean?*

"Oh. Pretending to be sick to get out of having to do something."

James smiled. "I know what 'malingering' means, Paul."

"You can't go wrong by stating the obvious," he answered, unwilling to expose the gap in Amy's vocabulary.

They coughed from both trying to speak at once. As usual, Paul deferred to Amy, since it was her body. "Jeffrey said the name of the firm. The lawyer is the daughter of someone Pepaw Doublet went to college with. What is it?" She was flapping their arms at their sides, as if she were keeping time. "Damn it, why can't I remember the name?"

James was shaking his head when he heard his daughter's voice say, "Goode at law."

"I hope they are." She saw the confusion on her father's face. "Paul says whoever they are, they're good at law."

"No! It's Paul. The firm is Goode at Law. I remember because I thought it was a clever name."

"What did you do with my phone, Dad? I need to call them."

He put a reassuring hand on her shoulder. "Not now, you don't. It's seven-thirty at night. And I'm keeping you here overnight." He smiled while she began to protest. "Amy Elizabeth, don't make me put an armed guard on your room."

Amy laughed out loud, "Get Mom to work on that with you. If she said it, it wouldn't have sounded so funny."

Paul noticed an abrupt blue light come on behind James. "What is that?"

The doctor turned to see. "You mean the UV light?" James took a tissue from the Kleenex box and held it out to the wall-mounted fixture; it glowed a psychedelic blue-tinged white. "These kill germs. There were some studies a few years ago that showed these bulbs kill *Clostridium difficile* and some other bugs that have become resistant to antibiotics, so we started installing them around 2027."

As he waved the tissue in the light, Paul thought to Amy *Psychedelic, man. Groovy.*

"We've got them all over the facility," Doctor Clear went on, "and really big ones in the operating rooms. They cycle on and off." He sniffed. "They make the rooms smell good, too."

Amy sniffed as well, and Paul said, "Ozone."

"Smells better than bleach. Mind you, hospitals still go through a lot of bleach, but these lights are a big help."

Amy said, "Hospital as tanning booth. Sign me up."

"I'll be back in the morning," James said. He stood, looking down at his grown daughter, and just for a moment he saw a glimpse of the little girl she once was. He bent over and kissed her on the forehead. "Good night, Pumpkin," he said. "'Night, Paul."

He flicked off the overhead light as he left. As Amy lay in the room, lit by the ghostly blue wash of the UV fixture, she thought to Paul, *When did he start calling me 'Pumpkin' again? I thought I cured him of that when I was a kid.*

Paul thought to her, *Calling Goode at Law, that's a great idea. Let's write that presentation and let them pay us to run Jeffrey down.*

With the calm, blue light and their body recuperating from the cutting and stitching, Amy finally began to relax. "Dad's right," she said aloud. "Can't do anything right now." A smile spread over her face. "Life's pretty good, you know?"

Yep, he thought back. *But it would be better if I could talk to Christine. She's going to get all worried when she hears we got stabbed.*

"She worries because she cares about us. She loves you. In case you haven't noticed."

They were beginning to drift toward sleep when Paul thought, *I'm sorry you lost your boyfriend. I liked Ryan.*

"Hmmm? Oh. He only shaved. That one. Time."

"That cut was deep," James Clear told his daughter, "so I want you to take these antibiotics for ten days. One pill, three times a day, got that?"

"Yes, Dad."

"Change the bandage every morning. If you see white goo or it smells foul, come see me again. Got that?"

"Yes, Dad."

"And I thought you were going to call your mother."

Amy was wearing her cut jeans with the blood-soaked leg, as well as the other clothes she had had on the day before. She was resting her right hand on a cane, and holding a plastic bag in her left; her doctor father kept dropping more supplies for her recuperation in the bag.

"You took my phone away," she answered, feeling defensive.

"Hmm, I guess I did. How do you feel, Pumpkin?"

"It's Paul. Amy feels fine. Don't you, Amy?"

"It's Amy. Yes, Paul, Amy feels great. Except that my leg is throbbing. But aside from that, Amy is doing fine."

Her father looked surprised. "What brought that on?" he asked, puzzled.

"Remember how I asked you not to call me 'Pumpkin' anymore?"

His mouth fell open. "That was—Oh, no. Have I really—did I— Oh, swee—Oh, Amy, I'm sorry." Amy didn't even try to hide her grin at his embarrassment. "It's just a parent thing. You're a grown woman,

I don't ask either of you questions when you mention boyfriends or girlfriends, but sometimes I look at you and—" he sighed "—and I see that precious child from way back when."

"I'm still that precious child," Amy laughed, "and you named me Amy." When she saw the wistful look on his face, she put her hand to her father's cheek. "Are you okay?"

He did that thing people do: he shook his head and said, "Yes. I'm fine." Then, "Maybe I'm getting old or something."

"It's Paul. Don't do that, okay?"

James rode the elevator with Amy, his arm around her as she tapped the floor impatiently with her cane. "Take it easy for a few days. The stitches will dissolve, but they'll probably itch before that. Don't scratch!"

"I know you love me, Dad. But sometimes you have a weird way of saying it." She was smiling.

When they got out at the main floor, James pointed and said, "I moved your car into the employee parking lot over there. And yes, Amy, I do love you." He kissed her on the cheek.

She smiled like a child. "I know. And I love you. Now let me figure out how to walk with a cane." She hobbled out the automatic door, into the hot New Orleans morning.

She found her car. Her father had left the door unlocked, and put the keys—in keeping with a long family tradition—under the front passenger seat floormat. Paul thought to her, *And if we're locked out of your folks' house, the key is under, what, the second flowerpot on the right?*

"I never remember which one," she said aloud. "I check under all of them until I find the key." She waited for the glow plug light to go out, then cranked the engine. "As soon as I get home, I'm going to call Goode at Law and set up a meeting. Then you are going to help me write the presentation."

"Breakfast first," he thought back to her. "Hospital food doesn't have the nutrition I need for creative insights."

After a stop at the Dot's Diner on Jefferson Highway, Paul led to get them back home to the Carrollton section of New Orleans. "It hurts to hit the brakes," he moaned. "How long before this cut heals up?"

"Dad says it'll quit hurting in four or five days. But he says I may have a limp for the rest of my life. I'm thirty, I'm too young to have things go wrong for the rest of my life."

"Yes, you are. Be glad you don't have a prostate gland, that was going to be trouble for the rest of my life. Well, I guess it was, for the rest of my body's life."

Inside her house, she lay on the futon to keep their sutured leg raised, and held her clipboard and pad. She opened her phone and called Goode at Law, LLC.

"Good morning," she said to the receptionist. "I'm Amy Clear, the investigator who worked with Jeff—uh, with Ryan Doublet and his son Lucas. Who is the attorney who just finished up with the grandfather's will?"

"You worked with Lucas?" the woman said, conspiratorially. "If he isn't the best-looking man I've ever seen, I'll take vows."

I'm not sure what that means, Paul thought to Amy. She snickered and said, "Yes, he's quite the hunk. Who was—"

"That was Melanie. I can transfer you."

"Wait, wait!" Amy called. "In case I get disconnected, what's her last name?"

"Melanie Goode. She's the chief partner. Hang on."

They were on hold, so Paul said aloud, "Since when does a senior partner handle a will? I thought they didn't get their hands dirty for less than seven digits."

They heard a click, then a brusque voice on a speaker phone, "Melanie. What?"

Amy introduced herself. "I've learned some disturbing things about our mutual client, Je—uh, Ryan Doublet. I'd like to come in and meet with you."

"Nah. Tell me now. What's so disturbing?"

This was not what Amy had anticipated. "Ryan Doublet has been dead for over a year. The person claiming to be Ryan is his twin brother, Jeffrey Doublet."

There was a loud click and suddenly Melanie Goode was speaking into the handset. "Tell me who you are again?"

She repeated her name. "I'm an ex-cop, now I'm a private investigator. Ryan Doublet hired me to find his runaway son, which I did. And now I've discovered the man who says he is Ryan Doublet can't be."

"Well, isn't that a double steaming plate of shit. Why are you telling me this?"

"I'd like to be your go-to person when you need to investigate potential clients."

Melanie Goode laughed until the laugh morphed into a protracted cough. There still was a smile in her voice when she finally was able to say, "You just broke a lot of rules of marketing. I hope you're a better detective."

Amy started, defensive, "Well, I don't know a—"

Another laugh from the lawyer. "You know where I am? Girod, it's catty-corner from LaFayette Square. Seventh floor. I can see you right after lunch."

"Uh, what are we—"

"And bring me what you've got on Doublet," Melanie said, and she hung up.

As she closed her phone, Amy said, "Did I just get hired?"

"More like we got a quick interview appointment," Paul replied aloud. "Where are our business cards? Dress to impress, we've got two hours to get there."

Their hair was dirty, but Amy didn't want to take a shower and risk getting her wound wet. She used half a container of some dry hair-cleaning powder, then coughed in the white cloud it made as she combed and brushed it out. *Guys don't realize,* Paul thought to her, *how much work goes into being beautiful.*

"Thanks, I think."

She picked a black suit with a long skirt, even though it left the bandage on her calf exposed. "So much for the ankle holster," she thought, and settled for the thigh holster she used with a maxi-skirt. She glanced in the mirror to make sure she was presentable. "Oh, Christ, it's time to whack the uni-brow again." Amy took a tweezer from the medicine chest and rinsed it, then set about plucking the errant hairs connecting the left and right eyebrows. She heard Paul think, *The Neanderthal genes—are they from your mom or your dad?*

You sleep on the couch tonight, she thought back. Like most people, Amy wasn't thrilled with her appearance; but the eyebrow was the one thing about which she was touchy.

They spent a precious ten minutes with the clipboard and pad, trying to think of additional clever lines to add to her presentation. She said, "How about the direct approach. 'Three years on the force, forty-one investigations, twenty-seven convictions, and only two acquittals.' For New Orleans, that's a great record."

From his days with a body as a market researcher, Paul did the math in his—uh, their—head. "That's a sixty-six percent conviction rate. What percent of murders does the Parish close? Forty percent?"

She checked her watch. "Let's call Christine while I've got time," she offered, and opened her phone.

"Paulette Where have you been Are you alright Is Amy okay I've been so worried!" came in a rush from the phone. "I'm here," he said. "You can relax, it's going to be okay."

"It scares me when I can't reach you," she offered, ruefully. "I worry about you. But you're okay, right?"

"Here I am, Honey. Amy's dad took the phone away yesterday, so I couldn't call until now."

There was a pause. "Wait. Why did Doctor Clear take the phone away from his thirty-year-old daughter? Did she stay out past curfew? Talk back? Forget to do her homework?"

"It's Amy. My client boyfriend went all psycho yesterday. I ended up in Dad's emergency room. We're—"

"Ohmygod!" Christine interrupted, "What happened? Is Paulette okay? Are you alright?"

"We're fine," Amy continued. She described the fight with Ryan, really Jeffrey, and its aftermath. "Seven stitches. I'll never get a tattoo, but someday I'll be in a circus sideshow as the scarred lady."

"Amy, you're so funny. So now you have a fallback career lined up."

Paul knew Christine always could tell which one of them was speaking, so he didn't bother to identify himself. "How's your mom doing?"

"It was great, Paulette," she said. "When I came back after lunch yesterday she called me by name! And then she thanked me for being there. Well, sort of, she's still having trouble with her speech. But she's talking!"

He let out a sigh of relief. "I'm so glad. And I'm sure it's because you and your brother have been helping her."

"Yeah. I'm so happy about this, Paulette. I was afraid that—well, you know."

Paul lifted their throbbing right leg up on the futon. "I know. But that's all gone now. What does the doctor say?"

"Umm, there are two of them. One of them said he's pleased. The other said it's a, a, it's a bleeping miracle."

"Bleeping?"

Christine lowered her voice to a whisper. "He said it's...it's a fucking miracle."

Amy said, "Do doctor's really say things like that?"

"This one did. It was so funny, even mom laughed."

"So, your mom is a miracle," Paul said. "I'm glad. Now what?"

They heard the sounds of Christine changing hands holding her phone. "First we wait to see if there's more improvement, I hope I hope I hope. Then Nathan and I have to decide if she can go home, or if she has to move in with him and Sheila, or if she goes, well, you know."

"This progress is wonderful, Honey," he told her. "May she improve more and more and more."

"Thanks. You know, I've been happy all day today. And your call made it even better."

"Anything I can do for you, you know that. Look, Amy has an interview in a little bit, so I've got to run. Let me—"

"Interview? Amy, are you taking a new job?"

"I'm in business for myself," she said, "I'm always looking for a new job. This is with the senior partner at a law firm."

"I'd hire you if I was him."

"Actually, it's a her."

"Better still. Good luck, Amy. I love you, Paulette."

He closed her phone. "Thank God. It would be wonderful if her mom recovers completely."

"It happens sometimes," Amy said. She was rubbing the bandage on her leg, trying to make the throbbing stop. "Think she'll come home soon?"

"Either that," Paul said, "or I'm putting in a chit to transfer to St. Louis."

"Time to go," Amy said. She picked up her clipboard, and her business cards, and the black purse she only used with this business suit. Cane in hand, she locked up behind her and got comfortable in her old yellow Benz. "My leg hurts," Amy said. "You drive."

The clock behind the receptionist at Goode at Law LLC said one-ten when Amy limped through the door. The woman was no more than twenty, disturbingly skinny, in a fashionable dress that just hung off her anorexic frame. Amy began, "Melanie Goode is—"

"It's about time you're here," she countered, getting up to come help Amy. "Melanie has been asking for you for half-an-hour." She took Amy's right arm, the one with the cane.

"Sorry, sister," Paul said, sounding just like Amy, "I need that hand for the cane. Here—" he handed her the clipboard and purse, "There. Thanks." The woman led, and Amy hobbled behind.

Melanie Goode was standing behind her desk, looking out the floor-to-ceiling window of her seventh floor office. The view would have been spectacular but for the New Orleans haze that limited visibility. Paul sized up the lawyer from behind: a tall woman, wide rear end, in a flowered dress that went to her knees.

"The detective is here," said the receptionist, and the woman turned to face them.

She was very pretty, with blue eyes, a small nose, and open lips even with her face at rest. Her Irish face was framed by healthy, curly hair to her shoulders. Amy thought she might be in her mid-forties. The woman coughed—a deep, productive cough—and then smiled. "Thanks for coming in. I want to see—hey, what's with the cane?"

"It keeps me from falling over," Paul said, annoyed. "I'm here to talk about Doublet."

She nodded and took her seat behind the enormous glass-topped desk. When she noticed Amy was still standing, she extended a hand to point at a chair. "Uh, please," she said.

This lady is all business, Paul thought to Amy.

"What's this shit about Ryan being Jeffrey?"

Amy settled in the chair and looked for a place to rest the cane, finally leaning it against the desk. "Have you known Ryan long?" she asked.

The lawyer made a dismissive sound. "We took baths together when I was three years old. My father and old Gasçon Doublet were friends from school."

"Ah, so you know what they look like naked." Melanie squinted at her as Amy went through the papers on her clipboard. "I got this from the medical examiner yesterday," as she handed over the printout of 'Jeffrey' Doublet's autopsy photo. "The birthmark?"

"Yeah. That's Ryan all right." Looking up she asked Amy, "So what's his fucking game?"

"Doctor Tallant—uh, the medical examiner—admits he might not have called the death a suicide if he had known that Ryan really was the dead man. And now, for whatever reason, the nephew that he's calling his son is in the hospital with blown-out kidneys."

"Did Ryan—uh, Jeffrey—hurt the boy?"

Shaking their head, Amy said, "Not that I know of. But that detective sixth sense tells me something is going on."

The lawyer stared at the photograph. "Aside from the stain, they really are identical twins. They were always playing games about which one was which."

Amy lifted their right leg and put the ankle over her left knee, trying to make the pulsing stitches quiet down. Melanie suddenly laughed and said, "I love your fashion sense. What is it you do?"

Confused, Amy began, "I'm not sure what—" until she realized she was still wearing her pink tennis shoes from the day before, complete with blood stains. "Oh, crap! I forgot to change shoes!"

"Do tell," Melanie said, with a laugh that morphed into another noisy cough.

"I'm embarrassed," Amy said. "Can I come back tomorrow and do this over again?"

Still coughing, the woman shook her head. "It's clear to me you care more about getting your shit done than making it look pretty. I like that."

Amy covered her tennis shoe with her skirt. "Where were we? Oh, yes. I'm worried that Jeffrey killed Ryan, and now is doing something to harm Lucas. He was unconcerned with how sick Lucas is, and actually got mad that I took the boy to the hospital."

"No shit?" the lawyer mused. "I have to say, when they were up here to settle Daddy Doublet's will, Lucas kept asking questions and Ryan—uh, Jeffrey—kept saying, "Just sign the damn thing.""

"So, now what?" Paul was rubbing the bandage through their skirt.

"For me, not a damn thing. My client was Lucas."

It annoyed Paul, that the lawyer's concern was so limited. "And what if your client dies?"

She thought. "Since there isn't a twenty-year-old in the state smart enough to have their own will, I'd say that Ryan—uh, Jeffrey— would inherit."

"That's it!" Amy shouted. She stood up, then fell back in the chair from the pain in their leg. "If I hadn't found Lucas," she went on, "the old man's legacy would have gone to a bunch of pussy cats. But once

Lucas signed whatever, now it's Jeffrey who gets the money." She pointed at the lawyer. "And he's always talking about how much he needs money."

Melanie opened a drawer in her desk and removed a box of Marlboros and a dirty ashtray. First she lit her cigarette, then motioned to Amy to take one. Amy shook her head.

"Since you're now a subcontracted employee," the lawyer said, "you would never in a million years tell your old colleagues at NOPD that I routinely ignore their stupid laws."

"I am?"

"Yeah. You seem to be incapable of bullshit. What do you charge?"

Amy struggled to remember. "Uh, two-fifty a day, plus expenses."

"I'll give you two hundred."

Paul took the lead. "Perhaps you didn't hear me," he said, of course with Amy's voice. "Two-fifty a day. Plus expenses."

Melanie stared through a few puffs on her cigarette. Paul maintained eye contact and a smile. He heard Amy think, *I need the work;* he thought back, *No, we need the money.*

Finally the lawyer coughed and smiled. "Shit. Two-fifty. You are a piece of work."

"Here's my card," Amy said, handing over several. "How often do you need a detective's help?"

"Usually a couple of times a month. Believe me, a friend's will is a tiny part of my business. Goode at Law LLC is one of the top criminal defense firms in Louisiana. Sometimes I need to find out if a client is innocent or not before I take the case."

"This will work," Amy said. "Good. Now, about Doublet?"

"Amy, is it? I appreciate the gossip, but it's not my concern." She stood up, indicating the interview was at an end. "I'll probably be the one who calls you. When I do, I'm going to want your ass here chop-chop." She smiled, cigarette in her mouth. "Got that?"

"Tell me what you need and then get out of my way," Amy said.

She struggled to their feet, this time grabbing the cane to stay upright. "Can I ask you something?"

"As long as I don't have to answer. What?"

"Are all your employee interviews like this?"

"Nah. Most of them, I kick them out after two minutes."

The telephone receptionist at the Jefferson Parish Medical Center answered Amy's question and told her Lucas Doublet was in room 431 North. "Let's pack up and head out," she said aloud to Paul when she had ended the call.

"What's the plan?" he asked.

"I don't know where Jeffrey is. I assume he knows where I live, so I'm going to stay at Christine's double. And—"

Wait. He never came here. Why would he know where we live?

"Oh. Well, we checked him out. I just assume he checked me out. But the important thing is that sooner or later he'll figure out where Lucas is. I'm afraid—"

Paul interrupted by thinking to her, *And he's going to want to finish the job of making Lucas dead.*

"You know, you just might have what it takes to become a detective," she said. "Who's your teacher?"

"Oh, I'll introduce you some time. She's young, pretty, and smart. Her name is Amy."

Amy giggled, "Yes, I'd like to compare notes with her. Does she have a dyad or does she work solo?" She was tossing underwear and shirts into her valise. "And I guess I'll stand guard over Lucas. I wonder where he'll go when he gets better?"

"Back to Kali," Paul answered aloud. "That's what I'd do. There's nothing left for him here."

She fastened her holster on her left hip, since her right hand would be occupied with the cane. Left-handed Paul was in charge of hand-held artillery.

Left-handed Paul got to lead to drive to Christine's double, where Amy put her suitcase in the bedroom. "It's empty without Christine," he complained.

"I'll keep you company," Amy said. "And—" she sniffed "—it smells like her. What's her perfume?"

"I don't know. Bacon, maybe?"

Paul led to drive out to the Jefferson Parish Medical Center to visit Lucas, and parked the old yellow Benz in the visitor lot. Amy leaned on the cane while she used their left hand to slam shut the car door. "I don't know which is worse," she muttered as she hobbled toward the medical center entrance, "getting cut, or using a cane. This is the twenty-first century, surely there's a better way."

She took the north wing elevator up to the fourth floor, and made her way to Lucas in room 431. The door was standing open, and the room beyond it was dark. She used her cane to knock on the door frame, then limped in. Lucas was asleep, with pipes from two IV bags disappearing in his arms.

She thought to Paul, *It's a relief to see him. He's safe, Dad's taking care of him. My dad.* Smiling, she bent over the sleeping man's bed and kissed his forehead. Then she backed into a chair and set her gear on the floor. "Now we wait," she said out loud.

When Christine called, Paul led and sat in the fourth floor waiting room to hear the news that her mother's speech was improving by the hour. Stretching the truth a little bit, he asked if he and Amy could stay at her apartment while they were hiding from Jeffrey Doublet. "Even if I'm not there," she said, "it's great that Paulette will be. Yes, hide out there. Tell Amy it's okay if she wears my clothes."

"Thanks, Christine," Amy responded, laughing. "I promise I'll do laundry."

Late in the afternoon, two nurses came in to change out the IV solutions. Amy asked, "Has anyone but my dad been in to see Lucas? Uhh—Doctor Clear?" They assured her no one else had been in. She thought to Paul, *Jeffrey hasn't figured out where he is yet. Good.*

They watched one nurse change out the saline IV, while the other wrestled with an intravenous antibiotic.

The nurses' activity roused Lucas. "Is that—is that Amy?" he croaked. A smile blossomed across his face.

"Hey, good-looking," she said, struggling to her feet and then swinging her butt onto the side of his bed. "How are you feeling? Is my father taking good care of you?"

"I feel like home-made crap," he said, "which is a lot better than the last time I saw you." His face screwed into a question mark. "Why were we going 'boom'?"

She leaned over him to hug him. "You sound fantastic! I'm so glad."

She didn't hear Paul think directly to him, *Left-handed me here. You were great. You were such a big help to Amy, getting you here. You done good.* As a result, she didn't know why a belated smile came over him.

"So you're still here?" he asked.

A cough, then "It's Paul. Wherever there's Amy, there's me."

"When can I go home?" he asked. He lifted his arms and wiggled the IV tubes.

"That's up to my dad. Where do you want to go? Back to Atlanta?"

"No. Uh, I don't think so. What's wrong with my father's place?"

Amy rubbed his chest through the blanket. "I guess you missed some of what happened."

A pause, until Lucas said, slowly, "Uh-oh."

"The nickel version is that your father died a year ago. The person calling himself Ryan really is Jeffrey. It's possible he killed your dad, and I'm afraid he means you harm."

There was no response from the man.

"Lucas? Is everything okay?"

"No!" he cried, frowning. "Not okay! My dad is dead? And Uncle Jeffrey wants to hurt me? I don't believe you."

"I don't blame you," Amy said. "Besides, your job is to get better. Did my dad say what was wrong with you?"

"Something about my kidneys. He had me on diala—diala—di what?"

"Dialysis," Amy prompted.

"That's it! Yeah. I don't hurt like I did before, but I'm still tired all the time. Your dad, he's funny. I like him."

She nodded. "I do, too." Then, seriously, she said, "I need to get you to do something very important." She saw he was staring at her, attentive. "If Jeffrey shows up, mash the nurse call button and keep at it until someone shows up. Then make them throw Jeffrey out."

"You really think he wants to hurt me?"

"Yes. Yes, I do. I can't be here every minute, so you have to be ready to do this. You hear me?"

"Uh, yeah. Yeah, I hear you."

Paul thought to her, *Poor kid! He looks like someone just told him his dog died.*

Worse, she thought back. *I just told him his dad's dead and his beloved uncle wants to kill him.*

Still sitting on his bed, Amy put her hand over one of his. "I have to get going, but I'll be back tomorrow. Can I bring you anything? Books? Magazines? Beer?"

"Would you? How about a *Car and Driver*, or *Road and Track*? Oh, and my cell phone? And the charger?"

"I can't promise the phone, but I'll try." She stood up and lurched back to the chair, where she was able to retrieve her cane. "Take care of yourself, Lucas. Remember what I told you."

Paul was leading as they drove back to the city from Jefferson Parish. Out loud she said, "Go by Jeffrey's place. If he's not home, I'll get Lucas' phone."

Are you crazy? he thought back. *If Jeffrey finds us there, he'll kill us. Really, I don't think this is such a good idea.*

Amy took the lead and turned off the Airline Highway to head for Jeffrey's house. "It may be a stupid idea," she hissed through clenched teeth, "but it's the idea I'm going with."

Amy drove past the front of Jeffrey's home and saw the driveway was empty. She parked her Benz up the side street, then used her cane to walk—uh, hobble—to the side gate. She heard Paul think, *I don't know.*

"Me, neither," she whispered, "but I'm going to find out."

Her key worked the side door. She headed straight for Lucas' room. "You see a phone?" she thought to Paul as she scanned the room.

"Charger is plugged in over there," he said, and pointed with their left hand. Amy bent over to pull the cord, and was pleasantly surprised to find the phone itself attached to the other end.

"Okay," she said. "I want to make one stop before we leave," and she began her three-point walk.

Surely we can find another bathroom! he thought.

She giggled. "Nuh-uh. I want to see the magic kitchen," and with that she pushed the door open with her cane.

The smell was overwhelming. There was a big puddle of mostly dried blood by the refrigerator, blood that she understood had once coursed through her own veins. There was more blood on the floor and cabinet doors by the sink. "He hasn't cleaned this up?" she asked, incredulous. Then, "You must have whacked him better than I thought."

Paul thought, *If we don't get out of here I'm going to hurl. Oh, that's nasty!*

Amy hobbled back past Lucas' room and out the side door. As she closed the side gate and turned up the side street toward her car, she saw Jeffrey's Volkswagen Passat turning in to his narrow driveway. *Crap,* she thought, *did he see me? Is he following me? Oh, crap crap crap.*

If I may quote that great philosopher, Speedy Gonzales, 'Andale! Ariba!'

I'm andale-ing as fast as I can, she thought, forcing herself to push her cane farther ahead and take longer strides, *but it hurts.* As she came alongside her car the cane slid forward and she fell on the sidewalk, arms stretched forward and protecting her face. She felt their knees scrape across the pavement, and pebbles digging into their palms. Their right calf throbbed.

Get up, get up! Amy thought to Paul. *I won't let my homicidal boyfriend catch me.* Still face down, she reached out with their right hand and felt the side of her car. "Get up!" she said out loud as she pushed themself up with their left hand. Still groping blindly, their right hand finally felt the door handle. She used it to hoist themself up.

Key, she thought. Paul retrieved it from their back pocket. He was focused on the key fob, struggling to find the right button to unlock the car. They heard noises to their right, from where they had left Jeffrey's side gate. *Please,* she thought, *Please get me in.*

The door lock clicked. She gave a quiet "Yay!" and struggled to push back far enough to open the door, wary of falling backwards. The cane lay about ten feet away. Amy threw herself into the car, mashing the glow plug button as she fell across the front seat. Painfully, she pulled their legs in and pushed themself upright. There was a dark shape in the rear view mirror, she couldn't tell if it was down the street or at her back bumper. "Get me out of here!" she shouted.

Paul slammed the car door and cranked the engine, but he had been too heavy on the fuel pedal; the car didn't start. Frantic, he turned the key again, and again. On the third try there was a loud backfire and a cloud of gray smoke as the engine turned over. He let out the clutch and drove off with the tires sounding like fingernails on a chalkboard.

Paul was controlling their eyes, watching the road as he drove. She used their peripheral vision to see what was in the side mirror. It looked like someone was waving her cane in the air.

Three blocks later Paul pulled in to a drugstore parking lot. "Why did you stop?" Amy asked.

"So we can catch our breath," Paul answered aloud in the privacy of the car. "I think we nearly got caught."

She nodded. "You were right, I was stupid."

"No! You had an idea I thought was dumb, but you're fine."

"You are the best dyad a girl could have," she smiled.

"And didn't Lucas ask for *Road & Track*?" He undid the seat belt and opened the car door, then sat sideways, feet hanging out over the asphalt. "Besides, we need a new cane."

Amy stepped slowly and gingerly, with a hand on whatever car was nearest. Their right calf was screaming, while their knees and palms vibrated with pain. She looked down at the damage. *Crap-and-a-half, that's the second pair of pants he's ruined.* Their fall had left their strawberry red knees exposed by ragged holes in her pants.

Slowly she shuffled their feet across the traffic lane of the parking lot until she made it to the front door. She reached a hand out to steady themself on it and nearly fell forward when the automatic door opened unexpectedly. She staggered into the store.

"Hey, lady, are you okay?" A black man in a red uniform with nametag called to her.

"I will be in a minute. Where do you have canes?"

"Canes I can help you with," he answered. "You need to know there's a laundromat across the street, and a thrift store up the block." He remained behind the counter.

"Do I look that bad?" she asked.

The man shrugged. "You sure you're going to be okay, now?"

"Where are the canes again?"

He pointed toward aisle four, and offered, "In back, by the pharmacy." Then he turned back to restocking double-A batteries.

At least he noticed us, Paul thought to her. *That's top-flight customer service right there.* She hobbled down aisle four with a hand on the right-hand shelves, knocking over the occasional package of Q-tips and condoms "ribbed for her pleasure." When she came to the display for canes, she stopped to catch her breath and wait for the pain in her calf to subside. She thought to Paul, *Dad will kill me if I ripped a stitch.*

And Jeffrey might have killed us if you hadn't risked it, he thought back. *Fair trade.*

She tried out several canes, then settled on one with a particularly wide crook. "Seems sturdy," Amy said, leaning on it. The attached label promised the large rubber tip would be reliable on any walking surface, wet or dry. She heard Paul think, *Does that include blood?*

She hefted the cane in one hand, patting it against the other palm. *What do you think?*

This would be better than that broomstick, Paul thought back.

It was an easier walk to the front of the store now that she had a cane. She fetched a little red shopping cart, then wheeled it off to find the magazine section. Paul muttered aloud, "*Road & Track*. And *Car & Driver*. There! And *Motor Trend*." Amy put the three periodicals in her cart.

Something I need over here, she thought, and happily wheeled her way to the side wall. She finally found the section for vodka and picked up a big bottle of 90 proof Taaka. "For medicinal purposes," she murmured.

We're going to Christine's, Paul thought. *Maybe some band-aids and merthiolate? I'm just saying.*

"Oh," she said aloud; then silently as she pushed the cart toward the first aid aisle, *Good thinking. Christine may not have these things. And I'd be a bad house guest to use up whatever she does have and not replace it.*

The same man was at the cash register when Amy wheeled the buggy to the counter. "You sure you're okay?" he asked again.

Paul glanced at the man's nametag. "I appreciate your concern, Malik. I fell, no big deal."

He began ringing up her items. "Good. I mean, I'm glad no one, uh, beat you up or anything." He kept his eyes aimed at the scanner on the countertop.

"No. Well, not since yesterday."

Even with the plastic bags loaded with supplies, Amy's walk back to the car was much easier because of the new, sturdy cane. When she got in the car she sat and took a deep breath. The scrapes on her knees still stung, but the knife wound on her calf had calmed down to a low, steady note of annoyance. "All I want to do is go to sleep," she said.

"It's going to be strange," Paul offered out loud in the closed vehicle, "being at Christine's without her there. I miss her. Can we go to St. Louis now?"

"I wish," she snickered. "She says her mom is doing much better. I hope she's able to come home soon." Silently she added, *I miss her, too*.

Paul led to drive to Christine's double in West End. The neighborhood was a checkerboard of old, large houses—many converted like hers into apartments—interrupted irregularly by vacant lots left behind by Katrina, by Rodrigo, by Bianca, and all the other hurricanes and floods of the past twenty-five years. "I'll help," he said when he parked, and led to begin carrying Amy's valise, then some groceries, and finally the liquid and first-aid supplies from the drug store. "If our leg worked," he said, "we could have done this in one trip."

She replied, "It could have been worse. If I was on crutches, I'd have a sack hanging around my neck to bring stuff from here to there." Then an afterthought, "If you're on crutches, how do you get a glass of water? Or dinner?"

Amy felt safe inside Christine's apartment. Her car was off the street, so Jeffrey wouldn't accidentally drive by and recognize it; he didn't know where Christine lived; she had her gun, which Paul had named Rosckette; and the door was locked.

With some effort she got her pants off, then sat on the side of the bathtub to examine her wounds. The knife cut on her calf had bled more, but wasn't doing so now. "Did we break a stitch?" Paul asked as she daubed at the area with gauze.

"I can't tell, but it doesn't look worse than this morning."

She moved on to her knees, first cleaning with a washcloth and then applying antiseptic. A small piece of cement came out as she washed their left knee. She moaned, "They haven't looked like this since I was eight years old."

When Amy finished her medical exam, she picked up her torn trousers. "Another pair of pants lost to a homicidal boyfriend." She thought, then added, "They were on sale at Marshalls. I think I paid twenty-nine bucks for them. Crap!" and she threw them down.

She poured herself half a glass of vodka, then poked around in Christine's refrigerator for something to use as mixer. "PowerAde Zero?" she said, holding up a bottle of light green liquid. "The color, it looks like nuclear waste." Even so, she opened the jar, sniffed, then filled the rest of the glass with it.

She hobbled to the bedroom with her drink. Paul took the lead to crouch and smooth the covers on his girlfriend's unmade bed, then fluffed the pillows against the wall so Amy would be able to sit up. Lying back, drink in hand, she let out a sigh and said, "This feels like heaven."

Her phone was giving off its eighth ring by the time Amy had hobbled to the bathroom to retrieve it from the pocket of her torn pants. "Hello?" she said, then shouted "Crap!" as the phone fell from her hand. "Okay, I'm here," she said when she had it securely in hand. "Who is this?"

"Miss Amy?" A woman's voice, slightly familiar but out of context.

"This is Amy Clear of Clear, Hodges and Owens. Who is this?" She was getting annoyed.

"You do not remember me. I am Sanjay Goswami's daughter."

Paul pushed to the lead. "Kali! I didn't recognize your voice. I was wondering when I'd hear from you."

"I did not know who else to call. I am worried about my Lucas."

Amy pulled Paul back and took the lead. "I remember he said he was calling you, when, last week? That you had emailed him."

"Yes. Yes, that is true," she said. "We talked two or three times on the phone. Then he did not call me like he said he would. And he has not answered my calls. I am worried about my Lucas."

"Oh, right, you don't know." Amy hobbled back to the bedroom and let herself down on the floor mattress. "He is very sick, in the hospital where my father works."

"No, no, no!" she exclaimed. "What is wrong with him? Is he all right?"

"My dad's not sure what happened, but his kidneys quit working. He's been on dialysis. He really has been terribly sick. I guess he didn't have a chance to tell you. And he won't get his phone back until tomorrow."

"This is not good. What—I mean, can I do anything?"

An idea popped into her head. First she thought to Paul, *You behave;* then she answered Kali, "Maybe. He's going to need someone to take care of him."

"You said he was going to be with his father. Is his father all right?"

Amy sighed. "A lot has happened down here. The man who said he was the father really was the uncle. The real father is dead. And now the uncle is sort-of on the lam."

"On the lamb? He rides sheep?"

Amy ignored Paul's silent laughter. "It's an expression. The uncle is in hiding, I think he killed Lucas' dad and has something to do with how sick our boy is."

"Tch! Oh, my poor Lucas."

"He's going to need someone to help him when he gets out of the hospital," she went on. "Are you still in school? And didn't he say you—"

"Summer semester is over. I can come down to help him." Amy felt relief that she had found someone else to take responsibility for Lucas.

"Well, then, come on down. You can stay with me for a while." They discussed some practical matters, like the size of the closet in Amy's guest bedroom, and the state of the bathroom. Neither woman was familiar with the weather in the other's city, so they went over wardrobe needs.

"This is the most girly conversation I've had in months," Amy said. "Thanks."

Even though Amy had no idea when Lucas would be discharged from the Jefferson Parish Medical Center, she talked Kali into flying down to New Orleans in four days. "Let me know your flight number and arrival time. I'll meet you at the baggage carousel."

Before they finished the call, Kali said, "My father thanks you for your kind words about his monograph. It pleased him that it was useful to a young student. And when I stay with you, Amy, will you then tell me if you've killed anyone?"

It was Paul who laughed out loud. "With luck, the number won't be higher by then."

When Amy closed her phone, she lay back against the pillows propped up against the wall, lying on Christine's floor bed. "That takes care of Lucas," she said aloud. "I didn't want to have to be his mommy."

"Where are we going to put Kali?" Paul asked.

"The guest room. Why, did you have some other idea, you naughty boy?"

"We're hiding here. You want to put Kali where Jeffrey may find her?"

"Oh." Amy drummed her fingers on her thigh, thinking. "Well, I guess she'll stay here."

"Christine doesn't have another bedroom. And I don't think Kali is the kind of woman who wants to sleep on a mattress on the floor."

"I could handle sharing the bed with her," Amy mused, "I'm used to you and Christine. But I don't know that Kali would be comfortable."

"Or me."

"Oh, don't kid me. You'd love being between the sheets with that beautiful woman."

Amy felt their face burning. Why was she blushing? Then she heard Paul think to her, *Yes, I would. But I won't be unfaithful to Christine.* They were quiet for a moment. He went on, *Be with another woman? In Christine's bed? You'd hate me for it almost as much as I would.*

She wrapped their arms around themself to hug Paul. "I didn't mean to tease you. I didn't realize you were serious. Look, we'll put her in the Motel 6 if we have to."

"Yeah. Okay. Thanks."

Amy took a long sip of her drink. She glanced at Christine's alarm clock and realized Kali's call had awakened her from a nap. She decided her nap wasn't over, that it should last at least until bedtime, if not until morning.

Amy spent much of the next two days in Lucas' hospital room, 431 North. She kept him company when he was awake, and guarded him when he wasn't. When he was taken downstairs for additional dialysis, she and Paul played rock, paper, scissors.

Except for Paul's sacrosanct appointments to talk with Christine. The news was better and better. Her mother had been discharged and was staying with Christine's brother Nathan and his wife Sheila so they could keep an eye on her and make sure she was ready to return to her own home alone. "She's so much better," Christine exclaimed with relief, "except she babbles on and on like a, like a drunk monkey. It's great and all, but she never stops."

Paul suggested, "She's probably thrilled to be alive."

"I am, too, Paulette, but I use periods when I talk."

"Maybe she's just making up for the time that she couldn't talk. She's got all these words she has to get out of her system."

Laughing, Christine said, "Then she won't wind down until Christmas."

"So, when are you coming home, Honey? I miss you."

Softly, the woman said, "I miss you, too. But I'm going to stay a few more days to look after Mom. Nathan and Sheila both work, and I don't want Mom to be alone until we're sure she's okay."

Paul took a deep breath. "That makes sense. I hate to go longer without you, but family comes first. I understand."

"And I'm glad you do. This would be so hard if you didn't."

After the call, Amy thought to Paul, *I hope she's back next week. I know you miss her.* She felt Paul nodding their head. "I miss her, too. Hey, do you think she'll like Kali?"

"I'm afraid to guess. Since she likes women, I'm sure she will. But if she guesses that my no-longer-existent man parts throb at the sight of her, maybe not. We'll find out."

Amy caught her father on rounds when he stepped into Lucas' room. Since the man was asleep, all James could do was look at the electronic clipboard to see vital signs and the previous day's test results. "What's the prognosis?" she asked him.

"Hey, swee-- uh, Amy. We've got him stable, but the damage is done. There's some chance his kidneys might recover some function, but in the meantime he'll need dialysis two or three times a week. And if function doesn't improve, it'll have to be a kidney transplant."

"Oh, that's awful," she moaned.

"The nurses say you've been here every day. What have you seen?"

"With Lucas? He's tired all the time, but he's not complaining about things hurting anymore. I swear, he can't stay awake more than thirty minutes at a time."

Doctor Clear nodded. "That should improve some, but no doubt about it, dead kidneys are debilitating."

"When do you think he'll be able to leave the hospital?"

"If all goes well, one or two more rounds of dialysis. Sometime next week. If he's lucky."

"L-L-Lucky?"

"Good morning, Mister Doublet," James said. "How are you feeling?"

"Tired." He tried to stretch, but one hand still was tethered to an IV pipe. "And I have to pee."

"That's a good sign," the doctor said, and he took a urinal off the nightstand. "Amy?"

"Uh, sure, dad." Around him she added, "Morning, Lucas. I'll be back in a minute."

It was a few minutes before her father called, "All clear!"

Amy walked in to find her father with his arm hanging down, his index finger hooked through the urinal's handle, around hip level. As he was giving Lucas a pep talk, the ultraviolet antiseptic fixture cycled on behind him.

"Whoa!" Paul said. "Is that supposed to be doing that?"

Doctor Clear turned to his daughter, confusion on his face. Paul pointed at the urinal. It—actually, its contents—were glowing a vivid turquoise.

The doctor stared at the turquoise torch. First he lifted it up, but when it left the field of the UV light the fluorescence disappeared. He knelt down with the urinal, until the glow returned, and he examined it with wonder.

Lucas hoisted himself up on one elbow to see what was going on. He repeated Paul's words: "Is that supposed to be doing that?"

"No, son, it's not." There was a smile on the doctor's face. "But now I think I know what happened to you. Do you pick mushrooms?"

"My dad does. Uh, I mean, Uncle Jeffrey does. He was going to teach me how to do it. Why?"

"I recall this from a class at Vandy Med School," he said, standing up. "There's a mushroom, when it's metabolized it makes urine glow turquoise under UV light. And it just so happens that it can take up to three weeks to eat out your kidneys." He turned to Lucas. "I've never seen it in a patient before, so I'm sending this to the lab for confirmation."

"No!" Paul cried. "Lucas and Amy and I were with Jeffrey a few weeks ago on the north shore. We helped him pick shant- shant what? Chanteuses?"

Amy continued; the voice was the same, and it came out of the same mouth, and James wasn't sure if it was Amy or Paul. "Chanterelles. I wouldn't eat any, but I watched Jeffrey eat a bunch of them." She thought a moment. "Dad, that was two, three weeks ago. Lucas didn't get sick until Monday."

Satisfied it was his daughter, the doctor began, "I don't remember which—"

"If you think you know what it is," Lucas interrupted, "then you know how to treat it?"

James was still holding the glowing urinal. He thought for a long moment, then told Lucas, "Yes, we do. We hope your kidneys start to recover, or we get you a kidney transplant. Your kidneys were being damaged before you felt sick. I've gotten your condition stable, and you'll be okay with regular dialysis." Lucas stared at him, mouth open. The doctor sighed, "There's no antidote. But you're out of the woods now."

The UV antiseptic fixture cycled off, and the urinal's contents returned to their usual appearance.

James said to his daughter, "The lab will tell us exactly what mushroom it was. Not that it matters." Then to Lucas, "I'll check in on you tomorrow. I'll let you know what they find out." He put his free hand on Amy's shoulder, then left the room.

Paul thought, *Well, this is awkward.* Silently, Amy nodded in agreement.

So Paul thought to Lucas, *You have three choices, big guy. You can go 'oh woe is me' and let yourself wallow in self-pity. Or you can be glad you're not dead, which you would be if Amy hadn't gotten you here when she did. Or, you can take that nice, new inheritance and buy yourself a kidney.*

Lucas shouted, "What?"

"Oh, crap," Amy said. "Paul thought something to you, didn't he? I can't hear him when he does that. What did he say?"

"He—he—he said—" Lucas sputtered.

"It's Paul. I told him to be glad he's not dead and to buy himself a kidney."

"That's—I mean—What—"

Amy sat on the side of his bed and placed her hands on Lucas' chest. "Take it easy. You can yell at Paul after you calm down." She smiled. To Paul she thought, *Something about him makes me want to mother him. I may adopt him.*

Lucas put his free hand on top of Amy's. He was staring at her, wearing an expression that was a plea.

"We're going to get you okay," she soothed. "They can replace a kidney if you need one. You'll be okay. You'll be normal."

He closed his eyes and let out a sigh. "Please." Suddenly he shook himself on the bed, lifting himself up on one elbow. "I want to be able to go back to work. Live on my own. Not have to get hooked up to a machine all the time."

"Sounds reasonable," she nodded. "We'll work on it, okay?"

She heard Paul ask, *Please tell me you're not thinking about donating one of our kidneys.*

Two hundred thousand dollars, she thought back. *I'll split it with you.*

No, no, no, no, no!

I'll keep it all then, suit yourself. And then she laughed. Out loud she said, "No, Paul, I'm not thinking about it."

"Thinking about what?" Lucas asked, startled.

"Private joke with left-handed me," she answered. "And you, young man," jabbing her index finger in his chest, "your job is to get better. Get your strength back, your stamina. Dad told me he'll probably discharge you next week."

He fell back on the bed, and ran his free hand through his hair. "To where? If I go to my old house, you say Uncle Jeffrey will try to kill me."

"I've got that all figured out. It's a surprise." She was grinning at the prospect of Kali showing up on Friday.

"I like you," Lucas said, "but you are the strangest lady I've ever known."

Paul responded silently, *You mean we're not the strangest _person_ you've ever known? I'm crushed.*

When visiting hours were over, one of the floor nurses came into Lucas' room to chase Amy out. "You can come back tomorrow, hee-hee-hee," the good-natured sister said, "but you have to leave now. I'll look after Mister Lucas, hee-hee-hee."

Amy slapped her thighs, then struggled to lift herself with her cane. "I'll be back tomorrow," she said to her charge. "Any requests?"

"Dialysis is so boring," he moaned, "and no one can visit me while that's going on. Can you bring me a crossword puzzle magazine?"

"Crossword puzzles, check," Amy smiled.

And in a whisper he added, "And a milkshake? Chocolate?"

"I don't know," the sister intruded. "Only if Doctor Clear says it's okay, hee-hee-hee." As Amy and the nurse turned to leave, Paul thought *Chocolate milkshake, check. See you tomorrow, Sport.*

When they got to the nurses' station, Amy reached out to pinch the sleeve fabric of the sister's uniform. 'Can I ask you for a favor?" she asked.

"You can't stay past visiting hours, hee-hee-hee."

"Oh, I understand," Amy responded. "I'd never ask you to break hospital rules. I mean, Doctor Clear is my father. I don't want to get anyone in trouble."

The nurse didn't say anything, but she appeared to be paying a lot of attention since Amy dropped the detail of her parentage. So she went on, "I'm a licensed detective. I'm a veteran of NOPD. No charges have been filed yet, but Lucas was the victim of an attack. Since I can't be here every minute, I'd like you keep an eye out in case his assailants come back. To finish the job."

"I'm no hero," she said, flustered. "I'm not going to tackle a bad guy, or punch out a criminal..." Her tone of voice indicated the woman would actually love to do either of those things.

"No, no, I wouldn't want you to put yourself in any danger. I'd just like you to call your security if either of his attackers shows up."

"Oh. Hee-hee-hee, I can do that."

"I know visitors check in here at the nurses' station. I'm worried about Jeffrey Doublet and Ryan Doublet."

Smart! Paul thought. *He might use either name.*

Or some other name, for that matter. Amy went on, "Yes, they are relatives, but they want to harm Lucas. If they come in, please call security. And as long as you feel safe, stay with them until security arrives so they can't do anything bad. You probably would save his life."

"I'm on night shift this week," Sister Hee-hee-hee said. "I'll watch out for the boy."

"Thank you, Nurse!" Amy gushed. She thought to Paul, *I'm bringing this woman a box of candy bars tomorrow.*

Box of candy bars, check.

"Where are we going to put Lucas when your dad discharges him?" Paul asked. They were sitting on Christine's floor bed, ignoring a newscast on the TV, and finishing off a bottle of sangria.

"I've been thinking about that," Amy answered. "We can't bring him here because there's not enough room. And he sure can't go back to the family manse, not with Jeffrey still on the loose."

"Our place? I've been thinking about that. Did you ever tell Ryan—or Jeffrey—where you live? Is there any reason he might know?"

She stopped with the glass of wine just inches from their lips. *Oh! I guess—I guess I just assumed that he knew.* Then she finished her sip. *Can he do a, what do you call it, a reverse look-up on the dedicated phone line for Clear, Owens & Hodges? The number's on the business card I gave him.*

"I don't think that's a problem," Paul said. "It's a VOIP number, not a land line. Pretty sure he'd need a warrant to get our address."

A smile spread across Amy's face. "Okay, then. We can put him and Kali in the spare bedroom." Suddenly the smile began to retreat. "Or if dad prescribes a hospital bed, they go in the living room. Crap, I'd hate to clog up the living room with a temporary infirmary ward."

Paul said, "So we don't really need to hide out here at Christine's place." When Amy had put the empty glass down by the equally empty bottle, Paul turned their head and buried their nose in the other pillow on the bed. He inhaled deeply, and moaned, "I miss Christine!"

Last report is her mom is doing better.

Paul rolled onto their back and parked their hands behind their head. "I like being here. The place smells like her. I can pretend she'll be here any minute."

Yes. And she will be here soon, when she gets her mother settled.

When Paul made no response, she added aloud, "We'll be busy entertaining Kali and Lucas. I predict the time will pass quickly."

A laugh. "Not too quickly, I hope. There's still the inconvenient matter of Jeffrey."

"Any idea where he might be hiding?" Amy was rubbing her left arm with her right hand, her way of feeling close and offering closeness. "I doubt he's living at the family castle, although if it were me I'd check in there frequently."

"I suppose he's got cash and credit cards, so he could be in any motel in the parish. Or sleeping at his job."

"And I'm sure he still wants to give Lucas a special gift of death." *And I feel guilty that I'm not sleeping on the floor in his hospital room.*

"We can't be everywhere," Paul said, stretching. "And I'm too old to be sleeping on floors. Uh, unless I'm really, really drunk." He paused. "At least Christine has this mattress, so we're not really on the floor, just almost. I can deal with that."

"Do you think that nurse will call the cavalry if Jeffrey turns up?"

"Yes!" Paul said, enthusiastically. "Something about her tone of voice, I think she's looking forward to a confrontation. Maybe she's got ninja skills from before she took orders."

Amy snickered. "And she's big enough to lift patients single-handedly. I think she'll be helpful." She reached out to turn off the desk lamp sitting on the floor next to the mattress. "Good. Now I'll be able to sleep."

Amy sat in one of the hard plastic chairs that edge the baggage claim area at Armstrong International Airport, looking at the empty baggage carrousels and idly tapping her cane on the plastic tile floor. She heard Paul think *Kali's flight is bound to be late. Everything from Atlanta is late.* Lucas' stunning model girlfriend was due on a 2:42 PM flight. Amy had invited her to take care of Lucas. Amy had teased Lucas about having a plan, but he would be surprised when the two women came to his hospital room later that afternoon. Amy hoped the surprise would be a good one.

Rock, Paper, Scissors? she thought back to him.

"Nah." He leaned them toward the vacant chair on the right, where a crumpled *Times-Picayune* was splayed out. "Let's look at the movie schedule. We have to entertain Kali until your dad discharges Lucas."

So they checked the movie schedule. The grocery sales at Rouse's. An article about how the Zephyrs were destined to win the Pacific Coast League baseball pennant, just not this year. Nor, as Paul pointed out, last year, nor the one before that, nor any year since before the short-lived experiment when the team was called the New Orleans Baby Cakes. *What marketing genius came up with that one? Feh!*

It was almost four o'clock when the airport public address system announced baggage from Delta flight 1951 from Atlanta would be on carrousel 14. Gradually people gathered around the metal oval, and a motley assortment of suitcases, duffel bags, golf clubs, and large cardboard boxes were slowly disgorged. "Looks like a sideways escalator," Paul muttered.

A tall, young, dark-skinned woman made her way toward the carrousel, looking around to see if she recognized anyone. *That's her!* Paul thought. He jammed their cane down and lifted themself to their feet.

"Kali! Kali!" Amy called as they limped towards her. When she heard her name she turned toward Amy, and her guarded expression turned into a broad smile. "I am so glad to see you," she said as she leaned in to place air kisses on either side of Amy's head. "I have never been here before. I was concerned."

"A delight to see you," Amy said, returning the grin. "Did you have a good flight?"

"A good flight is one that lands safely where you hoped to go. Yes, it was a good flight."

Good to see you again, Kali. Uh, it's Paul. I hope we get to be friends now. She made a small double-take, then said, "You are still up to your mischief, I see. You must teach me how you do that."

"Let's collect your baggage and go get you settled," Amy said. "It's pouring rain out there. Uh, I guess you know that."

Kali moved to the carrousel and started to wrestle a full-size suitcase with dull green hard sides. She pointed to a smaller red case, and Amy caught the crook of her cane in its handle. The case stayed on the carrousel, and Amy hopped to keep up with its circuit. *Let go,* Paul advised. *Kali can grab it when it comes around.* She retreated to where Kali was guarding the green case and said, "I couldn't get the other one. See if you can."

"Why are you limping?" she asked, ignoring her remaining suitcase with trailing cane that was whacking unsuspecting people as it went around carrousel 14. "You weren't limping in Atlanta."

"Lucas's relative hadn't stabbed me yet in Atlanta," Paul said out loud. "You'll have to be the stevedore until we get the cases up on their wheels."

"His father stabbed you?" Her pretty face was wide-eyed.

"Well, I got him pretty good with a broomstick. Do you want that other suitcase? Or should we leave it here?"

Kali threaded through the other survivors of flight 1951 who were trying to collect their own baggage and get on with the rest of their lives. When her red case came around she grappled it off the carrousel, and nabbed Amy's cane before it made yet another circuit.

The women prepared to leave baggage claim and brave New Orleans' 110% humidity on such a rainy day. They lifted the carrier handles and began making use of the built-in wheels. Amy was pushing the red case, the crook of her cane slipped through an unused strap buckle; Kali was pulling the bigger green suitcase behind her. Necessary small talk out of the way, Kali said, "How is Lucas? Is he doing better? When can I see him?"

"Better, yes," Amy answered. "But he's got a long way to get to well. And if the rain doesn't drown us, you can see him this evening." She smiled at the woman, while she thought to Paul, *I hope this is a good idea. What if Lucas doesn't want to see her?*

In that case we all drop dead in a pool of white-hot lava and the world ends. His tone of thought dropped the sarcasm to add, *He's not in any position to complain about a beautiful model choosing to help him recover. The boy probably needs a kidney transplant, for crying out loud.*

"I want to see him. I miss him." They walked out of the baggage claim section of the airport terminal and headed down the west sky bridge that led to the parking areas. The rain on the elevated walking tube sounded like a kindergarten class where the teacher had foolishly distributed drums to everyone.

"What?"

"I said, I want to see Lucas. I miss him."

Amy nodded. "When's the last time you spoke to him?"

"Two weeks ago? He wasn't feeling well, he said, but he was still at home."

Paul thought to her *Amy's dad is a doctor, so she knows some medical stuff. She realized how sick he was. Amy saved Lucas' life.*

Kali jerked her head to look at Amy, then slowly smiled. "You djinn," she said. Then, "Thank you for helping my Lucas."

Inside the short-term parking structure, they went down concrete aisles, wet from the rainwater that had been tracked in by countless cars. "Short-term parking was full," Paul said out loud. "We're in the next deck. The skywalk is down here somewhere."

"It's so humid!" Kali said as they walked. "I thought Atlanta was wet, but this, this is awful. My hair must be all pin-curls. I don't want my Lucas to see me like this."

"I predict," Amy said, laughing, "that your Lucas will be thrilled to see you. He won't care about your hair." She heard Paul think, *We hope that Lucas will be thrilled.* Then she went on, "When we get to my place you can take a shower and change clothes before we go to the hospital. Will that be better?"

"You are a woman. I knew you would understand."

Paul thought to her, *I have no comment.*

The skywalk let them out on the 4th level of the six-story long-term parking deck. The driveways were not as thoroughly wet, as long-term parking has less traffic than the short-term facility. Still, the humidity was making Kali's hair curl, making her posture sag, and making her mood turn dark. "Perhaps I should have used a parachute to go directly to your home," she said.

It was Paul who said, "Damn, I wish that had occurred to me. I could have given you my latitude and longitude, Delta could have delivered you like a Hellfire missile."

"You are laughing at me," and Amy could hear the woman's lower lip stuck out.

"Oh, yes," Amy said, "yes, I am." Paul added silently, *Me, too. Relax, Kali, we'll be back to civilization soon.*

"Oooh," Kali muttered. "I don't suppose you have any bhang at your house."

"Probably not, since I have no idea what that is." Amy kept pushing the suitcase, using it in place of her cane to help her walk. Paul asked, "What is that?"

"There's my car!" Amy shouted. She aimed her keys at the old yellow Benz and made the running lights blink with a soft honk. Kali pulled her suitcase as Amy pushed the bigger one to the back of the car and opened the trunk.

"Thanks be to Ganesh," Kali said, in a less-than-reverent tone of voice. As Amy struggled to get the big case in the trunk, Kali answered Paul, "Bhang. Like alcohol, a mild intoxicant. It's good for relaxing. If you stop laughing at me I will make some for you."

Amy retrieved her cane and stepped back so Kali could manoeuver the suitcase she'd been pulling and add it to the luggage compartment. "Make some? What's in it?" Mentally she was inventorying her kitchen appliances. Blender? Cuisinart? Double boiler?

"Fermented milk and cut up ganja leaves. It is simple."

Amy was still processing the Rastafarian euphemism when Paul said, "You flew here with marijuana in your luggage?"

"Of course not," she said, dropping the suitcase on top of the one Amy had interred. She turned toward them and said, "It is too valuable. I kept it in my purse."

What have I invited into my home? Amy thought to Paul.

By the time Kali was installed in Amy's spare room and everyone had showered and changed clothes, the rain had tapered to a drizzle. *You want to drive us to Dad's hospital?* Amy asked, and got the standard *Yes, yes, God, YES!* Paul had never recovered from the automotive deprivation of the first five or six years he spent in Amy's body, when she was too young even for a Louisiana Cheater's Permit—uh, learner's permit.

"I have been dying to ask you this since the first time I met you," Kali said from the passenger's seat. "How many people have you killed?"

"It's Paul. You've been asking all that time. What you're dying to know is the answer."

Kali snorted. "I'll have you know I have gotten B-plusses and As in English at Agnes Scott."

"He's just giving you a hard time because he likes you," Amy said. "When he had his own body he was a researcher and statistician, but somehow he can be quite the grammar Nazi."

"Had his own body? I wish you did not tease me like this." She was sitting with her arms folded across her chest.

In a childish sing-song Paul said, "Oh, no! That mean old Paul, he's making fun of me. Oh, woe, life is not fair." Switching to Amy's normal voice he went on, "Jill up, woman. Yes, I teased you about sentence construction. Big deal. Put on your big girl pants and maybe admit I am right."

"It's Amy. Truce, you two. I'll tell you, Kali, if you give Paul as good as he gives you, he'll leave you alone. Anyway, now what?"

Her arms still folded in front of her, Kali said, "Amy, You were a policeman, and now a detective. I'm sure you have had to kill criminals. How many have you killed?"

Amy and Paul both were smiling. Amy managed not to laugh out loud, in deference to Kali's touchy attitude. "I don't know for sure. It's like asking a gigilo how many women he's slept with. That's not the point of his job."

"A guess, perhaps?"

"I remember the first person I killed. A crazy drug kingpin had me cornered in his bunker. When he shot his brother a ricochet hit my left arm, so Paul couldn't do his manly gun thing. Anyway—"

"Never mind this Paul thing. What happened?" Kali had dropped her arms and was turned in her seat to look toward Amy.

"Anyway, I shot the guy. I got him in the hip, which was enough to, uh, neutralize the threat, as we used to say on the police force. But by the time reinforcements came, he had bled to death. Does that count?"

"I am a model. I make money because I have a pretty face, and I get to wear beautiful clothes. Being in school is important for the future, but it is waiting, it is not real life. But you! What you do is dangerous. You risk something important, your very life, to protect other people. You have even killed to do so. I—I—You make me feel so insignificant."

Wow, Paul thought to Amy. *You have a fan.*

"I appreciate that, Kali," Amy said. She showed down and moved into the curb lane, then pulled into the parking lot of the Firemen's Federal Credit Union on Napoleon Avenue.

"Why are we stopping?" Kali asked. "Is Lucas's hospital here?"

Amy shook her head. "No, we're not there yet. I just don't trust myself to be driving while we're having this conversation." She put out her arms and held Kali's left hand in both of hers.

"Since I was a detective, it didn't seem special or praiseworthy to me, it was just something I wanted to do Paul and I love to solve puzzles, figure out who the bad guy was and catch him. Your opinion of what I did—it's so different from my own, and I really do appreciate it. But—" Paul squirmed, settling their butt more comfortably as they were facing their passenger "—You. Don't sell yourself short. You're a lot younger than me, you haven't grown into who you'll be or what you'll do. Give yourself a chance! You told me you're majoring in what, physics? And—"

"Chemistry, actually," Kali corrected.

"Okay, in chemistry. Depending what specialty you go into, you may figure out something that improves life for millions of people. Saves zillions of dollars. Or even makes three people happier." *Time for your cliché, Paul. I cannot make myself say those words.* And so it was Paul who finished by saying, "It's all good."

"You are kind," Kali said, looking down for a moment. "But Lavoisier was 25 when he isolated oxygen as the cause of rust. Einstein wrote the special theory of relativity when he was 26. Galileo made the hydrostatic balance at 22. I am 22, and all I've done is adorn the cover of a magazine that was in everyone's trash a month later."

Ohmygod, Paul thought to Amy, *she's about to cry.*

Amy shook Kali's hand. "Sometimes I wish I were still twenty-two." Paul thought to Amy, *But then we'd have to make eight-years' worth of mistakes all over again.* Amy chuckled, which made Kali defensive, then went on, "You will do fine. If you have half your dad's brain, you will be a brilliant chemist."

"You are kind," she repeated, "but I am—"

Hurry up and wait, dingbat! Kali's sudden stop and puzzled expression told Amy her dyad had silently interrupted. She sighed, "Okay, what did Paul say to you? I can't hear him when he does that."

"You really don't know? How is it—"

"Kali, what did he say?"

"But it's impossible!"

Another sigh. "Yes, it's impossible. What did Paul say to you?"

The woman blinked a few times, absorbing Amy's insistence on the what instead of her own interest in the how. Finally she said, "He called me a name. And he told me I have to wait."

"Ah. 'Hurry up and wait.' Paul's been saying that to me since I was eleven. Unfortunately, he is correct. Sometimes all you can do is wait to see how things turn out." Amy smiled, then released Kali's hand. "As for calling you names, he is a foul-mouthed S-O-B, isn't he?"

Me? he thought to Amy. *Oh, I am cut to the quick. To the fucking quick, I tell you.*

Amy told Paul he could drive the rest of the way to the Jefferson Parish Medical Center, where her father had his private practice and where Lucas Doublet was putting up with dialysis three times a week. Although she had to keep her eyes on the road, as Paul needed to use them to drive, it freed up Amy's concentration to converse with Kali.

"I was earning an A at Agnes Scott," the woman explained, "but I became so distracted when you came to visit and took Lucas. My father was not pleased with my B-plus average. Or with a B-minus in German."

"When do you register for fall semester?" Amy asked.

"Two weeks ago. Except I didn't. I will stay here to look after my Lucas."

I hope that works for her, Paul thought to Amy. *Don't know that putting college on hold to be with your boyfriend is such a good idea.*

Maybe, she thought back. *But if Kali and Lucas get serious, maybe the trade is worth it. The question is, how angry is Kali over Lucas leaving her? And how frightened will Lucas be when this gorgeous surprise walks into his hospital room?*

Frightened?

What Lucas said on the airplane. Remember? That she was too intense for him? That he shut down when she got so emotional?

Amy felt Paul nod their head. The movement startled Kali, who asked, "Are you—is everything—I mean—okay?"

"Okay," Amy replied. "Paul was agreeing with something I said to him."

"Are we near your daddy's hospital? I want to see my Lucas."

"Not far. We'll make a left at Clearview and then it's a straight shot."

Kali nodded, and Amy went on, "I'm glad you're getting comfortable with me and Paul. You know, the left-handed me?"

Kali tilted her head, considering what Amy said. "I believe I am. He still calls me names, but not like he did in Atlanta. And other than this Paul, you seem so normal—" Amy heard Paul laugh silently "—so, yes. Comfortable. But I must tell you, you are the strangest person I have ever known."

"Yes. I hear that a lot."

Amy hobbled on her cane to lead Kali out of the elevator on the fourth floor of the Jefferson Parish Medical Center, ready to check in at the nurses' station. She saw James Clear, his back to her, as he wrote out something, probably on a patient charge form. "That's my dad!" she whispered to Kali, then shouted—breaking the serene quiet of a hospital floor—"Dad! Hey, Dad!"

James looked up, then turned his head until he found the source of the voice he knew so well. A broad smile spread across his face. "Pump—uh, Amy! Come here, Darling."

After their embrace, Amy said, "Dad, this is Kali. She's going to look after Lucas. And how is our boy today?"

Doctor Clear dipped his head to acknowledge Kali, but answered his daughter. "Tired. A four hour hemodialysis session is exhausting until you get used to it."

"Hemodialysis..." Kali whispered.

"I don't think he's asleep yet," James said, and he put his hands on both women's back to press them toward Lucas' room. "Kali, is it? Lucas can tell you all about it."

Amy entered first. She saw Lucas on his hospital bed, the head raised and a tray table in front of him. Sister Hee-hee-hee was adjusting the sheet over him, babbling all the while.

"Hey, good looking," Amy called. Lucas turned his head, then smiled weakly when he focused on her. "Amy," he said, softly. "Hi."

"I have some things for you. Here's..." she rummaged in a repurposed Rouses T-shirt bag, and held out as she said, "...the latest *Road and Track*. And a Dell crossword magazine. Oh, and a Hershey bar." She turned to the nurse, who was quiet now but still present, and held out another piece of candy, saying, "And one for you, too." She heard Paul think *The sister won't complain about breaking the rules for Lucas when you break them for her, too.*

That's the idea, yes.

Lucas placed the magazines on the tray table, and used the candy bar to hold them in place. "You remembered. Thank you."

"I brought something else. Some one else." Amy turned toward the doorway and motioned for Kali to enter the room.

She took two steps in, tentatively. She was wearing a loose black cotton tank top that fell to her hips, with lace trim at the neck and arm holes; it left her shoulders and dark arms exposed. Her wide-legged slacks, also black, were long enough to cover all but the toes that stuck out in her brown sandals. Kali's arms were crossed in front of her, each hand holding the opposite bicep. "Lucas?" she whispered.

Damn, she is a fox. Uh, don't tell Christine I said that.

Even though the head of his bed was raised, Lucas struggled to press his elbows down, trying to sit up straighter. "Kali?" His voice was the strongest yet. "Why? What?"

Amy thought to him, *I asked her to come down to look after you for awhile. You need more help than just me.*

"Amy asked you? And you came?"

Shyly, Kali went past Sister Hee-hee-hee, who was working on her chocolate, and demurely sat on the side of the bed. "Yes. She asked. I was worried when I did not hear from you. She explained what has happened to you."

"After everything that went down in Atlanta?" Feebly he let his left hand crawl over the sheet to touch Kali's. "You still—"

"Hush." She held an index finger to his lips. "My Lucas needs help. Of course I am here."

She's not freaking out anymore, Paul thought, *that's good. The worst I had to call her today is 'dingbat.'*

Silently, Amy responded, *I was pretty sure she'd be gold. What I'm worried about is Lucas. Is he still more boy than man?*

"Thank you for the candy bar," the nurse said to Amy. For the first time Amy actually looked at the name tag, then said, "You're welcome, Sister Janet. Look—" and she stood up, "can I talk to you about something?" She limped after the nurse and followed her to the station. From having a doctor as a father, Amy knew the nurse was not supposed to be licking her fingers, 72% dark chocolate or not.

"It must be tough," Amy said as they stood at the nurse's station. "Friends and relatives bring your patients goodies—flowers, muffulettas, daiquiris—and all you get to do is watch. That's not fair. You're taking care of Lucas, and I appreciate it. So, candy bar for you, too."

"That's so thoughtful," Janet said. "You know, the strangest things people have brought in were pets. Fish, a cat, a bunch of dogs. Well, one at a time, but a bunch of people did that." She rubbed her hands on a sani-wipe. "I have to say, your boyfriend is quite a looker."

"Lucas?" Amy shook, eyes wide open. "No, he's Kali's boyfriend. I mean, it's—" she coughed when Paul started to speak, and she stepped back internally to hear what he had to say. "Yeah, he's a looker, but you ought to see his father. That's my boyfriend." Amy added out loud, "Or the uncle. It's, uh, it's complicated."

"Didn't you tell me it was relatives that may come here to hurt Lucas?"

"Yes. Uncle or father. The boyfriend." Amy shook her head. "There's an estate legacy, and—"

"La-la-la-la," Sister Janet said, holding her palms against her ears. "No details, please." Amy was quiet, so the nurse went back to using her hands on tidying up the station. "There are days this job is a handful, just knowing what happened to someone to make them my patient. Hearing people's motivations would just make it unbearable."

Amy watched the woman do her custodial nursing tasks for a few moments. "Yes. I had some of that problem when I was a police detective." Paul added, "Trouble was, it was our job to know the motivations. Nah, I don't blame you a bit."

Shall we check on the lovebirds? Paul thought to Amy.

"Yes, we shall," she answered aloud. Then, "Thanks again for looking out for Lucas. If the evil relatives show up, just scream for security." As she started to walk back toward Lucas's room, Nurse Hee-hee-hee said, "They teach us to urinate on ourselves or vomit on an attacker." Amy cringed at the thought, while Paul remembered, *That's what that Godawful gender studies class you took at LSU Lakeshore said.*

I hope the curriculum's changed by now and they hand out 9 millimeters, Amy replied silently. *With free ammo and range time.*

Back in the hospital room, Kali was lying on top of the sheet, next to Lucas, with an arm over his chest. He was subdued from the trial of the day's dialysis, but he was trying to keep up with Kali's exuberance as they talked. As Amy sat she thought to Paul, *Why do I suddenly feel like a chaperone?*

You kids have a nice time, but no slow dancing! Paul thought back.

"Oh, Sister Agnetha! Those dances at Archbishop Rummel were like running through a mine field. Trying to get close to that boy, what was his name? Uh, Johnson, something Johnson. Just trying to get a kiss without him trying to get a feel, and you screaming in disgust over a boy trying to kiss me, and then Sister Agnetha scolding us, 'You're dancing too close! Make room for the Holy Ghost!'"

"Amy? What is it you are telling us?"

"Was that out loud? Sorry, Kali." Even as their face began to turn red in embarrassment Paul took the lead to add, "A random synapse fired and I was remembering a high school dance in Catholic school. Didn't mean to spook you or anything."

The woman laughed, "You have done many things to 'spook' me, but this is not one of them. You know, even though I am Hindu, I went to Catholic School in Kolkata, before we came to America."

"Were the nuns there crazy, too? Did they chaperone your dances?"

"I was only ten when my family moved to Atlanta. I do not remember chaperones or dances. But yes, the nuns were crazy."

Amy nodded. And she was glad to see the smile on Lucas's face. He'd been through a lot, and would deal with much more before a kidney transplant could restore his life to 'normal' (whatever that is); it was a relief to Amy that, even so, anything could make him smile. *Kali makes him smile* she thought to Paul. *It's almost enough to make me believe in romance.*

Almost, Paul thought back.

Kali asked, "When will Lucas be released? And where—" she turned to look at the man "—will we take him?"

"We'll bring him to my house. I figure he'll go in the guest bedroom where I set you up. And we'll do it as soon as Dad discharges him. Maybe this weekend."

So Amy and Paul silently observed while Kali and Lucas forgave each other and kept one another company.

"Closing time!" Sister Janet called from the doorway at 8 o'clock. "You don't have to go home, but you can't stay here. Hee-hee-hee."

Amy slapped her thighs and hoisted herself up with the cane. "Come on, Kali. Say good night and we'll be back in the morning."

"I just got here!" Kali cried, rubbing Lucas's face, feeling the stubble. "I want to stay with him."

"Only relatives or declared agents can stay," the nurse said. "But we'll have him all pretty for you in the morning. Visiting hours start at 10 o'clock."

"It's okay, Kali," Lucas whispered. "I'm wiped out. I think I fell asleep an hour ago and this is just a dream."

"Oh, you!" Kali laughed, and play slapped at his arm.

"I'm glad you're here. You...you are a gift, you know that? I'll..." he yawned, "...I'll still be here in the morning. No dialysis tomorrow, so I should feel better. For you."

Paul said, "Can we bring anything tomorrow?"

A weak smile, and he said, "Wasn't there something about a chocolate shake?"

Whoops, Paul thought to Lucas and to Amy. *Chocolate shake, check and check again.* Meanwhile Kali, who was not included on Paul's direct conference announcement, said, "Yes. Yes, I will bring you that shake. I promise."

"Come on, Kali," Amy repeated, standing by where the woman was lying on Lucas's bed. "We have to go."

"Thank you, Amy," Lucas said, smiling. "You saved my life and you keep saving it. Thank you."

"Let's not get too soppy here," Amy said, returning the man's smile. "It's Kali who's going to be your guardian angel."

On the drive to Amy's home Kali smiled without interruption. She was even smiling when she complained about the humidity. "Thank you for having me come to help Lucas," she said. "I was afraid I'd never see him again, but now we are like we were before."

"You mean before Amy came to Atlanta," Paul said out loud. "Still, it's great to see the two of you together. Your children will be like Adonis."

"Well! It's a little early to talk about children," Kali said, with a dull blush beneath her bronze skin that showed she indeed was thinking about children, or, at least, the usual way of begetting them.

"I'm happy for you," Amy said. "You can concentrate on helping Lucas get better, and I can concentrate on running down Jeffrey."

"Run him down? Are you going to kill him with your car?"

Paul swerved into the next lane of traffic but righted the car before the oncoming vehicle quit blowing its horn. *Still having some trouble with American idioms?* he thought to Kali.

"You djinn, today even you can not disturb me. My Lucas understands me."

"Agreed," Amy voiced, smiling. "And for the record, killing Jeffrey is not my plan."

She heard Paul think, *Just what is the plan?* about the same time Kali asked the same question, although their tones and inflections were quite different.

"I like him, okay?" Amy shouted. Then, in a normal voice, "I want him to leave Lucas alone and go back to being my lover." She nodded to herself. "Yes. That is the plan."

He stabbed you! Paul thought. *Amy Clear, you have never been the kind of woman who puts up with domestic abuse. What is going on?"*

"I—I thought you said he stabbed you."

"Yes, there is that. Excuse me, Kali, but I don't feel obliged to justify myself to you about this. My plan includes protecting Lucas, trust me on that." Kali blinked and obeyed the not-so-subtle order not to challenge Amy.

How about me? Can you explain your plan to me?

A sigh. *To you? I guess. I know you won't laugh at me, but I hope you don't lecture me, either.* Another sigh. *I like Jeffrey. He's interesting. He likes me—uh, when he's not stabbing me.* And yet another sigh. *And I don't remember the last time I had a boyfriend, a lover, a man I can hold and hug and kiss and everything like I wish I could do with you. Okay?*

In the nineteen years Paul had lived inside Amy's head, he learned some rules. First off, he was a guest; it was Amy's head, Amy's body, Amy's life. He could make his opinion known about anything, but it was Amy's decision that was final. If he tried to interfere by seizing the lead, she could punish him by tensing her muscles and preventing him having any access. And if he ever tried to gloat with a 'I told you so' she would just ignore him until he felt like he was locked inside a prison—he had first learned that the hard way when she was twelve, and there had been remedial lessons periodically after that.

Plus, Paul had Christine. He was in love with the mixed-blonde woman who now was tending her mama in St. Louis. Amy and Paul had an explicit agreement: Paul could be with Christine (assuming Christine wanted that, which boy howdy she does) if he would not interfere with Amy's romantic life. He had made his concern about Jeffrey's character and behavior known, and all he could do now was grit his teeth (figuratively, since Amy was using their/her teeth on a regular basis), hope for the best, and be ready to boost his dyad's spirit and confidence if this project were not successful. If a dangerous relationship was what she wanted, so be it. Amy had terrible judgement about men, but she wasn't a sucker for bad boys. Usually.

So Paul said, out loud, "Okay. Let's see if I can help you make this work."

"Djinn? Is that you? You think it's good that Amy wants to be with a stabbing stabber?"

He thought directly to her: *Amy doesn't need to justify herself to you, and neither do I.* Aloud he added, "She's the boss, and it's her life."

He parked in the gravel lane that ran up and down Amy's street, where utility construction was in its third year. NOPSI–New Orleans Public Service, Inc–was not expected by natives to be particularly efficient.

As Kali got out of the passenger door she looked inside her enormous purse. "I need bhang." she announced. "Shall I make enough for you, Amy?"

"No! Kali, I used to be a police detective, and my dad is a doctor. You may think it's stupid or square, but I don't use drugs."

Silently Paul thought to their guest, *I do.*

Amy didn't know why a smile spread across Kali's face. The woman said, "Oh, you are a little djinn, aren't you?" Hefting her purse, she asked Amy, "Will you show me where things are in your kitchen?"

Amy began to sputter, but Paul thought to her, *Go ahead, at least you'll keep her from burning down the house. You know she's going to do this as soon as you're not home.* Grudgingly Amy opened her front door and used her cane to push it open. "Sure. Come on," and led the way.

"I need a sauce pan," Kali said.

"In the cabinet next to the stove. No, the lower one."

She pulled out a pot and looked inside it. "You don't cook much, do you?" she asked as she took the pan to the sink and rinsed it.

Amy settled down at the breakfast table. "I don't starve or anything," she responded, "but Paul is the cook."

"Really? Djinn, is that so?"

Paul thought back, *Yes, I am the cook. Amy told you so. You should believe her when she tells you stuff.*

Kali laughed, and Amy rolled her eyes imagining what Paul must have thought to her. "Let me show you my recipe for bhang." She turned to the refrigerator and looked inside. "Butter, good. Not as good as ghee, but I confess, it's what I use most of the time. And—" still holding the refrigerator door open, she turned to face Amy "—No milk? You don't drink milk?"

"No. Lactose intolerant. I thought Asians had trouble with milk."

Kali turned back to the refrigerator. "Bhang doesn't use enough to matter. Ah!" and she reached into the appliance, "Yogurt. It's already fermented, good." She put the container on the table by Amy, near the butter. "Now, how about your spices?"

Well, this is fun, Paul thought.

"Above and next to the sink. What are you looking for?"

Kali opened the cabinet and pulled at the bottles, reading labels. "Cardamom. Nutmeg. Cinnamon. Anise."

"My God, all of those?" Amy thought to Paul, *Sounds like a purgative.*

"Ummm...No, just any one of them. How old is this cinnamon?"

"It's Paul. It's not old enough to drink, but I think it's registered to vote."

"It will have to do. Now, watch." The woman cut a hunk of butter, put it in the sauce pan, and turned the gas on medium. Then she reached into her purse; she fumbled around in it, then withdrew a cosmetic case. She unzipped it, and a cloud of talcum powder escaped. Paul thought to Amy, *Looks like the kitchen when my grandma made biscuits.*

Kali blew into the case, then tilted it so a small plastic container fell into her hand.

"Oh, great," Amy muttered. Then, to her houseguest, "You are so lucky I'm not a sworn officer these days!"

You never hassled Christine about her nightcaps when you were on the force, Paul protested.

Kali's different, Amy responded. *If I had turned Christine in, you would have left me.*

As the butter began to melt, Kali opened the container and sprinkled what she knew and Paul assumed and Amy guessed was ground marijuana. The woman stirred to mix the vegetable matter into the butter and let it simmer for a minute or so. Then she used the same spoon to lift yogurt into the pot, and kept stirring. "This would be much better if you had some cardamom," she said, "but the cinnamon will do." She pried open the lid of the McCormack's tin and sprinkled some of the sweet spice into the milky mixture, then stirred more and more and more.

"Do you do this a lot?" Amy asked.

"Heating it like this does not pasteurize it, so it will go sour in a few days. That's why I make it in small batches." She was still stirring, but with a huge smile on her face.

"No, what I mean is do you, uh, use this a lot?"

"Oh, yes," Kali answered. "It is very common in my culture. And it is very relaxing." She leaned over the stove to inhale the concoction, and pronounced, "It is done. Would you like some?"

"I said no."

Can you let me lead and try it? That way it won't affect you.

"If you stay up with Christine after I fall asleep, I wake up coughing with a clot of crud in my lungs."

"I—I'm sorry?" said Kali, confused, as she poured the potion into a drinking glass.

"No, not you," Amy said, then went on silently, *I will let you do this. The sooner you and Kali use up this stuff, the sooner my house won't have any contraband in it. But...*

Hmmm?

Kali took a sip of the brew. She looked up and smacked her lips, like a wine connoisseur evaluating a 1982 Bordeaux Cabernet Grand Cru. "Hmm, the cinnamon works with the yogurt."

"It's Paul. Amy says no, but I'd like to try."

Kali held out the glass in her left hand and the spoon in her right. "You don't have to pretend someone else is doing this, you know."

Spontaneously Amy thought to her, with her normal Amy voice, *I'm Amy.* And Paul chimed in, with the remains of his male voice, *I'm Paul.*

"I'm not schizophrenic. Paul and I are different people. We—"

"So you say."

"It's Paul. Please don't make fun of us. We are your hosts. If you want to think of us as loony toons, fine, but keep it to yourself. And may I have some more? That's interesting stuff right there. What did you call it? Bang?"

"Bhang. A little crunchy. I should have ground the ganja more."

Don't get too looped, Amy thought to her dyad. *You wanted to call Christine.*

"Amy, are you kidding? Christine will think this is hysterical. I wonder if she's ever heard of bhang." He took a third spoonful.

"Hey, djinn," Kali called, "leave some for me." Paul handed the paraphernalia back to her.

Amy asked, "What happens? What does this do for you?" She had never thought to ask Christine or Paul that question about their more, uh, American ingestion of cannabis.

"It takes a little while," Kali answered, "and it happens slowly." She thought for a moment. "First I notice I am relaxing. Maybe silly things seem funny. Unfortunately, maybe I get hungry."

"It's Paul. I feel the relaxing. Not hungry yet."

"Amy? Are you relaxed?"

"No," she said, shaking her head. "Letting you and Paul use this stuff inside my home is way outside my comfort zone."

The woman took another spoonful. "So, the djinn is relaxed, and you are not?"

"It's Paul. We keep telling you, we are different people. We just happen to live inside the same body."

She shook her head. "I think you had some bhang before I got here."

Let it go, Amy thought to Paul. *She talks like she doesn't believe we're a dyad, but she calls you djinn. It's not worth arguing about.*

Yeah, okay. Besides, I already feel too mellow to fight.

Mellow?

Out loud, he said, "I need to call Christine. She's probably waiting to hear from us. Kali, will you excuse us?"

"There's a little left," the woman said, holding out the glass with its residue of pied liquid.

"All yours, babe," he said. "I'm gonna talk to my girlfriend."

"Oh," Kali's eyes widened. "That's why—"

Amy thought to her, *No, don't even say it. Not unless you want to sleep on the patio.*

They left Kali to finish her bhang and (Amy hoped) clean up the kitchen, and retreated to the privacy of the bedroom. Amy sat up on top of the covers, leaning against a pillow on the headboard. Paul pushed the buttons on Amy's phone and listened to the electronic sound of a phone ringing in St. Louis.

Only two rings. "Paulette! It's so late I was afraid you weren't going to call How are you Hi, Amy," all in one breath.

"Wow, I didn't realize it was 11 o'clock already. Amy's been entertaining," Paul cooed to his lover. "How's Mom doing? How are you? I miss you."

"I took Mom to the doctor for a checkup today. He says he's amazed and happy at how well Mom is doing."

"That's wonderful, Hon—"

"He's prescribed some new medicine for her. It's supposed to, I think he said, thin her blood so she won't have another clot like last time."

"Christine, I'm so happy for you. For you both."

"Yeah." He heard her sigh. "That doll you and Amy gave me? It doesn't have any hair left, I've been holding it and rubbing it to feel you with me. It worked! You're so smart to think of that."

"Any idea when you're coming home, Sweetie? I miss you lots." And then, "It's Amy. I miss you, too. And that's great news about your mother, Christine."

"Nathan thinks mom's going to be okay on her own. And he and Sheila are here in town, so it's easier for them to deal with anything that comes up. Paulette, I'll be home next week!"

"I am so glad to hear that!" Paul shouted down the phone line. "When Amy and I stayed at your place, before we realized the bad guy doesn't know where we live, I liked how the apartment smells like you. What's your perfume?"

"Perfume? Paulette, I just use some grapefruit oil. Someone told me it makes girls smell young and wholesome."

"It makes you smell great."

"It's Amy. Paul guessed that your perfume was bacon because he liked it so much."

"Oh, Amy, boys can be so weird. But I love my Paulette."

"I've got a house guest," Amy went on. "When the son gets out of the hospital he's going to stay at my place. His girlfriend from Atlanta flew down to look after him."

"That's sweet."

"It's Paul. Sweeter still—have you ever heard of bhang?"

"What? 'Bang bang into the room'?[17]"

"Nah. It's a drink with marijuana in it. Very pleasant buzz."

"No. Amy! Have you come over to the dark side? We have cookies, you know."

Amy answered sternly, "No. I'm just letting Lucas's girlfriend use up what she brought with her so it's gone."

"Brought with her? What kind of person gets on an airplane with pot in her luggage?"

"Not her baggage," Paul corrected. "She said it was too valuable, so she brought it in her purse. In a makeup bag full of loose talcum powder."

"Paulette? Amy? Can I meet this girl when I come back?"

They coughed, the sound of both of them trying to talk at the same time. Over the phone they weren't able to think directly to Christine. Finally Paul said, "Sure, but I need to warn you. She's a model. She's tall, skinny, and gorgeous, and Lucas has no idea how lucky he is."

"Amy, don't you let her turn Paulette's head." It didn't sound like a joke. Although Christine was much healthier than when she and Paul first met years earlier, she still had a streak of insecurity that sometimes bubbled to the surface. Like right now.

"Not to worry," Amy answered. "He has demonstrated absolute loyalty to you. Now hurry home so he can show you!"

"Wednesday or Thursday," Christine said. "I miss you so much, Paulette, you're better than my medicine. You are my medicine. And I miss you, too, Amy."

---

[17] Jessie J with Ariana Grande & Nicki Minaj - "Bang Bang"

They ended the call with the usual and heartfelt protestations of love. As Amy put the phone down on her nightstand, Paul said, "Christine's coming home! We'll all be normal again."

Amy added, "As normal as three people in two bodies can be."

She opened the top left drawer in her bureau and pulled out a spare house key, then headed back to the kitchen.

They found Kali sitting at the kitchen table with a smile on her face and a red rubber glove on her right hand. She was clutching a sponge. "Interesting ensemble there," Paul said.

"Oh, yes. I was washing the dishes and suddenly the bhang told me to sit down or fall down. This has been such a-a-a wonderful day."

"Glad you took option A," Paul said. "And yeah, a great day." He retreated to let Amy say, "It was sweet to watch you and Lucas. You two are good for each other."

"I was afraid I'd never see him again when you took him away," she said dreamily. "It is fitting that you brought us back together."

Amy sat across from the woman and, with the back of her hand, slid the salt and pepper shakers to the side. Then she held out the spare house key, holding it by the blade. "You'll need this. Don't lose it. It's expensive to change all the locks."

Kali looked at it in Amy's fingers, then turned her gaze up to Amy's face. "You trust me with your key? I—I am overwhelmed. For Hindus, hospitality is very important." She glanced down at the key, then met Amy's eyes again. "I am touched that you trust me. I will not lose it."

"Well, good. Look, we'll be busy tomorrow," Amy said. "First thing, I'll help you rent a car. We'll—"

"Why would we do that?"

"'Chauffeur' is not part of my job description. I run a detective business, not an Uber. You'll have to get around on your own." Amy heard Paul think, *We run a business that is not all that busy just now.*

"Oh. Yes, okay."

"And we'll make sure it has a GPS so you don't get too lost. I'd hate to have to rescue you from the Pontchartrain Causeway, or from the New Orleans East swamp."

"There is a swamp in New Orleans?"

It was Paul who said, "All of New Orleans is a swamp. Only a few spots are above sea level, you know."

Amy led to continue, "And since we expect Dad will let Lucas out in a few days, you need to lay in some supplies. Food. *Road & Track Maga*—"

"Tch. I don't know why he reads that. Do you know he drives some boxy minivan?"

"It's Paul. Is there a mattress in the back?"

Immediately Kali's face flushed, and she stammered, "What does that matter?"

"It doesn't, but that's how I set up my minivan when I was in my twenties. Glad the old traditions continue with this new generation. Good for Lucas. And good for you, my lady."

Amy rolled her eyes while Paul was talking. After he finished, she added, "He tried so hard to be a bad boy, bless his heart. Uh, I doubt what he said is true."

Never let the truth interfere with a good story! he replied silently. *I wanted a van. And if I had gotten one, I would have carpeted the back and put in a mattress. Put up a bumper sticker that said 'If this van's a-rockin', don't come a-knockin'. Really, I would have.*

"Your djinn, he's funny." She waved the sponge in the air, dreamy smile on her face. "And so is my bhang. You really don't feel it?"

Amy swallowed her annoyance. "I don't feel it because I didn't have it. Paul is fantasizing about redecorating a 1972 VW camper that he never owned because he did have it." She stood up. "I'm going to get the vodka. Would you like any?"

Kali shook her head. "You can add that to bhang, it changes how you feel."

"That's what I'm counting on," Amy said as she rummaged through the cupboard that Paul referred to as her liquor cabinet.

Amy let Paul lead to drive up South Carrollton Avenue and navigate the spaghetti roads that snaked underneath the Pontchartrain Expressway. The Enterprise rental was the nearest place to rent a vehicle. Otherwise, one had to go to the airport or to the tourist part of the CBD. As they got out of Amy's old yellow Benz, she was grilling Kali, "You're sure your car insurance covers a rental?"

"I believe so. I think so. Why would it not?"

"It might not if you didn't ask your agent to include it, that's why not."

"I think you worry too much. What do they call that? Borrowing trouble?"

Amy opened the door to the single-story, stand-alone building and let Kali walk ahead. As Amy followed, walking awkwardly with her cane, she responded, "You can't rent a car yourself because you're not old enough. I'm going to co-sign, which means I'm going to be financially responsible. And if there's no insurance, and you wreck it, I'm on the hook for a car I never owned or drove. You bet I'm borrow—"

"What's this about wrecking a car?" asked the nattily dressed young man behind the counter. "Will this be an insurance rental?"

"Oh, hello," Amy said to him. "Not an insurance rental. I'm here to help my ward rent a car."

"Your ward?" The thin black man was wearing a tweed jacket with narrow lapels, and a narrow red-and-blue striped tie. He turned to Kali. "You are a ward?"

"I do not know what that means," Kali answered. "I need to rent a car and my friend will help me."

"I'm sure I can find the right vehicle for you," and he went into his description of what was available.

"I like that little Kia," Kali whispered to Amy. She thought back to the woman, *You'll be ferrying Lucas back and forth to doctors and dialysis. You might want something bigger.*

"Oh. I guess so."

The clerk said, "Excuse me?"

Amy replied, "We need something bigger. Any SUVs?"

"Of course." As he reached for brochures under the sales counter, he added, "There is an upcharge for them."

Kali turned to Amy with alarm on her face. "I don't have a lot of money," she said.

"It's Paul. We've got you covered."

"Excuse me?"

"Family code," Amy said, shaking her head. Then, to Kali, "That one looks big enough. Lucas may have a wheelchair when Dad discharges him."

"Yes. Yes, this one," Kali jammed an index finger on the full-size Tahoe.

The clerk began rattling off the fees: daily rate, gasoline surcharge, under-age surcharge, insurance. "Or do you have insurance on your own car?"

"Yes. Georgia requires it."

"Good. If you have both collision and liability coverage, we can waive our charge."

"I have liability insurance, that's what the law says. What is the other?"

"Collision. It covers damage to your vehicle. Minus the deductible, of course."

Kali turned to Amy again. "Do I have collision?"

"It's Paul. I know many things, but not the answer to that."

"Amy?"

"Well, what kind of car do you have? If you're still paying for it, you probably have collision insurance."

"Oh, no. My daddy gave it to me when I got into Agnes Scott. It's a, a, a—" her face screwed into creases as she tried to remember "—a 2021. A Subaru."

The clerk tried to be helpful when he said, "Subarus hold their value, so many people keep collision on them. But this is 2030, and a lot of people drop collision for a car that old."

Paul thought to Amy, *Well, ain't that a huge help.*

"I don't know. Amy, djinn, I don't know." She looked as if she were approaching tears.

Amy asked the agent, "Can I put Kali on my insurance?"

He slid a desk phone around to her and said, "Call your agent. Add her to your collision policy and we'll work something out."

Amy picked up the handset and froze, thinking to Paul, *My Benz is ancient. I've never had collision insurance on it. And I don't think I could afford it, anyway.*

She replaced the handset on the cradle. "It occurs to me that I don't have collision insurance. It's a 2017 Benz."

The clerk took the phone back and put it on a shelf under the counter. "So, we're adding insurance to the charges?"

Paul thought to Amy, *I used to rent cars every time I came to New Orleans for research projects. Car rental insurance is a scam. Let me, okay?*

"Sure thing," and she withdrew to let Paul lead.

"We offer a million dollars' worth—"

"Just the waiver, thanks."

"But—"

"Just the waiver, thanks."

"No, really, you—"

Paul channeled Amy's mother Tracey, who could give actress Maggie Smith lessons at being imperious. "Don't make me say it again." He peered at the name badge on the man's tweed jacket. "Don."

"I don't think you understand what a bargain we're offering. One million—"

"Come on, Kali," Paul said, putting their arm around the woman's shoulder. "I think there's an Avis by the Superdome."

"No, no, wait!" the clerk called, coming out from behind the security of the sales counter. Somehow his necktie had gotten loose and pulled to one side. "I apologize, ma'am, really. Let's get you set up with the insurance waiver so your ward here can get on the road." He wore an ingratiating smile, one hand held out as if to help them walk back to the counter, the paperwork, and the cash register.

You are a genius! Amy thought.

Once safely behind the counter, the agent said, "Damage waiver, on a Tahoe, let's see..." he pulled some pages out from under the counter, "...we add that, and—" now he was pounding the buttons on his desk calculator "—we get, uh, $101.15 a day."

Paul said, "Make it one hundred, and ditch the mileage charge."

"Yes, ma'am," Don said, and he kept working the calculator.

What? Why didn't you negotiate my mortgage?

Paul thought back, *I didn't realize that this is my superpower.*

The clerk slid paperwork across the counter with instructions. Kali signed there, there, there, and there; Amy followed suit. Don straightened his tie, and took everything to the copier.

"Thank you," Kali said quietly. "But that's still one hundred dollars a day. I cannot afford that."

It was Amy who said, "It's only until you get your own car. Buying costs more up front, but it's cheaper in the long run. And you already have some kind of auto insurance."

Paul thought to the woman, *And now you'll be able to take care of Lucas better. Amy's got a business to run, you know.*

Kali's beautiful face sprouted a beautiful smile. "Thank you, djinn. And thank you, Amy." The three people in two bodies stood looking at one another while Don was making copies. And then Kali said, "You mentioned my father, Sanji. We lost my mother a few years ago, and Daddy still works too hard. He could use a good woman. When we can, let us all go to Atlanta and I'll introduce you."

Amy heard Paul's silent laughter. *My God, she's trying to set you up with her dad!*

I take it as a compliment, Amy thought back. *It could be a plan B if I can't get Jeffrey to come around.*

"Amy?" Kali was rubbing the toe of her right sandal back and forth on the floor in front of her.

"You are a sweetheart," Amy said. "I've got some irons in the fire here, but I'm touched that you think I'd be worthy of your father. Thank you." She leaned forward and kissed the woman's cheek, then hugged her. "Thank you," she repeated.

"That credit card," the clerk said as he returned with his paperwork, "and I'll have the Tahoe brought out for you."

In the parking lot, Kali sat behind the wheel of the rental but with the driver's door open. Amy was standing beside the car, bent a bit to peer inside. "You know how to work the GPS?" she asked.

"My car at home has one," Kali replied. "This seems to work the same way." She pushed buttons and the display flashed different screens. "What is your address? I'll enter it as 'home'."

Amy dictated her house number on Cherokee Street. Kali pushed more buttons and finally said, "There! The hospital?"

"I don't know what the address is, but it's on Esplanade at the Suburban Canal."

"My GPS works on intersections, let's see...Ah, yes. Got it."

"Good. Sorry to throw you in the deep end of the pool, Kali, but I've got to get going. You need to start getting the supplies we talked about. Then, this afternoon, come out to the hospital to see our boy."

"With chocolate shake. I promised him."

Paul said, "Chocolate shake, check. Bring two. If we give one to the nurse, she won't bust us for bringing in contraband."

Amy thought to the woman, *I don't know what grocers you have at home, but—*

"Publix. And Kroger."

Down here it's Rouses I'm partial to the one on Tchoupitoulas Street.

Kali nodded. She cranked the ignition, even with the driver's door still open. "Will you be with Lucas?" she asked.

"After a while, yes. Why?"

"I will see you at his hospital, then." She closed the door, waved through the window, and drove off in the rental.

It's not Lucas' hospital, Amy thought to Paul as she stood watching the Tahoe disappear down the street. *It's Dad's.*

"She'll learn. Shall we?"

"Oh, yes, kind sir," she laughed. "Let us perambulate to my father's emporium of health. You can drive."

"Where's Kali?"

It was the first thing Lucas said when Amy entered his hospital room. She thought to Paul, *Okay! He's on board. This is going to work.*

All he needs is a donor kidney. Uh, not one of ours, thanks.

"Good morning, Lucas. She'll be here later. This morning we rented her a car, and now she's rounding up supplies for when Dad discharges you."

His hair was combed, his bare cheeks showed a fresh shave, and he was wearing street clothes as he lay propped up on his hospital bed. He seemed more energetic than the day before, when Amy and Kali had visited right after a dialysis session. He said, "I'm still glad to see you."

"Aren't you a charmer," Amy responded as she sat on the edge of his bed. She leaned toward him to offer a hug, but his eyes grew wide and he put up his hands to keep her at some distance. "The port is in my chest," he offered. "It hurts when it gets pushed."

She sat back up straight. "It's Paul. Funny, you look absolutely normal."

A sigh. "I remember normal. My dad was alive. Grampa Doublet was alive. And my uncle loved me and wasn't trying to kill me."

"Paul again. Ah, those good old days. Fun times, fun times."

"What?" Lucas frowned at Amy.

"That was Paul. He has a mean sense of humor. Sometimes he lets it out. But I agree that you look nor—uh, you look regular now. No hoses coming out of you, no machine going 'beep.' Aren't you feeling better than last week?" She was patting his foot inside its Adidas.

"Well, yeah, I guess." He smiled. "Kali's here, that makes me feel good."

"She's bringing your chocolate shake."

Nurse Hee-hee-hee came into the room, pushing an empty wheel chair. "Hello again, Mister Lucas," she called. "Doctor Clear wants you in the hemo lab for tests. Oh, good morning, Miss Clear."

"I can walk," Lucas protested as he swung his legs off the other edge of his bed.

"I'm sure you can," the sister replied, as she placed her hands on his shoulders and steered him to the wheelchair, "but you're not going to. Hee-hee-hee." Lucas sputtered a bit, but he let the nurse sit him down.

"Sister Janet," Amy asked, "What's he going to do?"

"Bunch of blood tests," she said while she arranged the foot rests on the wheelchair and manhandled Lucas' legs. "I don't know why. The doctors never tell the nurses anything."

I remember your dad saying he never told his nurses anything. I guess he wasn't kidding.

"How long will he be gone?"

The nurse stood up, then arched her back, hands in fists at the small of her back. "Let me see—" she took the clipboard from the pocket on the back of the chair "—umm huh, umm huh. Oh, and he's going to get some IV antibiotic. I'll bring him back, umm, an hour?"

"Okay, that gives me time to say 'hi' to my dad." She turned to Lucas and let Paul lead. He said, "I hope you pass your blood test. Did you study?"

All these years and you still crack me up, Amy thought.

Lucas said, "That's him, isn't it?"

"Guilty as charged, Sport. Maybe Kali will be here with your chocolate shake when you get back."

"I do not know what you are talking about. Hee-hee-hee." Sister Janet wheeled Lucas out of the room and out of sight.

Are we really going to pester James?

Nuh-uh, Amy thought back. *He's probably real busy with patients. I'll see Dad if he makes rounds while I'm here.*

So Amy hobbled to a chair by the doorway. She flicked off the ceiling light, then settled in to watch some soap opera on the room's muted TV. *Which one's the wife and which one's the girlfriend?* she thought to Paul. She leaned her cane against the corner behind the open door.

I can't tell. I don't think it matters.

Will you look at them. Soap opera women make me feel ugly.

"No, no, no," he said aloud; then silently, *People like us make them look like weird freaks. Nobody in real life looks like them.*

"Kali."

Paul thought back, *Okay, so one person in real life looks like that. I think you look great. I love that tooth, you know.*

She sucked on her slanted front tooth, a souvenir of her parents' distrust of orthodontia. Actually, Paul wasn't the only man who had told her he liked it. And she knew A. Trauring was crazy about it.

A shadow fell into the room from just beyond where she could see outside the doorway. The promised hour had not passed, and there was none of Nurse Hee-hee-hee's typical chatter. *What have we here?* she thought to Paul, and they waited.

Quietly, in tennis shoes and a hooded sweatshirt, someone entered the room. They crept toward the gurney, their back to Amy. The figure leaned over the empty bed and pushed the hood back.

"Aren't you going to say hello to me? Jeffrey?"

Doublet spun around, shocked. In the dim light cast by the TV set, Amy saw he was holding a pillow covered in plastic wrap. She heard Paul think, *If I was going to smother someone, that's the kind of gear I'd use.*

Amy turned on the floor lamp on her left, letting her see how swollen and black-and-blue Jeffrey's face was. Paul thought to her, *Boy, I did a number on him. Sweet.* She patted the chair on her right and said, "Let's talk. I won't bite."

Cautiously, he turned and backed in to the seat. Amy thought to Paul, *Keep your hand on Rosckette, but don't shoot him unless he's trying to kill me, okay?* She was smiling broadly at the man who wouldn't meet her gaze for more than a second. Instead he looked down at the pillow he was still holding. After several seconds of silence he dropped it on the floor beside his chair.

"I don't care that you're Jeffrey. I got to know <u>you</u>. I like you. Uh, all except the crazy knife fight in the kitchen. Have you cleaned up that mess yet? It was foul."

He said nothing. He parked his hands in his armpits, arms folded in front of his chest.

Amy went on, "You said you had everything planned. What kind of mushroom did you feed Lucas? He's your nephew, not your son."

Finally, he spoke. "Fool's Webcap. And I'm pretty sure he really is my son. I love Sammie. Every now and then I would pretend to be Ryan and go to her. I don't think I ever fooled her."

"It's Paul. Lucas said she insisted on calling you Jeffrey when y'all went to Jackson together."

"Yeah," and a smile grew between swollen lips. "They think she's crazy so no one there believes her." Then, "You can stop playing with this 'left-handed you' shit."

So Paul thought directly to him, with his man's voice, *Watch your language, twerp. There's a lady present and she's not me. Am I real or are you hallucinating?*

When she saw surprise bloom on Jeffrey's face, Amy said, "I hate when he does that," out loud. "What did Paul say? I can't hear him when he does that."

He turned in the seat. "You know, I think you're crazy, too. What if I tell people that you think you can talk to me without speaking?"

A smile. She thought to him, *What if I tell people you think you can hear me do it?*

He frowned and narrowed his eyes, staring at her.

She put her right hand on his arm. "It's okay, Jeffrey. The only reason Paul and I beat you up is because you pulled a knife. If you never do anything like that again, I promise I won't shoot you. Is that a deal?"

Amy heard Paul think, *What? Are you serious? You're really trying to be nice to him? Can't we find you a man who doesn't kill his brother, or try to kill the son he sires with his sister-in-law? Please?*

Jeffrey didn't know why Amy laughed, but he began to jiggle his legs nervously. He was blinking as fast as his heart was beating.

"A deal?" She leaned forward and tried to look up at his turned away face.

"I don't understand you," he finally said. "I know you carry a gun; I watched you shoot that snake. You could have killed me the other day. I'm glad you didn't, although I wish you hadn't kept hitting me with that broomstick. Why don't you hate me?"

"Do you hate me?"

He started to smile. "A little. But only a little."

"Great!" Amy leaned over to kiss the man, but he turned his head and her lips landed on his ear. Embarrassed, she sat up again. "Tell me about Ryan," she began. "Did you hate him?"

"Yes. No. Well, yes and no. He was the golden boy. To Dad, I was like the faithful son— he took me for granted. He never cooked the fatted calf for me."

Paul heard Amy think, *I get that! Sister Agnetha would be so proud of me.*

Out loud, to Jeffrey, she said, "How did he commit suicide in your house?"

"Most of what I told you is true. Ryan was terribly depressed after Lucas ran off. He drank way too much, he abandoned his job, he owed a ton of money to everyone from Iberville Bank to New Orleans Gas Light." Jeffrey shifted in the chair; it wasn't often he allowed himself to think about his brother. "He spent maybe three weeks saying he should kill himself. Even the part of me that loved him wanted to smack him." He turned to Amy with a creepy smile on his face. "So one night I decided to help him out of his misery. He was too much of a coward to do it on his own. I offered to help, and he said 'yes.'" Frowning, he went on, "It's what you'd do if your dog was that far gone. It was a mercy, I tell you what."

Well, that's not what I expected, Paul thought to Amy. *You really want to stay close to someone who doesn't know the difference between his brother and his dog?*

Softly, Amy said, "I just can't imagine it. Wanting to die." Shaking her head, "I hope I never understand it."

"Yeah. Me, neither, actually."

After a long pause Jeffrey said, "So, you're not going to arrest me? Shoot me? Turn me in?"

"I'm not a cop anymore," she answered. "And Melanie Goode doesn't care because Lucas is her client, not you or Ryan." She put a hand on his arm again and went on, "As long as you don't try to hurt Lucas, and you don't try to hurt me, I'm good."

Jeffrey nodded slowly. In his silence Amy heard Paul think, *You're not going to change him. That's fairy tale crazy. Killers kill; that's what they do.*

"Hush," she whispered, still touching Jeffrey.

"You're serious, aren't you? I mean, that—that guy in your head? You think he's real?"

Nodding, she answered, "Oh, I know he's real. Even if I am crazy, I haven't stabbed any babies, and you love Sammie."

He laughed.

"So, tell me, why were you coming to visit Lucas with a pillow covered in Saran Wrap?"

While she was asking they heard gurney wheels in the hallway getting louder and louder. Sister Janet, a/k/a Nurse Hee-hee-hee, was saying, "...and I'll have to wake you up to give you a sleeping pill. Hee-hee-hee. You like that?" Lucas was still as the sister brought him back from his blood tests and intravenous antibiotic session. "Oh, look, my boy," the nurse said, "You got company. My, is that your daddy? And there's your girlfriend." She bent over and easily transferred him from the gurney to his hospital bed.

Lucas recognized the man he now understood was his uncle. He was quiet but tense, and very watchful.

The nurse said, "Mister Lucas has done his work for today, hee-hee-hee. I'll check back in a little while, okay?" and she left the room; they could hear her "Hee-hee-hee, hee-hee-hee" fading as she walked back to the nurse's station.

"Hello, boy. How are you doing?"

Lucas sat up on his bed, with his legs pulled up and his knees under his chin. "Uncle Jeffrey. Are you going to try to kill me again?"

Easy, Lucas, she thought to him. *I'm negotiating with him. You're safe while I'm here.*

Jeffrey ignored the boy's response. He stood up, an angry look on his face. "God damn. God damn it to hell," he muttered. He turned to Amy and wagged his index finger at her, but seemed to change his mind about saying something.

"Don't go!" Amy called, and she reached her right hand out toward him. "We're just getting comfortable again."

Jeffrey's frown turned into a scowl. Amy took her cane and began the process of standing up. "You need to know I will be here all the time. I will not let you hurt Lucas again."

He pushed his palm against Amy's chest and knocked her back into the chair. "And God damn you, too!" he snarled, then left the room.

Lucas began shouting, "I hate you! You killed Dad! You tried to kill me!" at his uncle, even after the man had disappeared out of the hospital room.

Amy struggled back to her feet to follow Jeffrey. "Lock your door and make sure you know who's knocking before you let anyone in." With that she turned her attention to pursuit. Limping into the hallway, she saw Jeffrey open the exit door to the stairwell. *I hope he's going down the stairs,* Paul thought to her. *Our leg hurts too much to go up them.*

Amy called to the nurse's station, a rare raised voice in an environment of hushed tones. "Sister Janet! Call security! Call police!" Then she went out the same doorway Jeffrey had used.

"Shhh," Paul said. "Is he up or down?" They listened.

They heard heavy, fast footsteps from above. The paces stopped; there was the sound of Jeffrey trying the locked door to the fifth floor, and his "Shit!" The heavy, fast footsteps resumed as the man climbed higher.

Do we have to follow him? Paul moaned silently. *Our leg really hurts. Isn't there an elevator?*

She thought back, *We'd risk losing him. Hold this,* and she put her cane in their left hand. She grabbed the railing with her right hand and began working her way up the stairs. It took a few steps before she found the rhythm of hauling her body up with the least pain to her cut calf, but even so, her progress was anything but rapid. Jeffrey's pounding footsteps cast more of an echo as he got farther ahead of her, but she still heard him try the door to the sixth and seventh floors, with the same one word of frustration. She knew the seventh was the top floor of her father's hospital; only the roof was beyond that. The sound of Jeffrey's strides changed as he went from concrete to the metal stairs that finished the stairwell. She heard him open a door, and a rush of wind told her he had made it to the rooftop.

Out loud, Paul said, "Wait a minute. The cane—"

I need it! she shouted silently.

"The crook," he went on. "Can we put it in our belt? Around our neck? I'm afraid I'll lose it."

Amy stopped. She didn't like the way the cane felt hooked around her neck, so she put it over her left shoulder, with the shaft on her back. She went up a few steps to see if it would stay without harming her. "Better," Paul said. "Now I can get Rosckette if I need to."

Glad you're happy, she thought back to him as she resumed her slow climb. *I hope all of the doors on the roof are locked.*

"Wait. How will we get back down?"

I figure either he'll throw me off the roof, which would take care of that—

"Is that the good news or the bad news?" Paul asked.

—or Sister Hee-hee-hee will call John Law like I asked her to and we'll have plenty of company after a while.

"I vote for option number two."

Amy said, "Me, too."

She didn't bother to try the door to the fifth floor when she passed it. *Dad took me up to the roof one time to watch the Fourth of July fireworks,* she thought. *You know—I couldn't have been seven or eight. Hah! I remember something from before you came to me.* She put her weight on their right hand, on the stair railing, as she took the next step with their right foot; then threw her weight onto their left foot for the next step. The shaft of the cane bounced on their back. Each step made the stitched cut on their right leg throb, but it was bearable.

Do you miss being a police detective? Paul thought to her.

"I hate to say it, but yes." She concentrated on the next right step, then added, "I wish I could flash a badge and arrest Jeffrey. All I can do now—" another right step "—is a citizen's arrest. That's a good way to get in trouble."

Will it help if I shoot him?

"Listen to me!" she barked out loud. Another right step. Silently, *If he's not trying to kill me, don't even think about Rosckette. I'm trying to work something out with him.*

They passed the sixth floor. Amy kept going, slowly, methodically. Hand rail, right foot, then left foot; hand rail, right foot, then left foot.

They passed the seventh floor and turned to the galvanized metal stairs that led up to the roof. Paul said, "Tactics. When we open the door up there, we should have our gun drawn. Just in case Jeffrey is waiting to greet us."

Amy twisted their mouth while she considered it. "You're right. But as soon as I see everything is okay, you holster Rosckette.

Agreed?"

She heard him sigh silently. *Agreed.*

The metal stairs clanged and echoed as Amy worked her way to the top landing. She took her cane back in her right hand, and waited while Paul retrieved their pistol from the hip holster.

"Ready?"

"Ready."

Amy turned the doorknob, then used the cane to swing the door out. She felt a warm breeze, and smelled vaguely fish-scented moisture from Lake Pontchartrain. The sky was a hazy pale blue. She heard street traffic, and air conditioning condensers, and birds.

She bumped up the final step and threw their back against the inside of the open metal door, pistol pointed toward the non-existent assailant who was not waiting beside the doorway. A deep breath and she moved to the latch side of the open doorway, holding the gun toward the equally-not-there enemy hiding behind the door. Finally she took two steps onto the roof, weapon poised for the cunning adversary who, as it turned out, was not hovering over the doorway, ready to swoop down on her; and it was only his non-being that saved him from having his incorporeal body ventilated by several 9mm slugs.

Okay, Amy thought to him, *put Rosckette away. Where the hell is Jeffrey?*

"Do you hear anything?" he asked aloud.

"I hear a car horn. I hear footsteps." She paused to listen carefully. "Definitely footsteps. Over there."

She turned, back to the now-closed door for cover. The north section roof was punctuated by air conditioning units, elevator motor houses, satellite antennas, and a utilities room; about sixty feet away was the south section, somehow a few feet higher.

Amy moved sideways, keeping the raised doorway behind her so Jeffrey couldn't sneak up from behind. To the left, the end of the building was ten feet away. Another turn, maybe forty feet of black gritty roofing material, the large white cross marking the helipad landing site, and a man standing almost at the parapet and looking away.

"Oh, there you are," she called. "Why did you run away, you bad boy? I want to talk to you." Cane in hand, she began to limp toward Jeffrey.

He was silent until she was just a few feet away. "Why are you doing this?" he asked softly. He still was facing away from her.

"Because I like you, you dumb lunk," she smiled. "You're great company when you're not trying to kill me or Lucas." Using her cane, she limped to stand between him and the parapet so they could face each other.

Jeffrey blinked. "I don't understand. You guessed that I fed Lucas a poisonous mushroom. And you know good and well why I came here today."

"Yes. Stop it. Don't try to hurt him anymore. I like him."

"And Ryan?"

Amy looked down, tapping the cane on the top of her right foot. "Medical examiner said he hanged himself. You're off the hook. And I guess I don't care."

She took one gamey step toward Jeffrey, and he stepped back one pace. Amy said, "As long as I feel safe, I'm not going to cause any trouble. So, make sure I feel safe."

When he didn't respond for several seconds, Amy added, "And I don't feel safe standing on a rooftop with you until we finish this conversation."

"This doesn't make any sense," Jeffrey said, his battered face crunched in confusion. "You sound like you're propositioning me."

"Well, yes. Yes, I guess I am."

She heard Paul think, *You what? Are you crazy? Amy, hello?*

Jeffrey's eyes popped as wide as the swelling would allow. "My God, woman. Why?"

"I'm not very good at this," she said, nervously shuffling her cane from one hand to the other. "I have bad taste in men—I mean, you're kind of living proof—and I have trouble making things last." She took a deep breath. "I—I'm comfortable with you. I like being with you." She looked up at him and smiled. "I still want you."

"Even though I helped one man die and tried to kill another?"

"I've killed more than two. Of course, all of those were legal. No, as long as you stop doing that, I'm okay. You've got a past. I hope you've got a future."

Silently Paul screamed, *Amy!* He heard her think back, *Shush.*

Jeffrey rubbed his chin. "So, you're saying that, as long as I behave myself, you still want to, to be with me?"

"Yes!" She was smiling. "Yes, Jeffrey, yes. What do you say?"

No! Paul shouted, silently. *He's just admitted he killed Ryan and you want to marry him?*

The man looked uncomfortable. "I don't know. This is just too weird," Jeffrey said. "This includes that left-handed you?"

No, it doesn't, Paul thought directly to him. *She's crazy to do this.*

Jeffrey smiled. "Your other half doesn't sound on board about this."

"Oh, crap," she said, rolling her eyes. "Give me a minute." Then she thought to Paul, *What is your problem? Don't you want me to be happy?* She turned around to concentrate on their silent conversation.

If it's got to be one or the other, he thought back, *I'd rather see you alive.*

"It's my decision to make," she barked out loud, and stamped her left foot. Silently she went on, *It's too bad if you—*

It took her a couple of seconds to realize it was Jeffrey tackling her from behind that threw her down to the rooftop. The sand in the roofing paper ripped the scabs off her palms, and made her knees hurt. She felt Jeffrey climbing along her back until he was over her, knees on her buttocks, trying to wrap his hands around her neck. He was shouting, but even though his mouth was only inches from their ears, she couldn't make sense of the sounds.

Can I pull Rosckette now, boss? Paul thought to her.

Amy threw her right arm back, elbow extended, and hit Jeffrey in the stomach. "Yes!" she shouted to Paul out loud. She tried to fishtail her body to get out from under the man, flailing her legs with no regard to the pain. The man's weight suddenly left her back, and abruptly she felt him grab her by the armpits and lift her up. Jeffrey was pushing her toward the parapet.

She held out her right hand as a decoy, so that Jeffrey might be distracted long enough for Paul to draw Rosckette. He spun her around so they were face-to-face, his intent, wide eyes only inches from hers. "Get down!" he growled at her.

Paul got the gun clear of the holster, but before he could think about aiming Jeffrey had thrown them back. The top edge of the parapet struck Amy across the shoulder blades and knocked the wind from them. Jeffrey grabbed for the gun; he and Paul wrestled for it, someone fired a wild shot, and they heard the sound of metal bouncing off the top of the wall that separated the rooftop from seven stories of oblivion. Two seconds later came the faint thud of a pound-and-a-half of steel hitting the sidewalk beside the hospital.

Another sound rapidly overtook it. The whump-whump-whump of the Angel Flight helicopter got louder as it hovered over the helipad, the rotors kicking up a wind that blew roof grit and bird feathers everywhere. Amy shut her eyes to protect them from all the particles swirling in the air, but she couldn't save her ears from the air pressure changes caused by the 'copter blades.

He wanted to throw me off the roof! she thought to Paul. *You may be right. Crap. Double crap.*

Jeffrey sprang back, hands over his eyes, rubbing at the irritating grit. Without him holding her against the parapet, she slid down and sat on the roof, trying to catch her breath. She heard voices—people on the helicopter shouting something she couldn't quite hear—as the Angel Flight slowly lowered itself to the big white X of the helipad.

Four people jumped out of the vehicle, then carefully passed a litter from the passenger compartment down to the rooftop. The immobile lump under the blanket was child sized.

We don't want to fight in front of an audience, Amy thought to Jeffrey.

She slowly stood up, squinting as the rotors, now in low gear, continued to whip the air. Then she heard Paul think, *Let's follow them. I think they have a key.* Without her cane, and after the walk up the stairwell and the fight with Jeffrey, Amy hobbled slowly. "Hey! Hey!" she called, but the paramedics did not hear her. Still, she limped as fast as she could to reach what she imagined would be the safety of the group.

A hand on her shoulder spun her around to face Jeffrey. His eyes were bright red from the grit blown by the helicopter. "We're not done," he shouted over the noise of the rotors.

"I am," she yelled back. "You were going to throw me off the roof! It's bad enough I know you want Lucas dead, but trying to kill me—that's a deal breaker. Congratulations, Jeffrey, you managed to make me stop liking you. I'll never forgive you for that."

The noise from the helicopter rotor continued, as did the flying debris. "Lucas has to die," he screamed back. "Ryan owed money to everyone and his uncle. I need Dad's money to settle up."

Amy stepped back, away from the man. "I won't let you hurt him. I'm taking him."

"I'll find you," he shouted, following her.

"Hey! What are you doing?" A hospital security guard was in the raised doorway, some twenty feet behind Amy.

Slowly, Jeffrey backed away from Amy, and away from the guard. "I'll find you," he shouted again, "I'll find Lucas. You can't hide."

Still squinting against the helicopter-induced wind, Amy watched the man she thought she could have learned to love slowly get smaller as he continued to back away. He was about to say something when she saw a red halo around his head.

She rubbed her eyes. The halo was gone, as was Jeffrey Doublet's head. Blood and goo from the rear rotor splashed her face and chest. "Oh, my God," she shouted, while Paul silently yelled the exact same words. They heard the guard, just a few steps away, vomit on the rooftop.

She shook herself, then limped to the guard. "You okay?" she asked, bending down on her right knee and touching the man's back.

Paul thought to her, *Jeffrey's the one who needs help.*

He's beyond help, Amy thought back. *I can try to make this guy feel better.*

It was a few minutes before the medical crew came back to the roof. The guard, sitting next to Amy, shouted at them. The crew members looked at each other, puzzled, but came to where they sat.

Amy shouted, "Turn your helicopter off, okay?" She had slipped back into police mode.

"Uh, no, miss. We have to get back to our home base."

She shook her head. "Wait for the police. There's a guy over there who walked into the rotor."

The medic ran to Jeffrey's body, then turned away. He motioned to the rest of his crew to gather by Amy and the guard. She saw him lean in to say something to one of them; that one took a roundabout route to avoid the gore, and climbed into the cockpit to switch the engine off. Abruptly it was quiet and still on the roof.

Amy heard her phone ringing, so she dug it out of her back pocket. "Where the fuck have you been?" she heard, with the echo of a speakerphone. "I've been calling you for an hour."

"Hi, Melanie. It's been noisy here, I couldn't hear anything. What's up?"

"Got a job for you. A gentleman has been charged with making explosive devices, I need to know if he did it or not."

"Oh. Sure, I can do that."

"Get your ass here, I want to go over it with you."

Work! Amy shouted silently to Paul. Then she looked down at her gore-spattered shirt. "I better shower first."

"I don't care if you smell like the Saints' locker room, I know traffic is bad this hour of the day, but I want you here now."

"I'm kind of covered in homicidal boyfriend, it's going—"

"Stop bragging about your sex life!" the lawyer shouted. "If you want the job you'll be here an hour ago!"

"Mel, stop! Jeffrey Doublet just got killed and I'm waiting on Jefferson Parish police to get here." She bent over to scratch where the stiches in her calf itched. "They have first claim, you know that."

"Arrrgh!"

"Melanie?"

The lawyer said, "Call me if they arrest you. And if they don't, be here in the morning so I can brief you on this new client."

"Thanks, Mel. You're the best."

"Oh, go to hell. You, you, you better—you better—Arrgh," and she hung up.

Amy clearly had trouble standing. One of the paramedics grabbed her left arm and helped her up. "We need another cane," Paul said out loud.

The security guard said, "I've called the police. I think we all need to wait right here until they show up."

"Well done," Amy told the man. "I used to be an Orleans Parish police detective. You did the right thing." And turning to the Angel Flight crew, who were wishing they were anywhere but stuck on a rooftop at 12 noon on a New Orleans July day, she added, "If anyone leaves, the police assume they did the crime on purpose." The man who had turned off the helicopter engine shook his head, but he remained sitting in the black tar grit.

The hospital security guard said, "You're Doctor Clear's girl, right? I don't remember you having freckles," he observed. "And maybe you should change clothes."

"Oh, yes. Just as soon as I get home." Paul added, "I'll take a bath in Clorox. Yuck!" Then silently he thought to Amy: *I can't wait to tell Christine about this. She'll beg us to stop doing detective work, or at least limit ourself to lost dogs.* Amy heard his chuckle, and he finished, *I love how she thinks we're so brave. No—she knows we're so brave.* A pause. *You're so brave. You are, you know.*

Thanks for the reminder. I've got to tell Lucas he's safe. And Kali. Her phone was still in her hand, so she opened her contacts. She pushed a few buttons and waited for an answer.

"Hello?" The world could be ending, twelve-foot tall aliens methodically laying waste to everyone and everything on your street, but if your phone rang, you'd answer it with "Hello?"

"Lucas, it's Amy. You need—"

"What happened?" he yelled down the phone line. "Are you alright? Did you catch Uncle Jeffrey?"

"You are safe," she said, slowly. "Jeffrey is dead, and you are safe."

"Uncle Jeffrey dead?" It was barely a whisper. After all, the boy now was an orphan.

"Yes. I'm up on the roof of the hospital waiting for the police. When Kali gets there—"

"Does she know? She's not here yet."

"No, sir, you get to break the news to her." "It's Paul. Now you don't have to worry whether your relatives will like her."

Paul! That's just cruel.

There was a commotion at the doorway to the roof. "I have to ring off, Lucas; the police are here now. I'll try to visit when they're done with me, but I don't know how long this will take."

There was a long pause, where she heard the faint sound of his TV speaker. "Lucas?"

"Thank you for rescuing me, Amy. Promise me something. Promise me you won't die."

Paul laughed and answered, "That's not really in the cards. But it won't be today, that I can promise."

Amy took a last look across the roof, to the now-still helicopter and the bloody remains of her client and former boyfriend. Silently she said to Paul, *I've seen lots of dead people. This is gross, but it's not a lot worse than the stuff that got wheeled into dad's ER when he used to take me to work with him.* She shook her head and turned toward the propped-open doorway to face the four Jefferson Parish police officers and two EMTs, all squinting in the sun. *This won't be real until I get home.*

Then what? Paul asked.

I think... I think then I scream. A lot. What about you?

Too late, Paul thought back. *I can't tell what I'm feeling the most. Horrified? Grossed out? Sorry for you that it didn't work out?*

The EMT personnel ran past Amy and the Angel Flight people to face the task of dealing with Jeffrey Doublet's body. They were wearing day-glo yellow vests over black shirts that sported EMS patches.

The lead officer opened a small notepad and said to one of the Angel Flight crew members, "Are you in charge here?" Amy heard Paul laugh silently and think, *The joy of being a woman. The cops will hassle all those men before they bother with me.*

Amy nodded. Stiffly, without her cane for help, Amy sat on the gritty roof next to the hospital guard and waited for the standard police procedure to slowly make its way to her.

Crap and a half. I may be ready for you to marry Christine.

ᛉ Coming soon from Amy and Paul ᛉ
The Razor And The Gun

Her driver's side door wasn't closed yet when her tires squealed and she headed out into and down Richmond Place toward her idea of safety: some place where the lights were on, where seemingly nice people didn't wave guns around, and where adults knew better than to worry about a boogieman. Out loud Paul said, "I'm afraid Cody's lost a customer."

He holstered my Ruger and zipped it closed. We stood in the dim, chilly December afternoon, looking at the place where Miriam's car had been. "It's nice to relax," I said to the world.

Suddenly my back and butt felt warm. Before I could comprehend that unexpected change, and just about the time Paul was thinking *Uh-oh spaghetti-o*, I felt hot and cold—hot breath on the side of my neck, and cold steel at my neck.

"Don't move, sweetheart."

I recognized the voice. It was LY.

"You and me, we're going to wait for George. I've got a little something for him."

Shoot him! I heard Paul shout silently. *We can end this!*

As much as I love Paul, and even though he's the one who taught me to shoot and handle guns safely, he was never in law enforcement; in fact, although he's never explained the details to me, it seems he spent some time in his youth evading the law. People who don't get immersed in firearms skills mistakenly think a gun is an all-purpose tool, like an umpteen blade Swiss army knife. No. A chainsaw is a wonderful tool, but not when you're climbing a ladder. A hammer is great, but not when you're dealing with screws. And a gun is no help when a badguy with a straight razor has the drop on you. *I could shoot him,* I thought to Paul, *and his dying reflex would slit my throat and I'd die on top of him. We wait for a better moment.*

Oh. I'm glad he takes me seriously. He listens. Have I mentioned how I love—

"Introduce me to your friends," LY said, as he began pushing me toward those marble steps and the front door that I foolishly had left standing open. "I've got a score to settle with you and that limping guy."

I hoped I wasn't too far away from that limping guy when I thought *Cody! LY has me. Hide so he doesn't find you. Later you can surprise him and take him down.* After all, he heard me last night when I thought to him up in his bedroom.

"So, how's the bar business these days?" Paul said. I'd never have tried to provoke the man holding a razor to my throat. He has different ideas of negotiating tactics.

"Shut up, bitch!" LY growled as he pushed me up the stairs. "You and that friend of yours are the reason I'm broke and on the run. I could kill you for it." He pushed some more. "I can kill you for it."

Paul thought, *He's in for a shock when George and Duke get here.* I answered, *I hope I'm still alive to see it.*

I thought of something else Cody could do while he was hiding, assuming he heard me think to him from outside the house. *Call George. Have him tell Duke LY's holding me hostage with a razor and is waiting on your dad.* Duke and I had worked some nasty cases together and we saved each other's lives—a common enough story for working cops or detectives. I trust him. If anyone can get me out of this in one piece, it's Duke Cranston.

LY pushed me up the steps. Paul thought, *He's shorter than we are. He's having trouble keeping his razor in the danger zone while we're going up stairs.*

Maybe he'll make me climb a ladder inside. Then I can take him.

Sure! Paul enthused. *If a ceiling light blows, you can climb the— oh, right, he cut the power. Never mind.* I swear, if I were being marched to a hangman's noose, Paul could make me laugh over the trapdoor. It takes a morbid sense of humor to get through things like this. Well, it's our way of doing it.

Once we were inside, LY kept shoving and marching me toward the light of the hurricane lantern in the kitchen. Donna was alone, but she was holding a regular drinking glass that seemed to be half-full. On the island counter-top was an open bottle of Chateau Bayou Rouge. Paul said out loud, "Wine? We've got company. Get some more glasses."

"Shut up!" LY barked, and pushed me down onto one of the chairs. The razor stung at my neck, and I felt a drop of blood bead up.

"Who are you?" he said to Donna, in a remarkably calm and social tone.

She drained the glass and put it back on the counter top. "I'm Eustacia," she said. "Who are you?"

"Oh, call me LY. Do you have another glass? May I have some of your wine?"

Amazing, Paul thought. *He sounds like this is a Rotary Club social.*

Without speaking, Donna retrieved a wine glass from one of the cabinets and brought it to the island.

"Could I trouble you to pour me some?" He chuckled. "My hands are busy."

Can we think to Donna? I mean, without freaking her out?

I thought about that. When I worked with Duke on a few cases I convinced him I was the best ventriloquist in the world. Did that with Lieutenant Kowalski, too. But at the start they always were startled and confused.

Then I had an idea.

Since LY was standing behind me, he couldn't see my face. So I mouthed the words I thought to Donna, hoping she'd think I was whispering. *Donna, he can't hear me like this. Did Cody hide?—show me your palm if it's yes. Back of your hand for 'no.'*

A small smile flew across her face while she poured wine for my captor. As she put the bottle back on the counter top she held her right hand up, palm out.

Caleb too?

She rubbed her cheek with the back of her hand, showing me her palm.

What's going on? Paul thought to me. I explained my little ruse, to which he silently expressed vulgar and obscene approval.

"Excellent wine," LY said pleasantly, "thank you. I appreciate it. Now, tell me, do you have some clothesline I can use? Rope? I'd hate to have to rip up your towels."

"Rip up...what on earth are you talking about?" Donna asked. I think there was as much curiosity as anger in her voice.

"Why, I have to tie you up. And this lady here," tapping me lightly on the top of my head.

I was surprised to hear Paul say, "No."

"What?" LY moved his razor and I felt another drop of blood bead up. Oh, crap, he was going to get blood on my UNO sweatshirt. That's a tough stain to remove. Of course, if he went much deeper with that razor, mom and dad could just bury me in it.

Paul! I shouted silently. *This man wants to kill us! Don't provoke him!*

I've died once, he replied. *Next time I die I'll be on my feet, not on my knees.*

"I don't remember asking for your opinion," LY said, and his pleasant social voice was replaced by a raspy snarl. He took the razor away, then clamped his other arm around my neck. He looked up at Donna and said, "Rope. Now."

"No!" Paul said again. LY tightened his grip on my throat.

"You know I can kill you right here," he hissed in my ear.

"Then what?" Paul croaked.

I saw Donna's face go pale. I knew she didn't want to see a bloody mess all over her kitchen, but there was something else in her expression. I started to think to Paul, *What is she—*

"Stop." It was Cody's voice!

I could feel LY turn, probably to look at the source of the voice. His grip on me loosened just a little, so I was able to turn, too. Cody was no more than six feet away, holding my revolver with both hands, but shaking uncontrollably, like an opened can of cranberry sauce on a Thanksgiving platter. I heard Paul think, *Oh no! He looks like the kid at the beginning of* Pulp Fiction. *We're all gonna die.*

"Well, what have we here?" LY drawled. He extended his free hand, razor outstretched, toward Cody.

Cody's eyes were darting everywhere: LY, me, his mother, me, the clock. *This is not going to work*, I thought to Paul.

At which point Donna landed a rolling pin on the side of LY's head. It made a satisfying *thunk!* and some blood spurted, and L-Y dropped to the floor like, well, like he'd just been pole-axed. Paul said, "Williams Sonoma needs a customer testimonial from you."

Cody fell into a chair, letting my revolver fall to the floor; I was guessing his adrenalin was spent.

Freed from LY's sharpened steel, I knelt by the chair where Cody sat. "You are one brave man," I said, putting my hands around his available arm. "You saved me."

Very softly he said, "I have never been so scared in my life." Paul thought, *It showed.*

"Courage isn't the absence of fear," I counseled. "It's doing what needs to be done even when you're terrified. You are my hero," and I hugged his arm.

Donna was on the wall phone. From her end of the conversation I was glad to hear she was talking to Orleans Parish police. Good. The sooner they got LY out of here, the sooner we could call an electrician to fix what the son-of-a-bitch broke.

"Hey," I asked, "Where's Caleb?"

Donna chuckled, "He went out the back door. He may be in Arkansas by now." Then she turned to her gas range. "I'll make some coffee while we're waiting." She moved the hurricane lamp to have a better view of the jars in her cabinet.

"It's over, Cody," I said. "You were brave to distract LY. And your mom was brave to whack him. Thanks."

He finally opened his eyes, looking down to where I sat next to his chair. "I need to know—is every day with you like this?"

Paul laughed and said, "More than I like, but no, not very often at all."

"It's Amy. And with this job done, now I'm out of work."

He leaned over and planted a warm, wet, wonderful kiss on my lips. *Yes,* I thought to him. *Yes yes yes.*

Balanced against that physical warmth was a cold spot on the nape of my neck. As I heard LY growl something unpleasant, Paul said, "Oh, great. Our spare revolver. The one Cody dropped." Cody's head jerked up, and he kicked his chair away from me.

Slowly I turned to face LY. He kept the gun barrel pressed against my head the entire time, until it was fixed to my forehead while I looked at him. His eyes were all pupils, all black. Just like his heart.

"Now what?" Paul asked.

"Now we wait for George to come home. Then I kill you all."

"Now, young man!" Donna blurted.

When he swiveled to point the weapon at her, I threw my right arm up against his gun hand. By reflex he pulled the trigger, putting a .38 caliber hole in the kitchen ceiling. You always forget how LOUD it is when a gun goes off indoors, but it makes your ears tighten up and interferes with your hearing for a while. Sometimes it even hurts. Like now.

At that point it turned into a wrestling match between LY and me. I'm taller than him, but he's probably got sixty pounds on me. And he still had my revolver. So I did what any well-mannered retired little-lady police detective would do: I bit his gun hand. I mean, bit it hard enough to taste blood. He shouted, although it sounded like a muffled cough, and the gun fell to the hardwood floor. Cody kicked it away and then piled on me and LY. There was a vague buzz in the background that I took to be Donna screaming and wailing. I hoped she still had a good grip on that rolling pin.

Shoot him! Paul screamed silently. Ah, another thing people without law enforcement or combat training don't realize is that at close quarters, there is no such thing as *your* gun. In a hand-to-hand melee like I was in, it's *all y'all's* gun; it's impossible to be sure of your control of a weapon when your opponent isn't even six inches away from you. *Don't draw,* I shouted back at Paul.

Do men understand how much it hurts to get punched in a boob? Ouch! I mean, OUUUUCHH!

LY twisted to face Cody, who was a bigger physical threat to him. I threaded my right arm in front of him, and managed to raise it up to his neck. Then I had my right hand grab my left shoulder for leverage, and began squeezing the man's throat. *That serial killer at UNO Lakeside,* I thought to Paul, *the detective said just five pounds of pressure in the right place could kill someone*[18].

Yeah. This would qualify as self-defense, he thought back. *But I still want to shoot the fucker.*

Apparently my pressure was not it the right place, because LY wasn't dying. He squirmed, he kicked, he parried the punches Cody was throwing at him, he was gurgling, but he was definitely conscious and alive.

I squeezed harder.

More gurgling. Cody continued to pound him.

I squeezed as hard as I could; I thought my left shoulder was going to fall off.

---

[18] Paul's West Virginia Boy Scout troop may have taught him about quarterstaff (see *The Strawberry Birthmark*), but not judo. Amy didn't know the detective had talked about 'blood choke,' and she really didn't know how to apply it. No wonder it didn't work.

Even more weird sounds from him. And then Cody planted a roundhouse against his jaw.

At that L-Y stopped struggling.

Out of breath, I managed to wheeze, "Donna." Pant. "That rope." Pant.

Cody hoisted himself up to his knees, and lifted the limp LY off me. He threw the man down on the floor beside me and landed a gratuitous punch on his nose. LY didn't respond, unless you consider starting to bleed a response.

With LY's weight off me, I caught my breath. "Cody. Great. But stop hitting him, he's down." Even if you're into punishing an opponent, what's the punishment if they are unconscious and can't feel the pain you're inflicting?

Cody let himself fall onto the floor on the other side of me, facing up and breathing heavily. "I can't believe it. I can't believe what I just did." He turned his head to look at me, our noses only inches apart. "I can't believe what you've done."

"Yes," I said. "You were great. I'm—I'm proud of you, Cody. Thank you." I pushed my face forward and kissed him.

Donna cleared her throat. "The police should be here any minute. I want to clean up this mess before they get here."

Sheepish, I looked around. Chairs were on their backs and sides, and there were blood spatters over LY, and the floor, and Cody, and my precious UNO Lakeside sweatshirt. At least it wasn't our blood. "Okay, Donna," I said, standing up. My left boob still hurt, and for some reason, so did my left knee.

"Yes, Mom," her son said. He was up and straightening furniture. Donna smiled and said, "The coffee's ready. Do you take sugar and cream, Dear?"

I hugged the woman. "Thank you, Donna. You helped save us. Thank you thank you thankyou." I felt her patting my back. "Of course, Amy. You're important to Cody, and that makes you important to me. Now drink up your coffee before it gets cold."

I didn't know any of the four New Orleans police officers who showed up halfway through the cup of Cafe du Monde's finest. They seemed startled to see the three of us at the kitchen island, drinking coffee by the light of a hurricane lamp, while LY was stretched out on the floor with clothesline binding his hand and feet. My revolver was sitting on the countertop with the cylinder open.